MURDER
& OTHER ACTS OF
LITERATURE

MURDER &

OTHER ACTS OF
LITERATURE

TWENTY-FOUR UNFORGETTABLE
AND CHILLING STORIES BY SOME
OF THE WORLD'S BEST-LOVED,
MOST CELEBRATED WRITERS

EDITED BY MICHELE SLUNG

ST. MARTIN'S PRESS ✿ NEW YORK

MYS

A THOMAS DUNNE BOOK.
An imprint of St. Martin's Press.

MURDER AND OTHER ACTS OF LITERATURE. Copyright © 1997 by Michele Slung.
All rights reserved. Printed in the United States of America. No part of this book
may be used or reproduced in any manner whatsoever without written permission
except in the case of brief quotations embodied in critical articles or reviews. For
information, address St. Martin's Press, 175 Fifth Avenue, New York, N.Y. 10010.

Library of Congress Cataloging-in-Publication Data

Murder & other acts of literature / Michele Slung, editor.
    p. cm.
    "A Thomas Dunne book."
    ISBN 0-312-16937-X (hardcover)
    1. Detective and mystery stories.   I. Slung, Michele B., 1947–
    II. Title: Murder and other acts of literature.
PN6120.95.D45M77   1997
808.83'872—DC21   97-14677
                                          CIP

First published in United States by Book-of-the-Month Club

First St. Martin's Press Edition: September 1997

10 9 8 7 6 5 4 3 2

To Otto Penzler, a good friend in the world of mystery and an even better one in life.

Thanks also to Lorraine Shanley (as always), to Harold Augenbraum and the staff at The Mercantile Library and, especially, to Leslie Pockell.

After all, a criminal lawyer is not concerned with facts, he is concerned with probabilities. It is the novelist who is concerned with facts, whose job it is to say what a particular man did do on a particular occasion: the lawyer does not, cannot be expected to go further than to show what the ordinary man would be most likely to do under presumed circumstances.

—Richard Hughes, *A High Wind in Jamaica*

Tut! I have done a thousand dreadful things
As willingly as one would kill a fly.

—William Shakespeare, *Titus Andronicus*

TABLE OF CONTENTS

TABLE OF CONTENTS

EDITOR'S FOREWORD

S INCE MURDER is the grim stuff of daily headlines, it's a bit odd that the world into which many of us choose regularly to escape is filled with more of the same. Yet, even before popular fictional crime—the sort committed right there on the page, with characters imagined into life only so that they might brutally lose it—had become a genre all its own, there were those ready to regard certain manifestations of sudden death as a distinct form of artistic expression.

Thomas De Quincey, a nineteenth-century man of letters whose lively wit made him a favorite of the contemporary London coffeehouse circuit, grasped the ironic possibilities. "I am a very particular man in everything relating to murder," he declared with relish, gleefully shock-delighting the readers of *Blackwood's Magazine* where appeared in 1827 his essay "On Murder Considered as One of the Fine Arts."

First praising Cain ("the inventor of murder, and the father of the art"), for example, before approving of recent villains such as the reviled Edinburgh body snatchers Burke and Hare ("models of a perfect friendship"), he took as his central aesthetic position the notion that there must be "more . . . to the composition of a fine murder than two blockheads to kill and be killed—a knife—a purse—and a dark lane."

Fast-forward to the last decade of the twentieth century, where in cities across the country, shopfronts, many of them innocent enough looking on the outside, house bookshops stocked floor to ceiling with volumes containing the homicidal fantasies of thousands of law-abiding citizens. The clientele, meanwhile, is made up of those thousands of other citizens who happen to be as homicidally inclined but are (one hopes) equally sublimated. Loading briefcases and shopping bags with narratives of unspeakable mayhem attractively packaged, they will carry their purchases onto innocent-looking modes of transportation or home to equally innocent-looking residences, there best to savor them at leisure.

To apply the standards of De Quincey to this vast commercial production—of an industry that *truly* may be said to run on blood—is to risk disappointment, of course. There are, after all, no requirements to be met before setting oneself up as a professional practitioner of fictional murder—a fact, of course, that holds true for many careers. Still, few other callings demand such constant intimacy with the mechanics of small-scale annihilation or such ceaseless inventiveness in pursuit of its accomplishment.

Today, though the labels mystery, detective, suspense, and crime fiction are used almost interchangeably, sudden death remains the element most common to all. Its finality—the absolute unrecoverability of the life force of any departed soul—simply rivets the attention in ways no other plot device ever manages to equal. And the ensuing complications, the unavoidable ripple effects of even a single human demise (let alone larger body counts) not only inspire individual imaginations to create the stories clamored for by so many readers, they also ensure the distinction between those creations and filing cabinets stuffed with mere police reports.

But while, for over a century, we've had the territory of the murder arts increasingly well delineated—from the Victorian era's shilling shockers to the hard-boiled pulp magazines of the 1930s to today's proliferation of series detective characters—it was not the case in Thomas De Quincey's day. As he constructed his argument in favor of the snobbery of violence, he was forced to combine crimes both true and imagined in order simply to have material enough to make his points: Murder mystery specialty stores, weekends, cruises, and catalogs were phenomena still far in the future. Edgar Allan Poe, the putative father of the genre, one needs to remember, was still only a teenager.

Burke and Hare aside, when it came to literary citations, De Quincey, not having the possibility of Conan Doyle, Hammett, or Christie to hand, selected his references from classic sources that included the Bible, Milton, and Shakespeare. And, even though in the decades following, modern readers have had a far easier time of it seeking that particular De Quincey-ish sort of thrill, never has there been a monopoly held by mystery writers on the offering of such gratification.

In Dorothy L. Sayers's seminal historical anthology, *The Omnibus of Crime* (1929), she launched her own survey of the field by including, De Quincey-like, mystery tales from the *Apocrypha* and from Vergil's *Aeneid.* However, from today's perspective, it's not necessary to proceed that far back into literary mayhem; from the oeuvres of a diverse selection of distinguished writers one has no difficulty compiling what is virtually an open-ended list of literary plots featuring doom and destruction and driven by the ultimate cruelties and betrayals of humankind.

Think of Dickens or Dostoevsky or Kafka, to go for a few easy names, or remember, for that matter, the Argentine master Jorge Luis Borges, whose earliest works translated from Spanish into English appeared in the late 1940s in *Ellery Queen's Mystery Magazine.* The only thing often missing from these tales driven by crime is the formal (some would say, formulaic) structure of the detective story, although two I've included here— William Faulkner's "Monk" and Paul Theroux's "The Johore Murders"— employ versions of just those orderly puzzle-unravelings we've come to expect. And in "The Fat Man," Isak Dinesen's pair of amateur sleuths hoping to trap a child's killer would be right at home, as they carefully rig their bait, in almost any TV movie of the week, while A. A. Milne quite wickedly turns the conventions on their ear in "In Vino Veritas."

The most fun about compiling a book like this one is finding the stories themselves, with some tracked down like rare specimens and others hiding in plain sight. Once assembled, each one becomes subtly different, somehow, in the light of its fellows and the common theme. Suddenly one experiences the pleasure of seeing little flashes of never-intended resemblance between, say, Cornell Woolrich and Edith Wharton, whose portrait of a woman's gradual disintegration in "A Journey" is as hauntingly claustrophobic as anything by the noir star responsible for *Phantom Lady* and *The Bride Wore Black*. Or between Ngaio Marsh and Louisa May Alcott, whose "A Double Tragedy" prefigures the former's backstage thrillers, utilizing the same sorts of theatrical props while exploring, as Marsh was later to do, the dangerous passions that may lie concealed beneath a layer of greasepaint.

The always urbane, never-to-be underestimated William Trevor, here in a sinister mode, offers a situation of such elegant malevolence that even Ruth Rendell or Patricia Highsmith might envy it. And although one doesn't ordinarily seek Jim Thompson's or James M. Cain's brand of thwarted, volatile drifter—men at the edge of their own damnation—in the work of Eudora Welty, "The Hitch-Hikers" is as deceptively affectless and shaded by anomie as any of the tougher pulps.

In a cozier vein, Virginia Woolf's "The Widow and the Parrot: A True Story" provides a quaint village episode more reminiscent of Miss Marple than Mrs. Dalloway. Here, the crime isn't murder (the action begins with the body already interred) but rather those wrongs the resentful dead may perpetrate even beyond the grave. And since, in the usual way of things, one goes to Trollope for gentle Victorian satire, domestic complications, or the occasional worldly intrigue, he wouldn't be the author of choice for making the close-up acquaintance of a ruthless escaped convict with nothing to lose. "Aaron Trow," however, with its New World setting, offers just that: a hard-case hostage drama—*America's Most Wanted* in crinolines.

However, not every story equates crime with the breaking of the sixth commandment. The ninth, instead—"thou shalt not steal"— inspired Sir William S. Gilbert. And the skeptical English attitude toward the law, featured so amusingly in several of the librettos he created in collaboration with Sir Arthur Sullivan (*Iolanthe, Trial by Jury*), has a direct descendant in the legal comedies of John Mortimer. Nonetheless, it's as curious to come across "My Maiden Brief," with its positively Rumpolean air, as it's strange to find a Cheever narrator casually robbing Tiffany's.

Some of these stories begin with a crime; others end with one. In some, mystery persists even when, strictly speaking, there is no "mystery," when "who" and "how" and perhaps "why," too, are perfectly clear. Ambiguity, in fact, is probably the element most on view here in a way it might not be in a more traditional crime-and-murder anthology, irony, running a very close second. And, of course, there's the way *sui generis* writers have of appropriating conventions only to reinvent them, brilliantly.

Murder and Other Acts of Literature implies what we already know, that the pen can be lethal and that the book is indeed a blunt instrument. Thus, when those wielding these weapons are among the world's greatest and most honored literary figures, what more desirable fate than willingly, for a few hours, to allow oneself to become a victim of their artistry?

Dangerous though it may be, the greater risk by far lies . . . in *not* reading on.

—Michele Slung

MURDER
& OTHER ACTS OF
LITERATURE

JOHN CHEEVER

MONTRALDO

T HE FIRST TIME I robbed Tiffany's, it was raining. I bought
an imitation-diamond ring at a costume-jewelry place in
the Forties. Then I walked up to Tiffany's in the rain and
asked to look at rings. The clerk had a haughty manner. I looked at
six or eight diamond rings. They began at eight hundred and went up
to ten thousand. There was one priced at three thousand that looked
to me like the paste in my pocket. I was examining this when an
elderly woman—an old customer, I guessed—appeared on the other
side of the counter. The clerk rushed over to greet her, and I switched
rings. Then I called, "Thank you very much. I'll think it over." "Very
well," the clerk said haughtily, and I went out of the store. It was as
simple as pie. I walked down to the diamond market in the Forties
and sold the ring for eighteen hundred. No questions were asked.
Then I went to Thomas Cook and found that the *Conte di Salvini*
was sailing for Genoa at five. This was in August, and there was plenty of space on the eastbound crossing. I took a cabin in first class and
was standing at the bar when she sailed. The bar was not officially

open, of course, but the bar Jack gave me a Martini in a tumbler to hold me until we got into international waters. The *Salvini* had an exceptionally percussive whistle, and you may have heard it if you were anywhere near midtown, although who ever is at five o'clock on an August afternoon?

That night I met Mrs. Winwar and her elderly husband at the horse races. He promptly got seasick, and we plunged into the marvelous skulduggery of illicit love. The passed notes, the phony telephone calls, the affected indifference, and what happened when we were behind the closed door of my cabin made my theft of a ring seem guileless. Mr. Winwar recovered in Gibraltar, but this only seemed like a challenge, and we carried on under his nose. We said goodbye in Genoa, where I bought a secondhand Fiat and started down the coast.

I got to Montraldo late one afternoon. I stopped there because I was tired of driving. There was a semicircular bay, set within high stone cliffs, and one of those beaches that are lined with cafés and bathing houses. There were two hotels, a Grand and a National, and I didn't care for either one of them, and a waiter in a café told me I could rent a room in the villa on the cliff. It could be reached, he said, either by a steep and curving road or by a flight of stone steps—one hundred and twenty-seven, I discovered later—that led from the back garden down into the village. I took my car up the curving road. The cliff was covered with rosemary, and the rosemary was covered with the village laundry, drying in the sun. There were signs on the door in five languages, saying that rooms were for rent. I rang, and a thickset, bellicose servant opened the door. I learned that her name was Assunta. I never saw any relaxation of her bellicosity. In church, when she plunged up the aisle to take Holy Communion, she looked as if she were going to knock the priest down and mess up the acolyte. She said I could have a room if I paid a week's rent in advance, and I had to pay her before I was allowed to cross the threshold.

The place was a ruin, but the whitewashed room she showed me into was in a little tower, and through a broken window the room had a broad view of the sea. The one luxury was a gas ring. There was no toilet, and there was no running water; the water I washed in had to be hauled out of a well in a leaky marmalade can. I was obviously the only guest. That first afternoon, while Assunta was praising the healthfulness of the sea air, I heard a querulous and elegant voice calling to us from the courtyard. I went down the stairs ahead of the servant, and introduced myself to an old woman standing by the well. She was short, frail, and animated, and spoke such a flowery Roman that I wondered if this wasn't a sort of cultural or social dust thrown into one's eyes to conceal the fact that her dress was ragged and dirty. "I see you have a gold wristwatch," she said. "I, too, have a gold wristwatch. We will have this in common."

The servant turned to her and said, "Go to the devil!"

"But it is a fact. The gentleman and I do both have gold wristwatches," the old lady said. "It will make us sympathetic."

"Bore," the servant said. "Rot in hell."

"Thank you, thank you, treasure of my house, light of my life," the old lady said, and made her way toward an open door.

The servant put her hands on her hips and screamed, "Witch! Frog! Pig!"

"Thank you, thank you, thank you infinitely," the old lady said, and went in at the door.

That night, at the café, I asked about the signorina and her servant, and the waiter was fully informed. The signorina, he said, came from a noble Roman family, from which she had been expelled because of a romantic and unsuitable love affair. She had lived as a hermit in Montraldo for fifty years. Assunta had been brought here from Rome to be her *donna di servizio,* but all she did for the old lady these days was to go into the village and buy her some bread and wine. She had robbed the old woman of all her possessions—she had even taken the bed from her room—and she now kept her a prisoner in the villa. Both the Grand Hotel and the National were luxurious and commodious. Why did I stay in such a place?

I stayed because of the view, because I had paid my rent in advance, and because I was curious about the eccentric old spinster and her cranky servant. They began quarreling early the next morning. Assunta opened up with obscenity and abuse. The signorina countered with elaborate sarcasm. It was a depressing performance. I wondered if the old lady was really a prisoner, and later in the morning, when I saw her alone in the courtyard, I asked her if she would like to drive with me to Tambura, the next village up the coast. She said, in her flowery Roman, that she would be delighted to join me. She wanted to have her watch, her gold watch, repaired. The watch was of great value and beauty and there was only one man she dared entrust it to. He was in Tambura. While we were talking, Assunta joined us.

"Why do you want to go to Tambura?" she asked the old lady.

"I want to have my gold watch repaired," the old lady said.

"You don't have a gold watch," Assunta said.

"That is true," the old lady said. "I no longer have a gold watch, but I used to have a gold watch. I used to have a gold watch, and I used to have a gold pencil."

"You can't go to Tambura to have your watch repaired if you don't have a watch," Assunta said.

"That is true, light of my life, treasure of my house," the old lady said, and she went in at her door.

I spent most of my time on the beach and in the cafés. The fortunes of the resort seemed to be middling. The waiters complained about business, but then they always do. The smell of the sea was riggish but unfresh, and I used to think with homesickness of the wild and magnificent beaches of my own country. Gay Head is, I know, sinking into the sea, but the sinkage at Montraldo seemed to be spiritual—as if the waves were eroding the vitality of that place. The sea was incandescent; the light was clear but not brilliant. The flavor of Montraldo, as I remember it, was immutable, intimate, depleted—everything I detest; for shouldn't the soul of man be as limpid and cutting as a diamond? The waves spoke in French or Italian—now and then a word of dialect—but they seemed to speak without force.

One afternoon a remarkably beautiful woman came down the beach, followed by a boy of about eight, I should say, and an Italian woman dressed in black—a maid. They carried sandwich bags from the Grand Hotel, and my guess was that the boy lived mostly in hotels. He was pitiful. The maid took some toys from an assortment she carried in a string bag. They seemed to be all wrong for his age. There was a sand bucket, a shovel, some molds, a whiffle ball, and an old-fashioned pair of water wings. I suspected that the mother, stretched out on a blanket with an American novel, was a divorcée, and that she would presently have a drink with me in the café. With this in mind, I got to my feet and offered to play whiffle ball with the boy. He was delighted to have some company, but he could neither throw nor catch a ball, and, making a guess at his tastes, I asked, with one eye on the mother, if he would like me to build him a sand castle. He would. I built a water moat, then an escarpment with curved stairs, a dry moat, a crenelated wall with cannon positions, and a cluster of round towers with parapets. I worked as if the impregnability of the place was a reality, and when it was completed I set flags, made of candy wrappers, flying from every tower. I thought naïvely that it was beautiful, and so did the boy, but when I called his mother's attention to my feat she said, *"Andiamo."* The maid gathered up the toys, and off they went, leaving me, a grown man in a strange country, with a sand castle.

At Montraldo, the high point of the day came at four, when there was a band concert. This was the largesse of the municipality. The bandstand was wooden, Turkish in inspiration, and weathered by sea winds. The musicians sometimes wore uniforms, sometimes bathing suits, and their number varied from day to day, but they always played Dixieland. I don't think they were interested in the history of jazz. I just think they'd found some old arrangements in a trunk and were stuck with them. The music was comical, accelerated—they seemed to be playing for some ancient ballroom team. "Clarinet Marmalade," "China Boy," "Tiger Rag," "Careless Love"—how stirring it was to hear this old, old jazz explode in the salty air. The concert ended at five, when most of the musicians packed up their instruments and went out to sea with the sardine fleet and the bathers returned to the cafés and the village. Men, women, and children on a beach, band music, sea grass, and sandwich hampers remind me much more forcibly than classical landscapes of our legendary ties to paradise. So I would go up with the others to the café, where, one day, I befriended Lord and Lady Rockwell, who asked me for cocktails. You may wonder why I put these titles down so breathlessly, and the reason is that my father was a waiter.

He wasn't an ordinary waiter; he used to work at a dinner-dance spot in one of the big hotels. One night he lost his temper at a drunken brute, pushed his face into a plate of cannelloni, and left the premises. The union suspended him for three months, but he was, in a way, a hero, and when he went back to work they put him on the banquet shift, where he passed mushrooms to Kings and Presidents. He saw a lot of the world, but I sometimes wonder if the world ever saw much more of him than the sleeve of his red coat and his suave and handsome face, a little above the candlelight. It must have been like living in a world divided by a sheet of one-way glass. Sometimes

I am reminded of him by those pages and guards in Shakespeare who come in from the left and stand at a door, establishing by their costumes the fact that this is Venice or Arden. You scarcely see their faces, they never speak a line; nor did my father, and when the after-dinner speeches began he would vanish like the pages on stage. I tell people that he was in the administrative end of the hotel business, but actually he was a waiter, a banquet waiter.

The Rockwells' party was large, and I left at about ten. A hot wind was blowing off the sea. I was later told that this was the sirocco. It was a desert wind, and so oppressive that I got up several times during the night to drink some mineral water. A boat offshore was sounding its foghorn. In the morning, it was both foggy and suffocating. While I was making some coffee, Assunta and the signorina began their morning quarrel. Assunta started off with the usual "Pig! Dog! Witch! Dirt of the streets!" Leaning from an open window, the whiskery old woman sent down her flowery replies: "Dear one. Beloved. Blessed one. Thank you, thank you." I stood in the door with my coffee, wishing they would schedule their disputes for some other time of day. The quarrel was suspended while the signorina came down the stairs to get her bread and wine. Then it started up again: "Witch! Frog! Frog of frogs! Witch of witches!" etc. The old lady countered with "Treasure! Light! Treasure of my house! Light of my life!" etc. Then there was a scuffle—a tug-of-war over the loaf of bread. I saw Assunta strike the old woman cruelly with the edge of her hand. She fell on the steps and began to moan "Aiee! Aieee!" Even these cries of pain seemed florid. I ran across the courtyard to where she lay in a disjointed heap. Assunta began to scream at me, "I am not culpable, I am not culpable!" The old lady was in great pain. "Please, signore," she asked, "please find the priest for me!" I picked her up. She weighed no more than a child, and her clothing smelled of soil. I carried her up the stairs into a high-ceilinged room festooned with

cobwebs and put her onto a couch. Assunta was on my heels, screaming, "I am not culpable!" Then I started down the one hundred and
twenty-seven steps to the village.

The fog streamed through the air, and the African wind felt like a
furnace draft. No one answered the door at the priest's house, but I
found him in the church, sweeping the floor with a broom made of
twigs. I was excited and impatient, and the more excited I became, the
more slow-moving was the priest. First, he had to put his broom in a
closet. The closet door was warped and wouldn't shut, and he spent an
unconscionable amount of time trying to close it. I finally went outside and waited on the porch. It took him half an hour to get collected, and then, instead of starting for the villa, we went down into the
village to find an acolyte. Presently a young boy joined us, pulling on
a soiled lace soutane, and we started up the stairs. The priest negotiat-
ed ten steps and then sat down to rest. I had time to smoke a cigarette.
Then ten more steps and another rest, and when we were halfway up
the stairs, I began to wonder if he would ever make it. His face had
turned from red to purple, and the noises from his respiratory tract
were harsh and desperate. We finally arrived at the door of the villa.
The acolyte lit his censer. Then we made our way into that ruined
place. The windows were open. There was sea fog in the air. The old
woman was in great pain, but the notes of her voice remained genteel,
as I expect they truly were. "She is my daughter," she said. "Assunta.
She is my daughter, my child."

Then Assunta screamed, "Liar! Liar!"

"No, no, no," the old lady said, "you are my child, my only child.
That is why I have cared for you all my life."

Assunta began to cry, and stamped down the stairs. From the window, I saw her crossing the courtyard. When the priest began to
administer the last rites, I went out.

I kept a sort of vigil in the café. The church bells tolled at three, and a little later news came down from the villa that the signorina was dead. No one in the café seemed to suspect that they were anything but an eccentric old spinster and a cranky servant. At four o'clock the band concert opened up with "Tiger Rag." I moved that night from the villa to the Hotel National, and left Montraldo in the morning.

EUDORA WELTY

THE HITCH-HIKERS

*T*OM HARRIS, a thirty-year-old salesman traveling in office supplies, got out of Victory a little after noon and saw people in Midnight and Louise, but went on toward Memphis. It was a base, and he was thinking he would like to do something that night.

Toward evening, somewhere in the middle of the Delta, he slowed down to pick up two hitch-hikers. One of them stood still by the side of the pavement, with his foot stuck out like an old root, but the other was playing a yellow guitar which caught the late sun as it came in a long straight bar across the fields.

Harris would get sleepy driving. On the road he did some things rather out of a dream. And the recurring sight of hitch-hikers waiting against the sky gave him the flash of a sensation he had known as a child: standing still, with nothing to touch him, feeling tall and having the world come all at once into its round shape underfoot and rush and turn through space and make his stand very precarious and lonely. He opened the car door.

"How do you do?"

"How do you do?"

Harris spoke to hitch-hikers almost formally. Now resuming his speed, he moved over a little in the seat. There was no room in the back for anybody. The man with the guitar was riding with it between his legs. Harris reached over and flicked on the radio.

"Well, music!" said the man with the guitar. Presently he began to smile. "Well, we been there a whole day in that one spot," he said softly. "Seen the sun go clear over. Course, part of the time we laid down under that one tree and taken our ease."

They rode without talking while the sun went down in red clouds and the radio program changed a few times. Harris switched on his lights. Once the man with the guitar started to sing "The One Rose That's Left in My Heart," which came over the air, played by the Aloha Boys. Then in shyness he stopped, but made a streak on the radio dial with his blackly callused finger tip.

"I 'preciate them big 'lectric gittars some have," he said.

"Where are you going?"

"Looks like north."

"It's north," said Harris. "Smoke?"

The other man held out his hand.

"Well . . . rarely," said the man with the guitar.

At the use of the unexpected word, Harris's cheek twitched, and he handed over his pack of cigarettes. All three lighted up. The silent man held his cigarette in front of him like a piece of money, between his thumb and forefinger. Harris realized that he wasn't smoking it, but was watching it burn.

"My! Gittin' night agin," said the man with the guitar in a voice that could assume any social surprise.

"Anything to eat?" asked Harris.

The man gave a pluck to a low string and glanced at him.

"Dewberries," said the other man. It was his only remark, and it was delivered in a slow and pondering voice.

"Some nice little rabbit come skinnin' by," said the man with the guitar, nudging Harris with a slight punch to his side, "but it run off the way it come."

The other man was so bogged in inarticulate anger that Harris could imagine him running down a cotton row after the rabbit. He smiled but did not look around.

"Now to look out for a place to sleep—is that it?" he remarked doggedly.

A pluck of the strings again, and the man yawned.

There was a little town coming up; the lights showed for twenty miles in the flat land.

"Is that Dulcie?" Harris yawned too.

"I bet you ain't got no idea where all I've slep'," the man said, turning around in his seat and speaking directly to Harris, with laughter in his face that in the light of a road sign appeared strangely teasing.

"I could eat a hamburger," said Harris, swinging out of the road under the sign in some automatic gesture of evasion. He looked out of the window, and a girl in red pants leaped onto the running board.

"Three and three beers?" she asked, smiling, with her head poked in. "Hi," she said to Harris.

"How are you?" said Harris. "That's right."

"My," said the man with the guitar. "Red sailor-boy britches." Harris listened for the guitar note, but it did not come. "But not purty," he said.

The screen door of the joint whined, and a man's voice called, "Come on in, boys, we got girls."

Harris cut off the radio, and they listened to the nickelodeon which was playing inside the joint and turning the window blue, red and green in turn.

"Hi," said the car-hop again as she came out with the tray. "Looks like rain."

They ate the hamburgers rapidly, without talking. A girl came and looked out of the window of the joint, leaning on her hand. The same couple kept dancing by behind her. There was something brassy playing, a swing record of "Love, Oh Love, Oh Careless Love."

"Same songs ever'where," said the man with the guitar softly. "I come down from the hills. . . . We had us owls for chickens and fox for yard dogs but we sung true."

Nearly every time the man spoke Harris's cheek twitched. He was easily amused. Also, he recognized at once any sort of attempt to confide, and then its certain and hasty retreat. And the more anyone said, the further he was drawn into a willingness to listen. I'll hear him play his guitar yet, he thought. It had got to be a pattern in his days and nights, it was almost automatic, his listening, like the way his hand went to his pocket for money.

"That'n's most the same as a ballat," said the man, licking mustard off his finger. "My ma, she was the one for ballats. Little in the waist as a dirt-dauber, but her voice carried. Had her a whole lot of tunes. Long ago dead an' gone. Pa'd come home from the courthouse drunk as a wheelbarrow, and she'd just pick up an' go sit on the front step facin' the hill an' sing. Ever'thing she knowed, she'd sing. Dead an' gone, an' the house burned down." He gulped at his beer. His foot was patting.

"This," said Harris, touching one of the keys on the guitar. "Couldn't you stop somewhere along here and make money playing this?"

Of course it was by the guitar that he had known at once that they were not mere hitch-hikers. They were tramps. They were full blown, abandoned to this. Both of them were. But when he touched it he knew obscurely that it was the yellow guitar, that bold and gay burden in the tramp's arms, that had caused him to stop and pick them up.

The man hit it flat with the palm of his hand.

"This box? Just play it for myself."

Harris laughed delightedly, but somehow he had a desire to tease him, to make him swear to his freedom.

"You wouldn't stop and play somewhere like this? For them to dance? When you know all the songs?"

Now the fellow laughed out loud. He turned and spoke completely as if the other man could not hear him. "Well, but right now I got *him*."

"Him?" Harris stared ahead.

"He'd gripe. He don't like foolin' around. He wants to git on. You always git a partner got notions."

The other tramp belched. Harris laid his hand on the horn.

"Hurry back," said the car-hop, opening a heart-shaped pocket over her heart and dropping the tip courteously within.

"Aw river!" sang out the man with the guitar.

As they pulled out into the road again, the other man began to lift a beer bottle, and stared beseechingly, with his mouth full, at the man with the guitar.

"Drive back, mister. Sobby forgot to give her back her bottle. Drive back."

"Too late," said Harris rather firmly, speeding on into Dulcie, thinking, I was about to take directions from him.

Harris stopped the car in front of the Dulcie Hotel on the square.

"'Preciated it," said the man, taking up his guitar.

"Wait here."

They stood on the walk, one lighted by the street light, the other in the shadow of the statue of the Confederate soldier, both caved in and giving out an odor of dust, both sighing with obedience.

Harris went across the yard and up the one step into the hotel.

Mr. Gene, the proprietor, a white-haired man with little dark freckles all over his face and hands, looked up and shoved out his arm at the same time.

"If he ain't back." He grinned. "Been about a month to the day—I was just remarking."

"Mr. Gene, I ought to go on, but I got two fellows out front. O.K., but they've just got nowhere to sleep tonight, and you know that little back porch."

"Why, it's a beautiful night out!" bellowed Mr. Gene, and he laughed silently.

"They'd get fleas in your bed," said Harris, showing the back of his hand. "But you know that old porch. It's not so bad. I slept out there once, I forget how."

The proprietor let his laugh out like a flood. Then he sobered abruptly.

"Sure. O.K.," he said. "Wait a minute—Mike's sick. Come here, Mike, it's just old Harris passin' through."

Mike was an ancient collie dog. He rose from a quilt near the door and moved over the square brown rug, stiffly, like a table walking, and shoved himself between the men, swinging his long head from Mr. Gene's hand to Harris's and bearing down motionless with his jaw in Harris's palm.

"You sick, Mike?" asked Harris.

"Dyin' of old age, that's what he's doin'!" blurted the proprietor as if in anger.

Harris began to stroke the dog, but the familiarity in his hands changed to slowness and hesitancy. Mike looked up out of his eyes.

"His spirit's gone. You see?" said Mr. Gene pleadingly.

"Say, look," said a voice at the front door.

"Come in, Cato, and see poor old Mike," said Mr. Gene.

"I knew that was your car, Mr. Harris," said the boy. He was nervously trying to tuck a Bing Crosby cretonne shirt into his pants like a real shirt. Then he looked up and said, "They was tryin' to take your car, and down the street one of 'em like to bust the other one's head wide op'm with a bottle. Looks like you would 'a' heard the commotion. Everybody's out there. I said, 'That's Mr. Tom Harris's car, look at the out-of-town license and look at all the stuff he all time carries around with him, all bloody.'"

"He's not dead though," said Harris, kneeling on the seat of his car.

It was the man with the guitar. The little ceiling light had been turned on. With blood streaming from his broken head, he was slumped down upon the guitar, his legs bowed around it, his arms at either side, his whole body limp in the posture of a bareback rider. Harris was aware of the other face not a yard away: the man the guitar player had called Sobby was standing on the curb, with two men unnecessarily holding him. He looked more like a bystander than any of the rest, except that he still held the beer bottle in his right hand.

"Looks like if he was fixin' to hit him, *he* would of hit *him* with that gittar," said a voice. "That'd be a real good thing to hit somebody with. Whang!"

"The way I figure this thing out is," said a penetrating voice, as if a woman were explaining it all to her husband, "the men was left to 'emselves. So—that 'n' yonder wanted to make off with the car—he's the bad one. So the good one says, 'Naw, that ain't right.'"

Or was it the other way around? thought Harris dreamily.

"So the other one says bam! bam! He whacked him over the head. And so dumb—right where the movie was letting out."

"Who's got my car keys!" Harris kept shouting. He had, without realizing it, kicked away the prop, the guitar; and he had stopped the blood with something.

Nobody had to tell him where the ramshackle little hospital was—he had been there once before, on a Delta trip. With the constable scuttling along after and then riding on the running board, glasses held tenderly in one fist, the handcuffed Sobby dragged alongside by the other, with a long line of little boys in flowered shirts accompanying him on bicycles, riding in and out of the headlight beam, with the rain falling in front of him and with Mr. Gene shouting in a sort of plea from the hotel behind and Mike beginning to echo the barking of the rest of the dogs, Harris drove in all carefulness down the long tree-dark street, with his wet hand pressed on the horn.

The old doctor came down the walk and, joining them in the car, slowly took the guitar player by the shoulders.

"I 'spec' he gonna die though," said a colored child's voice mournfully. "Wonder who goin' to git his box?"

In a room on the second floor of the two-story hotel Harris put on clean clothes, while Mr. Gene lay on the bed with Mike across his stomach.

"Ruined that Christmas tie you came in." The proprietor was talking in short breaths. "It took it out of Mike, I'm tellin' you." He sighed. "First time he's barked since Bud Milton shot up that Chinese." He lifted his head and took a long swallow of the hotel whisky, and tears appeared in his warm brown eyes. "Suppose they'd done it on the porch."

The phone rang.

"See, everybody knows you're here," said Mr. Gene.

"Ruth?" he said, lifting the receiver, his voice almost contrite.

But it was for the proprietor.

When he had hung up he said, "That little peanut—he ain't ever goin' to learn which end is up. The constable. Got a nigger already in the jail, so he's runnin' round to find a place to put this fella of yours with the bottle, and damned if all he can think of ain't the hotel!"

"Hell, is he going to spend the night with me?"

"Well, the same thing. Across the hall. The other fella may die. Only place in town with a key but the bank, he says."

"What time is it?" asked Harris all at once.

"Oh, it ain't *late,*" said Mr. Gene.

He opened the door for Mike, and the two men followed the dog slowly down the stairs. The light was out on the landing. Harris looked out of the old half-open stained-glass window.

"Is that rain?"

"It's been rainin' since dark, but you don't ever know a thing like that—it's proverbial." At the desk he held up a brown package. "Here. I sent Cato after some Memphis whisky for you. He had to do something."

"Thanks."

"I'll see you. I don't guess you're goin' to get away very shortly in the mornin'. I'm real sorry they did it in your car if they were goin' to do it."

"That's all right," said Harris. "You'd better have a little of this."

"That? It'd kill me," said Mr. Gene.

In a drugstore Harris phoned Ruth, a woman he knew in town, and found her at home having a party.

"Tom Harris! Sent by heaven!" she cried. "I was wondering what I'd do about Carol—this *baby!*"

"What's the matter with her?"

"No date."

Some other people wanted to say hello from the party. He listened awhile and said he'd be out.

This had postponed the call to the hospital. He put in another nickel. . . . There was nothing new about the guitar player.

"Like I told you," the doctor said, "we don't have the facilities for giving transfusions, and he's been moved plenty without you taking him to Memphis."

Walking over to the party, so as not to use his car, making the only sounds in the dark wet street, and only partly aware of the indeterminate shapes of houses with their soft-shining fanlights marking them off, there with the rain falling mistlike through the trees, he almost forgot what town he was in and which house he was bound for.

Ruth, in a long dark dress, leaned against an open door, laughing. From inside came the sounds of at least two people playing a duet on the piano.

"He would come like this and get all wet!" she cried over her shoulder into the room. She was leaning back on her hands. "What's the matter with your little blue car? I hope you brought us a present."

He went in with her and began shaking hands, and set the bottle wrapped in the paper sack on a table.

"He never forgets!" cried Ruth.

"Drinkin' whisky!" Everybody was noisy again.

"So this is the famous 'he' that everybody talks about all the time," pouted a girl in a white dress. "Is he one of your cousins, Ruth?"

"No kin of mine, he's nothing but a vagabond," said Ruth, and led Harris off to the kitchen by the hand.

I wish they'd call me "you" when I've got here, he thought tiredly.

"More has gone on than a little bit," she said, and told him the news while he poured fresh drinks into the glasses. When she accused him of nothing, of no carelessness or disregard of her feelings, he was fairly sure she had not heard about the assault in his car.

She was looking at him closely. "Where did you get that sunburn?"

"Well, I had to go to the Coast last week," he said.

"What did you do?"

"Same old thing." He laughed; he had started to tell her about something funny in Bay St. Louis, where an eloping couple had flagged him down in the residential section and threatened to break up if he would not carry them to the next town. Then he remembered how Ruth looked when he mentioned other places where he stopped on trips.

Somewhere in the house the phone rang and rang, and he caught himself jumping. Nobody was answering it.

"I thought you'd quit drinking," she said, picking up the bottle.

"I start and quit," he said, taking it from her and pouring his drink. "Where's my date?"

"Oh, she's in Leland," said Ruth.

They all drove over in two cars to get her.

She was a slight little thing, with her nightgown in some sort of little bag. She came out when they blew the horn, before he could go in after her. . . .

"Let's go holler off the bridge," said somebody in the car ahead.

They drove over a little gravel road, miles through the misty fields, and came to the bridge out in the middle of nowhere.

"Let's dance," said one of the boys. He grabbed Carol around the waist, and they began to tango over the boards.

"Did you miss me?" asked Ruth. She stayed by him, standing in the road.

"Woo-hoo!" they cried.

"I wish I knew what makes it holler back," said one girl. "There's nothing anywhere. Some of my kinfolks can't even hear it."

"Yes, it's funny," said Harris, with a cigarette in his mouth.

"Some people say it's an old steamboat got lost once."

"Might be."

They drove around and waited to see if it would stop raining.

Back in the lighted rooms at Ruth's he saw Carol, his date, give him a strange little glance. At the moment he was serving her with a drink from the tray.

"Are you the one everybody's 'miratin' and gyratin' over?" she said, before she would put her hand out.

"Yes," he said. "I come from afar." He placed the strongest drink from the tray in her hand, with a little flourish.

"Hurry back!" called Ruth.

In the pantry Ruth came over and stood by him while he set more glasses on the tray and then followed him out to the kitchen. Was she at all curious about him? he wondered. For a moment, when they were simply close together, her lips parted, and she stared off at nothing; her jealousy seemed to let her go free. The rainy wind from the back porch stirred her hair.

As if under some illusion, he set the tray down and told her about the two hitch-hikers.

Her eyes flashed.

"What a—stupid thing!" Furiously she seized the tray when he reached for it.

The phone was ringing again. Ruth glared at him.

It was as though he had made a previous engagement with the hitch-hikers.

Everybody was meeting them at the kitchen door.

"Aha!" cried one of the men, Jackson. "He tried to put one over on you, girls. Somebody just called up, Ruth, about the murder in Tom's car."

"Did he die?" asked Harris, without moving.

"I knew all about it!" cried Ruth, her cheeks flaming. "He told me all about it. It practically ruined his car. Didn't it!"

"Wouldn't he get into something crazy like that?"

"It's because he's an angel," said the girl named Carol, his date, speaking in a hollow voice from her highball glass.

"Who phoned?" asked Harris.

"Old Mrs. Daggett, that old lady about a million years old that's always calling up. She was right there."

Harris phoned the doctor's home and woke the doctor's wife. The guitar player was still the same.

"This is so exciting, tell us all," said a fat boy. Harris knew he lived fifty miles up the river and had driven down under the impression that there would be a bridge game.

"It was just a fight."

"Oh, he wouldn't tell you, he never talks. I'll tell you," said Ruth. "Get your drinks, for goodness' sake."

So the incident became a story. Harris grew very tired of it.

"It's marvelous the way he always gets in with somebody and then something happens," said Ruth, her eyes completely black.

"Oh, he's my hero," said Carol, and she went out and stood on the back porch.

"Maybe you'll still be here tomorrow," Ruth said to Harris, taking his arm. "Will you be detained, maybe?"

"If he dies," said Harris.

He told them all good-bye.

"Let's all go to Greenville and get a Coke," said Ruth.

"No," he said. "Good night."

"'Aw river,'" said the girl in the white dress. "Isn't that what the little man said?"

"Yes," said Harris, the rain falling on him, and he refused to spend the night or to be taken in a car back to the hotel.

In the antlered lobby, Mr. Gene bent over asleep under a lamp by the desk phone. His freckles seemed to come out darker when he was asleep.

Harris woke him. "Go to bed," he said. "What was the idea? Anything happened?"

"I just wanted to tell you that little buzzard's up in 202. Locked and double-locked, handcuffed to the bed, but I wanted to tell you."

"Oh. Much obliged."

"All a gentleman could do," said Mr. Gene. He was drunk. "Warn you what's sleepin' under your roof."

"Thanks," said Harris. "It's almost morning. Look."

"Poor Mike can't sleep," said Mr. Gene. "He scrapes somethin' when he breathes. Did the other fella poop out?"

"Still unconscious. No change," said Harris. He took the bunch of keys which the proprietor was handing him.

"You keep 'em," said Mr. Gene.

In the next moment Harris saw his hand tremble and he took hold of it.

"A murderer!" whispered Mr. Gene. All his freckles stood out. "Here he came . . . with not a word to say . . ."

"Not a murderer yet," said Harris, starting to grin.

When he passed 202 and heard no sound, he remembered what old Sobby had said, standing handcuffed in front of the hospital, with nobody listening to him. "I was jist tired of him always uppin' an' makin' a noise about ever'thing."

In his room, Harris lay down on the bed without undressing or turning out the light. He was too tired to sleep. Half blinded by the unshaded bulb he stared at the bare plaster walls and the equally white surface of the mirror above the empty dresser. Presently he got up and turned on the ceiling fan, to create some motion and sound in the room. It was a defective fan which clicked with each revolution, on and on. He lay perfectly still beneath it, with his clothes on, unconsciously breathing in a rhythm related to the beat of the fan.

He shut his eyes suddenly. When they were closed, in the red darkness he felt all patience leave him. It was like the beginning of desire. He remembered the girl dropping money into her heart-shaped pocket, and remembered a disturbing possessiveness, which meant nothing, Ruth leaning on her hands. He knew he would not be held by any of it. It was for relief, almost, that his thoughts turned to pity, to wonder about the two tramps, their conflict, the sudden brutality when his back was turned. How would it turn out? It was in this suspense that it was more acceptable to him to feel the helplessness of his life.

He could forgive nothing in this evening. But it was too like other evenings, this town was too like other towns, for him to move out of this lying still clothed on the bed, even into comfort or despair. Even the rain—there was often rain, there was often a party, and there had been other violence not of his doing—other fights, not quite so pointless, but fights in his car; fights, unheralded confessions, sudden love-making—none of any of this his, not his to keep, but belonging to the people of these towns he passed through, coming out of their rooted pasts and their mock rambles, coming out of their time. He himself had no time. He was free; helpless. He wished he knew how the guitar player was, if he was still unconscious, if he felt pain.

He sat up on the bed and then got up and walked to the window.

"Tom!" said a voice outside in the dark.

Automatically he answered and listened. It was a girl. He could not see her, but she must have been standing on the little plot of grass that ran around the side of the hotel. Wet feet, pneumonia, he thought. And he was so tired he thought of a girl from the wrong town.

He went down and unlocked the door. She ran in as far as the middle of the lobby as though from impetus. It was Carol, from the party.

"You're wet," he said. He touched her.

"Always raining." She looked up at him, stepping back. "How are you?"

"O.K., fine," he said.

"I was wondering," she said nervously. "I knew the light would be you. I hope I didn't wake up anybody." Was old Sobby asleep? he wondered.

"Would you like a drink? Or do you want to go to the All-Nite and get a Coca-Cola?" he said.

"It's open," she said, making a gesture with her hand. "The All-Nite's open—I just passed it."

They went out into the mist, and she put his coat on with silent protest, in the dark street not drunken but womanly.

"You didn't remember me at the party," she said, and did not look up when he made his exclamation. "They say you never forget anybody, so I found out they were wrong about that anyway."

"They're often wrong," he said, and then hurriedly, "Who are you?"

"We used to stay at the Manning Hotel on the Coast every summer—I wasn't grown. Carol Thames. Just dances and all, but you had just started to travel then, it was on your trips, and you—you talked at intermission."

He laughed shortly, but she added:

"You talked about yourself."

They walked past the tall wet church, and their steps echoed.

"Oh, it wasn't so long ago—five years," she said. Under a magnolia tree she put her hand out and stopped him, looking up at him with her child's face. "But when I saw you again tonight I wanted to know how you were getting along."

He said nothing, and she went on.

"You used to play the piano."

They passed under a street light, and she glanced up as if to look for the little tic in his cheek.

"Out on the big porch where they danced," she said, walking on. "Paper lanterns . . ."

"I'd forgotten that, is one thing sure," he said. "Maybe you've got the wrong man. I've got cousins galore who all play the piano."

"You'd put your hands down on the keyboard like you'd say, 'Now this is how it really is!'" she cried, and turned her head away. "I guess

I was crazy about you, though."

"Crazy about me then?" He struck a match and held a cigarette between his teeth.

"No—yes, and now too!" she cried sharply, as if driven to deny him.

They came to the little depot where a restless switch engine was hissing, and crossed the black street. The past and present joined like this, he thought, it never happened often to me, and it probably won't happen again. He took her arm and led her through the dirty screen door of the All-Nite.

He waited at the counter while she sat down by the wall table and wiped her face all over with her handkerchief. He carried the black coffees over to the table himself, smiling at her from a little distance. They sat under a calendar with some picture of giant trees being cut down.

They said little. A fly bothered her. When the coffee was all gone he put her into the old Cadillac taxi that always stood in front of the depot.

Before he shut the taxi door he said, frowning, "I appreciate it. . . . You're sweet."

Now she had torn her handkerchief. She held it up and began to cry. "What's sweet about me?" It was the look of bewilderment in her face that he would remember.

"To come out, like this—in the rain—to be here . . . " He shut the door, partly from weariness.

She was holding her breath. "I hope your friend doesn't die," she said. "All I hope is your friend gets well."

But when he woke up the next morning and phoned the hospital, the guitar player was dead. He had been dying while Harris was sitting in the All-Nite.

"It *was* a murderer," said Mr. Gene, pulling Mike's ears. "That was just plain murder. No way anybody could call that an affair of honor."

The man called Sobby did not oppose an invitation to confess. He stood erect and turning his head about a little, and almost smiled at all the men who had come to see him. After one look at him Mr. Gene, who had come with Harris, went out and slammed the door behind him.

All the same, Sobby had found little in the night, asleep or awake, to say about it. "I done it, sure," he said. "Didn't ever'body see me, or was they blind?"

They asked him about the man he had killed.

"Name Sanford," he said, standing still, with his foot out, as if he were trying to recall something particular and minute. "But he didn't have nothing and he didn't have no folks. No more'n me. Him and me, we took up together two weeks back." He looked up at their faces as if for support. "He was uppity, though. He bragged. He carried a gittar around." He whimpered. "It was his notion to run off with the car."

Harris, fresh from the barbershop, was standing in the filling station where his car was being polished.

A ring of little boys in bright shirt-tails surrounded him and the car, with some colored boys waiting behind them.

"Could they git all the blood off the seat and the steerin' wheel, Mr. Harris?"

He nodded. They ran away.

"Mr. Harris," said a little colored boy who stayed. "Does you want the box?"

"The what?"

He pointed, to where it lay in the back seat with the sample cases. "The po' kilt man's gittar. Even the policemans didn't want it."

"No," said Harris, and handed it over.

T. H. WHITE

SUCCESS
OR FAILURE

*T*HE HOUSE they lived in was called Colenso. It was in a suburb of London near Wembley and was shaped like a wedge of cheese. The red, jerry-built roof sloped at a sharp angle which had been thought artistic in 1920. All the houses in the road had the same kind of roof. They were semi-detached. The road was called Laburnum Avenue. Each house had a rectangular strip of garden behind it, sixty feet by thirty feet, with wooden fences between them. They were cultivated in different ways. Some of the slatternly ones just had long grass and poles to hang out the washing, but many of them were proud of themselves, and tried to be better than their neighbors. The garden of Colenso began at the top, near the house, with a small strip of lawn carefully mowed. Then there was a neat patch of gooseberry and raspberry bushes, with three apple trees. Next there was a bed of potatoes and peas. At the bottom of the garden, there was a chicken house with eight hens in it and a little shed where Mr. Briant did his carpentry. In the summer, there was a fancy garden hammock or swingseat on the lawn, and some croquet hoops.

Everything about Colenso was beautifully kept. The linoleum in the hall and on the stairs shone with a wax finish. The brass bowl in the sitting-room window, with a fern in it, was polished twice a week. Nobody sat in the sitting-room, unless there were visitors, and then some imitation Crown Derby china was brought out for tea, while the visitors perched on the hard, tight, clean, Drage chairs, which smelled of new cloth and furniture cream. The kitchen, where the family life was really lived, was as shiny as the sitting-room. The grate was black-leaded every day, and its brass bits gleamed with Brasso, as did all the knickknacks—like copper letter-racks in the shape of galleons, toasting forks with the Lincoln Imp on them, bits of metal off the harness of cart-horses, miniature candlesticks bought as souvenirs with the arms of seaside towns in enamel, and a bellows in beaten brass showing a lighthouse and some seagulls. The pots and pans and kettles were speckless. There was a special mat and scraper in the scullery, where Mr. Briant had to take his boots off when he came in from the garden.

Nearly all the houses in Laburnum Avenue had television aerials, which stood up like a forest of modern statuary called "Political Prisoners," or like the bare masts of futuristic tankers in a busy port.

Mrs. Briant was an ex-schoolteacher and had married her husband for the sake of being married. She was a house-proud Lancashire woman, who had a faint moustache and rather a wild, avid look, as if she might go mad at any moment. She was inclined to be the "life and soul" at Christmas parties. She jollied people along in a loud "funny" voice, crying "Ee" and "Bye"—a sort of imitation Gracie Fields, with the same kind of screech—and she ordered everybody to sit down or stand up or hide in cupboards or take a pencil and write down the names of twelve fish beginning with W. Under this veneer of camaraderie, she was as hard as nails. She allowed her husband to have a bottle of stout with his meals—it kept him out of the pubs—and she cooked for him superbly—but he had to sleep in a separate bed because of "hygiene," and she had taught him to believe that all males were beastly. They had no children.

Mr. Briant—she had married him rather late in life, when it turned out that there was nobody else available—was in one way a source of shame to her. He was a sewer man. For this very reason—he washed himself so thoroughly before he came home—he was cleaner than most other people in Laburnum Avenue, but she did not let him forget that she had married beneath her, and that she was a cultured person whose father had been a farmer, while her husband was low enough to work in drains.

They were far from being unhappy together. Most marriages are desperate affairs sometimes, when the glamor has worn off, but these two did have a clean, comfortable, warm home, with excellent food, and a loyalty to each other which was based on economics.

Mr. Briant was a stocky man going bald, with thick, foxy hair on his forearms, and he wore an apron when he was doing the washing up. He had his own hobbies, which he conducted in the shed at the bottom of the garden. He had a project or daydream about adapting the shed so that he could keep racing pigeons in it. Also he was a Freemason. On Saturdays he was allowed to go to the Freemasons or to the Bowls Club, where croquet was also played, and on weekday evenings they either listened to the radio together or else he did carpentry in the shed. He made stools and ornamental bookshelves neatly, or sometimes a special tour-de-force, like a cage for his sister-in-law's budgerigar. When they listened to the radio, he often wished that they could have the boxing commentaries, but Mrs. Briant preferred the readings from Dickens or one of the "diaries" which go on and on in England as serials—the "Diary of a Doctor's Wife" or "An Everyday Story of Country Folk." Mr. Briant was clever with his blunt fingers, which had golden hair on the back of the lower joints, but he was not clever with his head. He admired his wife for her brains. She was the leader in the marriage, and he accepted this, as he accepted her superior birth and education and her disinclination to have children. She preferred the radio to the TV.

One evening while they were listening to the radio, there was a talk on the Third Programme about Imaginary Children. It told about Charles Lamb, Kipling and Sir James Barrie, who had all three written about childless people, and how their characters consoled themselves by daydreaming of the babies who had never existed—about the might-have-beens.

It was Mrs. Briant who suggested they might invent a baby for themselves. The idea did not appeal to her husband at first, but he did not oppose it, and after a bit he caught on, with surprising imagination for such a humdrum man. Perhaps he needed a son more than he knew.

Their idea was to imagine a baby, and to let it live on, day by day, having the adventures which it would normally have had if it had been a real one, just like a baby on the radio serials. Both of them preferred a boy.

Mrs. Briant was a thorough woman, and she insisted on going through the whole procedure from the beginning. She only announced her pregnancy after three months, when she was quite sure, and she speculated about sex and names and provided herself with a layette—pink or blue—for the full time before she consented to present her husband with the expected heir. They talked it out every evening, in front of the kitchen fire, inventing incidents and testing them for probability, rejecting some, accepting others, until Mr. Briant was as excited as she was, by the time the nine months were over.

The delivery was a normal one, and the boy was born on the twenty-fifth of April. They christened him Arthur, after Mrs. Briant's father, and Pendlebury, after a distant cousin who had risen to be a general. He was a healthy specimen, weighing nearly eight pounds, and Mr. Briant was amazed by his mauve color, his wrinkles, his bedraggled hair and the perfection of his fingernails. When he remarked that the baby was mauve, Mrs. Briant was furious. She said that all babies were this color, which was not mauve, and for a whole evening there were strained relations in Laburnum Avenue.

They were model parents, devoted to the little life which they had conceived between them, and from the start they were determined to make it a successful one. Mr. Briant gave up having stout with his meals and actually put the money which would have been spent on it—real money—into a teapot on the mantelpiece, afterward investing it in savings certificates whenever the teapot was full. He did this in fact, not in imagination.

Mrs. Briant proved to be a good mother, though a bit fussy and dainty, as was natural in a schoolteacher. Mr. Briant often chided her for coddling the boy. She was a fanatical sterilizer and boiler of things. Also she insisted on a meticulous diet and regular habits, while her husband grumbled that his own large family at Southend, where he had been born, had been brought up more natural, and none lost.

As the child grew older and survived the countless hazards and small troubles of infancy—the teething, the difficulties about food—he absolutely refused to eat vegetables or fat—and the day when he fell down in the toolshed and cut his forehead on a chisel which had carelessly been left about—Mr. Briant was full of remorse about this—they began to save up still more for him, again in real money, because Mrs. Briant insisted on a good education. In this she was not opposed by her husband. He knew the value of—he had before him, day by day, an example of—the power of education. Besides, he loved his son as much as she did. Nothing short of the best was to be good enough for Arthur.

The pool money, the stout money and all sorts of other luxuries were set aside, so that the boy could be sent to a preparatory school, as it is called in England, like a gentleman. Mrs. Briant had taught in a secondary school, which, instead of making her know better, had given her ideas about the other kind. She was an innocent creature in some ways. Mr. Briant, who could remember nothing about his own school except a girl called Mabel, accepted his wife's information on the subject. All the same, it was a struggle for them to pay the fees.

Luckily Arthur turned out to be clever. Probably he inherited it from his mother. He won a scholarship to Dulwich College.

He was clever, he was healthy in spite of the usual scares about mumps, chickenpox, etc., he was happy and—this was Mr. Briant's contribution—he was good at games. Mrs. Briant would not agree to his being the captain of the cricket team, but he played on it. All through the summer months, his father kept a record of his scores, grieving when he was out for nought and disputing the umpire's decision if he was given L.B.W. Mrs. Briant did not pay much attention to this, though she was pleased to hear of successes, in a general way.

They shared the usual disagreements of parents. Mrs. Briant was against corporal punishment on principle, while Briant was in favor of it—but he could not bring himself to do it, so there was no trouble about this. When Arthur was tiresome, as was perhaps natural in an only child, they talked it over quietly in the evening and made plans about how to cure him of it for the future.

One thing did lead to friction. Mrs. Briant did not want Arthur to be interested in girls or to do anything that was wrong. Mr. Briant absolutely refused to let him be a molly-coddle. He said that all boys were interested in girls—like Mabel. He said that any natural boy would tell lies sometimes and even pinch things, perhaps. They agreed on part of this eventually, as it gave them something to worry about. The girls were always a bone of contention.

Perhaps it was the girls who made the first rift in the lute.

As Arthur began to grow up and to be less dependent on his parents—less in need of his mother's protection—Mrs. Briant seemed to grow cooler toward him. It was not exactly that she was jealous of the girls. It was more as if she resented his being a male. She did not like it that he should have a life apart from hers. She lost interest in him as he ceased to belong to her protectorate, and even began to disapprove of him—perhaps to fear him, for being a man.

Mr. Briant seemed to love him all the more for being one.

It was at this point that husband and wife stopped imagining in harmony.

Being estranged from the masculine Arthur, Mrs. Briant ceased to wish the best for him. The point was that she had it in her power not to give it to him.

She explained to her husband, while they were washing up in the tight, hard kitchen, that daydreaming was wrong when it became a wish-fulfillment. He did not know what she meant by this word, but he felt defensive and beleaguered, and held the wet cup with a damp clutch, in his blunt, russet fingers.

She said that they were just imagining Arthur to be clever and successful and good at things because they wanted him to be so. But few real people were like that. It was betraying the truth of their creation, she said, to make Arthur a superman who always went from strength to strength, just because they hoped for it. It was more likely that he would fail sometimes. He might fail often. He might be a failure.

As a failure, of course, she would have got him back into her protection. But she may not have desired this. She may have dreaded his successes, or envied them.

Briant was forced to agree that people did not usually turn out to be supermen. He was not one himself. From now on he fought a long losing battle on behalf of Arthur, who began to go from bad to worse.

He went to London University, again on a scholarship assisted by his parents, but he slacked there and did not do well. Mrs. Briant pointed out that children who were brilliant too early often used up their powers too soon. Also, she suspected that those unlucky girls might have got hold of him in earnest. He began to show signs of being a rotter.

As Arthur began to go to the dogs, his parents began to fall out about his doings. They reproached each other about his upbringing, quarreling about the might-have-beens. The quarrels were one-sided in a way, because Mrs. Briant provided the noise while her husband sulked, in silent obstinacy.

The boy did not get a good job. The best they could do for him was a clerkship in a bank. It was badly paid. The inevitable happened, and he stole some money to bet on the horses. Mrs. Briant had been afraid of this.

His broken-hearted parents were working in the oblong garden at Wembley when matters came to a head. There was the patch of neat grass, thirty feet by fifteen, which Mr. Briant was mowing. There was the crazy path with alyssum growing on it, the border of lupins, the clothesline, some potatoes and scarlet runners, and the small toolshed. The pigeon house had never been finished.

"Prison!" cried Mr. Briant. "Oh, Arthur! He must not go to prison!"

"God is not mocked," she said.

"What can he do—what can he do when he comes out?"

"We shall have to move."

"But Arthur never meant no harm."

"He will find no work as an ex-convict. We shall have to support him forever."

Mr. Briant said: "I will get him on the sewers. I can ask Mr. Brownlow."

"A sewer man," she said bitterly. "And then I suppose he will marry a schoolteacher—like you did."

Mr. Briant went to the toolshed for his croquet mallet. He bashed her brains out with it. It only needed one thump. He had to do this, in defense of Arthur. He could not afford to have two failures in the family.

NAGUIB MAHFOUZ

BY A PERSON
UNKNOWN

*T*HERE was nothing unusual in the flat to attract attention, nothing that could be of any help to an investigator. It consisted of two rooms and an entrance hall, and in general was extremely simple. What was truly worthy of surprise was the fact that the bedroom should have remained in its natural state, retaining its normal tidiness despite the ghastly murder that had been committed there. Even the bed was undisturbed, or altered only to the extent that occurs when a bed has been slept in. However, the person lying on it was not asleep but had been murdered, the blood not yet dry. As evidenced by the mark of the cord around the neck and the protruding eyeballs, he had been strangled. Blood had coagulated around the nose and mouth, but apart from this there was no sign of any struggle or resistance in the bed, in the bedroom, or in the rest of the flat. Everything was normal, usual, familiar.

The officer in charge of the case stood aghast, his trained eyes searching out the corners, examining and noting, but achieving nothing. Without doubt he was standing before a crime, and there was no crime without a criminal, and the criminal could not be brought to light other than through some clue. Here all the windows were securely closed, so the murderer had come in and gone out by the door. Also, the murdered man had died of strangulation with a cord. How, then, had the murderer been able to wind the cord around the man's neck? Perhaps he had been able to do so while his victim was asleep. This was the acceptable explanation, there being no trace of any resistance. Another explanation was that he had taken his victim unawares from behind, done him in, laid him out on the bed, put everything back in order, and then gone off without leaving a trace. What a man! What nerves! He operated with patience, deliberation, calm, and precision, as happens only in fiction. In control of himself, of the murdered man, of the crime, and of the whole location—then off he goes, safe and sound! What a murderer!

In his mind the officer arranged the investigatory steps (the motive for the crime, the questioning of the concierge and the old servant woman), and also made a number of possible hypotheses. As much as he could he suppressed his strong emotions, then went back to thinking about the strange criminal who had crept into the flat, done away with a human being, and then gone off without a trace, like a delightful waft of breeze or shaft of sunlight. He searched the cupboard, the desk, and the clothes, and found a wallet containing ten pounds; he also came across the man's watch and a gold ring. It would seem that theft was not the motive for the crime. What, then, was the motive?

He asked for the concierge to be brought for questioning. He was an elderly Nubian who had worked in the small building on Barrad Street in Abbasiyya for many years. He made statements of some relevance. He said the murdered man had been a retired teacher named Hasan Wahbi. He was over seventy years of age and had lived alone ever since the death of his wife. He had a married daughter in Asyout and a son working as a doctor in Port Said. He himself was originally from Damietta and was being looked after by Umm Amina, who used to come at about ten in the morning and leave around five in the afternoon.

"And you, don't you sometimes perform services for him?"

"Not once in a year," said the old man quickly and emphatically. "I see him only at the door when he's going out and coming back."

"Tell me about yesterday."

"I saw him leaving the house at eight."

"He didn't ask you to clean the flat?"

With a certain asperity the man answered: "I've told you, not once in a year, not once in his lifetime. Umm Amina comes at ten to cook his food, clean the flat, and wash his clothes."

"Does she leave any windows open?"

"I don't know."

"Isn't it possible for someone to enter by the window?"

"As you can see, his flat is on the third floor, so it's not possible. Also, the building is faced on three sides by other buildings, while the fourth side overlooks Barrad Street itself."

"Go on with what you were saying."

"He left the house at eight, then returned at nine. This has been his usual routine every day for more than ten years. After that he stays in his flat until the next morning."

"Does no one visit him?"

"Except for his son and daughter, I don't remember seeing anyone visit him."

"When were they last here?"

"On the occasion of the feast of Greater Bairam."

"Doesn't the milkman or the paperman call?"

"The papers he brings back with him after going out in the morning. As for the yogurt, Umm Amina takes it in during the afternoon."

"Did she take it in yesterday?"

"Yes, I saw the boy going up to the flat and saw him leaving."

"When did Umm Amina leave the flat yesterday?"

"At about sunset."

"And when did she come today?"

"About ten. She rang the bell, and he didn't answer the door."

"Did he go out today as usual?"

"No, he didn't."

"Are you sure?"

"I didn't see him go out. I was sitting at my place by the door until Umm Amina arrived. Then, after a quarter of an hour, she returned to tell me he wasn't answering, so I went up with her. I rang the bell and knocked on the door, and when he didn't answer we went off to the police station. . . ."

The officer decided that this concierge was not capable of strangling a chicken, nor was Umm Amina, though they might make it possible for someone else to come in and go out. But why was Mr. Hasan Wahbi murdered? Was there some undiscovered theft? Had the wallet been left untouched for the purpose of putting the police off the scent? And was the presence of the key to the flat in the desk drawer another trick?

Umm Amina said she had been working in the schoolmaster's house for a quarter of a century—fifteen years during the lifetime of his wife and ten years following her death. The man had decided that she should spend the night at her own home ever since he had become a widower. She herself was a widow, she said, and the mother of six girls, all of whom were now married to workers or craftsmen; and she provided all their addresses.

"Yesterday he was in good health. He read through the newspapers, recited aloud a portion of the Koran, and when I left the flat, he was listening to the radio."

"What do you know of his family?"

"They are from Damietta, but he's hardly in touch with them and no one visits him except for his son and daughter at feast times and holidays."

"Do you know if he had any enemies?"

"None at all."

"No one used to visit him at home?"

"Never. Very rarely he would sit at the café on a Friday with some of his colleagues or former students."

The officer wondered how it was possible for the crime to have occurred without any motive or clues.

The necessary formalities were completed and, with the help of his assistant, the living quarters of the concierge were searched, as well as the homes of Umm Amina and her six daughters. Then the few friends of the deceased were summoned for examination, but not one of them gave evidence of any significance. The murder of the man appeared to be a complete and baffling mystery. The news of it spread through the street and later appeared in the papers, then the whole of Abbasiyya learned of it, and many people were saddened. The doctor, the murdered man's son, confirmed that his father possessed nothing of value and that his bank account had contained no more than the one hundred pounds he had saved in case of emergency and had in the end taken out. He also confirmed that the old man had had no enemies and that his murder might well have been from greed for some imaginary fortune the criminal had supposed him to have at his home. A thorough questioning of the concierge and Umm Amina took place and came to nothing, both of them being released without bail.

The investigating officer found himself in a fog of confusion and suffered from a sense of frustration he had not previously known. He had an honorable history in the fighting of crime, both in the towns and in the countryside, and was in general an officer with a high reputation. This was the first crime to defeat him so utterly and without his being accorded so much as a ray of hope or consolation. He sent off his scouts among the suspicious characters in the Muqattam Hills, on the borders of the district of Waili, and in Arab al-Mohammedi, but they all came back with nothing. The forensic doctor reported that Mr. Hasan Wahbi had died of strangulation, and he examined all his belongings in the hope of coming across a fingerprint or a hair or any clue that the criminal might have left behind him, but his efforts were in vain. Everyone found himself standing before a silent void.

Because of the severe defeat he had suffered, Officer Muhsin Abd al-Bari, who lived not far away, in a street that led to the police station, felt disconcerted, and his peace of mind was disturbed. When his wife noticed his depression, she said gently, "Don't get yourself into a state about it for nothing."

He retreated into silence and kept his mind off things by reading. He was fond of the mystical poets, such as Saadi, Ibn al-Farid, and Ibn al-Arabi, a rare enough hobby for a police investigation officer, and he therefore hid it even from his best friends.

The incident continued to be the talk of Abbasiyya, both because of its bewildering mystery and because the deceased had been the teacher of many of the young and middle-aged inhabitants of the district. But with the passing of a week or so the news became lost in the fearsome sea of oblivion, and even Muhsin Abd al-Bari entered it among the crimes committed by "person or persons unknown," saying to himself as he chewed over his bitter defeat, "Unknown! This one certainly is unknown!"

A month later the officer was called to an old mansion in the main street of Abbasiyya, the scene of a similar crime. It was as though the first crime had been repeated. Muhsin could hardly believe his eyes. The murdered man was a former army major general. He was living with his family, which consisted of a wife of sixty, a widowed sister also of sixty, and his youngest son, who was a twenty-year-old university student. Also living in the mansion were the concierge, the gardener, the chauffeur, the cook, and two other servants.

The major general was found one morning apparently asleep in bed as usual. It was, however, later than was normal, and it was this that had led his wife to come to see if he was all right. But he had not been sleeping, he had been strangled, the mark of the cord scored around his neck, his eyes bulging horribly, and sticky blood around his mouth and nose. As for the room, it was undisturbed, even the bed itself, and no sound had been heard during the night to awaken any of his family, who slept on the same floor. The long and short of it was that the officer found himself once again facing the deadly mystery that had crushed him a month before at the home of the teacher Hasan Wahbi, facing too the person unknown, with his silence, his obscureness, his singular cruelty, his preposterous mockery.

"Was anything stolen?"

"No."

"Did he have any enemies?"

"None."

"And the servants, did he have a good relationship with them?"

"Very good."

"Do you have any suspicions about anyone?"

"None at all."

The officer went through the formalities without hope. He examined the mansion thoroughly and questioned the family and the servants. He had a sensation of fear of some person unknown, and felt that a plot was being hatched in the dark to do away not only with many victims, but also with his reputation and all the values in his life. He likewise felt that there was some sort of an enigma that was about to suffocate him with the weight of its mystery, and that if once again he were to fail, he would not be able to face up to life, that life itself would not be worthwhile for anyone.

Owing to the status of the murdered man, a number of senior investigation officers came to take charge of the case. "There's certainly been a crime," said one of them in astonishment, "but it's as though it has been committed without a criminal."

"But the criminal's there all right, and maybe he's closer to us than we imagine."

"How did he do it?"

"He passed a thin cord around the neck, pulling it tight until the man was dead. But how did he reach the site of his crime? How did he get away without leaving a trace?"

"And what's the motive for the killing?"

"Motives for killing are as numerous as those for living!"

"Could he kill for no reason?"

"If he were mad he would kill for no reason—or without such reason as would convince us."

"What's the connection between the major general and the teacher?"

"Both were susceptible to death!"

The news was printed on the front pages of the newspapers in sensational headlines. Public opinion was shaken, in particular among the inhabitants of Abbasiyya, for the major general had been known since the time of the elections, having put himself forward as a candidate on a number of occasions and having once been elected to the Senate. Muhsin mobilized all the detectives on the force to investigate and make inquiries. He issued them strict instructions and applied himself to his work with a feverish desire to succeed. At the end of the night, he returned home utterly fatigued in body and spirit. He resolved to keep his worries from his wife, who had at the time begun to suffer the discomforts of pregnancy. The thing he feared most was that he would be transferred from the police station of al-Waili, bearing the mark of disgrace at his defeat, and be replaced by someone else, just as he had replaced others in the countryside at the time of his victories and successes. He tried to rid himself of his worries by reading poetry, but in vain, for his mind fixed itself solely on the crime that had become for him the symbol of his defeat.

Who could this terrible killer be? He was not a thief, or someone seeking revenge, nor even a madman—a madman might kill, but he would not carry out his crime with such devastating perfection. He was confronted by a strong, overpowering riddle from whose wantonness there was no escape. How, then, was he to bear the responsibility of protecting lives?

People, especially those of Abbasiyya, lost interest in the subject and calmed down slightly. The officer's apprehension turned into a composed sadness harbored within the depths of his soul.

It was then that the third murder occurred. It happened forty days after the death of the major general. The location was a medium-sized house in Bain al-Ganayen, its victim a young woman in her thirties, the wife of a small contractor and the mother of three children. As usual everything was normal, other than the livid mark of the cord around the neck, the blood around the mouth and nose, and the bulging eyeballs. Apart from this there was no trace of anything. Muhsin carried out his routine duties in a quiet spirit of despair, for he believed that his torture would never come to an end and that he had been set up as a target by some merciless power. The mother of the murdered woman had lived with her. "In the morning I went in to find out how she was and I found her . . . " She was choked by tears and kept silent until the outburst of crying had passed. "The poor thing had typhoid ten years ago. . . . "

"Typhoid!" Muhsin called out in surprise at this irrelevant piece of information.

"Yes, her condition was serious, but she was not to die from it."

"You were not aware of any movement during the night?"

"None at all. The children were asleep in this room, while I slept on that sofa close by her room so as to be within earshot if she called. I was the last to go to sleep and the first to wake up. I went into her room and found her, poor love, as you can see. . . ."

The husband came at noon, having returned from Alexandria in a state of extreme grief. It was some time before he found himself in a state to answer the officer's questions, and he had nothing to say that could help the inquiry. He had been in Alexandria on business, having spent the previous day at the Commercial Café with some people whom he named, and he had spent the night with one of them in Qabbari, where he received the calamitous telegram. Giving a deep sigh, the man exclaimed, "Officer, this is unbearable—it's not the first time. Before this the teacher and the major general were killed. What are the police doing about it? People aren't killed without there being a murderer. You should be arresting him!"

"We're not magicians," burst out Muhsin, unable to endure such an attack. "Don't you understand?"

He quickly regretted his words. He returned to the police station, saying to himself that in actual fact it was he who was the criminal's number one victim. He wished that he could somehow declare his sense of impotence. This criminal was like the air, though even the air left some trace of itself in houses, or like heat, yet it too left its trace. How long would the crimes continue to have to be recorded among those committed by "a person unknown"?

Meanwhile Abbasiyya was in the throes of a terror that set the press ablaze. There was no other subject for conversation in the cafés than the stranglings and the terrible unknown perpetrator. It was a peril that had suddenly made its appearance, and no one was safe. There was no longer any confidence in the security forces, and suspicions were centered on perverts and madmen, this being the fashion in those days. From investigations it appeared that none of the inmates of the mental asylum had escaped. The police station received letters from anonymous informants, as a result of which many houses were searched, but no one of any importance was discovered; most of those involved were elderly. Somebody reported a young man known for being crazy or abnormal, who lived in Sarayat Street. He was arrested and taken off for questioning, but it was established that on the night the major general was killed he had been in detention in Ezbekiyya for importuning a girl in the street, so he was released. All efforts came to nothing, and Muhsin said sadly, "The sole accused in this case is myself!"

And so it was in his view and that of the residents of Abbasiyya, and that of the newspaper readers. Rumors spread without anyone knowing how they did so. It was said that the murderer was known to the security men but that they were covering up for him because he was closely related to an important personality. It was also said that there was in fact no murderer and no crime, but that it was all the result of an unknown and dangerous disease and that the laboratories of the Ministry of Health were working night and day to uncover its secret. Confusion and uneasiness reigned.

One day, a month or thereabouts after the murder of the woman, the policeman on duty at the al-Waili station found a corpse in the lane alongside it. Nothing like this had ever been heard of before. Officer Muhsin Abd al-Bari hurried to the place where the corpse lay—though it would have been possible to see it from the window of his room, had he so wanted. He found it to be the almost naked body of a man, certainly a beggar, lying against the wall of the police station. From sheer agony he almost let out a scream as his eyes alighted on the mark of the cord round the neck. Good Lord! Even this beggar! He searched the man, as though there might be a hope of coming across something. The local district official was summoned, and he identified the body as that of a mendicant from al-Wailiyya al-Sughra, a man of no fixed abode though known to many people.

The investigations took their course, not with any hope in view but as a cover to humiliating defeat. The residents of the houses close by were questioned, but what could be expected? Why not also ask those at the police station, which adjoined the scene of the crime? Detectives took themselves off to areas of suspicion, but they were searching for nothing in particular—for a specter, a spirit. As a reaction to the rancor that overwhelmed people's hearts, dozens of perverts and dubious characters were rounded up and detained, till the whole of Abbasiyya was cleared of them. But what was achieved? In addition, the number of policemen patrolling the streets was increased, particularly during the hours of night. The Ministry of the Interior allocated a thousand pounds as a reward for anyone leading the police to the mysterious killer. The press took up the matter in emotionally powerful tones on its front pages. All of this served to exacerbate the situation in the minds of the inhabitants of Abbasiyya until it was turned into a crisis of frightening proportions. Terror ruled as people's minds were tortured by evil presentiments, conversations turned into hysterical ravings, and those who could left the district. Were it not for the housing crisis and the circumstances under which people lived, Abbasiyya would have been emptied of its population.

Perhaps, though, no one suffered quite as much as Officer Muhsin Abd al-Bari or his unfortunate pregnant wife. By way of consolation and encouragement, she said, "You're not to blame, this is something beyond man's imagining."

"There's no longer any point to staying on in my job."

"Tell me how you've been at fault," she said anxiously.

"Wasted effort and being at fault are one and the same thing so long as lives are not safeguarded."

"In the end you will triumph as usual."

"I doubt it. This is something quite out of the ordinary."

He did not sleep that night. He remained awake with his thoughts, overwhelmed by a desire to escape into the world of his mystic poetry, where calm and eternal truth lay, where lights melted into the ultimate unity of existence, where there was solace from the trials of life, its failures, its manipulations. Was it not extraordinary that both the worshiper of truth and this bestial killer should belong to one and the same life? We die because we waste our lives in concerning ourselves with ridiculous things. There is no life for us and no escape except by directing ourselves to the truth alone.

Hardly had two weeks gone by than an incident no less strange than the previous one occurred. A body fell from the last car of Tram 22, in front of Street Ten late at night. The conductor stopped the tram and went toward where the sound had come from, and the driver followed him. They saw on the ground a man dressed in a suit—they thought he must be drunk or under the effect of drugs and that he had stumbled. The driver flashed his torch at him and immediately let out a scream and pointed at the man's neck. "Look!"

The conductor saw the well-known mark of the cord. They called out, and a number of police and plainclothesmen posted throughout the nooks and crannies of the vicinity hurried toward them. Two people who happened to be passing close by were arrested on the spot and taken to the police station. The incident caused a terrible shock, and Muhsin had to expend yet more hopeless and drastic efforts to no avail. One of those arrested was released (it turned out that he was an Army officer in civilian clothes), while several others were questioned without result. Muhsin tasted the bitterness of defeat and frustration for the fifth time, and it seemed to him that the criminal had none other than him in mind with his devilish pranks. The personality of the criminal made him think of mysterious characters in fiction, or of those creatures which in films descend to Earth from other planets.

Inwardly raging with his affliction, he said to his wife, "It's only sensible for you to go to your father's house at the Pyramids, far from all this atmosphere charged with terror and torment."

"Isn't it wrong for me to leave you in this state?" she protested.

Sighing, he said, "I just wish I could find some good reason for putting the blame on myself or one of my assistants."

The matter was discussed at length in the press and in detailed articles by psychologists and men of religion. As for Abbasiyya, it was seized by panic. At sundown it became depopulated, its cafés and streets empty: it was as though everyone was expecting his own turn to come. The crisis reached its peak when a child at the preparatory school for girls was found strangled in the lavatories.

Incidents followed one upon another in horrifying fashion. People were stunned. No one any longer paid attention to the tedious details about the examinations and inquiries being made, or the opinions of the investigators as given to the press. All thoughts were directed to the impending danger that advanced heedless of anything, making no distinction between old and young, rich and poor, man and woman, healthy and sick, a home, a tram, or a street. A madman? An epidemic? A secret weapon? Some foolish fable? Gloom descended upon the semideserted district. Terror consumed it. People bolted their doors and windows. No one had any subject of conversation apart from death.

Muhsin Abd al-Bari roamed about the district like a man possessed, checking with the police and plainclothesmen, scrutinizing faces and places, wandering around in a state of utter despair, talking to himself about this despair and the pain of his defeat, wishing he could offer his neck to the murderer on condition that he would spare others from his devilish cord.

He visited the maternity hospital where his wife lay. He sat beside her bed for a while, gazing at her and the newborn child, relaxing his mouth into a smile for the first time recently. Then he kissed her on the forehead and left. He returned to the world in which he wished to be seen by no one. He felt something resembling vertigo. Life: terminated by the cord of some unknown person so that it becomes nothing. Yet without doubt it was something, and something of value: love and poetry and the newborn child; hopes whose beauty was limitless; being in life, merely being in life. Was there some error that had to be put right? And when to put it right? The feeling of vertigo intensified as when one suddenly awakes from a deep sleep.

Reports reached the station superintendent that it had been decided to transfer and replace Officer Muhsin Abd al-Bari. Extremely upset, the superintendent at once went to the room of the officer for whom he had such a high regard. He found him with his head flopped down on the desk as though asleep. He approached and softly called out, "Muhsin."

There was no answer. He called again, but the man still did not answer. He shook the officer to wake him, and the head tilted grotesquely. It was then that the superintendent spotted the drop of blood on the blotter. He looked at his colleague in terror and saw the mark of the infernal cord around his neck. The police station and its occupants were shattered.

A series of weighty meetings were held at the Governorate and urgent and important decisions were made. The director-general summoned all his assistants and told them in firm, rousing terms, "We shall declare unremitting war until the criminal is arrested." He thought momentarily and then went on. "There is something no less important than the apprehension of the criminal himself—it is to control the panic that has seized people."

"Yes sir."

"Life must go on as normal, people must go back to feeling that life is good." The questioning look in the probing eyes was answered by the director. "Not one word about this matter will be published in the press."

He discerned a certain listlessness in the men's eyes. "The fact is," he said, "that news disappears from the world once it disappears from the press." He scrutinized the faces. "No one will know anything, not even the people of Abbasiyya themselves."

Striking his desk with his fist, he declared, "No talking of death after today. Life must go on as usual, people must go back to feeling that life is good—and we shall not give up the investigation."

—Translated by Denys Johnson-Davies

ALICE WALKER

HOW DID I GET AWAY WITH KILLING ONE OF THE BIGGEST LAWYERS IN THE STATE? IT WAS EASY.

*M*Y MOTHER AND FATHER were not married. I never knew him. My mother must have loved him, though; she never talked against him when I was little. It was like he never existed. We lived on Poultry street. Why it was called Poultry street I never knew. I guess at one time there must have been a chicken factory somewhere along there. It was right near the center of town. I could walk to the state capitol in less than ten minutes. I could see the top—it was gold—of the capitol building from the front yard. When I was a little girl I used to think it was real gold, shining up there, and then they bought an eagle and put him on top, and when I used to walk up there I couldn't see the top of the building from the ground, it was so high, and I used to reach down and run my hand over the grass. It was like a rug, that grass was, so springy and silky and deep. They had these big old trees, too. Oaks and magnolias; and I thought the magnolia trees were beautiful and one night I climbed up in one of them and got a bloom and took it home. But the air in our house blighted it; it turned brown the minute I took it inside and the petals dropped off.

"Mama worked in private homes. That's how she described her job, to make it sound nicer. 'I work in private homes,' she would say, and that sounded nicer, she thought, than saying 'I'm a maid.'

"Sometimes she made six dollars a day, working in two private homes. Most of the time she didn't make that much. By the time she paid the rent and bought milk and bananas there wasn't anything left.

"She used to leave me alone sometimes because there was no one to keep me—and then there was an old woman up the street who looked after me for a while—and by the time she died she was more like a mother to me than Mama was. Mama was so tired every night when she came home I never hardly got the chance to talk to her. And then sometimes she would go out at night, or bring men home—but they never thought of marrying her. And they sure didn't want to be bothered with me. I guess most of them were like my own father; had children somewhere of their own that they'd left. And then they came to my Mama, who fell for them every time. And I think she may have had a couple of abortions, like some of the women did, who couldn't feed any more mouths. But she tried.

"Anyway, she was a nervous kind of woman. I think she had spells or something because she was so tired. But I didn't understand anything then about exhaustion, worry, lack of a proper diet; I just thought she wanted to work, to be away from the house. I didn't blame her. Where we lived people sometimes just threw pieces of furniture they didn't want over the railing. And there was broken glass and rags everywhere. The place stunk, especially in the summer. And children were always screaming and men were always cussing and women were always yelling about something. . . . It was nothing for a girl or woman to be raped. I was raped myself, when I was twelve, and my Mama never knew and I never told anybody. For, what could they do? It was just a boy, passing through. Somebody's cousin from the North.

"One time my Mama was doing day's work at a private home and took me with her. It was like being in fairyland. Everything was spotless and new, even before Mama started cleaning. I met the woman in the house and played with her children. I didn't even see the man, but he was in there somewhere, while I was out in the yard with the children. I was fourteen, but I guess I looked like a grown woman. Or maybe I looked fourteen. Anyway, the next day, he picked me up when I was coming from school and he said my Mama had asked him to do it. I got in the car with him . . . he took me to his law office, a big office in the middle of town, and he started asking me questions about 'how do you all live?' and 'what grade are you in?' and stuff like that. And then he began to touch me, and I pulled away. But he kept touching me and I was scared . . . he raped me. But afterward he told me he hadn't forced me, that I felt something for him, and he gave me some money. I was crying, going down the stairs. I wanted to kill him.

"I never told Mama. I thought that would be the end of it. But about two days later, on my way from school, he stopped his car again, and I got in. This time we went to his house; nobody was there. And he made me get into his wife's bed. After we'd been doing this for about three weeks, he told me he loved me. I didn't love him, but he had begun to look a little better to me. Really, I think, because he was so clean. He bathed a lot and never smelled even alive, to tell the truth. Or maybe it was the money he gave me, or the presents he bought. I told Mama I had a job after school baby-sitting. And she was glad that I could buy things I needed for school. But it was all from him.

"This went on for two years. He wouldn't let me get pregnant, he said, and I didn't. I would just lay up there in his wife's bed and work out algebra problems or think about what new thing I was going to buy. But one day, when I got home, Mama was there ahead of me, and she saw me get out of his car. I knew when he was driving off that I was going to get it.

"Mama asked me didn't I know he was a white man? Didn't I

know he was a married man with two children? Didn't I have good sense? And do you know what I told her? *I told her he loved me.* Mama was crying and praying at the same time by then. The neighbors heard both of us screaming and crying, because Mama beat me almost to death with the cord from the electric iron. She just hacked it off the iron, still on the ironing board. She beat me till she couldn't raise her arm. And then she had one of her fits, just twitching and sweating and trying to claw herself into the floor. This scared me more than the beating. That night she told me something I hadn't paid much attention to before. She said: 'On top of everything else, that man's daddy goes on the t.v. every night and says folks like us ain't even human.' It was his daddy who had stood in the schoolhouse door saying it would be over his dead body before any black children would come into a white school.

"But do you think that stopped me? No. I would look at his daddy on t.v. ranting and raving about how integration was a communist plot, and I would just think of how different his son Bubba was from his daddy! Do you understand what I'm saying. I thought he *loved* me. That *meant* something to me. What did I know about 'equal rights'? What did I care about 'integration'? I was sixteen! I wanted somebody to tell me I was pretty, and he was telling me that all the time. I even thought it was *brave* of him to go with me. History? What did I know about History?

"I began to hate Mama. We argued about Bubba all the time, for months. And I still slipped out to meet him, because Mama had to work. I told him how she beat me, and about how much she despised him—he was really pissed off that any black person could despise him—and about how she had these spells. . . . Well, the day I became seventeen, the *day* of my seventeenth birthday, I signed papers in his law office, and I had my mother committed to an insane asylum.

"After Mama had been in Carthage Insane Asylum for three

months, she managed somehow to get a lawyer. An old slick-headed man who smoked great big black cigars. People laughed at him because he didn't even have a law office, but he was the only lawyer that would touch the case, because Bubba's daddy was such a big deal. And we all gathered in the judge's chambers—because he wasn't about to let this case get out. Can you imagine, if it had? And Mama's old lawyer told the judge how Bubba's daddy had tried to buy him off. And Bubba got up and swore he'd never touched me. And then I got up and said Mama *was* insane. And do you know what? By that time it was true. Mama was insane. She had no mind left at all. They had given her shock treatments or something. . . . God knows what else they gave her. But she was as vacant as an empty eye socket. She just sat sort of hunched over, and her hair was white.

"And after all this, Bubba wanted us to keep going together. Mama was just an obstacle that he felt he had removed. But I just suddenly— in a way I don't even pretend to understand—woke up. It was like everything up to then had been some kind of dream. And I told him I wanted to get Mama out. But he wouldn't do it; he just kept trying to make me go with him. And sometimes—out of habit, I guess—I did. My body did what it was being paid to do. And Mama died. And I killed Bubba.

"How did I get away with killing one of the biggest lawyers in the state? It was easy. He kept a gun in his desk drawer at the office and one night I took it out and shot him. I shot him while he was wearing his thick winter overcoat, so I wouldn't have to see him bleed. But I don't think I took the time to wipe off my fingerprints, because, to tell the truth, I couldn't stand it another minute in that place. No one came after me, and I read in the paper the next day that he'd been killed by burglars. I guess they thought 'burglars' had stolen all that money Bubba kept in his safe—but I had it. One of the carrots Bubba always dangled before me was that he was going to send me to college:

I didn't see why he shouldn't do it.

"The strangest thing was, Bubba's wife came over to the house and asked me if I'd mind looking after the children while she went to Bubba's funeral. I did it, of course, because I was afraid she'd suspect something if I didn't. So on the day he was buried I was in his house, sitting on his wife's bed with his children, and eating fried chicken his wife, Julie, had cooked."

WILLIAM TREVOR

THE HOTEL
OF THE
IDLE MOON

*T*HE WOMAN called Mrs. Dankers placed a rose-tipped cigarette between her lips and lit it from the lighter on the
dashboard. The brief spurt of light revealed a long, handsome face with a sharpness about it that might often have been reminiscent of the edge of a chisel. In the darkness a double funnel of
smoke streamed from her nostrils, and she gave a tiny gasp of satisfaction. On a grass verge two hundred miles north of London the car
was stationary except for the gentle rocking imposed by the wind.
Above the persistent lashing of the rain the radio played a popular
tune of the thirties, quietly and without emotion. It was two minutes
to midnight.

"Well?"

The car door banged and Dankers was again beside her. He smelt
of rain; it dripped from him on to her warm knees.

"Well?" Mrs. Dankers repeated.

He started the engine. The car crept on to the narrow highway, its
wipers slashing at the rain, its powerful headlights drawing the stream-

ing foliage startlingly near. He cleared the windscreen with his arm. "It'll do," he murmured. He drove on slowly, and the sound of the engine was lost in a medley of wind and rain and the murmur of music and the swish of the wipers.

"It'll do?" said Mrs. Dankers. "Is it the right house?"

He twisted the car this way and that along the lane. The lights caught an image of pillars and gates, closed in upon them and lost them as the car swung up the avenue.

"Yes," he murmured. "It's the right house."

Within that house, an old man lying stiffly in bed heard the jangle of the bell at the hall door and frowned over this unaccustomed sound. At first he imagined that the noise had been caused by the wind, but then the bell rang again, sharply and in a peremptory manner. The old man, called Cronin, the only servant in the house, rose from his bed and dragged a coat on to his body, over his pyjamas. He descended the stairs, sighing to himself.

The pair outside saw a light go on in the hall, and then they heard the tread of Cronin's feet and the sound of a bar being pulled back on the door. Dankers threw a cigarette away and prepared an expression for his face. His wife shivered in the rain.

"It's so late," the old man in pyjamas said when the travellers had told him their tale. "I must wake the Marstons for guidance, sir. I can't do this on my own responsibility."

"It's wet and cold as well," Dankers murmured, smiling at the man through his widely spread moustache. "No night to be abroad, really. You must understand our predicament."

"No night to be standing on a step," added Mrs. Dankers. "At least may we come in?"

They entered the house and were led to a large drawing-room. "Please wait," the man invited. "The fire is not entirely out. I'll question the Marstons as you warm yourselves."

The Dankerses did not speak. They stood where the man had left them, staring about the room. Their manner one to the other had an edge of hostility to it, as though they were as suspicious in this relationship as they were of the world beyond it.

"I am Sir Giles Marston," said another old man. "You've sustained some travelling difficulty?"

"Our car has let us down—due, I suppose, to some penetration of the weather. We left it by your gates. Sir Giles, we're at your mercy. Dankers the name is. The lady is my good wife." Dankers stretched his arm towards his host in a manner that might have suggested to an onlooker that he, and not Sir Giles, was the welcomer.

"Our need is simple," said Mrs. Dankers. "A roof over our heads."

"Some outhouse maybe," Dankers hazarded, overplaying his part. He laughed. "Anywhere we can curl up for an hour or two. We cannot be choosers."

"I'd prefer a chair," his wife interceded sharply. "A chair and a rug would suit me nicely."

"I'm sure we can do better than that. Prepare two beds, Cronin; and light our guests a fire in their room."

Sir Giles Marston moved into the centre of the room and in the greater light the Dankerses saw a small, hunched man, with a face like leather that has been stretched for a lifetime and is suddenly slackened; as lined as a map.

"Oh, really," Dankers protested in his soft voice, "you mustn't go to such trouble. It's imposition enough to rouse you like this."

"We'll need sheets," Cronin said. "Sheets and bedding: God knows where I shall find them, sir."

"Brandy," Sir Giles suggested. "Am I right, Mrs. Dankers, in thinking that strong refreshment would partly answer the situation?"

Cronin left the room, speaking to himself. Sir Giles poured the brandy. "I'm ninety years of age," he told his guests, "but yet aware that inhospitality is a sin to be ashamed of. I bid you good-night."

"Who are they?" Lady Marston asked in the morning, having heard the tale from her husband.

"My dear, they are simply people. They bear some unpleasant name. More than that I do not really wish to know."

"It's a sunny day by the look of it. Your guests will have breakfasted and gone by now. I'm sorry in a way, for I would welcome fresh faces and a different point of view. We live too quiet a life, Giles. We are too much thrown in upon each other. It's hardly a healthy manner in which to prepare for our dying."

Sir Giles, who was engaged in the drawing up of his trousers, smiled. "Had you seen these two, my dear, you would not have said they are the kind to make our going any easier. The man has a moustache of great proportions, the woman you would describe as smart."

"You're intolerant, love. And so high-handed that you didn't even discover the reason for this visit."

"They came because they could move in neither direction. Trouble with their motor-car."

"They've probably left with all our little bits and pieces. You're a sitting bird for a confidence trick. Oh, Giles, Giles!"

Sir Giles departed, and in the breakfast-room below discovered the pair called Dankers still at table.

"Your man has been most generous," Dankers said. "He's fed us like trenchermen: porridge, coffee, bacon and eggs. Two for me, one for my good wife. And toast and marmalade. And this delicious butter."

"Are you trying to say that an essential commodity was lacking? If so, I fear you must be more precise. In this house we are now past subtlety."

"You've made a fool of yourself," Mrs. Dankers said to her husband. "Who wishes to know what two strangers have recently digested?"

"Pardon, pardon," murmured Dankers. "Sir Giles, forgive a rough diamond!"

"Certainly. If you have finished, please don't delay on my account. Doubtless you are anxious to be on your way."

"My husband will attend to the car. Probably it's necessary to send for help to a garage. In the meantime I'll keep you company if I may."

Dankers left the room, passing on the threshold an elderly lady whom he did not address, wishing to appear uncertain in his mind as to her identity.

"This is the woman who came in the night," Sir Giles said to his wife. "Her husband is seeing to their motor-car so that they may shortly be on their way. Mrs. Dankers, my wife, Lady Marston."

"We're more than grateful, Lady Marston. It looked as though we were in for a nasty night."

"I hope Cronin made you comfortable. I fear I slept through everything. 'My dear, we have two guests,' my husband said to me this morning. You may imagine my surprise."

Cronin entered and placed plates of food before Sir Giles and Lady Marston.

Conversationally, Mrs. Dankers said: "You have a fine place here."

"It's cold and big," Sir Giles replied.

The Marstons set about their breakfast, and Mrs. Dankers, unable to think of something to say, sat in silence. The smoke from her cigarette was an irritation to her hosts, but they did not remark on it, since they accepted its presence as part of the woman herself. When he returned Dankers sat beside his wife again. He poured some coffee and said: "I am no mechanic, Sir Giles. I would like to use your phone to summon help."

"We are not on the telephone."

"Not?" murmured Dankers in simulated surprise, for he knew the fact already. "How far in that case is the nearest village? And does it boast a garage?"

"Three miles. As to the presence of a garage, I have had no cause to establish that point. But I imagine there is a telephone."

"Giles, introduce me please. Is this man Mrs. Dankers' husband?"

"He claims it. Mr. Dankers, my wife, Lady Marston."

"How d'you do?" Dankers said, rising to shake the offered hand. "I'm afraid we're in a pickle."

"You should walk it in an hour," Sir Giles reminded him.

"There's no way of forwarding a message?"

"No."

"The postman?"

"He hardly ever comes. And then brings only a circular or two."

"Perhaps your man?"

"Cronin's days as Hermes are over. You must see that surely for yourself?"

"In that case there's nothing for it but a tramp."

This conclusion of Dankers' was received in silence.

"Walk, Mr. Dankers," Lady Marston said eventually, and added to her husband's dismay, "and return for lunch. Afterwards you can leave us at your leisure."

"How kind of you," the Dankerses said together. They smiled in unison too. They rose and left the room.

Cronin watched and listened to everything. "Prepare two beds," his master had said, and from that same moment Cronin had been on his guard. He had given them breakfast in the morning, and had hoped that once they had consumed it they would be on their way. He took them to be commercial travellers, since they had the air of people who were used to moving about and spending nights in places. "You have a fine place here," Mrs. Dankers had said to the Marstons, and Cronin had narrowed his eyes, wondering why she had said it, wondering why she was sitting there, smoking a cigarette while the Marstons breakfasted. He had examined their motor-car and had thought it somehow typical of the people. They were people, thought Cronin, who would know what to do with all the knobs and gadgets on the motor-car's dashboard; they would take to that dashboard like ducks to water.

For forty-eight years Cronin had lived in the house, serving the Marstons. Once, there had been other servants, and in his time he had watched over them and over the house itself. Now he contented himself with watching over the Marstons. "Some outhouse maybe," Dankers had said, and Cronin had thought that Dankers was not a man who knew much about outhouses. He saw Dankers and Mrs. Dankers sitting together in a café connected with a cinema, a place such as he had himself visited twenty-odd years ago and had not cared for. He heard Dankers asking the woman what she would take to eat, adding that he himself would have a mixed grill with chips, and a pot of strong tea, and sliced bread and butter. Cronin observed these people closely and memorized much of what they said.

"Clearly," Dankers remarked at lunch, "we're not in training. Or perhaps it was the fascination of your magnificent orchard."

"Are you saying you didn't walk to the village?" Sir Giles inquired, a trifle impatiently.

"Forgive these city folk," cried Dankers loudly. "Quite frankly, we got no distance at all."

"What are you to do then? Shall you try again this afternoon? There are, of course, various houses on the route. One of them may have a telephone."

"Your orchard has greatly excited us. I've never seen such trees."

"They're the finest in England."

"A pity," said Mrs. Dankers, nibbling at fish on a fork, "to see it in such rack and ruin."

Dankers blew upwards into his moustache and ended the activity with a smile. "It is worth some money, that orchard," he said.

Sir Giles eyed him coolly. "Yes, sir; it is worth some money. But time is passing and we are wasting it in conversation. You must see to the affair of your motor-car."

The storm had brought the apples down. They lay in their thousands in the long grass, damp and glistening, like immense, unusual jewels in the afternoon sun. The Dankerses examined them closely, strolling through the orchard, noting the various trees and assessing their yield. For the purpose they had fetched Wellington boots from their car and had covered themselves in waterproof coats of an opaque plastic material. They did not speak, but occasionally, coming across a tree that pleased them, they nodded.

"A lot could be done, you know," Dankers explained at dinner. "It is a great orchard and in a mere matter of weeks it could be set on the road to profit and glory."

"It has had its glory," replied Sir Giles, "and probably its profit too. Now it must accept its fate. I cannot keep it up."

"Oh, it's a shame! A terrible shame to see it as it is. Why, you could make a fortune, Sir Giles."

"You didn't get to the village?" Lady Marston asked.

"We could not pass the orchard!"

"Which means," Sir Giles said, "that you'll be with us for another night."

"Could you bear it?" Mrs. Dankers smiled a thin smile. "Could you bear to have us all over again?"

"Of course, of course," said Lady Marston. "Perhaps tomorrow you'll feel a little stronger. I understand your lethargy. It's natural after an unpleasant experience."

"They have been through neither flood nor fire," her husband reminded her. "And the village will be no nearer tomorrow."

"Perhaps," Dankers began gently, "the postman will call in the morning—"

"We have no living relatives," Sir Giles cut in, "and most of our friends are gone. The circulars come once a month or so."

"The groceries then?"

"I have inquired of Cronin about the groceries. They came yesterday. They will come again next week."

"The daily milk is left at the foot of the avenue. Cronin walks to fetch it. You could leave a message there," Lady Marston suggested. "It is the arrangement we have for emergencies, such as summoning the doctor."

"The doctor? But surely by the time he got here—?"

"In greater emergency one of the three of us would walk to the nearest house. We do not," Sir Giles added, "find it so difficult to pass one leg before the other. Senior though we may be."

"Perhaps the milk is an idea," Lady Marston said.

"Oh no, we could never put anyone to so much trouble. It would be too absurd. No, tomorrow we shall have found our feet."

But tomorrow when it came was a different kind of day, because with something that disagreed with him in his stomach Sir Giles died in the night. His heart was taxed by sharp little spasms of pain and in the end they were too much for it.

"We're going to see to you for a bit," Mrs. Dankers said after the funeral. "We'll pop you in your room, dear, and Cronin shall attend to all your needs. You can't be left to suffer your loss alone; you've been so kind to us."

Lady Marston moved her head up and down. The funeral had been rather much for her. Mrs. Dankers led her by the arm to her room.

"Well," said Dankers, speaking to Cronin with whom he was left, "so that's that."

"I was his servant for forty-eight years, sir."

"Indeed, indeed. And you have Lady Marston, to whom you may devote your whole attention. Meals in her room, Cronin, and pause now and then for the occasional chat. The old lady'll be lonely."

"I'll be lonely myself, sir,"

"Indeed. Then all the more reason to be good company. And you, more than I, understand the business of being elderly. You know by instinct what to say, how best to seem soothing."

"Your car is repaired, sir? At least it moved today. You'll be on your way? Shall I pack some sandwiches?"

"Come, come, Cronin, how could we leave two lonely people so easily in the lurch? Chance has sent us to your side in this hour of need: we'll stay to do what we can. Besides, there are Sir Giles's wishes."

What's this? thought Cronin, examining the eyes of the man who had come in the night and had stayed to see his master buried. They were eyes he would not care to possess himself, for fear of what went with them. He said:

"His wishes, sir?"

"That his orchard should again be put in use. The trees repaired and pruned. The fruit sold for its true value. An old man's dying wish won't go unheeded."

"But, sir, there's so much work in it. The trees run into many hundreds—"

"Quite right, Cronin. That's observant of you. Many men are needed to straighten the confusion and waste. There's much to do."

"Sir Giles wished this, sir?" said Cronin, playing a part, knowing that Sir Giles could never have passed on to Dankers his dying wish. "It's unlike him, sir, to think about his orchard. He watched it failing."

"He wished it, Cronin. He wished it, and a great deal else. You who have seen some changes in your time are in for a couple more. And now, my lad, a glass of that good brandy would not go down amiss. At a time like this one must try to keep one's spirits up."

Dankers sat by the fire in the drawing-room, sipping his brandy and writing industriously in a notebook. He was shortly joined by his wife, to whom he handed from time to time a leaf from this book so that she might share his plans. When midnight had passed they rose and walked through the house, measuring the rooms with a practised eye and noting their details on paper. They examined the kitchens and outhouses, and in the moonlight they walked the length of the gardens. Cronin watched them, peeping at them in all their activity.

"There's a pretty little room next to Cronin's that is so much sunnier," Mrs. Dankers said. "Cosier and warmer, dear. We'll have your things moved there, I think. This one is dreary with memories. And you and Cronin will be company for one another."

Lady Marston nodded, then changing her mind said: "I like this room. It's big and beautiful and with a view. I've become used to it."

"Now, now, my dear, we mustn't be morbid, must we? And we don't always quite know what's best. It's good to be happy, dear, and you'll be happier there."

"I'll be happier, Mrs. Dankers? Happier away from all my odds and ends, and Giles's too?"

"My dear, we'll move them with you. Come, now, look on the bright side. There's the future too, as well as the past."

Cronin came, and the things were moved. Not quite everything though, because the bed and the wardrobe and the heavy dressing-table would not fit in the new setting.

In the orchard half a dozen men set about creating order out of chaos. The trees were trimmed and then treated, paths restored, broken walls rebuilt. The sheds were cleared and filled with fruit-boxes in readiness for next year's harvest.

"There's a wickedness here," Cronin reported to Lady Marston. "There's a cook in the kitchen, and a man who waits on them. My only task, they tell me, is to carry your food and keep your room in order."

"And to see to yourself, Cronin, to take it easy and to watch your rheumatics. Fetch a pack of cards."

Cronin recalled the house as it once had been, a place that was lively with weekend guests and was regularly wallpapered. Then there had come the years of decline and the drifting towards decay, and now there was a liveliness of a different order; while the days passed by, the liveliness established itself like a season. Mrs. Dankers bustled from room to room, in tune with the altered world. Dankers said: "It's good to see you seeming so sprightly, Cronin. The weather suits you, eh? And now that we've made these few little changes life is easier, I think." Cronin replied that it was certainly true that he had less to do. "So you should have less to do," said Dankers. "Face the facts: you cannot hope to undertake a young chap's work." He smiled, to release the remark of its barb.

Cronin was worried about the passive attitude of Lady Marston. She had gone like a lamb to the small room, which now served as her sitting-room and bedroom combined. She had not stirred from the top of the house since the day of the move; she knew nothing save what he told her of all that was happening.

"The builders are here," he had said; but quite often, midway through a game of cards, she would pause with her head a little to one side, listening to the distant sound of hammering. "It is the noise of the builders," he would remind her; and she would place a card on the table and say: "I did not know that Sir Giles had ordered the builders." In the mornings she was well aware of things, but as the day passed on she spoke more often of Sir Giles; of Sir Giles's plans for the orchard and the house. Cronin feared that, day by day, Lady Marston was sinking into her dotage; the morning hours of her clarity were shrinking even as he thought about it.

One afternoon, walking to the foot of the avenue to stretch his legs, Cronin found a small, elegantly painted board secured to one of the pillars. It faced the road, inviting those who passed to read the words it bore. He read them himself and expostulated angrily, muttering the words, repeating them as he made his way back to the house.

"M'lady, this cannot happen. They've turned your house into an hotel."

Lady Marston looked at Cronin, whom she had known for so many years, who had seen with her and her husband a thousand details of change and reconstruction. He was upset now, she could see it. His white, sparse hair seemed uncombed, which was unusual for Cronin. There was a blush of temper on his cheeks; and in his eyes a wildness one did not associate with so well-trained a servant.

"What is it, Cronin?"

"There's a notice at the gate announcing 'The Hotel of the Idle Moon.'"

"Well?"

"The Dankerses—"

"Ah, the Dankerses. You talk so much about the Dankerses, Cronin. Yet as I remember them they are surely not worth it. Sir Giles said the man had repeated to him every mouthful of his breakfast. In the end he had to make short shrift of the pair."

"No, no—"

"Yes, Cronin: they tried his patience. He gave them their marching orders, reminding them that the night was fine and the moon was full. There was a coolness between us, for I believed he had gone too far."

"No, no. You must remember: the Dankerses are still here. They've tidied up the orchard and now have turned your house into an hotel."

Lady Marston made her impatient little shaking of the head. "Of course, of course. Cronin, I apologize. You must find me very trying."

"It has no meaning: The Hotel of the Idle Moon. Yet I fear, m'lady, it may in time mean much to us."

Lady Marston laughed quite gaily. "Few things have meaning,

Cronin. It is rather much to expect a meaning for everything."

They played three games of cards, and the matter was not again referred to. But in the night Lady Marston came to Cronin's bedside and shook him by the shoulder. "I'm upset," she said, "by what you tell me. This isn't right at all. Cronin, listen carefully: tomorrow you must inform Sir Giles. Tell him of our fears. Beg him to reconsider. I'm far too old to act. I must leave it all to you."

The house was busy then with visitors, and cars up and down the avenue. It thrived as the orchard thrived; it had a comfortable and sumptuous feel, and Cronin thought again of the past.

"Ah, Cronin," Mrs. Dankers said, pausing on the back stairs one day. "Tell me, how is poor Lady Marston? She does not come down at all, and we're so on the go here that it's hard to find time to make the journey to the top of the house."

"Lady Marston is well, madam."

"She's welcome in the lounges. Always welcome. Would you be good enough to tell her, Cronin?"

"Yes, madam."

"But keep an eye on her, like a good man. I would not like her upsetting the guests. You understand?"

"Yes, madam. I understand. I don't think Lady Marston is likely to make use of the lounges."

"She would find the climb up and down too much, I dare say."

"Yes, madam. She would find it too much."

Cronin made many plans. He thought that one day when Dankers was away he would approach the orchard with Sir Giles's rifle and order the men to cut down the trees. That at least would bring one part of the sadness to an end. He saw the scene quite clearly: the trees toppling one against the other, their branches webbed as they hung in the air above the fresh stumps. But when he searched for the rifle he could not find it. He thought that he might wreak great damage in the house, burning carpets and opening up the upholstery. But for this he found neither opportunity nor the strength it demanded. Stropping his razor one morning, he hit upon the best plan of all: to creep into the Dankerses' bedroom and cut their throats. It had once been his master's bedroom and now it was theirs; which made revenge the sweeter. Every day for forty-eight years he had carried to the room a tray of tea-cups and a pot of Earl Grey tea. Now he would carry his sharpened razor; and for the rest of his life he would continue his shaving with it, relishing every scrape. The idea delighted him. Sir Giles would have wished to see the last of them, to see the last of all these people who strayed about the house and grounds, and to see the orchard settle down again to being the orchard he had left behind. And was not he, Cronin, the living agent of the dead Sir Giles? Was he not now companion to his wife? And did she not, in an occasional moment of failure, address him as she had her husband? Yet when he shared his plans with Lady Marston she did not at all endorse them.

"Take the will for the deed, Cronin. Leave these people be."

"But they are guilty. They may have killed Sir Giles."

"They may have. And does it matter this way or that—to chop off a few dwindling years?"

Cronin saw no reason in her words. He pitied her, and hardened himself in his resolve.

"I am sorry to speak to you like this, Cronin," Dankers said, "but I cannot, you know, have you wandering about the house in this manner. There have been complaints from the guests. You have your room, with Lady Marston to talk to; why not keep more to the region we have set aside for you?"

"Yes, sir."

"Of late, Cronin, you've become untidy in your appearance. You have a dishevelled look and often seem—well, frankly, Cronin, dirty. It's not good for business. Not good at all."

The moon shall not be idle, Cronin thought. The moon shall be agog to see. The moon shall clear the sky of clouds that the stars may ponder on the pillows full of blood.

"Mr. Dankers, sir, why is this place called the Idle Moon?"

Dankers laughed. "A foible of my good wife's. She liked the sound of it. Quite telling, don't you think?"

"Yes, sir." The moon shall like the sound of her. A shriek in a severed throat, a howl of pain.

"See to it, Cronin, eh?"

"Yes, sir."

So Cronin kept to his room, descending the back stairs only for his food and Lady Marston's. The weeks passed, and more and more he sat entranced with the duty he had set himself. Sometimes, as though drunk with it, he found himself a little uncertain as to its exactitudes. That was when he felt tired; when he dropped off into a doze as he sat by his small window, staring at the sky and listening to the faraway hum from the house below.

Then one morning Cronin discovered that Lady Marston had died in her sleep. They carried her off, and he put away the pack of cards.

"It's a sad day for us all," Dankers said, and in the distance Cronin could hear Mrs. Dankers giving some brisk order to a servant. He returned to his room and for a moment there was an oddness in his mind and he imagined that it was Sir Giles who had said that the day was sad. Then he remembered that Sir Giles was dead too and that he was the only one left.

In the months that followed he spoke to no one but himself, for he was concentrating on the details of his plan. They kept slipping away, and increasingly he had a struggle to keep them straight.

When the razor was there the faces on the pillows were vague and empty, and he could not remember whose he had planned they should be. There was the pattern of moonlight, and the red stain on the bed-clothes, but Cronin could not often now see what any of it meant. It made him tired, thinking the trouble out. And when, in the end, the shreds of his plan came floating back to him he smiled in some astonishment, seeing only how absurd it had been that late in his life he should have imagined himself a match for the world and its conquerors.

ANTHONY TROLLOPE

AARON TROW

*I*WOULD wish to declare, at the beginning of this story, that I shall never regard that cluster of islets which we call Bermuda as the Fortunate Islands of the Ancients. Do not let professional geographers take me up, and say that no one has so accounted them, and that the ancients have never been supposed to have gotten themselves so far westwards. What I mean to assert is this—that, had any ancient been carried thither by enterprise or stress of weather, he would not have given those islands so good a name. That the Neapolitan sailors of King Alonzo should have been wrecked here, I consider to be more likely. The vexed Bermoothes is a good name for them. There is no getting in or out of them without the greatest difficulty, and a patient, slow navigation, which is very heart-rending. That Caliban should have lived here I can imagine; that Ariel would have been sick of the place is certain; and that Governor Prospero should have been willing to abandon his governorship, I conceive to have been only natural. When one regards the present state of the place, one is tempted to doubt whether any of the governors have been conjurors since his days.

Bermuda, as all the world knows, is a British colony at which we maintain a convict establishment. Most of our outlying convict establishments have been sent back upon our hands from our colonies, but here one is still maintained. There is also in the islands a strong military fortress, though not a fortress looking magnificent to the eyes of civilians as do Malta and Gibraltar. There are also here some six thousand white people and some six thousand black people, eating, drinking, sleeping, and dying.

The convict establishment is the most notable feature of Bermuda to a stranger, but it does not seem to attract much attention from the regular inhabitants of the place. There is no intercourse between the prisoners and the Bermudians. The convicts are rarely seen by them, and the convict islands are rarely visited. As to the prisoners themselves, of course it is not open to them—or should not be open to them—to have intercourse with any but the prison authorities.

There have, however, been instances in which convicts have escaped from their confinement, and made their way out among the islands. Poor wretches! As a rule, there is but little chance for any that can so escape. The whole length of the cluster is but twenty miles, and the breadth is under four. The prisoners are, of course, white men, and the lower orders of Bermuda, among whom alone could a runagate have any chance of hiding himself, are all negroes; so that such a one would be known at once. Their clothes are all marked. Their only chance of a permanent escape would be in the hold of an American ship; but what captain of an American or other ship would willingly encumber himself with an escaped convict? But, nevertheless, men have escaped; and in one instance, I believe, a convict got away, so that of him no further tidings were ever heard.

For the truth of the following tale I will not by any means vouch. If one were to inquire on the spot one might probably find that the ladies all believe it, and the old men; that all the young men know exactly how much of it is false and how much true; and that the steady, middle-aged, well-to-do islanders are quite convinced that it is romance from beginning to end. My readers may range themselves with the ladies, the young men, or the steady, well-to-do, middle-aged islanders, as they please.

Some years ago, soon after the prison was first established on its present footing, three men did escape from it, and among them a certain notorious prisoner named Aaron Trow. Trow's antecedents in England had not been so villainously bad as those of many of his fellow-convicts, though the one offence for which he was punished had been of a deep dye: he had shed man's blood. At a period of great distress in a manufacturing town he had led men on to riot, and with his own hand had slain the first constable who had endeavored to do his duty against him. There had been courage in the doing of the deed, and probably no malice; but the deed, let its moral blackness have been what it might, had sent him to Bermuda, with a sentence against him of penal servitude for life. Had he been then amenable to prison discipline—even then, with such a sentence against him as that—he might have won his way back, after the lapse of years, to the children, and, perhaps, to the wife, that he had left behind him; but he was amenable to no rules—to no discipline. His heart was sore to death with an idea of injury, and he lashed himself against the bars of his cage with a feeling that it would be well if he could so lash himself till he might perish in his fury.

And then a day came in which an attempt was made by a large body of convicts, under his leadership, to get the better of the officers of the prison. It is hardly necessary to say that the attempt failed. Such attempts always fail. It failed on this occasion signally, and Trow, with two other men, were condemned to be scourged terribly and then kept in solitary confinement for some lengthened term of months. Before, however, the day of scourging came, Trow and his two associates had escaped.

I have not the space to tell how this was effected, nor the power to describe the manner. They did escape from the establishment into the islands, and though two of them were taken after a single day's run at liberty, Aaron Trow had not been yet retaken even when a week was over. When a month was over he had not been retaken, and the officers of the prison began to say that he had got away from them in a vessel to the States. It was impossible, they said, that he should have remained in the islands and not been discovered. It was not impossible that he might have destroyed himself, leaving his body where it had not yet been found. But he could not have lived on in Bermuda during that month's search. So, at least, said the officers of the prison. There was, however, a report through the islands that he had been seen from time to time; that he had gotten bread from the negroes at night, threatening them with death if they told of his whereabouts; and that all the clothes of the mate of a vessel had been stolen while the man was bathing, including a suit of dark blue cloth, in which suit of clothes, or in one of such a nature, a stranger had been seen skulking about the rocks near St. George. All this the governor of the prison affected to disbelieve, but the opinion was becoming very rife in the islands that Aaron Trow was still there.

A vigilant search, however, is a task of great labour, and cannot be kept up for ever. By degrees it was relaxed. The wardens and gaolers ceased to patrol the island roads by night, and it was agreed that Aaron Trow was gone, or that he would be starved to death, or that he would in time be driven to leave such traces of his whereabouts as must lead to his discovery; and this at last did turn out to be the fact.

There is a sort of prettiness about these islands which, though it never rises to the loveliness of romantic scenery, is nevertheless attractive in its way. The land breaks itself into little knolls, and the sea runs up, hither and thither, in a thousand creeks and inlets; and then, too, when the oleanders are in bloom, they give a wonderfully bright colour to the landscape. Oleanders seem to be the roses of Bermuda, and are cultivated round all the villages of the better class through the islands. There are two towns, St. George and Hamilton, and one main high road, which connects them; but even this high road is broken by a ferry, over which every vehicle going from St. George to Hamilton must be conveyed. Most of the locomotion in these parts is done by boats, and the residents look to the sea with its narrow creeks, as their best highway from their farms to their best market. In those days—and those days were not very long since—the building of small ships was their chief trade, and they valued their land mostly for the small scrubby cedar-trees with which this trade was carried on.

As one goes from St. George to Hamilton the road runs between two seas; that to the right is the ocean; that on the left is an inland creek, which runs up through a large portion of the islands, so that the land on the other side of it is near to the traveller. For a considerable portion of the way there are no houses lying near the road, and there is one residence, some way from the road, so secluded that no other house lies within a mile of it by land. By water it might probably be reached within half a mile. This place was called Crump Island, and here lived, and had lived for many years, an old gentleman, a native of Bermuda, whose business it had been to buy up cedar wood and sell it to the ship-builders at Hamilton. In our story we shall not have very much to do with old Mr. Bergen, but it will be necessary to say a word or two about his house.

It stood on what would have been an island in the creek, had not a narrow causeway, barely broad enough for a road, joined it to that larger island on which stands the town of St. George. As the main road approaches the ferry it runs through some rough, hilly, open ground, which on the right side towards the ocean has never been cultivated. The distance from the ocean here may, perhaps, be a quarter of a mile, and the ground is for the most part covered with low furze. On the left of the road the land is cultivated in patches, and here, some half mile or more from the ferry, a path turns away to Crump Island. The house cannot be seen from the road, and, indeed, can hardly be seen at all, except from the sea. It lies, perhaps, three furlongs from the high road, and the path to it is but little used, as the passage to and from it is chiefly made by water.

Here, at the time of our story, lived Mr. Bergen, and here lived Mr. Bergen's daughter. Miss Bergen was well known at St. George as a steady, good girl, who spent her time in looking after her father's household matters, in managing his two black maid-servants and the black gardener, and who did her duty in that sphere of life to which she had been called. She was a comely, well-shaped young woman, with a sweet countenance, rather large in size, and very quiet in demeanor. In her earlier years, when young girls usually first bud forth into womanly beauty, the neighbours had not thought much of Anastasia Bergen, nor had the young men of St. George been wont to stay their boats under the window of Crump Cottage in order that they might listen to her voice or feel the light of her eye; but slowly, as years went by, Anastasia Bergen became a woman that a man might well love; and a man learned to love her who was well worthy of a woman's heart. This was Caleb Morton, the Presbyterian minister of St. George; and Caleb Morton had been engaged to marry Miss Bergen for the last two years past, at the period of Aaron Trow's escape from prison.

Caleb Morton was not a native of Bermuda, but had been sent thither by the synod of his church from Nova Scotia. He was a tall, handsome man, at this time of some thirty years of age, of a presence which might almost have been called commanding. He was very strong, but of a temperament which did not often give him opportunity to put forth his strength; and his life had been such that neither he nor others knew of what nature might be his courage. The greater part of his life was spent in preaching to some few of the white people around him, and in teaching as many of the blacks as he could get to hear him. His days were very quiet, and had been altogether without excitement until he had met with Anastasia Bergen. It will suffice for us to say that he did meet her, and that now, for two years past, they had been engaged as man and wife.

Old Mr. Bergen, when he heard of the engagement, was not well pleased at the information. In the first place, his daughter was very necessary to him, and the idea of her marrying and going away had hardly as yet occurred to him; and then he was by no means inclined to part with any of his money. It must not be presumed that he had amassed a fortune by his trade in cedar wood. Few tradesmen in Bermuda do, as I imagine, amass fortunes. Of some few hundred pounds he was possessed, and these, in the course of nature, would go to his daughter when he died; but he had no inclination to hand any portion of them over to his daughter before they did go to her in the course of nature. Now, the income which Caleb Morton earned as a Presbyterian clergyman was not large, and, therefore, no day had been fixed as yet for his marriage with Anastasia.

But, though the old man had been from the first averse to the match, his hostility had not been active. He had not forbidden Mr. Morton his house, or affected to be in any degree angry because his daughter had a lover. He had merely grumbled forth an intimation that those who marry in haste repent at leisure—that love kept nobody warm if the pot did not boil; and that, as for him, it was as much as he could do to keep his own pot boiling at Crump Cottage. In answer to this Anastasia said nothing. She asked him for no money, but still kept his accounts, managed his household, and looked patiently forward for better days.

Old Mr. Bergen himself spent much of his time at Hamilton, where he had a woodyard with a couple of rooms attached to it. It was his custom to remain here three nights of the week, during which Anastasia was left alone at the cottage; and it happened by no means seldom that she was altogether alone, for the negro whom they called the gardener would go to her father's place at Hamilton, and the two black girls would crawl away up to the road, tired with the monotony of the sea at the cottage. Caleb had more than once told her that she was too much alone, but she had laughed at him, saying that solitude in Bermuda was not dangerous. Nor, indeed, was it; for the people are quiet and well-mannered, lacking much energy, but being, in the same degree, free from any propensity to violence.

"So you are going," she said to her lover, one evening, as he rose from the chair on which he had been swinging himself at the door of the cottage which looks down over the creek of the sea. He had sat there for an hour talking to her as she worked, or watching her as she moved about the place. It was a beautiful evening, and the sun had been falling to rest with almost tropical glory before his feet. The bright oleanders were red with their blossoms all around him, and he had thoroughly enjoyed his hour of easy rest. "So you are going," she said to him, not putting her work out of her hand as he rose to depart.

"Yes; and it is time for me to go. I have still work to do before I can get to bed. Ah, well; I suppose the day will come at last when I need not leave you as soon as my hour of rest is over."

"Come; of course it will come. That is, if your reverence should choose to wait for it another ten years or so."

"I believe you would not mind waiting twenty years."

"Not if a certain friend of mine would come down and see me of evenings when I'm alone after the day. It seems to me that I shouldn't mind waiting as long as I had that to look for."

"You are right not to be impatient," he said to her, after a pause, as he held her hand before he went. "Quite right. I only wish I could school myself to be as easy about it."

"I did not say I was easy," said Anastasia. "People are seldom easy in this world, I take it. I said I could be patient. Do not look in that way, as though you pretended that you were dissatisfied with me. You know that I am true to you, and you ought to be very proud of me."

"I am proud of you, Anastasia—" on hearing which she got up and curtseyed to him. "I am proud of you; so proud of you that I feel you should not be left here all alone, with no one to help you if you were in trouble."

"Women don't get into trouble as men do, and do not want any one to help them. If you were alone in the house you would have to go to bed without your supper, because you could not make a basin of boiled milk ready for your own meal. Now, when your reverence has gone, I shall go to work and have my tea comfortably." And then he did go, bidding God bless her as he left her. Three hours after that he was disturbed in his own lodgings by one of the negro girls from the cottage rushing to his door, and begging him in Heaven's name to come down to the assistance of her mistress.

When Morton left her, Anastasia did not proceed to do as she had said, and seemed to have forgotten her evening meal. She had been working sedulously with her needle during all that last conversation; but when her lover was gone, she allowed the work to fall from her hands, and sat motionless for awhile, gazing at the last streak of colour left by the setting sun; but there was no longer a sign of its glory to be traced in the heavens around her. The twilight in Bermuda is not long and enduring as it is with us, though the daylight does not depart suddenly, leaving the darkness of night behind it without any intermediate time of warning, as is the case farther south, down among the islands of the tropics. But the soft, sweet light of the evening had waned and gone, and night had absolutely come upon her, while Anastasia was still seated before the cottage with her eyes fixed upon the white streak of motionless sea which was still visible through the gloom. She was thinking of him, of his ways of life, of his happiness, and of her duty towards him. She had told him, with her pretty feminine falseness, that she could wait without impatience; but now she said to herself that it would not be good for him to wait longer. He lived alone and without comfort, working very hard for his poor pittance, and she could see and feel and understand that a companion in his life was to him almost a necessity. She would tell her father that all this must be brought to an end. She would not ask him for money, but she would make him understand that her services must, at any rate in part, be transferred. Why should not she and Morton still live at the cottage when they were married? And so thinking, and at last resolving, she sat there till the dark night fell upon her.

She was at last disturbed by feeling a man's hand upon her shoulder. She jumped from her chair and faced him—not screaming, for it was especially within her power to control herself, and to make no utterance except with forethought. Perhaps it might have been better for her had she screamed, and sent a shrill shriek down the shore of that inland sea. She was silent, however, and with awe-struck face and outstretched hands gazed into the face of him who still held her by the shoulder. The night was dark; but her eyes were now accustomed to the darkness, and she could see indistinctly something of his features. He was a low-sized man, dressed in a suit of sailor's blue clothing, with a rough cap of hair on his head, and a beard that had not been clipped for many weeks. His eyes were large, and hollow, and frightfully bright, so that she seemed to see nothing else of him; but she felt the strength of his fingers as he grasped her tighter and more tightly by the arm.

"Who are you?" she said, after a moment's pause.

"Do you know me?" he asked.

"Know you? No." But the words were hardly out of her mouth

before it struck her that the man was Aaron Trow, of whom every one in Bermuda had been talking.

"Come into the house," he said, "and give me food." And he still held her with his hand as though he would compel her to follow him.

She stood for a moment thinking what she would say to him; for even then, with that terrible man standing close to her in the darkness, her presence of mind did not desert her. "Surely," she said, "I will give you food if you are hungry. But take your hand from me. No man would lay his hands on a woman."

"A woman!" said the stranger. "What does the starved wolf care for that? A woman's blood is as sweet to him as that of a man. Come into the house, I tell you." And then she preceded him through the open door into the narrow passage, and thence to the kitchen. There she saw that the back door, leading out on the other side of the house, was open, and she knew that he had come down from the road and entered on that side. She threw her eyes round, looking for the negro girls; but they were away, and she remembered that there was no human being within sound of her voice but this man who had told her that he was as a wolf thirsty after her blood!

"Give me food at once," he said.

"And will you go if I give it you?" she asked.

"I will knock out your brains if you do not," he replied, lifting from the grate a short, thick poker which lay there. "Do as I bid you at once. You also would be like a tiger if you had fasted for two days, as I have done."

She could see, as she moved across the kitchen, that he had already searched there for something that he might eat, but that he had searched in vain. With the close economy common among his class in the islands, all comestibles were kept under close lock and key in the house of Mr. Bergen. Their daily allowance was given day by day to the negro servants, and even the fragments were then gathered up and locked away in safety. She moved across the kitchen to the accustomed cupboard, taking the keys from her pocket, and he followed close upon her. There was a small oil lamp hanging from the low ceiling which just gave them light to see each other. She lifted her hand to this to take it from its hook, but he prevented her. "No, by Heaven!" he said, "you don't touch that till I've done with it. There's light enough for you to drag out your scraps."

She did drag out her scraps and a bowl of milk, which might hold perhaps a quart. There was a fragment of bread, a morsel of cold potato-cake, and the bone of a leg of kid. "And is that all?" said he. But as he spoke he fleshed his teeth against the bone as a dog would have done.

"It is the best I have," she said; "I wish it were better, and you should have had it without violence, as you have suffered so long from hunger."

"Bah! Better; yes! You would give the best no doubt, and set the hell hounds on my track the moment I am gone. I know how much I might expect from your charity."

"I would have fed you for pity's sake," she answered.

"Pity? Who are you, that you should dare to pity me? By——my young woman, it is I that pity you. I must cut your throat unless you give me money. Do you know that?"

"Money? I have got no money."

"I'll make you have some before I go. Come; don't move till I have done." And as he spoke to her he went on tugging at the bone, and swallowing the lumps of stale bread. He had already finished the bowl of milk. "And, now," said he, "tell me who I am."

"I suppose you are Aaron Trow," she answered, very slowly.

He said nothing on hearing this, but continued his meal, standing close to her so that she might not possibly escape from him out into the darkness. Twice or thrice in those few minutes she made up her mind to make such an attempt, feeling that it would be better to leave him in possession of the house, and make sure, if possible, of her own life. There was no money there; not a dollar! What money her father kept in his possession was locked up in his safe at Hamilton. And might he not keep to his threat, and murder her, when he found that she could give him nothing? She did not tremble outwardly, as she stood there watching him as he ate, but she thought how probable it might be that her last moments were very near. And yet she could scrutinise his features, form, and garments, so as to carry away in her mind a perfect picture of them. Aaron Trow—for of course it was the escaped convict—was not a man of frightful, hideous aspect. Had the world used him well, giving him when he was young ample wages and separating him from turbulent spirits, he also might have used the world well; and then women would have praised the brightness of his eye and the manly vigour of his brow. But things had not gone well with him. He had been separated from the wife he had loved, and the children who had been raised at his knee—separated by his own violence; and now, as he had said of himself, he was a wolf rather than a man. As he stood there satisfying the craving of his appetite, breaking up the large morsels of food, he was an object very sad to be seen. Hunger had made him gaunt and yellow, he was squalid with the dirt of his hidden lair, and he had the look of a beast—that look to which men fall when they live like the brutes of prey, as outcasts from their brethren. But still there was that about his brow which might have redeemed him—which might have turned her horror into pity, had he been willing that it should be so.

"And now give me some brandy," he said.

There was brandy in the house—in the sitting-room which was close at their hand, and the key of the little press which held it was in her pocket. It was useless, she thought, to refuse him; and so she told him that there was a bottle partly full, but that she must go to the next room to fetch it him.

"We'll go together, my darling," he said. "There's nothing like good company." And he again put his hand upon her arm as they passed into the family sitting-room.

"I must take the light," she said. But he unhooked it himself, and carried it in his own hand.

Again she went to work without trembling. She found the key of the side cupboard and, unlocking the door, handed him a bottle which might contain about half-a-pint of spirits. "And is that all?" he said.

"There is a full bottle here," she answered, handing him another; "but if you drink it, you will be drunk, and they will catch you."

"By Heavens, yes; and you would be the first to help them; would you not?"

"Look here," she answered. "If you will go now, I will not say a word to any one of your coming, nor set them on your track to follow you. There, take the full bottle with you. If you will go, you shall be safe from me."

"What, and go without money!"

"I have none to give you. You may believe me when I say so. I have not a dollar in the house."

Before he spoke again he raised the half empty bottle to his mouth, and drank as long as there was a drop to drink. "There," said he, putting the bottle down, "I am better after that. As to the other you are right, and I will take it with me. And now, young woman, about the money?"

"I tell you that I have not a dollar."

"Look here," said he, and he spoke now in a softer voice, as though he would be on friendly terms with her. "Give me ten sovereigns, and I will go. I know you have it, and with ten sovereigns it is possible that I may save my life. You are good, and would not wish that a man should die so horrid a death. I know you are good. Come, give me the money." And he put his hands up, beseeching her, and looked into her face with imploring eyes.

"On the word of a Christian woman I have not got money to give you," she replied.

"Nonsense!" And as he spoke he took her by the arm and shook her. He shook her violently so that he hurt her, and her breath for a moment was all but gone from her. "I tell you you must make dollars before I leave you, or I will so handle you that it would have been better for you to coin your very blood."

"May God help me at my need," she said, "as I have not above a few penny pieces in the house."

"And you expect me to believe that? Look here! I will shake the teeth out of your head, but I will have it from you." And he did shake her again, using both his hands and striking her against the wall.

"Would you—murder me?" she said, hardly able now to utter the words.

"Murder you, yes; why not? I cannot be worse than I am, were I to murder you ten times over. But with money I may possibly be better."

"I have it not."

"Then I will do worse than murder you. I will make you such an object that all the world shall loath to look on you." And so saying he took her by the arm and dragged her forth from the wall against which she had stood.

Then there came from her a shriek that was heard far down the shore of that silent sea, and away across to the solitary houses of those living on the other side—a shriek very sad, sharp, and prolonged—which told plainly to those who heard it of woman's woe when in her extremest peril. That sound was spoken of in Bermuda for many a day after that, as something which had been terrible to hear. But then, at that moment, as it came wailing through the dark, it sounded as though it were not human. Of those who heard it, not one guessed from whence it came, nor was the hand of any brother put forward to help that woman at her need.

AARON TROW

"Did you hear that?" said the young wife to her husband, from the far side of the arm of the sea.

"Hear it? Oh Heaven, yes! Whence did it come?" The young wife could not say from whence it came, but clung close to her husband's breast, comforting herself with the knowledge that that terrible sorrow was not hers.

But aid did come at last, or rather that which seemed as aid. Long and terrible was the fight between that human beast of prey and the poor victim which had fallen into his talons. Anastasia Bergen was a strong, well-built woman, and now that the time had come to her when a struggle was necessary, a struggle for life, for honour, for the happiness of him who was more to her than herself, she fought like a tigress attacked in her own lair. At such a moment as this she also could become wild and savage as the beast of the forest. When he pinioned her arms with one of his, as he pressed her down upon the floor, she caught the first joint of the forefinger of his other hand between her teeth till he yelled in agony, and another sound was heard across the silent water. And then, when one hand was loosed in the struggle, she twisted it through his long hair, and dragged back his head till his eyes were nearly starting from their sockets. Anastasia Bergen had hitherto been a sheer woman, all feminine in her nature. But now the foam came to her mouth, and fire sprang from her eyes, and the muscles of her body worked as though she had been trained to deeds of violence. Of violence, Aaron Trow had known much in his rough life, but never had he combated with harder antagonist than her whom he now held beneath his breast.

"By——I will put an end to you," he exclaimed, in his wrath, as he struck her violently across the face with his elbow. His hand was occupied, and he could not use it for a blow, but, nevertheless, the violence was so great that the blood gushed from her nostrils, while the back of her head was driven with violence against the floor. But yet she did not lose her hold of him. Her hand was still twined closely through his thick hair, and in every move he made she clung to him with all her might. "Leave go my hair," he shouted at her, but she still kept her hold, though he again dashed her head against the floor.

There was still light in the room, for when he first grasped her with both his hands, he had put the lamp down on a small table. Now they were rolling on the floor together, and twice he had essayed to kneel on her that he might thus crush the breath from her body, and deprive her altogether of her strength; but she had been too active for him, moving herself along the ground, though in doing so she dragged him with her. But by degrees he got one hand at liberty, and with that he pulled a clasp knife out of his pocket and opened it. "I will cut your head off, if you do not let go my hair," he said. But still she held fast by him. He then stabbed at her arm, using his left hand and making short ineffectual blows. Her dress partly saved her, and partly also the continual movement of all her limbs; but, nevertheless, the knife wounded her. It wounded her in several places about the arm, covering them both with blood—but still she hung on. So close was her grasp in her agony, that, as she afterwards found, she cut the skin of her own hand with her own nails. Had the man's hair been less thick or strong, or her own tenacity less steadfast, he would have murdered her before any interruption could have saved her.

And yet he had not purposed to murder her, or even, in the first instance, to inflict on her any bodily harm. But he had been determined to get money. With such a sum of money as he had named, it might, he thought, be possible for him to win his way across to America. He might bribe men to hide him in the hold of a ship, and thus there might be for him, at any rate, a possibility of escape. That there must be money in the house, he had still thought when first he laid hands on the poor woman; and then, when the struggle had once begun, when he had felt her muscles contending with his, the passion of the beast was aroused within him, and he strove against her as he would have striven against a dog. But yet, when the knife was in his hand, he had not driven it against her heart.

Then suddenly, while they were yet rolling on the floor, there was a sound of footsteps in the passage. Aaron Trow instantly leaped to his feet, leaving his victim on the ground, with huge lumps of his thick clotted hair in her hand. Thus, and thus only, could he have liberated himself from her grasp. He rushed at the door with the open knife still in his hand, and there he came against the two negro servant-girls who had returned down to their kitchen from the road on which they had been straying. Trow, as he half saw them in the dark, not knowing how many there might be, or whether there was a man among them, rushed through them, upsetting one scared girl in his passage. With the instinct and with the timidity of a beast, his impulse now was to escape, and he hurried away back to the road and to his lair, leaving the three women together in the cottage. Poor wretch! As he crossed the road, not skulking in his impotent haste, but running at his best, another pair of eyes saw him, and when the search became hot after him, it was known that his hiding-place was not distant.

It was some time before any of the women were able to act, and when some step was taken, Anastasia was the first to take it. She had not absolutely swooned, but the reaction, after the violence of her efforts, was so great, that for some minutes she had been unable to speak. She had risen from the floor when Trow left her, and had even followed him to the door; but since that she had fallen back into her father's old armchair, and there she sat gasping not only for words, but for breath also. At last she bade one of the girls to run into St. George, and beg Mr. Morton to come to her aid. The girl would not stir without her companion; and even then, Anastasia, covered as she was with blood, with dishevelled hair and her clothes half torn from her body, accompanied them as far as the road. There they found a negro lad still hanging about the place, and he told them that he had seen the man cross the road, and run down over the open ground towards the rocks of the sea-coast. "He must be there," said the lad, pointing in the direction of a corner of the rocks; "unless he swim across the mouth of the ferry." But the mouth of that ferry is an arm of the sea, and it was not probable that a man would do that when he might have taken the narrow water by keeping on the other side of the road.

At about one that night Caleb Morton reached the cottage breathless with running, and before a word was spoken between them, Anastasia had fallen on his shoulder and had fainted. As soon as she was in the arms of her lover, all her power had gone from her. The spirit and passion of the tiger had gone, and she was again a weak woman shuddering at the thought of what she had suffered. She remembered that she had had the man's hand between her teeth, and by degrees she found his hair still clinging to her fingers; but even then she could hardly call to mind the nature of the struggle she had undergone. His hot breath close to her own cheek she did remember, and his glaring eyes, and even the roughness of his beard as he pressed his face against her own; but she could not say whence had come the blood, nor till her arm became stiff and motionless did she know that she had been wounded.

It was all joy with her now, as she sat motionless without speaking, while he administered to her wants and spoke words of love into her ears. She remembered the man's horrid threat, and knew that by God's mercy she had been saved. And he was there caressing her, loving her, comforting her! As she thought of the fate that had threatened her, of the evil that had been so imminent, she fell forward on her knees, and with incoherent sobs uttered her thanksgivings, while her head was still supported on his arms.

It was almost morning before she could induce herself to leave him and lie down. With him she seemed to be so perfectly safe; but the moment he was away she could see Aaron Trow's eyes gleaming at her across the room. At last, however, she slept; and when he saw that she was at rest, he told himself that his work must then begin. Hitherto Caleb Morton had lived in all respects the life of a man of peace; but now, asking himself no questions as to the propriety of what he would do, using no inward arguments as to this or that line of conduct, he girded the sword on his loins, and prepared himself for war. The wretch who had thus treated the woman whom he loved should be hunted down like a wild beast, as long as he had arms and legs with which to carry on the hunt. He would pursue the miscreant with any weapons that might come to his hands; and might Heaven help him at his need, as he dealt forth punishment to that man, if he caught him within his grasp. Those who had hitherto known Morton in the island, could not recognise the man as he came forth on that day, thirsty after blood, and desirous to thrust himself into personal conflict with the wild ruffian who had injured him. The meek Presbyterian minister had been a preacher, preaching ways of peace, and living in accordance with his own doctrines. The world had been very quiet for him, and he had walked quietly in his appointed path. But now the world was quiet no longer, nor was there any preaching of peace. His cry was for blood; for the blood of the untamed savage brute who had come upon his young doe in her solitude, and striven with such brutal violence to tear her heart from her bosom.

He got to his assistance early in the morning some of the constables from St. George, and before the day was over, he was joined by two or three of the wardens from the convict establishment. There was with him also a friend or two, and thus a party was formed, numbering together ten or twelve persons. They were of course all armed, and therefore it might be thought that there would be but small chance for the wretched man if they should come upon his track. At first they all searched together, thinking, from the tidings which had reached them, that he must be near to them; but gradually they spread themselves along the rocks between St. George and the ferry, keeping watchmen on the road, so that he should not escape unnoticed into the island.

Ten times during the day did Anastasia send from the cottage up to Morton, begging him to leave the search to others, and come down to her. But not for a moment would he lose the scent of his prey. What! should it be said that she had been so treated, and that others had avenged her? He sent back to say that her father was with her now, and that he would come when his work was over. And in that job of work the life-blood of Aaron Trow was counted up.

Towards evening they were all congregated on the road near to the spot at which the path turns off towards the cottage, when a voice was heard hallooing to them from the summit of a little hill which lies between the road and the sea on the side towards the ferry, and presently a boy came running down to them full of news. "Danny Lund has seen him," said the boy, "he has seen him plainly in among the rocks." And then came Danny Lund himself, a small negro lad about fourteen years of age, who was known in those parts as the idlest, most dishonest, and most useless of his race. On this occasion, however, Danny Lund became important, and every one listened to him. He had seen, he said, a pair of eyes moving down in a cave of the rocks which he well knew. He had been in the cave often, he said, and could get there again. But not now; not while that pair of eyes was moving at the bottom of it. And so they all went up over the hill, Morton leading the way with hot haste. In his waistband he held a pistol, and his hand grasped a short iron bar with which he had armed himself. They ascended the top of the hill, and when there, the open sea was before them on two sides, and on the third was the narrow creek over which the ferry passed. Immediately beneath their feet were the broken rocks; for on that side, towards the sea, the earth and grass of the hill descended but a little way towards the water. Down among the rocks they all went, silently, Caleb Morton leading the way, and Danny Lund directing him from behind.

"Mr. Morton," said an elderly man from St. George, "had you not better let the warders of the gaol go first; he is a desperate man, and they will best understand his ways?"

In answer to this Morton said nothing, but he would let no one put a foot before him. He still pressed forward among the rocks, and at last came to a spot from whence he might have sprung at one leap into the ocean. It was a broken cranny on the sea-shore into which the sea beat, and surrounded on every side but the one by huge broken fragments of stone, which at first sight seemed as though they would have admitted of a path down among them to the water's edge; but which, when scanned more closely, were seen to be so large in size, that no man could climb from one to another. It was a singularly romantic spot, but now well known to them all there, for they had visited it over and over again that morning.

"In there," said Danny Lund, keeping well behind Morton's body, and pointing at the same time to a cavern high up among the rocks, but quite on the opposite side of the little inlet of the sea. The mouth of the cavern was not twenty yards from them where they stood, but at the first sight it seemed as though it must be impossible to reach it. The precipice on the brink of which they all now stood, ran down sheer into the sea, and the fall from the mouth of the cavern on the other side was as steep. But Danny solved the mystery by pointing upwards, and showing them how he had been used to climb to a projecting rock over their heads, and from thence creep round by certain vantages of the stone till he was able to let himself down into the aperture. But now, at the present moment, he was unwilling to make essay of his prowess as a cragsman. He had, he said, been up on that projecting rock thrice, and there had seen the eyes moving in the cavern. He was quite sure of the fact of the pair of eyes, and declined to ascend the rock again.

Traces soon became visible to them by which they knew that some one had passed in and out of the cavern recently. The stone, when examined, bore those marks of friction which passage and repassage over it will always give. At the spot from whence the climber left the platform and commenced his ascent, the side of the stone had been rubbed by the close friction of a man's body. A light boy like Danny Lund might find his way in and out without leaving such marks behind him, but no heavy man could do so. Thus before long they all were satisfied that Aaron Trow was in the cavern before them.

Then there was a long consultation as to what they would do to carry on the hunt, and how they would drive the tiger from his lair. That he should not again come out, except to fall into their hands, was to all of them a matter of course. They would keep watch and ward there, though it might be for days and nights. But that was a process which did not satisfy Morton, and did not indeed well satisfy any of them. It was not only that they desired to inflict punishment on the miscreant in accordance with the law, but also that they did not desire that the miserable man should die in a hole like a starved dog, and that then they should go after him to take out his wretched skeleton. There was something in that idea so horrid in every way, that all agreed that active steps must be taken. The warders of the prison felt that they would all be disgraced if they could not take their prisoner alive. Yet who would get round that perilous ledge in the face of such an adversary? A touch to any man while climbing there would send him headlong down among the waves? And then his fancy told to each what might be the nature of an embrace with such an animal as that, driven to despair, hopeless of life, armed, as they knew, at any rate, with a knife! If the first adventurous spirit should succeed in crawling round that ledge, what would be the reception which he might expect in the terrible depth of that cavern?

They called to their prisoner, bidding him come out, and telling him that they would fire in upon him if he did not show himself; but not a sound was heard. It was indeed possible that they should send their bullets to, perhaps, every corner of the cavern; and if so, in that way they might slaughter him; but even of this they were not sure. Who could tell that there might not be some protected nook in which he could lay secure? And who could tell when the man was struck, or whether he were wounded?

"I will get to him," said Morton, speaking with a low dogged voice, and so saying he clambered up to the rock to which Danny Lund had pointed. Many voices at once attempted to restrain him, and one or two put their hands upon him to keep him back, but he was too quick for them, and now stood upon the ledge of rock. "Can you see him?" they asked below.

"I can see nothing within the cavern," said Morton.

"Look down very hard, Massa," said Danny, "very hard indeed, down in deep dark hole, and then see him big eyes moving!"

Morton now crept along the ledge, or rather he was beginning to do so, having put forward his shoulders and arms to make a first step in advance from the spot on which he was resting, when a hand was put forth from one corner of the cavern's mouth—a hand armed with a pistol—and a shot was fired. There could be no doubt now but that Danny Lund was right, and no doubt now as to the whereabouts of Aaron Trow.

A hand was put forth, a pistol was fired, and Caleb Morton still clinging to a corner of the rock with both his arms, was seen to falter. "He is wounded," said one of the voices from below; and then they all expected to see him fall into the sea. But he did not fall, and after a moment or two, he proceeded carefully to pick his steps along the ledge. The ball had touched him, grazing his cheek and cutting through the light whiskers that he wore; but he had not felt it, though the blow had nearly knocked him from his perch. And then four or five shots were fired from the rocks into the mouth of the cavern. The man's arm had been seen, and indeed one or two declared that they had traced the dim outline of his figure. But no sound was heard to come from the cavern, except the sharp crack of the bullets against the rock, and the echo of the gunpowder. There had been no groan as of a man wounded, no sound of a body falling, no voice wailing in despair. For a few seconds all was dark with the smoke of the gunpowder, and then the empty mouth of the cave was again yawning before their eyes. Morton was now near it, still cautiously creeping. The first danger to which he was exposed was this; that his enemy within the recess might push him down from the rocks with a touch. But on the other hand, there were three or four men ready to fire, the moment that a hand should be put forth; and then Morton could swim—was known to be a strong swimmer—whereas of Aaron Trow it was already declared by the prison gaolers that he could not swim. Two of the warders had now followed Morton on the rocks, so that in the event of his making good his entrance into the cavern, and holding his enemy at bay for a minute, he would be joined by aid.

It was strange to see how those different men conducted themselves as they stood on the opposite platform watching the attack. The officers from the prison had no other thought but of their prisoner, and were intent on taking him alive or dead. To them it was little or nothing what became of Morton. It was their business to encounter peril, and they were ready to do so—feeling, however, by no means sorry to have such a man as Morton in advance of them. Very little was said by them. They had their wits about them, and remembered that every word spoken for the guidance of their ally would be heard also by the escaped convict. Their prey was sure, sooner or later, and had not Morton been so eager in his pursuit, they would have waited till some plan had been devised of trapping him without danger. But the townsmen from St. George, of whom some dozen were now standing there, were quick and eager and loud in their counsels. "Stay where you are, Mr. Morton—stay awhile for the love of God—or he'll have you down." "Now's your time, Caleb; in on him now, and you'll have him." "Close with him, Morton, close with him at once; it's your only chance." "There's four of us here; we'll fire on him if he as much as shows a limb." All of which words as they were heard by that poor wretch within, must have sounded to him as the barking of a pack of hounds thirsting for his blood. For him at any rate there was no longer any hope in this world.

My reader, when chance has taken you into the hunting-field, has it ever been your lot to sit by on horseback, and watch the digging out of a fox? The operation is not an uncommon one, and in some countries it is held to be in accordance with the rules of fair sport. For myself, I think that when the brute has so far saved himself, he should be entitled to the benefit of his cunning; but I will not now discuss the propriety or impropriety of that practice in venery. I can never, however, watch the doing of that work without thinking much of the agonising struggles of the poor beast whose last refuge is being torn from over his head. There he lies within a few yards of his arch enemy, the huntsman. The thick breath of the hounds make hot the air within his hole. The sound of their voices is close upon his ears. His breast is nearly bursting with the violence of that effort which at last has brought him to his retreat. And then pickaxe and mattock are plied above his head, and nearer and more near to him press his foes—his double foes, human and canine—till at last a huge hand grasps him, and he is dragged forth among his enemies. Almost as soon as his eyes have seen the light the eager noses of a dozen hounds have moistened themselves in his entrails. Ah me! I know that he is vermin, the vermin after whom I have been risking my neck, with a bold ambition that I might ultimately witness his death-struggles; but, nevertheless, I would fain have saved him that last half hour of gradually diminished hope.

And Aaron Trow was now like a hunted fox, doomed to be dug out from his last refuge, with this addition to his misery, that these hounds when they caught their prey, would not put him at once out of his misery. When first he saw that throng of men coming down from the hill top and resting on the platform, he knew that his fate was come. When they called to him to surrender himself he was silent, but he knew that his silence was of no avail. To them who were so eager to be his captors the matter seemed to be still one of considerable difficulty; but, to his thinking, there was no difficulty. There were there some score of men, fully armed, within twenty yards of him. If he but showed a trace of his limbs he would become a mark for their bullets. And then if he were wounded, and no one would come to him! If they allowed him to lie there without food till he perished! Would it not be well for him to yield himself? Then they called again and he was still silent. That idea of yielding is very terrible to the heart of a man. And when the worst had come to the worst, did not the ocean run deep beneath his cavern's mouth?

But as they yelled at him and halloa-ed, making their preparations for his death, his presence of mind deserted the poor wretch. He had stolen an old pistol on one of his marauding expeditions, of which one barrel had been loaded. That in his mad despair he had fired; and now, as he lay near the mouth of the cavern, under the cover of the projecting stone, he had no weapon with him but his hands. He had had a knife, but that had dropped from him during the struggle on the floor of the cottage. He had now nothing but his hands, and was considering how he might best use them in ridding himself of the first of his pursuers. The man was near him, armed, with all the power and majesty of right on his side; whereas on his side, Aaron Trow had nothing—not a hope. He raised his head that he might look forth, and a dozen voices shouted as his face appeared above the aperture. A dozen weapons were levelled at him, and he could see the gleaming of the muzzles of the guns. And then the foot of his pursuer was already on the corner stone at the cavern's mouth. "Now, Caleb, on him at once!" shouted a voice. Ah me! it was a moment in which to pity even such a man as Aaron Trow.

"Now, Caleb, at him at once!" shouted the voice. No, by heavens; not so, even yet! The sound of triumph in those words roused the last burst of energy in the breast of that wretched man; and he sprang forth, head foremost, from his prison house. Forth he came, manifest enough before the eyes of them all, and with head well down, and hands outstretched, but with his wide glaring eyes still turned towards his pursuers as he fell, he plunged down into the waves beneath him. Two of those who stood by, almost unconscious of what they did, fired at his body as it made its rapid way to the water; but, as they afterwards found, neither of the bullets struck him. Morton, when his prey thus leaped forth, escaping him for awhile, was already on the verge of the cavern—had even then prepared his foot for that onward spring which should bring him to the throat of his foe. But he arrested himself, and for a moment stood there watching the body as it struck the water, and hid itself at once beneath the ripple. He stood there for a moment watching the deed and its effect, and then, leaving his hold upon the rock, he once again followed his quarry. Down he went, head foremost, right on to the track in the waves which the other had made; and when the two rose to the surface together, each was struggling in the grasp of the other.

It was a foolish, nay, a mad deed to do. The poor wretch who had first fallen could not have escaped. He could not even swim, and had therefore flung himself to certain destruction when he took that leap from out of the cavern's mouth. It would have been sad to see him perish beneath the waves—to watch him as he rose gasping for breath, and then to see him sinking again, to rise against and then to go for ever. But his life had been fairly forfeit—and why should one so much more precious have been flung after it? It was surely with no view of saving that pitiful life that Caleb Morton had leaped after his enemy. But the hound, hot with the chase, will follow the stag over the precipice and dash himself to pieces against the rocks. The beast thirsting for blood, will rush in even among the weapons of men. Morton in his fury had felt but one desire, burned with but one passion. If the Fates would but grant him to fix his clutches in the throat of the man who had ill-used his love—for the rest it might all go as it would!

In the earlier part of the morning, while they were all searching for their victim, they had brought a boat up into this very inlet among the rocks; and the same boat had been at hand during the whole day. Unluckily, before they had come hither, it had been taken round the headland to a place among the rocks at which a government skiff is always moored. The sea was still so quiet that there was hardly a ripple on it, and the boat had been again sent for when first it was supposed that they had at last traced Aaron Trow to his hiding-place. Anxiously now were all eyes turned to the headland, but as yet no boat was there.

The two men rose to the surface, each struggling in the arms of the other. Trow, though he was in an element to which he was not used, though he had sprung thither as another suicide might spring to certain death beneath a railway engine, did not altogether lose his presence of mind. Prompted by a double instinct, he had clutched hold of Morton's body when he encountered it beneath the waters. He held on to it, as to his only protection, and he held on to him also as to his only enemy. If there was a chance for a life struggle, they would share that chance together; and if not, then together would they meet that other fate.

Caleb Morton was a very strong man, and though one of his arms was altogether encumbered by his antagonist, his other arm and his legs were free. With these he seemed to succeed in keeping his head above the water, weighted as he was with the body of his foe. But

Trow's efforts were also used with the view of keeping himself above the water. Though he had purposed to destroy himself in taking that leap, and now hoped for nothing better than that they might both perish together, he yet struggled to keep his head above the waves. Bodily power he had none left to him, except that of holding on to Morton's arm and plunging with his legs; but he did hold on, and thus both their heads remained above the surface.

But this could not last long. It was easy to see that Trow's strength was nearly spent, and that when he went down Morton must go with him. If indeed they could be separated—if Morton could once make himself free from that embrace into which he had been so anxious to leap—then indeed there might be a hope. All round that little inlet the rock fell sheer down into the deep sea, so that there was no resting place for a foot; but round the headlands on either side, even within forty or fifty yards of that spot, Morton might rest on the rocks, till a boat should come to his assistance. To him that distance would have been nothing, if only his limbs had been at liberty.

Upon the platform of rock they were all at their wits' ends. Many were anxious to fire at Trow; but even if they hit him, would Morton's position have been better? Would not the wounded man have still clung to him who was not wounded? And then there could be no certainty that any one of them would hit the right man. The ripple of the waves, though it was very slight, nevertheless sufficed to keep the bodies in motion; and then, too, there was not among them any marksman peculiar for his skill.

Morton's efforts in the water were too severe to admit of his speaking, but he could hear and understand the words which were addressed to him. "Shake him off, Caleb." "Strike him from you with your foot." "Swim to the right shore; swim for it, even if you take him with you." Yes; he could hear them all; but hearing and obeying were very different. It was not easy to shake off that dying man; and as for swimming with him, that was clearly impossible. It was as much as he could do to keep his head above water, let alone any attempt to move in one settled direction.

For some four or five minutes they lay thus battling on the waves before the head of either of them went down. Trow had been twice below the surface, but it was before he had succeeded in supporting himself by Morton's arm. Now it seemed as though he must sink again—as though both must sink. His mouth was barely kept above the water, and as Morton shook him with his arm, the tide would pass over him. It was horrid to watch from the shore the glaring upturned eyes of the dying wretch, as his long streaming hair lay back upon the wave. "Now, Caleb, hold him down. Hold him under," was shouted in the voice of some eager friend. Rising up on the water, Morton made a last effort to do as he was bid. He did press the man's head down—well down below the surface—but still the hand clung to him, and as he struck out against the water, he was powerless against that grasp.

Then there came a loud shout along the shore, and all those on the platform, whose eyes had been fixed so closely on that terrible struggle beneath them, rushed towards the rocks on the other coast. The sound of oars was heard close to them—an eager pressing stroke, as of men who knew well that they were rowing for the salvation of a life. On they came, close under the rocks, obeying with every muscle of their bodies the behests of those who called to them from the shore. The boat came with such rapidity—was so recklessly urged—that it was driven somewhat beyond the inlet; but in passing, a blow was struck which made Caleb Morton once more the master of his own life. The two men had been carried out in their struggle towards the open sea; and as the boat curved in, so as to be as close as the rocks would allow, the bodies of the men were brought within the sweep of the oars. He in the bow—for there were four pulling in the boat—had raised his oar as he neared the rocks—had raised it high above the water; and now, as they passed close by the struggling men, he let it fall with all its force on the upturned face of the wretched convict. It was a terrible, frightful thing to do—thus striking one who was so stricken; but who shall say that the blow was not good and just? Methinks, however, that the eyes and face of that dying man will haunt for ever the dreams of him who carried that oar!

Trow never rose again to the surface. Three days afterwards his body was found at the ferry, and then they carried him to the convict island and buried him. Morton was picked up and taken into the boat. His life was saved; but it may be a question how the battle might have gone had not that friendly oar been raised in his behalf. As it was, he lay at the cottage for days before he was able to be moved, so as to receive the congratulations of those who had watched that terrible conflict from the shore. Nor did he feel that there had been anything in that day's work of which he could be proud—much rather of which it behoved him to be thoroughly ashamed. Some six months after that he obtained the hand of Anastasia Bergen, but they did not remain long in Bermuda. "He went away, back to his own country," my informant told me; "because he could not endure to meet the ghost of Aaron Trow, at that point of the road which passes near the cottage." That the ghost of Aaron Trow may be seen there and round the little rocky inlet of the sea, is part of the creed of every young woman in Bermuda.

ISAK DINESEN

THE FAT MAN

ON ONE NOVEMBER evening a horrible crime was committed in Oslo, the capital of Norway. A child was murdered in an uninhabited house on the outskirts of town.

The newspapers brought long and detailed accounts of the murder. In the short, raw November days people stood in the street outside the house and stared up at it. The victim had been a workman's child, resentment of ancient wrongs stirred in the minds of the crowd.

The police had got but one single clue. A shopkeeper in the street told them that as he was closing up his shop on the evening of the murder he saw the murdered child walk by, her hand in the hand of a fat man.

The police had arrested some tramps and vagabonds and shady persons, but such people as a rule are not fat. So they looked elsewhere, among tradesmen and clerks of the neighborhood. Fat men were stared at in the streets. But the murderer had not been found.

In this same month of November a young student named Kristoffer

Lovunden in Oslo was cramming for his examination. He had come down to the town from the north of Norway, where it is day half the year and night the other half and where people are different from other Norwegians. In a world of stone and concrete Kristoffer was sick with longing for the hills and the salt sea.

His people up in Norland were poor and could have no idea of what it cost to live in Oslo, he did not want to worry them for money. To be able to finish his studies he had taken a job as bartender at the Grand Hotel, and worked there every night from eight o'clock till midnight. He was a good-looking boy with gentle and polite manners, conscientious in the performance of his duties, and he did well as a bartender. He was abstinent himself, but took a kind of scientific interest in the composition of other people's drinks.

In this way he managed to keep alive and to go on with his lessons. But he got too little sleep and too little time for ordinary human intercourse. He read no books outside his textbooks, and not even the newspapers, so that he did not know what was happening in the world around him. He was aware himself that this was not a healthy life, but the more he disliked it the harder he worked to get it over.

In the bar he was always tired, and he sometimes fell asleep standing up, with open eyes. The brilliant light and the noises made his head swim. But as he walked home from the Grand Hotel after midnight the cold air revived him so that he entered his small room wide awake. This he knew to be a dangerous hour. If now a thing caught his mind it would stick in it with unnatural vividness and keep him from sleep, and he would be no good for his books the next day. He had promised himself not to read at this time, and while he undressed to go to bed he closed his eyes.

All the same, one night his glance fell on a newspaper wrapped round a sausage that he had brought home with him. Here he read of the murder. The paper was two days old, people would have been talking about the crime around him all the time, but he had not heard what they said. The paper was torn, the ends of the lines were missing, he had to make them up from his own imagination. After that the thing would not leave him. The words "a fat man" set his mind running from one to another of the fat men he had ever known till at last it stopped at one of them.

There was an elegant fat gentleman who often visited the bar. Kristoffer knew him to be a writer, a poet of a particular, refined, half-mystical school. Kristoffer had read a few of his poems and had himself been fascinated by their queer, exquisite choice of words and symbols. They seemed to be filled with the colors of old precious stained glass. He often wrote about medieval legends and mysteries. This winter the theater was doing a play by him named *The Werewolf,* which was in parts macabre, according to its subject, but more remarkable still for its strange beauty and sweetness. The man's appearance too was striking. He was fat, with wavy dark hair, a large white face, a small red mouth, and curiously pale eyes. Kristoffer had been told that he had lived much abroad. It was the habit of this man to sit with his back to the bar, developing his exotic theories to a circle of young admirers. His name was Oswald Senjen.

Now the poet's picture took hold of the student. All night he seemed to see the big face close to his, with all kinds of expressions. He drank much cold water but was as hot as before. This fat man of the Grand Hotel, he thought, was the fat man of the newspaper.

It did not occur to him, in the morning, to play the part of a detective. If he went to the police they would send him away, since he had no facts whatever, no argument or reason even, to put before them. The fat man would have an alibi. He and his friends would laugh, they would think him mad or they would be indignant and complain to the manager of the hotel, and Kristoffer would lose his job.

So for three weeks the odd drama was played between the two

actors only: the grave young bartender behind the bar and the smiling poet before it. The one was trying hard all the time to get out of
it, the other knew nothing about it. Only once did the parties look
each other in the face.

A few nights after Kristoffer had read about the murder, Oswald
Senjen came into the bar with a friend. Kristoffer had no wish to spy
upon them—it was against his own will that he moved to the side of
the bar where they sat.

They were discussing fiction and reality. The friend held that to a
poet the two must be one, and that therefore his existence must be
mysteriously happy. The poet contradicted him. A poet's mission in
life, he said, was to make others confound fiction with reality in order
to render them, for an hour, mysteriously happy. But he himself must,
more carefully than the crowd, hold the two apart. "Not as far as enjoyment of them is concerned," he added, "I enjoy fiction, I enjoy reality
too. But I am happy because I have an unfailing instinct for distin-
guishing one from the other. I know fiction where I meet it. I know
reality where I meet it."

This fragment of conversation stuck in Kristoffer's mind, he went
over it many times. He himself had often before pondered on the idea
of happiness and tried to find out whether such a thing really existed.
He had asked himself if anybody was happy and, if so, who was happy.
The two men at the bar had repeated the word more than once—they
were probably happy. The fat man, who knew reality when he saw it,
had said that he was happy.

Kristoffer remembered the shopkeeper's evidence. The face of the
little girl Mattea, he had explained, when she passed him in the rainy
street, had looked happy, as if, he said, she had been promised something, or was looking forward to something, and was skipping along
toward it. Kristoffer thought: "And the man by her side?" Would his
face have had an expression of happiness as well? Would he too have

been looking forward to something? The shopkeeper had not had time to look the man in the face, he had seen only his back.

Night after night Kristoffer watched the fat man. At first he felt it to be a grim jest of fate that he must have this man with him wherever he went, while the man himself should hardly be aware of his existence. But after a time he began to believe that his unceasing observation had an effect on the observed, and that he was somehow changing under it. He grew fatter and whiter, his eyes grew paler. At moments he was as absent-minded as Kristoffer himself. His pleasing flow of speech would run slower, with sudden unneeded pauses, as if the skilled talker could not find his words.

If Oswald Senjen stayed in the bar till it closed, Kristoffer would slip out while he was being helped into his furred coat in the hall, and wait for him outside. Most often Oswald Senjen's large car would be there, and he would get into it and glide off. But twice he slowly walked along the street, and Kristoffer followed him. The boy felt himself to be a mean, wild figure in the town and the night, sneaking after a man who had done him no harm, and about whom he knew nothing, and he hated the figure who was dragging him after it. The first time it seemed to him that the fat man turned his head a little to one side and the other as if to make sure that there was nobody close behind him. But the second time he walked on looking straight ahead, and Kristoffer then wondered if that first slight nervous movement had not been a creation of his own imagination.

One evening in the bar the poet turned in his deep chair and looked at the bartender.

Toward the end of November Kristoffer suddenly remembered that his examination was to begin within a week. He was dismayed and seized with pangs of conscience, he thought of his future and of his people up in Norland. The deep fear within him grew stronger. He must shake off his obsession or he would be ruined by it.

At this time an unexpected thing happened. One evening Oswald Senjen got up to leave early, his friends tried to hold him back but he would not stay. "Nay," he said, "I want a rest. I want to rest." When he had gone, one of his friends said: "He was looking bad tonight. He is much changed. Surely he has got something the matter with him." One of the others answered: "It is that old matter from when he was out in China. But he ought to look after himself. Tonight one might think that he would not last till the end of the year."

As Kristoffer listened to these assertions from an outside and real world he felt a sudden, profound relief. To this world the man himself, at least, was a reality. People talked about him.

"It might be a good thing," he thought, "it might be a way out if I could talk about the whole matter to somebody else."

He did not choose a fellow student for his confidant. He could imagine the kind of discussion this would bring about and his mind shrank from it. He turned for help to a simple soul, a boy two or three years younger than himself, who washed up at the bar and who was named Hjalmar.

Hjalmar was born and bred in Oslo, he knew all that could be known about the town and very little about anything outside it. He and Kristoffer had always been on friendly terms, and Hjalmar enjoyed a short chat with Kristoffer in the scullery, after working hours, because he knew that Kristoffer would not interrupt him. Hjalmar was a revolutionary spirit, and would hold forth on the worthless rich customers of the bar, who rolled home in big cars with gorgeous women with red lips and nails, while underpaid sailors hauled tarred ropes, and tired laborers led their plowhorses to the stable. Kristoffer wished that he would not do so, for at such times his nostalgia for boats and tar, and for the smell of a sweaty horse, grew so strong that it became a physical pain. And the deadly horror that he felt at the idea of driving home with one of the women Hjalmar described proved to him that his nervous system was out of order.

As soon as Kristoffer mentioned the murder to Hjalmar he found that the scullery boy knew everything about it. Hjalmar had his pockets filled with newspaper cuttings, from which he read reports of the crime and of the arrests, and angry letters about the slowness of the police.

Kristoffer was uncertain how to explain his theory to Hjalmar. In the end he said: "Do you know, Hjalmar, I believe that the fat gentleman in the bar is the murderer." Hjalmar stared at him, his mouth open. The next moment he had caught the idea, and his eyes shone.

After a short while Hjalmar proposed that they should go to the police, or again to a private detective. It took Kristoffer some time to convince his friend, as he had convinced himself, that their case was too weak, and that people would think them mad.

Then Hjalmar, more eager even than before, decided that they must be detectives themselves.

To Kristoffer it was a strange experience, both steadying and alarming, to face his own nightmare in the sharp white light of the scullery, and to hear it discussed by another live person. He felt that he was holding on to the scullery boy like a drowning man to a swimmer; every moment he feared to drag his rescuer down with him, into the dark sea of madness.

The next evening Hjalmar told Kristoffer that they would find some scheme by which to surprise the murderer and make him give himself away.

Kristoffer listened to his various suggestions for some time, then smiled a little. He said: "Hjalmar, thou art even such a man . . . " He stopped. "Nay," he said, "you will not know this piece, Hjalmar. But let me go on a little, all the same—!

I have heard
that guilty creatures sitting at a play
have by the very cunning of the scene
been struck so to the soul that presently
they have proclaim'd their malefactions.
For murder, though it have no tongue, will speak.

"I understand that very well," said Hjalmar.

"Do you, Hjalmar?" asked Kristoffer. "Then I shall tell you one thing more:

the play's the thing
wherein we'll catch the conscience of the king.

"Where have you got that from?" asked Hjalmar. "From a play called *Hamlet*," said Kristoffer. "And how do you mean to go and do it?" asked Hjalmar again. Kristoffer was silent for some time.

"Look here, Hjalmar," he said at last, "you told me that you have got a sister."

"Yes," said Hjalmar, "I have got five of them."

"But you have got one sister of nine," said Kristoffer, "the same age as Mattea?"

"Yes," said Hjalmar.

"And she has got," Kristoffer went on, "a school mackintosh with a hood to it, like the one Mattea had on that night?"

"Yes," said Hjalmar.

Kristoffer began to tremble. There was something blasphemous in the comedy which they meant to act. He could not have gone on with it if he had not felt that somehow his reason hung upon it.

"Listen, Hjalmar," he said, "we will choose an evening when the man is in the bar. Then make your little sister put on her mackintosh, and make one of your big sisters bring her here. Tell her to walk straight from the door, through all the room, up to the bar, to me, and to give me something—a letter or what you will. I shall give her a shilling for doing it, and she will take it from the counter when she has put the letter there. Then tell her to walk back again, through the room."

"Yes," said Hjalmar.

"If the manager complains," Kristoffer added after a while, "we will explain that it was all a misunderstanding."

"Yes," said Hjalmar.

"I myself," said Kristoffer, "must stay at the bar. I shall not see his face, for he generally sits with his back to me, talking to people. But you will leave the washing up for a short time, and go round and keep guard by the door. You will watch his face from there."

"There will be no need to watch his face," said Hjalmar, "he will scream or faint, or jump up and run away, you know."

"You must never tell your sister, Hjalmar," said Kristoffer, "why we made her come here."

"No, no," said Hjalmar.

On the evening decided upon for the experiment, Hjalmar was silent, set on his purpose. But Kristoffer was in two minds. Once or twice he came near to giving up the whole thing. But if he did so, and even if he could make Hjalmar understand and forgive—what would become of himself afterwards?

Oswald Senjen was in his chair in his usual position, with his back to the bar. Kristoffer was behind the bar, Hjalmar was at the swinging door of the hall, to receive his sister.

Through the glass door Kristoffer saw the child arrive in the hall, accompanied by an elder sister with a red feather in her hat, for in these winter months people did not let children walk alone in the streets at night. At the same time he became aware of something in the room that he had not noticed before. "I can never, till tonight," he told himself, "have been quite awake in this place, or I should have noticed it." To each side of the glass door there was a tall looking glass, in which he could see the faces turned away from him. In both of them he now saw Oswald Senjen's face.

The little girl in her mackintosh and hood had some difficulty opening the door, and was assisted by her brother. She walked straight up to the bar, neither fast nor slow, placed the letter on the counter, and collected her shilling. As she did so she lifted her small pale face in the hood slightly, and gave her brother's friend a little pert, gentle grin of acquittal—now that the matter was done with. Then she turned and walked back and out of the door, neither fast nor slow.

"Was it right?" she asked her brother who had been waiting for her by the door. Hjalmar nodded, but the child was puzzled at the expression of his face and looked at her big sister for an explanation. Hjalmar remained in the hall till he had seen the two girls disappear in the rainy street. Then the porter asked him what he was doing there, and he ran round to the back entrance and to his tub and glasses.

The next guest who ordered a drink at the bar looked at the bartender and said: "Hello, are you ill?" The bartender did not answer a word. He did not say a word either when, an hour later, as the bar closed, he joined his friend in the scullery.

"Well, Kristoffer," said Hjalmar, "he did not scream or faint, did he?"

"No," said Kristoffer.

Hjalmar waited a little. "If it is him," he said, "he is tough."

Kristoffer stood quite still for a long time, looking at the glasses. At last he said: "Do you know why he did not scream or faint?"

"No," said Hjalmar, "why was it?"

Kristoffer said: "Because he saw the only thing he expected to see. The only thing he ever sees now. All the other men in the bar gave some sign of surprise at the sight of a little girl in a mackintosh walking in here. I watched the fat man's face in the mirror, and saw that he looked straight at her as she came in, and that his eyes followed her as she walked out, but that his face did not change at all."

"What?" said Hjalmar. After a few moments he repeated very low: "What?"

"Yes, it is so," said Kristoffer. "A little girl in a mackintosh is the only thing he sees wherever he looks. She has been with him here in the bar before. And in the streets. And in his own house. For three weeks."

There was a long silence.

"Are we to go to the police now, Kristoffer?" Hjalmar asked.

"We need not go to the police," said Kristoffer. "We need not do anything in the matter. You and I are too heavy, or too grown up, for that. Mattea does it as it ought to be done. It is her small light step that has followed close on his own all the time. She looks at him, just as your sister looked at me, an hour ago. He wanted rest, he said. She will get it for him before the end of the year."

EVELYN WAUGH

MR. LOVEDAY'S
LITTLE OUTING

*Y*OU WILL NOT FIND your father greatly changed," remarked Lady Moping, as the car turned into the gates of the County Asylum.

"Will he be wearing a uniform?" asked Angela.

"No, dear, of course not. He is receiving the very best attention."

It was Angela's first visit and it was being made at her own suggestion.

Ten years had passed since the showery day in late summer when Lord Moping had been taken away; a day of confused but bitter memories for her; the day of Lady Moping's annual garden party, always bitter, confused that day by the caprice of the weather which, remaining clear and brilliant with promise until the arrival of the first guests, had suddenly blackened into a squall. There had been a scuttle for cover; the marquee had capsized; a frantic carrying of cushions and chairs; a table-cloth lofted to the boughs of the monkey-puzzler, fluttering in the rain; a bright period and the cautious emergence of guests onto the soggy lawns; another squall; another twenty minutes of sunshine. It had been an abominable afternoon, culminating at about six o'clock in her father's attempted suicide.

Lord Moping habitually threatened suicide on the occasion of the garden party; that year he had been found black in the face, hanging by his braces in the orangery; some neighbours, who were sheltering there from the rain, set him on his feet again, and before dinner a van had called for him. Since then Lady Moping had paid seasonal calls at the asylum and returned in time for tea, rather reticent of her experience.

Many of her neighbours were inclined to be critical of Lord Moping's accommodation. He was not, of course, an ordinary inmate. He lived in a separate wing of the asylum, specially devoted to the segregation of wealthier lunatics. These were given every consideration which their foibles permitted. They might choose their own clothes (many indulged in the liveliest fancies), smoke the most expensive brands of cigars, and on the anniversaries of their certification entertain any other inmates for whom they had an attachment, to private dinner parties.

The fact remained, however, that it was far from being the most expensive kind of institution; the uncompromising address, "COUNTY HOME FOR MENTAL DEFECTIVES" stamped across the notepaper, worked on the uniforms of their attendants, painted, even, upon a prominent hoarding at the main entrance, suggested the lowest associations. From time to time, with less or more tact, her friends attempted to bring to Lady Moping's notice particulars of seaside nursing homes, of "qualified practitioners with large private grounds suitable for the charge of nervous or difficult cases," but she accepted them lightly; when her son came of age he might make any changes that he thought fit; meanwhile she felt no inclination to relax her economical régime; her husband had betrayed her basely on the one day in the year when she looked for loyal support, and was far better off than he deserved.

A few lonely figures in great-coats were shuffling and loping about the park.

"Those are the lower class lunatics," observed Lady Moping. "There is a very nice little flower garden for people like your father. I sent them some cuttings last year."

They drove past the blank, yellow brick façade to the doctor's private entrance and were received by him in the "visitors room," set aside for interviews of this kind. The window was protected on the inside by bars and wire netting; there was no fireplace; when Angela nervously attempted to move her chair further from the radiator, she found that it was screwed to the floor.

"Lord Moping is quite ready to see you," said the doctor.

"How is he?"

"Oh, very well, very well indeed, I'm glad to say. He had rather a nasty cold some time ago, but apart from that his condition is excellent. He spends a lot of his time in writing."

They heard a shuffling, skipping sound approaching along the flagged passage. Outside the door a high peevish voice, which Angela recognized as her father's, said: "I haven't the time, I tell you. Let them come back later."

A gentler tone, with a slight rural burr, replied, "Now come along. It is a purely formal audience. You need stay no longer than you like."

Then the door was pushed open (it had no lock or fastening) and Lord Moping came into the room. He was attended by an elderly little man with full white hair and an expression of great kindness.

"That is Mr. Loveday who acts as Lord Moping's attendant."

"Secretary," said Lord Moping. He moved with a jogging gait and shook hands with his wife.

"This is Angela. You remember Angela, don't you?"

"No, I can't say that I do. What does she want?"

"We just came to see you."

"Well, you have come at an exceedingly inconvenient time. I am very busy. Have you typed out that letter to the Pope yet, Loveday?"

"No, my lord. If you remember, you asked me to look up the figures about the Newfoundland fisheries first?"

"So I did. Well, it is fortunate, as I think the whole letter will have to be redrafted. A great deal of new information has come to light since luncheon. A great deal . . . You see, my dear, I am fully occupied." He turned his restless, quizzical eyes upon Angela. "I suppose you have come about the Danube. Well, you must come again later. Tell them it will be all right, quite all right, but I have not had time to give my full attention to it. Tell them that."

"Very well, Papa."

"Anyway," said Lord Moping rather petulantly, "it is a matter of secondary importance. There is the Elbe and the Amazon and the Tigris to be dealt with first, eh, Loveday? . . . *Danube* indeed. Nasty little river. I'd only call it a stream myself. Well, can't stop, nice of you to come. I would do more for you if I could, but you see how I'm fixed. Write to me about it. That's it. *Put it in black and white.*"

And with that he left the room.

"You see," said the doctor, "he is in excellent condition. He is putting on weight, eating and sleeping excellently. In fact, the whole tone of his system is above reproach."

The door opened again and Loveday returned.

"Forgive my coming back, sir, but I was afraid that the young lady might be upset at his Lordship's not knowing her. You mustn't mind him, miss. Next time he'll be very pleased to see you. It's only to-day he's put out on account of being behindhand with his work. You see, sir, all this week I've been helping in the library and I haven't been able to get all his Lordship's reports typed out. And he's got muddled with his card index. That's all it is. He doesn't mean any harm."

EVELYN WAUGH

"What a nice man," said Angela, when Loveday had gone back to his charge.

"Yes. I don't know what we should do without old Loveday. Everybody loves him, staff and patients alike."

"I remember him well. It's a great comfort to know that you are able to get such good warders," said Lady Moping; "people who don't know, say such foolish things about asylums."

"Oh, but Loveday isn't a warder," said the doctor.

"You don't mean he's cuckoo, too?" said Angela.

The doctor corrected her.

"He is an *inmate*. It is rather an interesting case. He has been here for thirty-five years."

"But I've never seen anyone saner," said Angela.

"He certainly has that air," said the doctor, "and in the last twenty years we have treated him as such. He is the life and soul of the place. Of course he is not one of the private patients, but we allow him to mix freely with them. He plays billiards excellently, does conjuring tricks at the concert, mends their gramophones, valets them, helps them in their crossword puzzles and various—er—hobbies. We allow them to give him small tips for services rendered, and he must by now have amassed quite a little fortune. He has a way with even the most troublesome of them. An invaluable man about the place."

"Yes, but why is he here?"

"Well, it is rather sad. When he was a very young man he killed somebody—a young woman quite unknown to him, whom he knocked off her bicycle and then throttled. He gave himself up immediately afterwards and had been here ever since."

"But surely he is perfectly safe now. Why is he not let out?"

"Well, I suppose if it was to anyone's interest, he would be. He has no relatives except a step-sister who lives in Plymouth. She used to visit him at one time, but she hasn't been for years now. He's perfectly happy here and I can assure you *we* aren't going to take the first steps in turning him out. He's far too useful to us."

"But it doesn't seem fair," said Angela.

"Look at your father," said the doctor. "He'd be quite lost without Loveday to act as his secretary."

"It doesn't seem fair."

2

Angela left the asylum, oppressed by a sense of injustice. Her mother was unsympathetic.

"Think of being locked up in a looney bin all one's life."

"He attempted to hang himself in the orangery," replied Lady Moping, "*in front of the Chester-Martins.*"

"I don't mean Papa. I mean Mr. Loveday."

"I don't think I know him."

"Yes, the looney they have put to look after papa."

"Your father's secretary. A very decent sort of man, I thought, and eminently suited to his work."

Angela left the question for the time, but returned to it again at luncheon on the following day.

"Mums, what does one have to do to get people out of the bin?"

"The bin? Good gracious, child, I hope that you do not anticipate your father's return *here.*"

"No, no. Mr. Loveday."

"Angela, you seem to me to be totally bemused. I see it was a mistake to take you with me on our little visit yesterday."

After luncheon Angela disappeared to the library and was soon immersed in the lunacy laws as represented in the encyclopædia.

She did not re-open the subject with her mother, but a fortnight later, when there was a question of taking some pheasants over to her father for his eleventh Certification Party she showed an unusual willingness to run over with them. Her mother was occupied with other interests and noticed nothing suspicious.

Angela drove her small car to the asylum, and after delivering the game, asked for Mr. Loveday. He was busy at the time making a crown for one of his companions who expected hourly to be anointed Emperor of Brazil, but he left his work and enjoyed several minutes' conversation with her. They spoke about her father's health and spirits. After a time Angela remarked, "Don't you ever want to get away?"

Mr. Loveday looked at her with his gentle, blue-grey eyes. "I've got very well used to the life, miss. I'm fond of the poor people here, and I think that several of them are quite fond of me. At least, I think they would miss me if I were to go."

"But don't you ever think of being free again?"

"Oh, yes, miss, I think of it—almost all the time I think of it."

"What would you do if you got out? There must be *something* you would sooner do than stay here."

The old man fidgeted uneasily. "Well, miss, it sounds ungrateful, but I can't deny I should welcome a little outing, once, before I get too old to enjoy it. I expect we all have our secret ambitions, and there *is* one thing I often wish I could do. You mustn't ask me what . . . It wouldn't take long. But I do feel that if I had done it, just for a day, an afternoon even, then I would die quiet. I could settle down again easier, and devote myself to the poor crazed people here with a better heart. Yes, I do feel that."

There were tears in Angela's eyes that afternoon as she drove away. "He *shall* have his little outing, bless him," she said.

3

From that day onwards for many weeks Angela had a new purpose in life. She moved about the ordinary routine of her home with an abstracted air and an unfamiliar, reserved courtesy which greatly disconcerted Lady Moping.

"I believe the child's in love. I only pray that it isn't that uncouth Egbertson boy."

She read a great deal in the library, she cross-examined any guests who had pretensions to legal or medical knowledge, she showed extreme goodwill to old Sir Roderick Lane-Foscote, their Member. The names "alienist," "barrister" or "government official" now had for her the glamour that formerly surrounded film actors and professional wrestlers. She was a woman with a cause, and before the end of the hunting season she had triumphed. Mr. Loveday achieved his liberty.

The doctor at the asylum showed reluctance but no real opposition. Sir Roderick wrote to the Home Office. The necessary papers were signed, and at last the day came when Mr. Loveday took leave of the home where he had spent such long and useful years.

His departure was marked by some ceremony. Angela and Sir Roderick Lane-Foscote sat with the doctors on the stage of the gymnasium. Below them were assembled everyone in the institution who was thought to be stable enough to endure the excitement.

Lord Moping, with a few suitable expressions of regret, presented Mr. Loveday on behalf of the wealthier lunatics with a gold cigarette case; those who supposed themselves to be emperors showered him with decorations and titles of honour. The warders gave him a silver watch and many of the nonpaying inmates were in tears on the day of the presentation.

The doctor made the main speech of the afternoon. "Remember," he remarked, "that you leave behind you nothing but our warmest good wishes. You are bound to us by ties that none will forget. Time will only deepen our sense of debt to you. If at any time in the future you should grow tired of your life in the world, there will always be a welcome for you here. Your post will be open."

A dozen or so variously afflicted lunatics hopped and skipped after him down the drive until the iron gates opened and Mr. Loveday stepped into his freedom. His small trunk had already gone to the station; he elected to walk. He had been reticent about his plans, but he was well provided with money, and the general impression was that he would go to London and enjoy himself a little before visiting his stepsister in Plymouth.

It was to the surprise of all that he returned within two hours of his liberation. He was smiling whimsically, a gentle, self-regarding smile of reminiscence.

"I have come back," he informed the doctor. "I think that now I shall be here for good."

"But, Loveday, what a short holiday. I'm afraid that you have hardly enjoyed yourself at all."

"Oh yes, sir, thank you, sir, I've enjoyed myself *very much*. I'd been promising myself one little treat, all these years. It was short, sir, but *most* enjoyable. Now I shall be able to settle down again to my work here without any regrets."

Half a mile up the road from the asylum gates, they later discovered an abandoned bicycle. It was a lady's machine of some antiquity. Quite near it in the ditch lay the strangled body of a young woman, who, riding home to her tea, had chanced to overtake Mr. Loveday, as he strode along, musing on his opportunities.

PAUL THEROUX

THE JOHORE MURDERS

*T*HE FIRST VICTIM was a British planter, and everyone at the Club said what a shame it was that after fifteen years in the country he was killed just four days before he planned to leave. He had no family, he lived alone; until he was murdered no one knew very much about him. Murder is the grimmest, briefest fame. If the second victim, a month later, had not been an American I probably would not have given the Johore murders a second thought, and I certainly would not have been involved in the business. But who would have guessed that Ismail Garcia was an American?

The least dignified thing that can happen to a man is to be murdered. If he dies in his sleep he gets a respectful obituary and perhaps a smiling portrait; it is how we all want to be remembered. But murder is the great exposer: here is the victim in his torn underwear, face down on the floor, unpaid bills on his dresser, a meager shopping list, some loose change, and worst of all the fact that he is alone. Investigation reveals what he did that day—it all matters—his habits are examined, his behavior scrutinized, his trunks rifled, and a balance sheet is drawn up at the hospital giving the contents of his stomach. Dying, the last private act we perform, is made public: the murder victim has no secrets.

So, somewhere in Garcia's house, a passport was found, an American one, and that was when the Malaysian police contacted the Embassy in Kuala Lumpur. I was asked to go down for the death certificate, personal effects, and anything that might be necessary for the report to his next of kin. I intended it to be a stopover, a day in Johore, a night in Singapore, and then back to Ayer Hitam. Peeraswami had a brother in Johore; Abubaker, my driver, said he wanted to pray at the Johore mosque; we pushed off early one morning, Abubaker at the wheel, Peeraswami playing with the car radio. I was in the back seat going over newspaper clippings of the two murders.

In most ways they were the same. Each victim was a foreigner, unmarried, lived alone in a house outside town, and had been a resident for some years. In neither case was there any sign of a forced entry or a robbery. Both men were poor, both men had been mutilated. They looked to me like acts of Chinese revenge. But on planters? In Malaysia it was the Chinese *towkay* who was robbed, kidnaped, or murdered, not the expatriate planters who lived from month to month on provisioners' credit and chit-signing in bars. There were two differences: Tibbets was British and Ismail Garcia was American. And one other known fact: Tibbets, at the time of his death, was planning to go back to England.

A two-hour drive through rubber estates took us into Johore, and then we were speeding along the shore of the Straits, past the lovely casuarina trees and the high houses on the leafy bluff that overlooks the swampland and the marshes on the north coast of Singapore. I dropped Peeraswami at his brother's house, which was in one of the wilder suburbs of Johore and with a high chain-link fence around it to assure even greater seclusion. Abubaker scrambled out at the mosque after giving me directions to the police headquarters.

Garcia's effects were in a paper bag from a Chinese shop. I signed for them and took them to a table to examine a cheap watch, a cheap ring, a copy of the Koran, a birth certificate, the passport.

"We left the clothes behind," said Detective-Sergeant Yusof. "We just took the valuables."

Valuables: there wasn't five dollars' worth of stuff in the bag.

"Was there any money?"

"He had no money. We're not treating it as robbery."

"What *are* you treating it as?"

"Homicide, probably by a friend."

"Some friend."

"He knew the murderer, so did Tibbets. You will believe me when you see the houses."

I almost did. Garcia's house was completely surrounded by a high fence, and Yusof said that Tibbets's fence was even higher. It was not unusual; every large house in Malaysian cities had an unclimbable fence or a wall with spikes of glass cemented on to the top.

"The lock wasn't broken, the house wasn't tampered with," said Yusof. "So we are calling it a sex crime."

"I thought you were calling it a homicide."

Yusof smirked at me. "We have a theory. The Englishmen who live here get funny ideas. Especially the ones who live alone. Some of them take Malay mistresses, the other ones go around with Chinese boys."

"Not Malay boys?"

Yusof said, "We do not do such things."

"You say Englishmen do, but Garcia was an American."

"He was single," said Yusof.

"I'm single," I said.

"We couldn't find any sign of a mistress."

"I thought you were looking for a murderer."

"That's what I'm trying to say," said Yusof. "These queers are very secretive. They get jealous. They fight with their boyfriends. The body was mutilated—that tells me a Chinese boy is involved."

"So you don't think it had anything to do with money?"

"Do you know what the rubber price is?"

"As a matter of fact, I do."

"And that's not all," said Yusof. "This man Garcia—do you know what he owed his provisioner? Eight hundred-over dollars! Tibbets was owing five hundred."

I said, "Maybe the provisioner did it."

"Interesting," said Yusof. "We can work on that."

Tibbets was English, so over lunch I concentrated on Garcia. There was a little dossier on him from the Alien Registration Office. Born 1922 in the Philippines; fought in World War II; took out American citizenship in Guam, came to Malaysia in 1954, converted to Islam and changed his name. From place to place, complicating his identity, picking up a nationality here, a name there, a religion somewhere else. And why would he convert? A woman, of course. No man changed his religion to live with another man. I didn't believe he was a homosexual, and though there was no evidence to support it I didn't rule out the possibility of robbery. In all this there were two items that interested me—the birth certificate and the passport. The birth certificate was brown with age, the passport new and unused.

Why would a man who had changed his religion and lived in a country for nearly twenty years have a new passport?

After lunch I rang police headquarters and asked for Yusof.

"We've got the provisioner," he said. "I think you might be right. He was also Tibbets's provisioner—both men owed him money. He is helping us with our inquiries."

"What a pompous phrase for torture," I said, but before Yusof could reply I added, "About Garcia—I figure he was planning to leave the country."

Yusof cackled into the phone. "Not at all! We talked to his employer—Garcia had a permanent and pensionable contract."

"Then why did he apply for a passport two weeks ago?"

"It is the law. He must be in possession of a valid passport if he is an expatriate."

I said, "I'd like to talk to his employer."

Yusof gave me the name of the man, Tan See Leng, owner of the Tai-Hwa Rubber Estate. I went over that afternoon. At first Tan refused to see me, but when I sent him my card with the consulate address and the American eagle on it, he rushed out of his office and apologized. He was a thin evasive man with spiky hair, and though he pretended not to be surprised when I said Garcia was an American national I could tell this was news to him. He said he knew nothing about Garcia, apart from the fact that he'd been a good foreman. He'd never see him socially. He confirmed that Garcia lived behind an impenetrable fence.

"Who owned the house?"

"He did."

"That's something," I said. "I suppose you knew he was leaving the country."

"He was not leaving. He was wucking."

"It would help if you told me the truth," I said.

Tan's bony face tightened with anger. He said, "Perhaps he intended to leave. I do not know."

"I take it business isn't so good."

"The rubber price is low, some planters are switching to oil palm. But the price will rise if we are patient."

"What did you pay Garcia?"

"Two thousand a month. He was on permanent terms—he signed

one of the old contracts. We were very generous in those days with expatriates."

"But he could have broken the contract."

"Some men break."

"Up in Ayer Hitam they have something called a 'golden hand-shake.' If they want to get rid of a foreigner they offer him a chunk of money as compensation for loss of career."

"That is Ayer Hitam," said Tan. "This is Johore."

"And they always pay cash, because it's against the law to take that much money out of the country. No banks. Just a suitcase full of Straits dollars."

Tan said nothing.

I said, "I don't think Garcia or Tibbets were queer. I think this was robbery, pure and simple."

"The houses were not broken into."

"So the papers say," I said. "It's the only thing I don't understand. Both men were killed at home during the day."

"Mister," said Tan. "You should leave this to the police."

"You swear you didn't give Garcia a golden handshake?"

"That is against the law, as you say."

"It's not as serious as murder, is it?"

In the course of the conversation, Tan had turned to wood. I was sure he was lying, but he stuck to his story. I decided to have nothing more to do with the police or Yusof and instead to go back to the house of Peeraswami's brother, to test a theory of my own.

The house bore many similarities to Garcia's and to what I knew of Tibbets's. It was secluded, out of town, rather characterless, and the high fence was topped with barbed wire. Sathya, Peeraswami's broth-er, asked me how I liked Johore. I told him that I liked it so much I wanted to spend a few days there, but that I didn't want the Embassy to know where I was. I asked him if he would put me up.

"Oh, yes," he said. "You are welcome. But you would be more comfortable in a hotel."

"It's much quieter here."

"It is the country life. We have no car."

"It's just what I'm looking for."

After I was shown to my bedroom I excused myself and went to the offices of the *Johore Mail*, read the classified ads for the previous few weeks and placed an ad myself. For the next two days I explored Johore, looked over the Botanical Gardens and the Sultan's mosque, and ingratiated myself with Sathya and his family. I had arrived on a Friday. On Monday I said to Sathya, "I'm expecting a phone call today."

Sathya said, "This is your house."

"I feel I ought to do something in return," I said. "I have a driver and a car—I don't need them today. Why don't you use them? Take your wife and children over to Singapore and enjoy yourself."

He hesitated, but finally I persuaded him. Abubaker, on the other hand, showed an obvious distaste for taking an Indian family out for the day.

"Peeraswami," I said. "I'd like you to stay here with me."

"*Tuan*," he said, agreeing. Sathya and the others left. I locked the gate behind them and sat by the telephone to wait.

There were four phone calls. Three of the callers I discouraged by describing the location, the size of the house, the tiny garden, the work I said had to be done on the roof. And I gave the same story to the last caller, but he was insistent and eager to see it. He said he'd be right over.

Rawlins was the name he gave me. He came in a new car, gave me a hearty greeting, and was not at all put off by the slightly ramshackle appearance of the house. He smoked a cheroot which had stained his teeth and the center swatch of his mustache a sticky yellow, and he walked around with one hand cupped, tapping ashes into his palm.

"You're smart not to use an agent," he said, looking over the house. "These estate agents are bloody thieves."

I showed him the garden, the lounge, the kitchen.

He sniffed and said, "You like curry."

"My cook's an Indian." He went silent, glanced around suspiciously, and I added, "I gave him the day off."

"You lived here long?"

"Ten years. I'm chucking it. I've been worried about selling this place ever since I broke my contract."

"Rubber?" he said, and spat a fragment of the cheroot into his hand.

"Yes," I said. "I was manager of an estate up in Kluang."

He asked me the price and when I told him he said, "I can manage that." He took out a checkbook. "I'll give you a deposit now and the balance when contracts are exchanged. We'll put our lawyers in touch and Bob's your uncle. Got a pen?"

I went to the desk and opened a drawer, but as I rummaged he said, "Okay, turn around slow and put your hands up."

I did as I was told and heard the cheroot hitting the floor. Above the kris Rawlins held his face was fierce and twisted. In such an act a man reverts; his face was pure monkey, threatening teeth and eyes. He said, "Now hand it over."

"What is this?" I said. "What do you want?"

"Your money, all of it, your handshake."

"I don't have any money."

"They always lie," he said. "They always fight, and then I have to do them. Just make it easy this time. The money—"

But he said no more, for Peeraswami in his bare feet crept behind him from the broom cupboard where he had been hiding and brought a cast-iron frying pan down so hard on his skull that I thought for a moment I saw a crack show in the man's forehead. We tied Rawlins up with Sathya's neckties and then I rang Yusof.

On the way to police headquarters, where Yusof insisted the corpse be delivered, I said, "This probably would not have happened if you didn't have such strict exchange control regulations."

"So it was robbery," said Yusof, "but how did he know Tibbets and Garcia had had golden handshakes?"

"He guessed. There was no risk involved. He knew they were leaving the country because they'd put their houses up for sale. Expatriates who own houses here have been in the country a long time, which means they're taking a lot of money out in a suitcase. You should read the paper."

"I read the paper," said Yusof. "Malay and English press."

"I mean the classified ads, where it says, 'Expatriate-owned house for immediate sale. Leaving the country. No agents.' Tibbets and Garcia placed that ad, and so did I."

Yusof said, "I should have done that. I could have broken this case."

"I doubt it—he wouldn't have done business with a Malay," I said. "But remember, if a person says he wants to buy your house you let him in. It's the easiest way for a burglar to enter—through the front door. If he's a white man in this country no one suspects him. We're supposed to trust each other. As soon as I realized it had something to do with the sale of a house I knew the murderer would be white."

"He didn't know they were alone."

"The wife and kids always fly out first, especially if daddy's breaking currency regulations."

"You foreigners know all the tricks."

"True," I said. "If he was a Malay or a Chinese I probably wouldn't have been able to catch him." I tapped my head. "I understand the mind of the West."

EDITH WHARTON

A JOURNEY

AS SHE LAY in her berth, staring at the shadows overhead, the rush of the wheels was in her brain, driving her deeper and deeper into circles of wakeful lucidity. The sleeping car had sunk into its night silence. Through the wet windowpane she watched the sudden lights, the long stretches of hurrying blackness. Now and then she turned her head and looked through the opening in the hangings at her husband's curtains across the aisle. . . .

She wondered restlessly if he wanted anything and if she could hear him if he called. His voice had grown very weak within the last months and it irritated him when she did not hear. This irritability, this increasing childish petulance seemed to give expression to their imperceptible estrangement. Like two faces looking at one another through a sheet of glass they were close together, almost touching, but they could not hear or feel each other: the conductivity between them was broken. She, at least, had this sense of separation, and she fancied sometimes that she saw it reflected in the look with which he supplemented his failing words. Doubtless the fault was hers. She was too impenetrably healthy to be touched by the irrelevancies of disease. Her self-reproachful tenderness was tinged with the sense of his irrationality: she had a vague feeling that there was a purpose in his helpless tyrannies. The suddenness of the change had found her so unprepared. A year ago their pulses had beat to one robust measure; both had the same prodigal confidence in an exhaustless future. Now their energies no longer kept step: hers still bounded ahead of life, pre-empting unclaimed regions of hope and activity, while his lagged behind, vainly struggling to overtake her.

When they married, she had such arrears of living to make up: her days had been as bare as the whitewashed schoolroom where she forced innutritious facts upon reluctant children. His coming had broken in on the slumber of circumstance, widening the present till it became the encloser of remotest chances. But imperceptibly the horizon narrowed. Life had a grudge against her: she was never to be allowed to spread her wings.

At first the doctors had said that six weeks of mild air would set him right; but when he came back this assurance was explained as having of course included a winter in a dry climate. They gave up their pretty house, storing the wedding presents and new furniture, and went to Colorado. She had hated it there from the first. Nobody knew her or cared about her; there was no one to wonder at the good match she had made, or to envy her the new dresses and the visiting cards which were still a surprise to her. And he kept growing worse. She felt herself beset with difficulties too evasive to be fought by so direct a temperament. She still loved him, of course; but he was gradually, undefinably ceasing to be himself. The man she had married had been strong, active, gently masterful: the male whose pleasure it is to clear a way through the material obstructions of life; but now it was she who was the protector, he who must be shielded from importunities and given his drops or his beef juice though the skies were falling. The routine of the sickroom bewildered her; this punctual administering of medicine seemed as idle as some uncomprehended religious mummery.

There were moments, indeed, when warm gushes of pity swept away her instinctive resentment of his condition, when she still found his old self in his eyes as they groped for each other through the dense medium of his weakness. But these moments had grown rare. Sometimes he frightened her: his sunken expressionless face seemed that of a stranger; his voice was weak and hoarse; his thin-lipped smile a mere muscular contraction. Her hand avoided his damp soft skin, which had lost the familiar roughness of health: she caught herself furtively watching him as she might have watched a strange animal. It frightened her to feel that this was the man she loved; there were hours when to tell him what she suffered seemed the one escape from her fears. But in general she judged herself more leniently, reflecting that she had perhaps been too long alone with him, and that she would feel differently when they were at home again, surrounded by her robust and buoyant family. How she had rejoiced when the doctors at last gave their consent to his going home! She knew, of course, what the decision meant; they both knew. It meant that he was to die; but they dressed the truth in hopeful euphemisms, and at times, in the joy of preparation, she really forgot the purpose of their journey, and slipped into an eager allusion to next year's plans.

At last the day of leaving came. She had a dreadful fear that they would never get away; that somehow at the last moment he would fail her; that the doctors held one of their accustomed treacheries in reserve; but nothing happened. They drove to the station, he was installed in a seat with a rug over his knees and a cushion at his back, and she hung out of the window waving unregretful farewells to the acquaintances she had really never liked till then.

The first twenty-four hours had passed off well. He revived a little and it amused him to look out of the window and to observe the humors of the car. The second day he began to grow weary and to chafe under the dispassionate stare of the freckled child with the lump of chewing gum. She had to explain to the child's mother that her husband was too ill to be disturbed: a statement received by that lady with a resentment visibly supported by the maternal sentiment of the whole car. . . .

That night he slept badly and the next morning his temperature frightened her: she was sure he was growing worse. The day passed slowly, punctuated by the small irritations of travel. Watching his tired face, she traced in its contractions every rattle and jolt of the train, till her own body vibrated with sympathetic fatigue. She felt the others observing him too, and hovered restlessly between him and the line of interrogative eyes. The freckled child hung about him like a fly; offers of candy and picture books failed to dislodge her; she twisted one leg around the other and watched him imperturbably. The porter, as he passed, lingered with vague proffers of help, probably inspired by phil-anthropic passengers swelling with the sense that "something ought to be done"; and one nervous man in a skull cap was audibly concerned as to the possible effect on his wife's health.

The hours dragged on in a dreary inoccupation. Towards dusk she sat down beside him and he laid his hand on hers. The touch startled her. He seemed to be calling her from far off. She looked at him help-lessly and his smile went through her like a physical pang.

"Are you very tired?" she asked.

"No, not very."

"We'll be there soon now."

"Yes, very soon."

"This time tomorrow—"

He nodded and they sat silent. When she had put him to bed and crawled into her own berth she tried to cheer herself with the thought that in less than twenty-four hours they would be in New York. Her people would all be at the station to meet her—she pictured their round unanxious faces pressing through the crowd. She only hoped they would not tell him too loudly that he was looking splendidly and would be all right in no time: the subtler sympathies developed by long contact with suffering were making her aware of a certain coarseness of texture in the family sensibilities.

Suddenly she thought she heard him call. She parted the curtains and listened. No, it was only a man snoring at the other end of the car. His snores had a greasy sound, as though they passed through tallow. She lay down and tried to sleep. . . . Had she not heard him move? She started up trembling. . . . The silence frightened her more than any sound. He might not be able to make her hear—he might be calling her now. . . . What made her think of such things? It was merely the familiar tendency of an overtired mind to fasten itself on the most intolerable chance within the range of its forebodings. . . . Putting her head out, she listened: but she could not distinguish his breathing from that of the other pairs of lungs about her. She longed to get up and look at him, but she knew the impulse was a mere vent for her restlessness, and the fear of disturbing him restrained her. . . . The regular movement of his curtain reassured her, she knew not why; she remembered that he had wished her a cheerful good night; and the sheer inability to endure her fears a moment longer made her put them from her with an effort of her whole sound-tired body. She turned on her side and slept.

She sat up stiffly, staring out at the dawn. The train was rushing through a region of bare hillocks huddled against a lifeless sky. It looked like the first day of creation. The air of the car was close, and she pushed up her window to let in the keen wind. Then she looked at her watch: it was seven o'clock, and soon the people about her would be stirring. She slipped into her clothes, smoothed her disheveled hair and crept to the dressing room. When she had washed her face and adjusted her dress she felt more hopeful. It was always a struggle for her not to be cheerful in the morning. Her cheeks burned deliciously under the coarse towel and the wet hair about her temples broke into strong upward tendrils. Every inch of her was full of life and elasticity. And in ten hours they would be at home!

She stepped to her husband's berth: it was time for him to take his early glass of milk. The window shade was down, and in the dust of the curtained enclosure she could just see that he lay sideways, with his face away from her. She leaned over him and drew up the shade. As she did so she touched one of his hands. It felt cold. . . .

She bent closer, laying her hand on his arm and calling him by name. He did not move. She spoke again more loudly; she grasped his shoulder and gently shook it. He lay motionless. She caught hold of his hand again: it slipped from her limply, like a dead thing. A dead thing?

Her breath caught. She must see his face. She leaned forward, and hurriedly, shrinkingly, with a sickening reluctance of the flesh, laid her hands on his shoulders and turned him over. His head fell back; his face looked small and smooth; he gazed at her with steady eyes.

She remained motionless for a long time, holding him thus; and they looked at each other. Suddenly she shrank back: the longing to scream, to call out, to fly from him, had almost overpowered her. But a strong hand arrested her. Good God! If it were known that he was dead they would be put off the train at the next station—

In a terrifying flash of remembrance there arose before her a scene she had once witnessed in traveling, when a husband and wife, whose child had died in the train, had been thrust out at some chance station. She saw them standing on the platform with the child's body between them; she had never forgotten the dazed look with which they followed the receding train. And this was what would happen to her. Within the next hour she might find herself on the platform of some strange station, alone with her husband's body. . . . Anything but that! It was too horrible—She quivered like a creature at bay.

As she cowered there, she felt the train moving more slowly. It was coming then—they were approaching a station! She saw again the husband and wife standing on the lonely platform; and with a violent gesture she drew down the shade to hide her husband's face.

Feeling dizzy, she sank down on the edge of the berth, keeping away from his outstretched body, and pulling the curtains close, so that he and she were shut into a kind of sepulchral twilight. She tried to think. At all costs she must conceal the fact that he was dead. But how? Her mind refused to act: she could not plan, combine. She could think of no way but to sit there, clutching the curtains, all day long. . . .

She heard the porter making up her bed; people were beginning to move about the car; the dressing-room door was being opened and shut. She tried to rouse herself. At length with a supreme effort she rose to her feet, stepping into the aisle of the car and drawing the curtains tight behind her. She noticed that they still parted slightly with the motion of the car, and finding a pin in her dress she fastened them together. Now she was safe. She looked round and saw the porter. She fancied he was watching her.

"Ain't he awake yet?" he inquired.

"No," she faltered.

"I got his milk all ready when he wants it. You know you told me to have it for him by seven."

She nodded silently and crept into her seat.

At half-past eight the train reached Buffalo. By this time the other passengers were dressed and the berths had been folded back for the day. The porter, moving to and fro under his burden of sheets and pillows, glanced at her as he passed. At length he said: "Ain't he going to get up? You know we're ordered to make up the berths as early as we can."

She turned cold with fear. They were just entering the station.

"Oh, not yet," she stammered. "Not till he's had his milk. Won't you get it, please?"

"All right. Soon as we start again."

When the train moved on he reappeared with the milk. She took it from him and sat vaguely looking at it: her brain moved slowly from one idea to another, as though they were stepping-stones set far apart across a whirling flood. At length she became aware that the porter still hovered expectantly.

"Will I give it to him?" he suggested.

"Oh, no," she cried, rising. "He—he's asleep yet, I think—"

She waited till the porter had passed on; then she unpinned the curtains and slipped behind them. In the semiobscurity her husband's face stared up at her like a marble mask with agate eyes. The eyes were dreadful. She put out her hand and drew down the lids. Then she remembered the glass of milk in her other hand: what was she to do with it? She thought of raising the window and throwing it out; but to do so she would have to lean across his body and bring her face close to his. She decided to drink the milk.

She returned to her seat with the empty glass and after a while the porter came back to get it.

"When'll I fold up his bed?" he asked.

"Oh, not now—not yet; he's ill—he's very ill. Can't you let him stay as he is? The doctor wants him to lie down as much as possible."

He scratched his head. "Well, if he's *really* sick—"

He took the empty glass and walked away, explaining to the passengers that the party behind the curtains was too sick to get up just yet.

She found herself the center of sympathetic eyes. A motherly woman with an intimate smile sat down beside her.

"I'm real sorry to hear your husband's sick. I've had a remarkable amount of sickness in my family and maybe I could assist you. Can I take a look at him?"

"Oh, no—no, please! He mustn't be disturbed."

The lady accepted the rebuff indulgently.

"Well, it's just as you say, of course, but you don't look to me as if you'd had much experience in sickness and I'd have been glad to assist you. What do you generally do when your husband's taken this way?"

"I—I let him sleep."

"Too much sleep ain't any too healthful either. Don't you give him any medicine?"

"Y—yes."

"Don't you wake him to take it?"

"Yes."

"When does he take the next dose?"

"Not for—two hours—"

The lady looked disappointed. "Well, if I was you I'd try giving it oftener. That's what I do with my folks."

After that many faces seemed to press upon her. The passengers were on their way to the dining car, and she was conscious that as they passed down the aisle they glanced curiously at the closed curtains. One lantern-jawed man with prominent eyes stood still and tried to shoot his projecting glance through the division between the folds. The freckled child, returning from breakfast, waylaid the passers with a buttery clutch, saying in a loud whisper, "He's sick"; and once the conductor came by, asking for tickets. She shrank into her corner and looked out of the window at the flying trees and houses, meaningless hieroglyphs of an endlessly unrolled papyrus.

Now and then the train stopped, and the newcomers on entering the car stared in turn at the closed curtains. More and more people seemed to pass—their faces began to blend fantastically with the images surging in her brain. . . .

Later in the day a fat man detached himself from the mist of faces. He had a creased stomach and soft pale lips. As he pressed himself into the seat facing her she noticed that he was dressed in black broadcloth, with a soiled white tie.

"Husband's pretty bad this morning, is he?"

"Yes."

"Dear, dear! Now that's terribly distressing, ain't it?" An apostolic smile revealed his gold-filled teeth. "Of course you know there's no such thing as sickness. Ain't that a lovely thought? Death itself is but a deloosion of our grosser senses. On'y lay yourself open to the influx of the sperrit, submit yourself passively to the action of the divine force, and disease and dissolution will cease to exist for you. If you could indooce your husband to read this little pamphlet—"

The faces about her again grew indistinct. She had a vague recollection of hearing the motherly lady and the parent of the freckled child ardently disputing the relative advantages of trying several medicines at once, or of taking each in turn; the motherly lady maintaining that the competitive system saved time; the other objecting that you couldn't tell which remedy had effected the cure; their voices went on and on, like bell buoys droning through a fog. . . . The porter came up now and then with questions that she did not understand, but somehow she must have answered since he went away again without repeating them; every two hours the motherly lady reminded her that her husband ought to have his drops; people left the car and others replaced them. . . .

Her head was spinning and she tried to steady herself by clutching at her thoughts as they swept by, but they slipped away from her like bushes on the side of a sheer precipice down which she seemed to be falling. Suddenly her mind grew clear again and she found herself vividly picturing what would happen when the train reached New York. She shuddered as it occurred to her that he would be quite cold and that someone might perceive he had been dead since morning.

She thought hurriedly: "If they see I am not surprised they will suspect something. They will ask questions, and if I tell them the truth they won't believe me—no one would believe me! It will be terrible"—and she kept repeating to herself—"I must pretend I don't know. I must pretend I don't know. When they open the curtains I must go up to him quite naturally—and then I must scream!" She had an idea that the scream would be very hard to do.

Gradually new thoughts crowded upon her, vivid and urgent: she tried to separate and restrain them, but they beset her clamorously, like her schoolchildren at the end of a hot day, when she was too tired to silence them. Her head grew confused, and she felt a sick fear of forgetting her part, of betraying herself by some unguarded word or look.

"I must pretend I don't know," she went on murmuring. The words had lost their significance, but she repeated them mechanically, as though they had been a magic formula, until suddenly she heard herself saying: "I can't remember, I can't remember!"

Her voice sounded very loud, and she looked about her in terror; but no one seemed to notice that she had spoken.

As she glanced down the car her eye caught the curtains of her husband's berth, and she began to examine the monotonous arabesques woven through their heavy folds. The pattern was intricate and difficult to trace; she gazed fixedly at the curtains and as she did so the thick stuff grew transparent and through it she saw her husband's face—his dead face. She struggled to avert her look, but her eyes refused to move and her head seemed to be held in a vise. At last, with an effort that left her weak and shaking, she turned away; but it was of no use; close in front of her, small and smooth, was her husband's face. It seemed to be suspended in the air between her and the false braids of the woman who sat in front of her. With an uncontrollable gesture she stretched out her hand to push the face away, and suddenly she felt the touch of his smooth skin. She repressed a cry and half started from her seat. The woman with the false braids looked around, and feeling that she must justify her movement in some way she rose and lifted her traveling bag from the opposite seat. She unlocked the bag and looked into it; but the first object her hand met was a small flask of her husband's thrust there at the last moment, in the haste of departure. She locked the bag and closed her eyes . . . his face was there again, hanging between her eyeballs and lids like a waxen mask against a red curtain. . . .

She roused herself with a shiver. Had she fainted or slept? Hours seemed to have elapsed; but it was still broad day, and the people about her were sitting in the same attitudes as before.

A sudden sense of hunger made her aware that she had eaten nothing since morning. The thought of food filled her with disgust, but she dreaded a return of faintness, and remembering that she had some biscuits in her bag she took one out and ate it. The dry crumbs choked her, and she hastily swallowed a little brandy from her husband's flask. The burning sensation in her throat acted as a counterirritant, momentarily relieving the dull ache of her nerves. Then she felt a gently-stealing warmth, as though a soft air fanned her, and the swarming fears relaxed their clutch, receding through the stillness that enclosed her, a stillness soothing as the spacious quietude of a summer day. She slept.

Through her sleep she felt the impetuous rush of the train. It seemed to be life itself that was sweeping her on with headlong inexorable force—sweeping her into darkness and terror, and the awe of unknown days.—Now all at once everything was still—not a sound, not a pulsation. . . . She was dead in her turn, and lay beside him with smooth upstaring face. How quiet it was!—and yet she heard feet coming, the feet of the men who were to carry them away. . . . She could feel too—she felt a sudden prolonged vibration, a series of hard shocks, and then another plunge into darkness: the darkness of death this time—a black whirlwind on which they were both spinning like leaves, in wild uncoiling spirals, with millions and millions of the dead. . . .

She sprang up in terror. Her sleep must have lasted a long time, for the winter day had paled and the lights had been lit. The car was in confusion, and as she regained her self-possession she saw that the passengers were gathering up their wraps and bags. The woman with the false braids had brought from the dressing room a sickly ivy plant in a bottle, and the Christian Scientist was reversing his cuffs. The porter passed down the aisle with his impartial brush. An impersonal figure with a gold-banded cap asked for her husband's ticket. A voice shouted, "Baiggage *express!*" and she heard the clicking of metal as the passengers handed over their checks.

Presently her window was blocked by an expanse of sooty wall, and the train passed into the Harlem tunnel. The journey was over; in a few minutes she would see her family pushing their joyous way through the throng at the station. Her heart dilated. The worst terror was past. . . .

"We'd better get him up now, hadn't we?" asked the porter, touching her arm.

He had her husband's hat in his hand and was meditatively revolving it under his brush.

She looked at the hat and tried to speak; but suddenly the car grew dark. She flung up her arms, struggling to catch at something, and fell face downward, striking her head against the dead man's berth.

GABRIEL GARCÍA MÁRQUEZ

MISS FORBES'S
SUMMER OF HAPPINESS

HEN WE CAME back to the house in the afternoon, we found an enormous sea serpent nailed by the neck to the door frame. Black and phosphorescent, it looked like a Gypsy curse with its still-flashing eyes and its sawlike teeth in gaping jaws. I was about nine years old at the time, and at the sight of that vision out of a delirium I felt a terror so intense that I lost my voice. But my brother, who was two years younger, dropped the oxygen tanks, the masks, the fins, and fled, screaming in panic. Miss Forbes heard him from the tortuous stone steps that wound along the reefs from the dock to the house, and she ran to us, panting and livid, yet she had only to see the beast crucified on the door to understand the cause of our horror. She always said that when two children were together they were both guilty of what each did alone, and so she scolded the two of us for my brother's screams and continued to reprimand us for our lack of self-control. She spoke in German, not in the English stipulated in her tutor's contract, perhaps because she too was frightened and refused to admit it. But as soon as she caught her breath she returned to her stony English and her pedagogical obsession.

"It is a *Muraena helena*," she told us," so called because it was an animal sacred to the ancient Greeks."

All at once Oreste, the local boy who taught us how to swim in deep waters, appeared behind the agave plants. He was wearing his diving mask on his forehead, a minuscule bathing suit, and a leather belt that held six knives of different shapes and sizes, for he could conceive of no other way to hunt underwater than by engaging in hand-to-hand combat with his prey. He was about twenty years old and spent more time at the bottom of the sea than on solid ground, and with motor oil always smeared over his body he even looked like a sea animal. When she saw him for the first time, Miss Forbes told my parents that it was impossible to imagine a more beautiful human being. But his beauty could not save him from her severity: He too had to endure a reprimand, in Italian, for having hung the moray eel on the door, with no other possible reason than his desire to frighten the children. Then Miss Forbes ordered him to take it down with the respect due a mythical creature, and told us to dress for supper.

We did so without delay, trying not to commit a single error, because after two weeks under the regime of Miss Forbes we had learned that nothing was more difficult than living. As we showered in the dim light of the bathroom, I knew that my brother was still thinking about the moray. "It had people's eyes," he said. I agreed, but made him think otherwise and managed to change the subject until I finished washing. Yet when I stepped out of the shower he asked me to stay and keep him company.

"It's still daytime," I said.

I opened the curtains. It was the middle of August, and through the window you could see the burning lunar plain all the way to the other side of the island, and the sun that had stopped in the sky.

"That's not why," my brother said. "I'm just scared of being scared."

But when we came down to the table he seemed calm, and he had done everything with so much care that he earned special praise from Miss Forbes and two more points in the week's good-conduct report. I, on the other hand, lost two of the five points I had already earned, because at the last minute I permitted myself to hurry and came into the dining room out of breath. Every fifty points entitled us to a double portion of dessert, but neither of us had earned more than fifteen. It was a shame, really, because we never again tasted any desserts as delicious as those made by Miss Forbes.

Before beginning supper we would stand and pray behind our empty plates. Miss Forbes was not Catholic, but her contract stipulated that she would have us pray six times a day, and she had learned our prayers in order to fulfill those terms. Then the three of us would sit down, and we held our breath while she scrutinized our deportment down to the slightest detail, and only when everything seemed perfect would she ring the bell. Then the cook, Fulvia Flaminea, came in, carrying the eternal vermicelli soup of that abominable summer.

At first, when we were alone with our parents, meals were a fiesta. Fulvia Flaminea giggled all around the table as she served us, with a vocation for disorder that brought joy to our lives, and then sat down with us and ate a little bit from everyone's plate. But ever since Miss Forbes had taken charge of our destiny, she served in such dark silence that we could hear the bubbling of the soup as it boiled in the tureen. We ate with our spines against the back of our chairs, chewing ten times on one side and ten times on the other, never taking our eyes off the iron, languid, autumnal woman who recited etiquette lessons by heart. It was just like Sunday Mass, but without the consolation of people singing.

On the day we found the moray eel hanging from the door, Miss Forbes spoke to us of our patriotic obligations. After the soup, Fulvia Flaminea, almost floating on the air rarefied by our tutor's voice, served a broiled fillet of snowy flesh with an exquisite aroma. I have always preferred fish to any other food on land or in the sky, and that memory of our house in Guacamayal eased my heart. But my brother refused the dish without tasting it.

"I don't like it," he said.

Miss Forbes interrupted her lesson.

"You cannot know that," she told him. "You have not even tasted it."

She shot a warning glance at the cook, but it was too late.

"Moray is the finest fish in the world, *figlio mio*," Fulvia Flaminea told him. "Try it and see."

Miss Forbes remained calm. She told us, with her unmerciful methodology, that moray had been a delicacy of kings in antiquity and that warriors fought over its bile because it gave them supernatural courage. Then she repeated, as she had so often in so short a time, that good taste was not an innate faculty, nor was it taught at any particular age; rather, it was imposed from infancy. Therefore we had no valid reason not to eat. I had tasted the moray before I knew what it was, and remembered the contradiction forever after: It had a smooth, rather melancholy taste, yet the image of the serpent nailed to the door frame was more compelling than my appetite. My brother made a supreme effort with his first bite, but he could not bear it: He vomited.

"You will go to the bathroom," Miss Forbes told him without losing her calm, "you will wash yourself with care, and you will come back to eat."

I felt great anguish for him, because I knew how difficult he found it to cross the entire house in the early darkness and stay alone in the bathroom for the time he needed to wash. But he returned very soon in a clean shirt, pale and quivering with a hidden tremor, and he bore up very well under the rigorous inspection of his cleanliness. Then Miss Forbes sliced a piece of moray and ordered us to continue. I just managed a second bite. But my brother did not even pick up his knife and fork.

"I'm not going to eat it," he said.

His determination was so obvious that Miss Forbes withdrew.

"All right," she said, "but you will have no dessert."

My brother's relief filled me with courage. I crossed my knife and fork on my plate, just as Miss Forbes had taught us to do when we were finished, and said:

"I won't have dessert either."

"And you will not watch television," she replied.

"And we will not watch television," I said.

Miss Forbes placed her napkin on the table, and the three of us stood to pray. Then she sent us to our bedroom, with the warning that we had to be asleep by the time she finished eating. All our good-conduct points were canceled, and only after we had earned twenty more would we again enjoy her cream cakes, her vanilla tarts, her exquisite plum pastries, the likes of which we would not taste again for the rest of our lives.

The break was bound to come sooner or later. For an entire year we had looked forward to a summer of freedom on the island of Pantelleria, at the far southern end of Sicily, and that is what it really had been for the first month, when our parents were with us. I still remember as if it were a dream the solar plain of volcanic rock, the eternal sea, the house painted with quicklime up to the brickwork; on windless nights you could see from its windows the luminous beams of lighthouses in Africa. Exploring the sleeping ocean floor around the island with our father, we had discovered a row of yellow torpedoes, half buried since the last war; we had brought up a Greek amphora almost a meter high, with petrified garlands and the dregs of an immemorial and poisonous wine in its depths; we had bathed in a steaming pool of waters so dense you almost could walk on them. But the most dazzling revelation for us had been Fulvia Flaminea. She looked like a cheerful bishop and was always accompanied by a troop of sleepy cats who got in her way when she walked. But she said she put up with them not out of love but to keep from being devoured by rats. At night, while our parents watched programs for adults on television, Fulvia Flaminea took us to her house, less than a hundred meters from ours, and taught us to distinguish the remote babbling, the songs, the outbursts of weeping on the winds from Tunis. Her husband was a man too young for her, who worked in the summer at the tourist hotels on the far end of the island and came home only to sleep. Oreste lived a little farther away with his parents, and always appeared at night with strings of fish and baskets of fresh-caught lobster, which he hung in the kitchen so that Fulvia Flaminea's husband could sell them the next day at the hotels. Then he would put his diving lantern back on his forehead and take us to catch the field rats as big as rabbits that lay in wait for kitchen scraps. Sometimes we came home after our parents had gone to bed, and it was hard for us to sleep with the racket the rats made as they fought over the garbage in the courtyards. But even that annoyance was a magical ingredient in our happy summer.

The decision to hire a German governess could have occurred only to my father, a writer from the Caribbean with more presumption than talent. Dazzled by the ashes of the glories of Europe, he always seemed too eager to excuse his origins, in his books as well as in real life, and he had succumbed to the fantasy that no vestige of his own past would remain in his children. My mother was still as unassuming as she had been when she was an itinerant teacher in Alta Guajira, and she never imagined her husband could have an idea that was less than providential. And therefore they could not have asked themselves in their hearts what our lives would be like with a sergeant from Dortmund intent on inculcating in us by force the most ancient, stale habits of European society, while they and forty other fashionable writers participated in a five-week cultural encounter on the islands of the Aegean Sea.

Miss Forbes arrived on the last Saturday in July on the regular boat from Palermo, and from the moment we first saw her we knew the party was over. She arrived in that southern heat wearing combat boots, a dress with overlapping lapels, and hair cut like a man's under her felt hat. She smelled of monkey urine. "That's how every European smells, above all in summer," our father told us. "It's the smell of civilization." But despite her military appearance, Miss Forbes was a poor creature who might have awakened a certain compassion in us if we had been older or if she had possessed any trace of tenderness. The world changed. Our six hours in the ocean, which from the beginning of the summer had been a continual exercise of our imagination, were turned into one identical hour repeated over and over again. When we were with our parents we had all the time we wanted to swim with Oreste and be astonished at the art and daring with which he confronted octopuses in their own environment murky with ink and blood, using no other weapons than his combat knives. He still arrived as always at eleven o'clock in his little outboard motorboat, but Miss Forbes did not allow him to stay with us a minute longer than required for our lesson in deep-sea diving. She forbade us to go to Fulvia Flaminea's house at night because she considered it excessive familiarity with servants, and we had to devote the hours we had once spent in the pleasurable hunting of rats to analytical readings of Shakespeare. Accustomed to stealing mangoes from courtyards and stoning dogs to death on the burning streets of Guacamayal, we could not imagine a crueler torture than that princely life.

But we soon realized that Miss Forbes was not as strict with herself as she was with us, and this was the first chink in her authority. In the beginning she stayed on the beach under the multicolored umbrella, dressed for war and reading ballads by Schiller, while Oreste taught us to dive, and then, for hours and hours, she gave us theoretical lectures on proper behavior in society, until it was time for lunch.

One day she asked Oreste to take her in his boat to the hotel tourist shops, and she came back with a one-piece bathing suit as black and iridescent as a sealskin, yet she never went in the water. She sunbathed on the beach while we swam, and wiped away the perspiration with a towel but did not take a shower, so that after three days she looked like a boiled lobster and the smell of her civilization had become unbreathable.

At night she gave vent to her emotions. From the very start of her reign we heard someone walking through the house, feeling his way in the darkness, and my brother was tormented by the idea that it was one of the wandering drowning victims that Fulvia Flaminea had told us so much about. We soon discovered, however, that it was Miss Forbes, who spent the night living her real life as a lonely woman, which she herself would have censured during the day. One morning at dawn we surprised her in the kitchen in her schoolgirl's nightdress, preparing her splendid desserts. Her entire body, including her face, was covered with flour, and she was drinking a glass of port with a mental abandon that would have scandalized the other Miss Forbes. By then we knew that after we were in bed she did not go to her bedroom but went down to swim in secret, or stayed in the living room until very late, watching movies forbidden to minors on television, with the sound turned off, eating entire cakes and even drinking from the bottle of special wine that my father saved with so much devotion for memorable occasions. In defiance of her own sermons on austerity and composure, she wolfed everything down, choking on it with a kind of uncontrolled passion. Later we heard her talking to herself in her room, we heard her reciting complete excerpts from *Die Jungfrau von Orleans* in melodious German, we heard her singing, we heard her sobbing in her bed until dawn, and then she would appear at breakfast, her eyes swollen with tears, more gloomy and authoritarian than ever. My brother and I were never again as unhappy as we were then, but I was prepared to endure her to the end, for I knew that in any case her word would prevail over ours. My brother, however, confronted her with all the force of his character, and the summer of happiness became hellish for us. The episode of the moray eel was the final straw. That same night, as we lay in our beds listening to the incessant coming and going of Miss Forbes in the sleeping house, my brother released all the hatred rotting in his soul.

"I'm going to kill her," he said.

I was surprised, not so much by his decision as by the fact that I had been thinking the same thing since supper. I tried, however, to dissuade him.

"They'll cut off your head," I told him.

"They don't have guillotines in Sicily," he said. "Besides, nobody will know who did it."

I thought about the amphora salvaged from the water, where the dregs of fatal wine still lay. My father had kept it because he wanted a more thorough analysis to determine the nature of the poison, which could not be the product of the simple passage of time. Using the wine on Miss Forbes would be so easy that nobody would think it was not an accident or suicide. And so at dawn, when we heard her collapse, exhausted by the rigors of her vigil, we poured wine from the amphora into my father's bottle of special wine. From what we had heard, that dose was enough to kill a horse.

We ate breakfast in the kitchen at nine o'clock sharp, Miss Forbes herself serving us the sweet rolls that Fulvia Flaminea left on the top of the stove very early in the morning. Two days after we had substituted the wine, while we were having breakfast, my brother let me know with a disillusioned glance that the poisoned bottle stood untouched on the sideboard. That was a Friday, and the bottle remained untouched over the weekend. Then on Tuesday night, Miss Forbes drank half the wine while she watched dissolute movies on television.

Yet on Wednesday she came to breakfast with her customary punctuality. As usual, her face looked as if she had spent a bad night; as always, her eyes were uneasy behind the heavy glasses, and they became even more uneasy when she found a letter with German stamps in the basket of rolls. She read it while she drank her coffee, which she had told us so many times one must not do, and while she read, flashes of light radiating from the written words passed over her face. Then she removed the stamps from the envelope and put them in the basket with the remaining rolls so that Fulvia Flaminea's husband could have them for his collection. Despite her initial bad experience, she accompanied us that day in our exploration of the ocean depths, and we wandered through a sea of delicate water until the air in our tanks began to run out, and we went home without our lesson in good manners. Not only was Miss Forbes in a floral mood all day, but at supper she seemed even more animated. My brother, however, could not tolerate his disappointment. As soon as we received the order to begin, he pushed away the plate of vermicelli soup with a provocative gesture.

"This worm water gives me a pain in the ass," he said.

It was as if he had tossed a grenade on the table. Miss Forbes turned pale, her lips hardened until the smoke of the explosion began to clear away, and the lenses of her glasses blurred with tears. Then she took them off, dried them with her napkin, placed the napkin on the table with the bitterness of an inglorious defeat, and stood up.

"Do whatever you wish," she said. "I do not exist."

She was locked in her room from seven o'clock on. But before midnight, when she supposed we were asleep, we saw her pass by in her schoolgirl's nightdress, carrying half a chocolate cake and the bottle with more than four fingers of poisoned wine back to her bedroom. I felt a tremor of pity.

"Poor Miss Forbes," I said.

My brother did not breathe easy.

"Poor us if she doesn't die tonight," he said.

That night she talked to herself again for a long time, declaimed Schiller in a loud voice inspired by a frenetic madness, and ended with a final shout that filled the entire house. Then she sighed many times from the depths of her soul and succumbed with a sad, continuous whistle like a boat adrift. When we awoke, still exhausted by the tension of the night, the sun was cutting through the blinds but the house seemed submerged in a pond. Then we realized it was almost ten and we had not been awakened by Miss Forbes's morning routine. We did not hear the toilet flush at eight, or the faucet turn in the sink, or the noise of the blinds, or the metallic sound of her boots, or the three mortal blows on the door with the flat of her slave driver's hand. My brother put his ear to the wall, held his breath in order to detect the slightest sign of life from the next room, and at last breathed a sigh of liberation.

"That's it!" he said. "All you can hear is the ocean."

We prepared our breakfast a little before eleven, and then, before Fulvia Flaminea arrived with her troop of cats to clean the house, we went down to the beach with two air tanks each and another two as spares. Oreste was already on the dock, gutting a six-pound gilthead he had just caught. We told him we had waited for Miss Forbes until eleven, and since she was still sleeping we decided to come down to the ocean by ourselves. We told him too that she had suffered an attack of weeping at the table the night before, and perhaps she had not slept well and wanted to stay in bed. Just as we expected, Oreste was not very interested in our explanation, and he accompanied us on our pillaging of the ocean floor for a little more than an hour. Then he told us we should go up for lunch, and left in his boat to sell the gilthead at the tourist hotels. We waved good-bye from the stone steps, making him think we were about to climb up to the house, until he disappeared around the cliff. Then we put on our air tanks and continued to swim without anyone's permission.

The day was cloudy and there was a rumble of dark thunder on the horizon, but the sea was smooth and clear and its own light was enough. We swam on the surface to the line of the Pantelleria lighthouse, then turned a hundred meters to the right and dove at the spot where we calculated we had seen the torpedoes at the beginning of the summer. There they were: six of them, painted sun-yellow with their serial numbers intact, and lying on the volcanic bottom in an order too perfect to be accidental. We kept circling the lighthouse, looking for the submerged city that Fulvia Flaminea had told us about so often, and with so much awe, but we could not find it. After two hours, convinced there were no new mysteries to discover, we surfaced with our last gulp of oxygen.

A summer storm had broken while we were swimming, the sea was rough, and a flock of bloodthirsty birds flew with fierce screams over the trail of dying fish on the beach. Yet without Miss Forbes the afternoon light seemed brand-new and life was good. But when we finished struggling up the steps cut into the cliff, we saw a crowd of people at the house and two police cars by the door, and for the first time we were conscious of what we had done. My brother began to tremble and tried to turn back.

"I'm not going in," he said.

I, on the other hand, had the confused notion that if we just looked at the body we would be safe from all suspicion.

"Take it easy," I told him. "Take a deep breath, and think about just one thing: We don't know anything."

No one paid attention to us. We left our tanks, masks, and flippers at the gate and went to the side veranda, where two men sat on the floor next to a stretcher and smoked. Then we realized there was an ambulance at the back door, and several soldiers armed with rifles. In the living room women from the area were sitting on chairs that had been pushed against the wall and praying in dialect, while their men crowded into the courtyard talking about anything that did not have to do with death. I squeezed my brother's hard, icy hand even tighter, and we walked into the house through the back door. Our bedroom door was open, and the room was just as we had left it that morning. In Miss Forbes's room, which was next to ours, an armed *carabineriere* stood guarding the entrance, but the door was open. We walked toward it with heavy hearts, and before we had a chance to look in, Fulvia Flaminea came out of the kitchen like a bolt of lightning and shut the door with a scream of horror:

"For God's sake, *figlioli*, don't look at her!"

It was too late. Never, for the rest of our lives, would we forget what we saw in that fleeting instant. Two plainclothesmen were measuring the distance from the bed to the wall with a tape, while another was taking pictures with a black-sleeve camera like the ones park photographers used. Miss Forbes was not on the unmade bed. She was stretched on her side, naked in a pool of dried blood that had stained the entire floor, and her body was riddled by stab wounds. There were twenty-seven fatal cuts, and by their number and brutality one could see that the attack had been made with the fury of a love that found no peace, and that Miss Forbes had received it with the same passion, without even screaming or crying, reciting Schiller in her beautiful soldier's voice, conscious of the fact that this was the inexorable price of her summer of happiness.

—Translated by Edith Grossman

JAMES THURBER

THE MACBETH
MURDER MYSTERY

*I*T WAS A STUPID mistake to make," said the American woman I
had met at my hotel in the English lake country, "but it was on
the counter with the other Penguin books—the little sixpenny
ones, you know, with the paper covers—and I supposed of course it
was a detective story. All the others were detective stories. I'd read all
the others, so I bought this one without really looking at it carefully.
You can imagine how mad I was when I found it was Shakespeare." I
murmured something sympathetically. "I don't see why the Penguin-
books people had to get out Shakespeare's plays in the same size and
everything as the detective stories," went on my companion. "I think
they have different-colored jackets," I said. "Well, I didn't notice that,"
she said. "Anyway, I got real comfy in bed that night and all ready to
read a good mystery story and here I had *The Tragedy of Macbeth*—a
book for high-school students. Like *Ivanhoe*." "Or *Lorna Doone*," I
said. "Exactly," said the American lady. "And I was just crazy for a good
Agatha Christie, or something. Hercule Poirot is my favorite detective." "Is he the rabbity one?" I asked. "Oh, no," said my crime-fiction

expert. "He's the Belgian one. You're thinking of Mr. Pinkerton, the one that helps Inspector Bull. He's good, too."

Over her second cup of tea my companion began to tell the plot of a detective story that had fooled her completely—it seems it was the old family doctor all the time. But I cut in on her. "Tell me," I said. "Did you read *Macbeth*?" "I *had* to read it," she said. "There wasn't a scrap of anything else to read in the whole room." "Did you like it?" I asked. "No, I did not," she said, decisively. "In the first place, I don't think for a moment that Macbeth did it." I looked at her blankly. "Did what?" I asked. "I don't think for a moment that he killed the King," she said. "I don't think the Macbeth woman was mixed up in it, either. You suspect them the most, of course, but those are the ones that are never guilty—or shouldn't be, anyway." "I'm afraid," I began, "that I—" "But don't you see?" said the American lady. "It would spoil everything if you could figure out right away who did it. Shakespeare was too smart for that. I've read that people never *have* figured out *Hamlet*, so it isn't likely Shakespeare would have made *Macbeth* as simple as it seems." I thought this over while I filled my pipe. "Who do you suspect?" I asked, suddenly. "Macduff," she said, promptly. "Good God!" I whispered, softly.

"Oh, Macduff did it, all right," said the murder specialist. "Hercule Poirot would have got him easily." "How did you figure it out?" I demanded. "Well," she said, "I didn't right away. At first I suspected Banquo. And then, of course, he was the second person killed. That was good right in there, that part. The person you suspect of the first murder should always be the second victim." "Is that so?" I murmured. "Oh, yes," said my informant. "They have to keep surprising you. Well, after the second murder I didn't know *who* the killer was for a while." "How about Malcolm and Donalbain, the King's sons?" I asked. "As I remember it, they fled right after the first murder. That looks suspicious." "Too suspicious," said the American lady. "Much too suspicious. When they flee, they're never guilty. You can count on that." "I believe," I said, "I'll have a brandy," and I summoned the waiter. My companion leaned toward me, her eyes bright, her teacup quivering. "Do you know who discovered Duncan's body?" she demanded. I said I was sorry, but I had forgotten. "Macduff discovers it," she said, slipping into the historical present. "Then he comes running downstairs and shouts, 'Confusion has broke open the Lord's anointed temple' and 'Sacrilegious murder had made his masterpiece' and on and on like that." The good lady tapped me on the knee. "All that stuff was *rehearsed*," she said. "You wouldn't say a lot of stuff like that, offhand, would you—if you had found a body?" She fixed me with a glittering eye. "I—" I began. "You're right!" she said. "You wouldn't! Unless you had practiced it in advance. 'My God, there's a body in here!' is what an innocent man would say." She sat back with a confident glare.

I thought for a while. "But what do you make of the Third Murderer?" I asked. "You know, the Third Murderer has puzzled *Macbeth* scholars for three hundred years." "That's because they never thought of Macduff," said the American lady. "It was Macduff, I'm certain. You couldn't have one of the victims murdered by two ordinary thugs—the murderer always has to be somebody important." "But what about the banquet scene?" I asked, after a moment. "How do you account for Macbeth's guilty actions there, when Banquo's ghost came in and sat in his chair?" The lady leaned forward and tapped me on the knee again. "There wasn't any ghost," she said. "A big, strong man like that doesn't go around seeing ghosts—especially in a brightly lighted banquet hall with dozens of people around. Macbeth was *shielding somebody!*" "Who was he shielding?" I asked. "Mrs. Macbeth, of course," she said. "He thought she did it and he was going to take the rap himself. The husband always does that when the wife is suspected." "But what," I demanded, "about the sleepwalking scene, then?" "The same thing, only the other way around," said my companion. "That time *she* was shielding *him*. She wasn't asleep at all. Do you remember where it says, 'Enter Lady Macbeth with a taper'?" "Yes," I said. "Well, people who walk in their sleep *never carry lights!*" said my fellow-traveller. "They have second sight. Did you ever hear of a sleepwalker carrying a light?" "No," I said, "I never did." "Well, then, she wasn't asleep. She was acting guilty to shield Macbeth." "I think," I said, "I'll have another brandy," and I called the waiter. When he brought it, I drank it rapidly and rose to go. "I believe," I said, "that you have got hold of something. Would you lend me that *Macbeth*? I'd like to look it over tonight. I don't feel, somehow, as if I'd ever really read it." "I'll get it for you," she said. "But you'll find that I am right."

I read the play over carefully that night, and the next morning, after breakfast, I sought out the American woman. She was on the putting green, and I came up behind her silently and took her arm. She gave an exclamation. "Could I see you alone?" I asked, in a low voice. She nodded cautiously and followed me to a secluded spot. "You've found out something?" she breathed. "I've found out," I said, triumphantly, "the name of the murderer!" "You mean it wasn't Macduff?" she said. "Macduff is as innocent of those murders," I said, "as Macbeth and the Macbeth woman." I opened the copy of the play, which I had with me, and turned to Act II, Scene 2. "Here," I said, "you will see where Lady Macbeth says, 'I laid their daggers ready. He could not miss 'em. Had he not resembled my father as he slept, I had done it.' Do you see?" "No," said the American woman, bluntly, "I don't." "But it's simple!" I exclaimed. "I wonder I didn't see it years ago. The reason Duncan resembled Lady Macbeth's father as he slept is that it *actually was her father!*" "Good God!" breathed my companion, softly. "Lady Macbeth's father killed the King," I said, "and, hearing someone coming, thrust the body under the bed and crawled into the bed himself." "But," said the lady, "you can't have a murderer who only appears in the story once. You can't have that." "I know that," I said, and I turned to Act II, Scene 4. "It says here, 'Enter Ross with an old Man.' Now, that old man is never identified and it is my contention he was old Mr. Macbeth, whose ambition it was to make his daughter Queen. There you have your motive." "But even then," cried the American lady, "he's still a minor character!" "Not," I said, gleefully, "when you realize that he was also *one of the weird sisters in disguise!*" "You mean one of the three witches?" "Precisely," I said. "Listen to this speech of the old man's. 'On Tuesday last, a falcon towering in her pride of place, was by a mousing owl hawk'd at and kill'd.' Who does that sound like?" "It sounds like the way the three witches talk," said my companion, reluctantly. "Precisely!" I said again. "Well," said the American woman, "maybe you're right, but —" "I'm sure I am," I said. "And do you know what I'm going to do now?" "No," she said. "What?" "Buy a copy of *Hamlet*, I said, "and solve *that!*" My companion's eyes brightened. "Then," she said, "you don't think Hamlet did it?" "I am," I said, "absolutely positive he didn't." "But who," she demanded, "do you suspect?" I looked at her cryptically. "Everybody," I said, and disappeared into a small grove of trees as silently as I had come.

LOUISA MAY ALCOTT

A DOUBLE TRAGEDY: AN ACTOR'S STORY

CHAPTER I

CLOTILDE was in her element that night, for it was a Spanish play, requiring force and fire in its delineation, and she threw herself into her part with an *abandon* that made her seem a beautiful embodiment of power and passion. As for me I could not play ill, for when with her my acting was not art but nature, and I *was* the lover that I seemed. Before she came I made a business, not a pleasure, of my profession, and was content to fill my place, with no higher ambition than to earn my salary with as little effort as possible, to resign myself to the distasteful labor to which my poverty condemned me. She changed all that; for she saw the talent I neglected, she understood the want of motive that made me indifferent, she pitied me for the reverse of fortune that placed me where I was; by her influence and example she roused a manlier spirit in me, kindled every spark of talent I possessed, and incited me to win a success I had not cared to labor for till then.

She was the rage that season, for she came unheralded and almost unknown. Such was the power of beauty, genius, and character, that she made her way at once into public favor, and before the season was half over had become the reigning favorite. My position in the theatre threw us much together, and I had not played the lover to this beautiful woman many weeks before I found I was one in earnest. She soon knew it, and confessed that she returned my love; but when I spoke of marriage, she answered with a look and tone that haunted me long afterward.

"Not yet, Paul; something that concerns me alone must be settled first. I cannot marry till I have received the answer for which I am waiting; have faith in me till then, and be patient for my sake."

I did have faith and patience; but while I waited I wondered much and studied her carefully. Frank, generous, and deephearted, she won all who approached her; but I, being nearest and dearest, learned to know her best, and soon discovered that some past loss, some present anxiety or hidden care, oppressed and haunted her. A bitter spirit at times possessed her, followed by a heavy melancholy, or an almost fierce unrest, which nothing could dispel but some stormy drama, where she could vent her pent-up gloom or desperation in words and acts which seemed to have a double significance to her. I had vainly tried to find some cause or explanation of this one blemish in the nature which, to a lover's eyes, seemed almost perfect, but never had succeeded till the night of which I write.

The play was nearly over, the interest was at its height, and Clotilde's best scene was drawing to a close. She had just indignantly refused to betray a state secret which would endanger the life of her lover; and the Duke had just wrathfully vowed to denounce her to the Inquisition if she did not yield, when I her lover, disguised as a monk, saw a strange and sudden change come over her. She should have trembled at a threat so full of terror, and have made one last appeal to the stern old man before she turned to defy and dare all things for her lover. But she seemed to have forgotten time, place, and character, for she stood gazing straight before her as if turned to stone. At first I thought it was some new presentiment of fear, for she seldom played a part twice alike, and left much to the inspiration of the moment. But an instant's scrutiny convinced me that this was not acting, for her face paled visibly, her eyes dilated as they looked beyond the Duke, her lips fell apart, and she looked like one suddenly confronted by a ghost. An inquiring glance from my companion showed me that he, too, was disturbed by her appearance, and fearing that she had over-exerted herself, I struck into the dialogue as if she had made her appeal. The sound of my voice seemed to recall her; she passed her hand across her eyes, drew a long breath, and looked about her. I thought she had recovered herself and was about to resume her part, but, to my great surprise, she only clung to me, saying in a shrill whisper, so full of despair, it chilled my blood—

"The answer, Paul, the answer: it has come!"

The words were inaudible to all but myself; but the look, the gesture were eloquent with terror, grief and love; and taking it for a fine piece of acting, the audience applauded loud and long. The accustomed sound roused Clotilde, and during that noisy moment a hurried dialogue passed between us.

"What is it? Are you ill?" I whispered.

"He is here, Paul, alive; I saw him. Heaven help us both!"

"Who is here?"

"Hush! not now; there is no time to tell you."

"You are right; compose yourself; you must speak in a moment."

"What do I say? Help me, Paul; I have forgotten every thing but that man."

She looked as if bewildered; and I saw that some sudden shock had entirely unnerved her. But actors must have neither hearts nor nerves while on the stage. The applause was subsiding, and she must speak. Fortunately I remembered enough of her part to prompt her as she struggled through the little that remained; for, seeing her condition, Denon and I cut the scene remorselessly, and brought it to a close as soon as possible. The instant the curtain fell we were assailed with questions, but Clotilde answered none; and though hidden from her sight, still seemed to see the object that had wrought such an alarming change in her. I told them she was ill, took her to her dressing-room, and gave her into the hands of her maid, for I must appear again, and delay was impossible.

How I got through my part I cannot tell, for my thoughts were with Clotilde; but an actor learns to live a double life, so while Paul Lamar suffered torments of anxiety Don Felix fought a duel, killed his adversary, and was dragged to judgment. Involuntarily my eyes often wandered toward the spot where Clotilde's had seemed fixed. It was one of the stage-boxes, and at first I thought it empty, but presently I caught the glitter of a glass turned apparently on myself. As soon as possible I crossed the stage, and as I leaned haughtily upon my sword while the seconds adjusted the preliminaries, I searched the box with a keen glance. Nothing was visible, however, but a hand lying easily on the red cushion; a man's hand, white and shapely; on one finger shone a ring, evidently a woman's ornament, for it was a slender circlet of diamonds that flashed with every gesture.

"Some fop, doubtless; a man like that could never daunt Clotilde," I thought. And eager to discover if there was not another occupant in the box, I took a step nearer, and stared boldly into the soft gloom that filled it. A low derisive laugh came from behind the curtain as the hand gathered back as if to permit me to satisfy myself. The act showed me that a single person occupied the box, but also effectually concealed that person from my sight; and as I was recalled to my duty by a warning whisper from one of my comrades, the hand appeared to wave me a mocking adieu. Baffled and angry, I devoted myself to the affairs of Don Felix, wondering the while if Clotilde would be able to reappear, how she would bear herself, if that hidden man was the cause of her terror, and why? Even when immured in a dungeon, after my arrest,

I beguiled the tedium of a long soliloquy with these questions, and executed a better stage-start than any I had ever practised, when at last she came to me, bringing liberty and love as my reward.

I had left her haggard, speechless, overwhelmed with some mysterious woe, she reappeared beautiful and brilliant, with a joy that seemed too lovely to be feigned. Never had she played so well; for some spirit, stronger than her own, seemed to possess and rule her royally. If I had ever doubted her love for me, I should have been assured of it that night, for she breathed into the fond words of her part a tenderness and grace that filled my heart to overflowing, and inspired me to play the grateful lover to the life. The last words came all too soon for me, and as she threw herself into my arms she turned her head as if to glance triumphantly at the defeated Duke, but I saw that again she looked beyond him, and with an indescribable expression of mingled pride, contempt, and defiance. A soft sound of applause from the mysterious occupant of that box answered the look, and the white hand sent a superb bouquet flying to her feet. I was about to lift and present it to her, but she checked me and crushed it under foot with an air of the haughtiest disdain. A laugh from behind the curtain greeted this demonstration, but it was scarcely observed by others; for that first bouquet seemed a signal for a rain of flowers, and these latter offerings she permitted me to gather up, receiving them with her most gracious smiles, her most graceful obeisances, as if to mark, for one observer at least, the difference of her regard for the givers. As I laid the last floral tribute in her arms I took a parting glance at the box, hoping to catch a glimpse of the unknown face. The curtains were thrown back and the door stood open, admitting a strong light from the vestibule, but the box was empty.

Then the green curtain fell, and Clotilde whispered, as she glanced from her full hands to the rejected bouquet—

"Bring that to my room; I must have it."

I obeyed, eager to be enlightened; but when we were alone she flung down her fragrant burden, snatched the stranger's gift, tore it apart, drew out a slip of paper, read it, dropped it, and walked to and fro, wringing her hands, like one in a paroxysm of despair. I seized the note and looked at it, but found no key to her distress in the enigmatical words—

"I shall be there. Come and bring your lover with you, else—"

There it abruptly ended; but the unfinished threat seemed the more menacing for its obscurity, and I indignantly demanded,

"Clotilde, who dares address you so? Where will this man be? You surely will not obey such a command? Tell me; I have a right to know."

"I cannot tell you, now; I dare not refuse him; he will be at Keen's; we *must* go. How will it end! How will it end!"

I remembered then that we were all to sup *en costume*, with a brother actor, who did not play that night. I was about to speak yet more urgently, when the entrance of her maid checked me. Clotilde composed herself by a strong effort—

"Go and prepare," she whispered; "have faith in me a little longer, and soon you shall know all."

There was something almost solemn in her tone; her eye met mine, imploringly, and her lips trembled as if her heart were full. That assured me at once; and with a reassuring word I hurried away to give a few touches to my costume, which just then was fitter for a dungeon than a feast. When I rejoined her there was no trace of past emotion; a soft color bloomed upon her cheek, her eyes were tearless and brilliant, her lips were dressed in smiles. Jewels shone on her white forehead, neck, and arms, flowers glowed in her bosom; and no charm that art or skill could lend to the rich dress or its lovely wearer, had been forgotten.

"What an actress!" I involuntarily exclaimed, as she came to meet me, looking almost as beautiful and gay as ever.

"It is well that I am one, else I should yield to my hard fate without a struggle. Paul, hitherto I have played for money, now I play for love;

help me by being a calm spectator to-night, and whatever happens promise me that there shall be no violence."

I promised, for I was wax in her hands; and, more bewildered than ever, followed to the carriage, where a companion was impatiently awaiting us.

CHAPTER II

We were late; and on arriving found all the other guests assembled. Three strangers appeared; and my attention was instantly fixed upon them, for the mysterious "he" was to be there. All three seemed gay, gallant, handsome men; all three turned admiring eyes upon Clotilde, all three were gloved. Therefore, as I had seen no face, my one clue, the ring, was lost. From Clotilde's face and manner I could learn nothing, for a smile seemed carved upon her lips, her drooping lashes half concealed her eyes, and her voice was too well trained to betray her by a traitorous tone. She received the greetings, compliments, and admiration of all alike, and I vainly looked and listened till supper was announced.

As I took my place beside her, I saw her shrink and shiver slightly, as if a chilly wind had blown over her, but before I could ask if she were cold a bland voice said,

"Will Mademoiselle Varian permit me to drink her health?"

It was one of the strangers; mechanically I offered her glass; but the next instant my hold tightened till the slender stem snapped, and the rosy bowl fell broken to the table, for on the handsome hand extended to fill it shone the ring.

"A bad omen, Mr. Lamar. I hope my attempt will succeed better," said St. John, as he filled another glass and handed it to Clotilde, who merely lifted it to her lips, and turned to enter into an animated conversation with the gentleman who sat on the other side. Some one addressed St. John, and I was glad of it; for now all my interest and attention was centered in him. Keenly, but covertly, I examined him, and soon felt that in spite of that foppish ornament he was a man to daunt a woman like Clotilde. Pride and passion, courage and indomitable will met and mingled in his face, though the obedient features wore whatever expression he imposed upon them. He was the handsomest, most elegant, but least attractive of the three, yet it was hard to say why. The others gave themselves freely to the enjoyment of a scene which evidently possessed the charm of novelty to them; but St. John unconsciously wore the half sad, half weary look that comes to those who have led lives of pleasure and found their emptiness. Although the wittiest, and most brilliant talker at the table, his gaiety seemed fitful, his manner absent at times. More than once I saw him knit his black brows as he met my eye, and more than once I caught a long look fixed on Clotilde—a look full of the lordly admiration and pride which a master bestows upon a handsome slave. It made my blood boil, but I controlled myself, and was apparently absorbed in Miss Damareau, my neighbor.

We seemed as gay and care-free a company as ever made midnight merry; songs were sung, stories told, theatrical phrases added sparkle to the conversation, and the varied costumes gave an air of romance to the revel. The Grand Inquisitor still in his ghostly garb, and the stern old Duke were now the jolliest of the group; the page flirted violently with the princess; the rivals of the play were bosom-friends again, and the fair Donna Olivia had apparently forgotten her knightly lover, to listen to a modern gentleman.

Clotilde sat leaning back in a deep chair, eating nothing, but using her fan with the indescribable grace of a Spanish woman. She was very lovely, for the dress became her, and the black lace mantilla falling from her head to her shoulders, heightened her charms by half concealing them; and nothing could have been more genial and gracious than the air with which she listened and replied to the compliments of the youngest stranger, who sat beside her and was all devotion.

I forgot myself in observing her till something said by our opposite neighbors arrested both of us. Some one seemed to have been joking St. John about his ring, which was too brilliant an ornament to pass unobserved.

"Bad taste, I grant you," he said, laughing, "but it is a *gage d'amour,* and I wear it for a purpose."

"I fancied it was the latest Paris fashion," returned Keen. "And apropos to Paris, what is the latest gossip from the gay city?"

A slow smile rose to St. John's lips as he answered, after a moment's thought and a quick glance across the room.

"A little romance; shall I tell it to you? It is a love story, ladies, and not long."

A unanimous assent was given; and he began with a curious glitter in his eyes, a stealthy smile coming and going on his face as the words dropped slowly from his lips.

"It begins in the old way. A foolish young man fell in love with a Spanish girl much his inferior in rank, but beautiful enough to excuse his folly, for he married her. Then came a few months of bliss; but Madame grew jealous. Monsieur wearied of domestic tempests, and, after vain efforts to appease his fiery angel, he proposed a separation. Madame was obdurate, Monsieur rebelled; and in order to try the soothing effects of absence upon both, after settling her in a charming chateau, he slipped away, leaving no trace by which his route might be discovered."

"Well, how did the experiment succeed?" asked Keen. St. John shrugged his shoulders, emptied his glass, and answered tranquilly.

"Like most experiments that have women for their subjects, for the amiable creatures always devise some way of turning the tables, and defeating the best laid plans. Madame waited for her truant spouse till rumors of his death reached Paris, for he had met with mishaps, and sickness detained him long in an obscure place, so the rumors seemed confirmed by his silence, and Madame believed him dead. But instead of dutifully mourning him, this inexplicable woman shook the dust of the chateau off her feet and disappeared, leaving everything, even to her wedding ring, behind her."

"Bless me, how odd! what became of her?" exclaimed Miss Damareau, forgetting the dignity of the Princess in the curiosity of the woman.

"The very question her repentant husband asked when, returning from his long holiday, he found her gone. He searched the continent for her, but in vain; and for two years she left him to suffer the torments of suspense."

"As he had left her to suffer them while he went pleasuring. It was a light punishment for his offence."

Clotilde spoke; and the sarcastic tone, for all its softness, made St. John wince, though no eye but mine observed the faint flush of shame or anger that passed across his face.

"Mademoiselle espouses the lady's cause, of course, and as a gallant man I should do likewise, but unfortunately my sympathies are strongly enlisted on the other side."

"Then you know the parties?" I said, impulsively, for my inward excitement was increasing rapidly, and I began to feel rather than to see the end of this mystery.

"I have seen them, and cannot blame the man for claiming his beautiful wife, when he found her," he answered, briefly.

"Then he did find her at last? Pray tell us how and when," cried Miss Damareau.

"She betrayed herself. It seems that Madame had returned to her old profession, and fallen in love with an actor; but being as virtuous as she was fair, she would not marry till she was assured beyond a doubt of her husband's death. Her engagements would not allow her to enquire in person, so she sent letters to various places asking for proofs of his demise; and as ill, or good fortune would have it, one of these letters fell into Monsieur's hands, giving him an excellent clue to her whereabouts, which he followed indefatigably till he found her."

"Poor little woman, I pity her! How did she receive Monsieur De Trop?" asked Keen.

"You shall know in good time. He found her in London playing at one of the great theatres, for she had talent, and had become a star. He saw her act for a night or two, made secret inquiries concerning her, and fell more in love with her than ever. Having tried almost every novelty under the sun he had a fancy to attempt something of the dramatic sort, so presented himself to Madame at a party."

"Heavens! what a scene there must have been," ejaculated Miss Damareau.

"On the contrary, there was no scene at all, for the man was not a Frenchman, and Madame was a fine actress. Much as he had admired her on the stage he was doubly charmed with her performance in private, for it was superb. They were among strangers, and she received him like one, playing her part with the utmost grace and self-control, for with a woman's quickness of perception, she divined his purpose, and knowing that her fate was in his hands, endeavored to propitiate him by complying with his caprice. Mademoiselle, allow me to send you some of those grapes, they are delicious."

As he leaned forward to present them he shot a glance at her that caused me to start up with a violence that nearly betrayed me. Fortunately the room was close, and saying something about the heat, I threw open a window, and let in a balmy gust of spring air that refreshed us all.

"How did they settle it, by duels and despair, or by repentance and reconciliation all round, in the regular French fashion?"

"I regret that I'm unable to tell you, for I left before the affair was arranged. I only know that Monsieur was more captivated than before, and quite ready to forgive and forget, and I suspect that Madame, seeing the folly of resistance, will submit with a good grace, and leave the stage to play 'The Honey Moon' for a second time in private with a husband who adores her. What is the Mademoiselle's opinion?"

She had listened, without either question or comment, her fan at rest, her hands motionless, her eyes downcast; so still it seemed as if she had hushed the breath upon her lips, so pale despite her rouge, that I wondered no one observed it, so intent and resolute that every feature seemed under control—every look and gesture guarded. When St. John addressed her, she looked up with a smile as bland as his own, but fixed her eyes on him with an expression of undismayed defiance and supreme contempt that caused him to bite his lips with ill-concealed annoyance.

"My opinion?" she said, in her clear, cold voice, "I think that Madame, being a woman of spirit, would *not* endeavor to propitiate that man in any way except for her lover's sake, and having been once deserted would not subject herself to a second indignity of that sort while there was a law to protect her."

"Unfortunately there is no law for her, having once refused a separation. Even if there were, Monsieur is rich and powerful, she is poor and friendless; he loves her, and is a man who never permits himself to be thwarted by any obstacle; therefore, I am convinced it would be best for this adorable woman to submit without defiance or delay—and I do think she will," he added, significantly.

"They seem to forget the poor lover; what is to become of him?" asked Keen.

"*I* do not forget him," and the hand that wore the ring closed with an ominous gesture, which I well understood. "Monsieur merely claims his own, and the other, being a man of sense and honor, will doubtless withdraw at once; and though 'desolated,' as the French say, will soon console himself with a new *inamorata*. If he is so unwise as to oppose Monsieur, who by the by is a dead shot, there is but one way in which both can receive satisfaction."

A significant emphasis on the last word pointed his meaning, and the smile that accompanied it almost goaded me to draw the sword I wore, and offer him that satisfaction on the spot. I felt the color rise to my forehead, and dared not look up, but leaning on the back of Clotilde's chair, I bent as if to speak to her.

"Bear it a little longer for my sake, Paul," she murmured, with a look of love and despair, that wrung my heart. Here some one spoke of a long rehearsal in the morning, and the lateness of the hour.

"A farewell toast before we part," said Keen. "Come, Lamar, give us a sentiment, after that whisper you ought to be inspired."

"I am. Let me give you—The love of liberty and the liberty of love."

"Good! That would suit the hero and heroine of St. John's story, for Monsieur wished much for his liberty, and, no doubt, Madame will for her love," said Denon, while the glasses were filled.

Then the toast was drunk with much merriment and the party broke up. While detained by one of the strangers, I saw St. John approach Clotilde, who stood alone by the window, and speak rapidly for several minutes. She listened with half-averted head, answered briefly and, wrapping the mantilla closely about her, swept away from him with her haughtiest mien. He watched for a moment, then followed, and before I could reach her, offered his arm to lead her to the carriage. She seemed about to refuse it, but something in the expression of his face restrained her; and accepting it, they went down together. The hall and little ante-room were dimly lighted, but as I slowly followed, I saw her snatch her hand away, when she thought they were alone; saw him draw her to him with an embrace as fond as it was irresistible; and turning her indignant face to his, kiss it ardently, as he said in a tone, both tender and imperious—

"Good night, my darling. I give you one more day, and then I claim you."

"Never!" she answered, almost fiercely, as he released her. And wishing me pleasant dreams, as he passed, went out into the night, gaily humming the burden of a song Clotilde had often sung to me.

The moment we were in the carriage all her self-control deserted her, and a tempest of despairing grief came over her. For a time, both words and caresses were unavailing, and I let her weep herself calm before I asked the hard question—

"Is all this true, Clotilde?"

"Yes, Paul, all true, except that he said nothing of the neglect, the cruelty, the insult that I bore before he left me. I was so young, so lonely, I was glad to be loved and cared for, and I believed that he would never change. I cannot tell you all I suffered, but I rejoiced when I thought death had freed me; I would keep nothing that reminded me of the bitter past, and went away to begin again, as if it had never been."

"Why delay telling me this? Why let me learn it in such a strange and sudden way?"

"Ah, forgive me! I am so proud I could not bear to tell you that any man had wearied of me and deserted me. I meant to tell you before our marriage, but the fear that St. John was alive haunted me, and till it was set at rest I would not speak. Tonight there was no time, and I was forced to leave all to chance. He found pleasure in tormenting me through you, but would not speak out, because he is as proud as I, and does not wish to hear our story bandied from tongue to tongue."

"What did he say to you, Clotilde?"

"He begged me to submit and return to him, in spite of all that has passed; he warned me that if we attempted to escape it would be at the peril of your life, for he would most assuredly follow and find us, to whatever corner of the earth we might fly; and he will, for he is as relentless as death."

"What did he mean by giving you one day more?" I asked, grinding my teeth with impatient rage as I listened.

"He gave me one day to recover from my surprise, to prepare for my departure with him, and to bid you farewell."

"And will you, Clotilde?"

"No!" she replied, clenching her hands with a gesture of dogged resolution, while her eyes glittered in the darkness. "I never will submit; there must be some way of escape; I shall find it, and if I do not—I can die."

"Not yet, dearest; we will appeal to the law first; I have a friend whom I will consult to-morrow, and he may help us."

"I have no faith in law," she said, despairingly, "money and influence so often outweigh justice and mercy. I have no witnesses, no friends, no wealth to help me; he has all, and we shall only be defeated. I must devise some surer way. Let me think a little; a woman's wit is quick when her heart prompts it."

I let the poor soul flatter herself with vague hopes; but I saw no help for us except in flight, and that she would not consent to, lest it should endanger me. More than once I said savagely within myself, "I will kill him," and then shuddered at the counsels of the devil, so suddenly roused in my own breast. As if she divined my thought by instinct, Clotilde broke the heavy silence that followed her last words, by clinging to me with the imploring cry,

"Oh, Paul, shun him, else your fiery spirit will destroy you. He promised me he would not harm you unless we drove him to it. Be careful, for my sake, and if any one must suffer let it be miserable me."

I soothed her as I best could, and when our long, sad drive ended, bade her rest while I worked, for she would need all her strength on the morrow. Then I left her, to haunt the street all night long, guarding her door, and while I paced to and fro without, I watched her shadow come and go before the lighted window as she paced within, each racking our brains for some means of help till day broke.

CHAPTER III

Early on the following morning I consulted my friend, but when I laid the case before him he gave me little hope of a happy issue should the attempt be made. A divorce was hardly possible, when an unscrupulous man like St. John was bent on opposing it; and though no decision could force her to remain with him, we should not be safe from his vengeance, even if we chose to dare everything and fly together. Long and earnestly we talked, but to little purpose, and I went to rehearsal with a heavy heart.

Clotilde was to have a benefit that night, and what a happy day I had fancied this would be; how carefully I had prepared for it; what delight I had anticipated in playing Romeo to her Juliet; and how eagerly I had longed for the time which now seemed to approach with such terrible rapidity, for each hour brought our parting nearer! On the stage I found Keen and his new friend amusing themselves with fencing, while waiting the arrival of some of the company. I was too miserable to be dangerous just then, and when St. John bowed to me with his most courteous air, I returned the greeting, though I could not speak to him. I think he saw my suffering, and enjoyed it with the satisfaction of a cruel nature, but he treated me with the courtesy of an equal, which new demonstration surprised me, till, through Denon, I discovered that having inquired much about me he had learned that I was a gentleman by birth and education, which fact accounted for the change in his demeanor. I roamed restlessly about the gloomy green room and stage, till Keen, dropping his foil, confessed himself out-fenced and called to me.

"Come here, Lamar, and try a bout with St. John. You are the best fencer among us, so, for the honor of the company, come and do your best instead of playing Romeo before the time."

A sudden impulse prompted me to comply, and a few passes proved that I was the better swordsman of the two. This annoyed St. John, and though he complimented me with the rest, he would not own himself outdone, and we kept it up till both grew warm and excited. In the midst of an animated match between us, I observed that the button was off his foil, and a glance at his face assured me that he was aware of it, and almost at the instant he made a skillful thrust, and the point pierced my flesh. As I caught the foil from his hand and drew it out with an exclamation of pain, I saw a gleam of exultation pass across his face, and knew that his promise to Clotilde was but idle breath. My comrades surrounded me with anxious inquiries, and no one was more surprised and solicitous than St. John. The wound was trifling, for a picture of Clotilde had turned the thrust aside, else the force with which it was given might have rendered it fatal. I made light of it, but hated him with a redoubled hatred for the cold-blooded treachery that would have given to revenge the screen of accident.

The appearance of the ladies caused us to immediately ignore the mishap, and address ourselves to business. Clotilde came last, looking so pale it was not necessary for her to plead illness; but she went through her part with her usual fidelity, while her husband watched her with the masterful expression that nearly drove me wild. He haunted her like a shadow, and she listened to him with the desperate look of a hunted creature driven to bay. He might have softened her just resentment by a touch of generosity or compassion, and won a little gratitude, even though love was impossible; but he was blind, relentless, and goaded her beyond endurance, rousing in her fiery Spanish heart a dangerous spirit he could not control. The rehearsal was over at last, and I approached Clotilde with a look that mutely asked if I should leave her. St. John said something in a low voice, but she answered sternly, as she took my arm with a decided gesture.

"This day is mine; I will not be defrauded of an hour," and we went away together for our accustomed stroll in the sunny park.

A sad and memorable walk was that, for neither had any hope with which to cheer the other, and Clotilde grew gloomier as we talked. I told her of my fruitless consultation, also of the fencing match; at that her face darkened, and she said, below her breath, "I shall remember that."

We walked long together, and I proposed plan after plan, all either unsafe or impracticable. She seemed to listen, but when I paused she answered with averted eyes—

"Leave it to me; I have a project; let me perfect it before I tell you. Now I must go and rest, for I have had no sleep, and I shall need all my strength for the tragedy to-night."

All that afternoon I roamed about the city, too restless for anything but constant motion, and evening found me ill prepared for my now doubly arduous duties. It was late when I reached the theatre, and I dressed hastily. My costume was new for the occasion, and not till it was on did I remember that I had neglected to try it since the finishing touches were given. A stitch or two would remedy the defects, and, hurrying up to the wardrobe room, a skillful pair of hands soon set me right. As I came down the winding-stairs that led from the lofty chamber to a dimly-lighted gallery below, St. John's voice arrested me, and pausing I saw that Keen was doing the honors of the theatre in defiance of all rules. Just as they reached the stair-foot someone called to them, and throwing open a narrow door, he said to his companion—

"From here you get a fine view of the stage; steady yourself by the rope and look down. I'll be with you in a moment."

He ran into the dressing-room from whence the voice proceeded, and St. John stepped out upon a little platform, hastily built for the launching of an aerial-car in some grand spectacle. Glad to escape meeting him, I was about to go on, when, from an obscure corner, a dark figure glided noiselessly to the door and leaned in. I caught a momentary glimpse of a white extended arm and the glitter of steel, then came a cry of mortal fear, a heavy fall; and flying swiftly down the gallery the figure disappeared. With one leap I reached the door, and looked in; the raft hung broken, the platform was empty. At that instant Keen rushed out, demanding what had happened, and scarcely knowing what I said, I answered hurriedly,

"The rope broke and he fell."

Keen gave me a strange look, and dashed down stairs. I followed, to find myself in a horror-stricken crowd, gathered about the piteous object which a moment ago had been a living man. There was no need to call a surgeon, for that headlong fall had dashed out life in the drawing of a breath, and nothing remained to do but to take the poor body tenderly away to such friends as the newly-arrived stranger possessed. The contrast between the gay crowd rustling before the curtain and the dreadful scene transpiring behind it, was terrible; but the house was filling fast; there was no time for the indulgence of pity or curiosity, and soon no trace of the accident remained but the broken rope above, and an ominous damp spot on the newly-washed boards below. At a word of command from our energetic manager, actors and actresses were sent away to retouch their pale faces with carmine, to restoring their startled nerves with any stimulant at hand, and to forget, if possible, the awesome sight just witnessed.

I returned to my dressing-room hoping Clotilde had heard nothing of this sad, and yet for us most fortunate accident, though all the while a vague dread haunted me, and I feared to see her. Mechanically completing my costume, I looked about me for the dagger with which poor Juliet was to stab herself, and found that it was gone. Trying to recollect where I put it, I remembered having it in my hand just before I went up to have my sword-belt altered; and fancying that I must have inadvertently taken it with me, I reluctantly retraced my steps. At the top of the stairs leading to that upper gallery a little white object caught my eye, and, taking it up, I found it to be a flower. If it had been a burning coal I should not have dropped it more hastily than I did when I recognized it was one of a cluster I had left in Clotilde's room because she loved them. They were a rare and delicate kind, no one but herself was likely to possess them in that place, nor was she likely to have given one away, for my gifts were kept with jealous care; yet how came it there? And as I asked myself the question, like an answer returned the remembrance of her face when she said, "I shall remember this." The darkly-shrouded form was a female figure, the white arm a woman's, and horrible as was the act, who but that sorely-tried and tempted creature would have committed it. For a moment my heart stood still, then I indignantly rejected the black thought, and thrusting the flower into my breast went on my way, trying to convince myself that the foreboding fear which oppressed me was caused by the agitating events of the last half hour. My weapon was not in the wardrobe-room; and as I returned, wondering what I had done with it, I saw Keen standing in the little doorway with a candle in his hand. He turned and asked what I was looking for. I told him, and explained why I was searching for it there.

"Here it is; I found it at the foot of these stairs. It is too sharp for a stage-dagger, and will do mischief unless you dull it," he said, adding, as he pointed to the broken rope, "Lamar, that was cut; I have examined it."

The light shone full in my face, and I knew that it changed, as did my voice, for I thought of Clotilde, and till that fear was at rest resolved to be dumb concerning what I had seen, but I could not repress a shudder as I said, hastily,

"Don't suspect me of any deviltry, for heaven's sake. I've got to go on in fifteen minutes, and how can I play unless you let me forget this horrible business."

"Forget it then, if you can; I'll remind you of it to-morrow." And, with a significant nod, he walked away, leaving behind him a new trial to distract me. I ran to Clotilde's room, bent on relieving myself, if possible, of the suspicion that would return with redoubled pertinacity since the discovery of the dagger, which I was sure I had not dropped where it was found. When I tapped at her door, her voice, clear and sweet as ever, answered, "Come!" and entering, I found her ready, but alone. Before I could open my lips she put up her hand as if to arrest the utterance of some dreadful intelligence.

"Don't speak of it; I have heard, and cannot bear a repetition of the horror. I must forget it till to-morrow, then——." There she stopped abruptly, for I produced the flower, asking as naturally as I could—

"Did you give this to any one?"

"No; why ask me that?" and she shrunk a little, as I bent to count the blossoms in the cluster on her breast. I gave her seven; now there were but six, and I fixed on her a look that betrayed my fear, and mutely demanded its confirmation or denial. Other eyes she might have evaded or defied, not mine; the traitorous blood dyed her face, then fading, left it colorless; her eyes wandered and fell, she clasped her hands imploringly, and threw herself at my feet, crying in a stifled voice,

"Paul, be merciful; that was our only hope, and the guilt is mine alone!"

But I started from her, exclaiming with mingled incredulity and horror—

"Was this the tragedy you meant? What devil devised and helped you execute a crime like this?"

"Hear me! I did not plan it, yet I longed to kill him, and all day the thought would haunt me. I have borne so much, I could bear no more, and he drove me to it. To-night the thought still clung to me, till I was half mad. I went to find you, hoping to escape it; you were gone, but on your table lay the dagger. As I took it in my hand I heard his voice, and forgot every thing except my wrongs and the great happiness one blow could bring us. I followed then, meaning to stab him in the dark; but when I saw him leaning where a safer stroke would destroy him, I gave it, and we are safe."

"Safe!" I echoed. "Do you know you left my dagger behind you? Keen found it; he suspects me, for I was near; and St. John has told him something of the cause I have to wish you free."

She sprung up, and seemed about to rush away to proclaim her guilt, but I restrained her desperate purpose, saying sternly—

"Control yourself and be cautious. I may be mistaken; but if either must suffer, let it be me. I can bear it best, even if it comes to the worst, for my life is worthless now."

"And I have made it so? Oh, Paul, can you never forgive me and forget my sin?"

"Never, Clotilde; it is too horrible."

I broke from her trembling hold, and covered up my face, for suddenly the woman whom I once loved had grown abhorrent to me. For many minutes neither spoke nor stirred; my heart seemed dead within me, and what went on in that stormy soul I shall never know. Suddenly I was called, and as I turned to leave her, she seized both my hands in a despairing grasp, covered them with tender kisses, wet them with repentant tears, and clung to them in a paroxysm of love, remorse, and grief, till I was forced to go, leaving her alone with the memory of her sin.

That night I was like one in a terrible dream; every thing looked unreal, and like an automaton I played my part, for always before me I seemed to see that shattered body and to hear again that beloved voice confessing a black crime. Rumors of the accident had crept out, and damped the spirits of the audience, yet it was as well, perhaps, for it made them lenient to the short-comings of the actors, and lent another shadow to the mimic tragedy that slowly darkened to its close. Clotilde's unnatural composure would have been a marvel to me had I not been past surprise at any demonstration on her part. A wide gulf now lay between us, and it seemed impossible for me to cross it. The generous, tender woman whom I first loved, was still as beautiful and dear to me as ever, but as much lost as if death had parted us. The desperate, despairing creature I had learned to know within an hour, seemed like an embodiment of the murderous spirit which had haunted me that day, and though by heaven's mercy it had not conquered me, yet I now hated it with remorseful intensity. So strangely were the two images blended in my troubled mind that I could not separate them, and they exerted a mysterious influence over me. When with Clotilde she seemed all she had ever been, and I enacted the lover with a power I had never known before, feeling the while that it might be for the last time. When away from her the darker impression returned, and the wildest of the poet's words were not too strong to embody my own sorrow and despair. They told me long afterwards that never had the tragedy been better played, and I could believe it, for the hapless Italian lovers never found better representatives than in us that night.

Worn out with suffering and excitement, I longed for solitude and silence with a desperate longing, and when Romeo murmured, "With a kiss I die," I fell beside the bier, wishing that I too was done with life. Lying there, I watched Clotilde, through the little that remained, and so truly, tenderly, did she render the pathetic scene that my heart softened; all the early love returned strong, and warm as ever, and I felt that I *could* forgive. As she knelt to draw my dagger, I whispered, warningly,

"Be careful, dear, it is very sharp."

"I know it," she answered with a shudder, then cried aloud,.

"Oh happy dagger! this is thy sheath; there rust, and let me die."

Again I saw the white arm raised, the flash of steel as Juliet struck the blow that was to free her, and sinking down beside her lover, seemed to breathe her life away.

"I thank God it's over," I ejaculated, a few minutes later, as the curtain slowly fell. Clotilde did not answer, and feeling how cold the cheek that touched my own had grown, I thought she had given way at last.

"She has fainted; lift her, Denon, and let me rise," I cried, as Count Paris sprang up with a joke.

"Good God, she has hurt herself with that cursed dagger!" he exclaimed, as raising her he saw a red stain on the white draperies she wore.

I staggered to my feet, and laid her on the bier she had just left, but no mortal skill could heal that hurt, and Juliet's grave-clothes were her own. Deaf to the enthusiastic clamor that demanded our re-appearance, blind to the confusion and dismay about me, I leaned over her passionately, conjuring her to give me one word of pardon and farewell. As if my voice had power to detain her, even when death called, the dark eyes, full of remorseful love, met mine again, and feebly drawing from her breast a paper, she motioned Keen to take it, murmuring in a tone that changed from solemn affirmation to the tenderest penitence,

"Lamar is innocent—I did it. This will prove it. Paul, I have tried to atone—oh, forgive me, and remember me for my love's sake."

I did forgive her, and she died, smiling on my breast. I did remember her through a long, lonely life, and never played again since the night of that DOUBLE TRAGEDY.

FAY WELDON

UN CRIME MATERNEL

HAT DID THEY call you? Miss Jacobs? I find that very strange. Only a mother, surely, can understand a mother. What is their purpose in having me see you? If anyone is crazy, it's the law, not me. If it asks for psychiatric reports, which frankly I see as both demeaning to me and damaging to my children, it might at least find someone competent to do the reporting. Or do they have to scrape the barrel for people such as yourself? I don't suppose it's a barrel of laughs, coming here to Holloway and sitting in this horrid little airless green room smelling of cabbage with a locked door and not even a window. In fact the room is rather like the inside of my head used to be before I battered my way out of it, made a hole to let in the air and the light.

Fortunately I can wear my own clothes, being on remand; I don't have to wear their nasty dingy dresses. There isn't an iron available but I keep my skirt beneath my mattress overnight, so the pleats stay in. I like to be smart. I am in the habit of being smart. It's so important to set an example to the children, don't you think? But I suppose you wouldn't know.

Now listen, Miss Jacobs, I will have to make do with you since you're all I have to work with. It is absolutely imperative, do you understand, that you declare me of sound mind. It would do Janet and Harvey no good at all to believe that their mother was insane. It would be too big a burden for them to bear. They are already having to cope with the loss of their father, and Janet's birthday is tomorrow—she will be eight—and she will be disturbed enough that for the first birthday ever I'm not there by her bed when she wakes to say "Happy birthday, darling." She may begin to worry, or doubt what she's been told; which is, very sensibly, that I'm on holiday in Greece getting over Peter's death and will be back soon. When I'm out of here I'll be able to talk the whole thing through with the pair of them. It's so important to tell children the truth: if you do, their trust in you is never diminished. Time passes so slowly for children: it is vital that I get back to them as soon as possible: that all this silly and unnecessary fuss comes to an immediate end. They're with Peter's parents, and though Graham and Jenny are not quite as child-centred as I'd like them to be, for people of that generation they're not bad. I can be confident they'll have the sense not to let Janet see the newspapers and of course Harvey isn't reading yet. I used to worry about Harvey's slowness at letters—Janet read at four, and he's already six—but I admit it has its advantages, however unexpected. Crime maternel must be recognized in this country, as crime passionnel is in France. To kill for one's children is no crime: rather, it is something for which a mother should be honoured. I want a medal, Miss Jacobs, not to be had up on a murder charge and remanded without bail for psychiatric reports. I did what it was my duty to do. I chose my children's interests over my husband's interests. Their lives, after all, were just beginning. We do give children this precedence as a matter of course.

It is imperative that I stand trial as a sane person and am properly acquitted, Miss Jacobs, because then the children can deal with it. It may mean moving house and changing schools and names afterwards, of course, but that is nothing compared to the avoidance of trauma. You must see, Miss Jacobs, that I did the only thing I could, in the circumstances I was in.

I had a troubled childhood myself. A father who molested me, a mother who let it happen. I was fostered when I was twelve by a very kind and pleasant family. I know there is good as well as bad in the world. I always wanted to have children, and to give them a perfect life. What is there more important in the world than this? I became a nurse and did well in my profession, but always with my future role as a mother in mind. I am not bad looking, and could, and indeed would, have married on several occasions, but each time I felt the man involved would not make a good enough father. He would have to be loving, kind, genial, patient, intelligent, sensitive to children's needs, and able to provide the proper male authority role within the family group. I began to think I'd never meet the perfect father. I could settle, even happily, for less than perfection for myself, but not for my unborn children!

And finally I met him! Peter! He fulfilled all my requirements, as I did his. He looked for the perfect mother, as I looked for the perfect father. We married, and agreed we would wait a year before starting a family so the children would be born into a settled and secure domestic framework. And that year, I may say, was exceedingly happy. I had always felt, because of my early experience, that sex was not for me. That year with Peter proved me wrong! Then, according to plan, I became pregnant with Janet, and of course after she was born sex became impossible. She could only sleep if she was in the bed with us, and then only if she was at the breast, and I got an ulcer, and you know how it is with small babies. Well, you don't, do you. Let me just say Janet was a sensitive baby, and cried a lot, and then when Harvey came along he turned out to be hyperactive, and I'm sorry to say Peter's views on child-rearing began to change: they simply did not coincide any more with mine.

Does this sound like the tale of a mad woman? I promise you I am not mad.

Peter was teaching at the time, and spent far too much time away from home. I know he had obligations to pupils and college, but he had obligations to his children as well. I insisted that he always be home by bathtime. It is imperative that children have the reassurance that a rock-solid routine provides. But sometimes, on some spurious ground or other, he would be absent. I would have to watch their little faces fall. Splashing about in the water, so important to the development of their tactile responses, their creative drive, just wasn't the same without Daddy. And so he and I began to quarrel. The atmosphere in the home became tense, and that's so very bad for children. They pick up really quickly on vibes.

Peter could, and would, sometimes even in front of them, say terrible things to me. "Why do you always ask those children questions?" he'd yell. "Why do you say, 'Are you sleepy? Would you like to go in your cot?' Why don't you say, 'You do feel sleepy, darling. Now I'm putting you in your cot'?" And of course the answer was so obvious! For one thing, children are not there for the parents' convenience, to be shut up; for another, even with the smallest child it is important to develop consciousness of self. The child knows what it feels; it is up to the parent to decipher those feelings and act upon them. I don't *tell* my child it is hungry: I require it to give me an accurate account of what's going on in its head. That way it learns self-expression. How else? Peter would accuse me of unforgivable things—of over-stimulating the children, of depriving them of pleasure—by which he only meant he'd shut them up if he could by shoving ice lollies in their mouths which would rot their teeth and give them a liking for sweet things which might stay with them all their lives, for all he knew. Or, I'm sorry to say, cared. Please don't think he was a bad father, he wasn't. He loved Janet and Harvey immoderately, and they loved him, which was of course the trouble. I'd feel like tucking them under my arm and running off with them, but how could I? Within two minutes they'd be grizzling and pining for their father.

The upshot of our disagreements over child-care, together with the actuality of those two small lively children, meant I was easily riled and distressed, and spent quite a lot of time in tears which I could not control. Try as I would to be brave and bright for the children's sake, I failed. They would see me red-eyed and depressed, and hear Peter shouting. It couldn't go on. It is the most traumatic and damaging thing for children to hear their parents rowing. Unforgivable to let it happen but it was not my doing. It began to look as if we had to part. Between us we had to provide two loving and caring environments between which Harvey and Janet would travel, since we could not make one. Now I knew I would do my part in this. But I was not convinced he would do his. Already Peter was seeing another woman, a junk-food addict whose idea of an afternoon out with the children was to go to McDonald's on the way to the zoo—can you imagine, a *zoo?*—the torment of those poor wild caged creatures—and Janet and Harvey actively encouraged to gawp and throw peanuts. Now I'm well aware that it's best for children to see their parents happy, and Peter's sex drive was such that he could only be happy if it was more or less satisfied. I had no grudge whatsoever against his girlfriends, one or all of them, so don't be misled by anyone who says mine was a crime passionnel. It was most definitely—if crime it was—a crime maternel. An act committed for the sake of the children which involves the death and/or disenabling of an incompetent and/or damaging parent. It wasn't Peter's *fault* that this was what he was. Blame God, if you must blame anyone, for creating parents and children whose emotional interests overlap but do not coincide. But there it was. I could see no other way out of an impossible bind.

Divorce, when it comes to it, is so crippling to the child's psyche, is it not? The children suffer appallingly when a family breaks up. Statistics show that a paternal death has a less damaging effect on the children than divorce, so long as the family home is maintained and family income does not fall. So what else could I do, Miss Jacobs? In my children's interests?

I insured Peter's life and he and I, his girlfriend and the children went for a country walk and we picked mushrooms, including a death cap, and I made a beef casserole that evening, and he and she ate it—I am a vegetarian and I never let the children eat beef because of the possibility of mad cow disease but Peter of course would never renounce beef: what he liked he had to have—and it proved as fatal as the books said. Don't worry—I got the pair of them into hospital promptly so the children witnessed nothing nasty. I hadn't realized how suspicious coroners and police can be—I supposed I do tend to think everyone is as child-centred as I am. But this is not insanity, Miss Jacobs, is it? I was doing my best for my children, as the statistics in our society suggest the best to be: and I must get back to them as soon as is humanly possible, for their sake. I presume the court won't be so stupid as not to understand that? What do you think?

RUDYARD KIPLING

MARY POSTGATE

OF MISS MARY POSTGATE, Lady McCausland wrote that she was "thoroughly conscientious, tidy, companionable, and ladylike. I am very sorry to part with her, and shall always be interested in her welfare."

Miss Fowler engaged her on this recommendation, and to her surprise, for she had had experience of companions, found that it was true. Miss Fowler was nearer sixty than fifty at the time, but though she needed care she did not exhaust her attendant's vitality. On the contrary, she gave out, stimulatingly and with reminiscences. Her father had been a minor Court official in the days when the Great Exhibition of 1851 had just set its seal on Civilization made perfect. Some of Miss Fowler's tales, none the less, were not always for the young. Mary was not young, and though her speech was as colourless as her eyes or her hair, she was never shocked. She listened unflinchingly to every one; said at the end, "How interesting!" or "How shocking!" as the case might be, and never again referred to it, for she prided herself on a trained mind, which "did not dwell on these things."

She was, too, a treasure at domestic accounts, for which the village tradesmen, with their weekly books, loved her not. Otherwise she had no enemies; provoked no jealousy even among the plainest; neither gossip nor slander had ever been traced to her; she supplied the odd place at the Rector's or the Doctor's table at half an hour's notice; she was a sort of public aunt to very small children of the village street, whose parents, while accepting everything, would have been swift to resent what they called "patronage"; she served on the Village Nursing Committee as Miss Fowler's nominee when Miss Fowler was crippled by rheumatoid arthritis, and came out of six months' fortnightly meetings equally respected by all the cliques.

And when Fate threw Miss Fowler's nephew, an unlovely orphan of eleven, on Miss Fowler's hands, Mary Postgate stood to her share of the business of education as practised in private and public schools. She checked printed clotheslists, and unitemized bills of extras; wrote to head and house masters, matrons, nurses and doctors, and grieved or rejoiced over half-term reports. Young Wyndham Fowler repaid her in his holidays by calling her "Gatepost," "Postey," or "Packthread," by thumping her between her narrow shoulders, or by chasing her bleating, round the garden, her large mouth open, her large nose high in the air, at a stiff-necked shamble very like a camel's. Later on he filled the house with clamour, argument, and harangues as to his personal needs, likes and dislikes, and the limitations of "you women," reducing Mary to tears of physical fatigue, or, when he chose to be humorous, of helpless laughter. At crises, which multiplied as he grew older, she was his ambassadress and his interpretress to Miss Fowler, who had no large sympathy with the young; a vote in his interest at the councils on his future; his sewing-woman, strictly accountable for mislaid boots and garments; always his butt and his slave.

And when he decided to become a solicitor, and had entered an office in London; when his greeting had changed from "Hullo, Postey, you old beast," to "Mornin', Packthread," there came a war which, unlike all wars that Mary could remember, did not stay decently outside England and in the newspapers, but intruded on the lives of people whom she knew. As she said to Miss Fowler, it was "most vexatious." It took the Rector's son who was going into business with his elder brother; it took the Colonel's nephew on the eve of fruit-farming in Canada; it took Mrs. Grant's son who, his mother said, was devoted to the ministry; and, very early indeed, it took Wynn Fowler, who announced on a postcard that he had joined the Flying Corps and wanted a cardigan waistcoat.

"He must go, and he must have the waistcoat," said Miss Fowler. So Mary got the proper-sized needles and wool, while Miss Fowler told the men of her establishment—two gardeners and an odd man, aged sixty—that those who could join the Army had better do so. The gardeners left. Cheape, the odd man, stayed on, and was promoted to the gardener's cottage. The cook, scorning to be limited in luxuries, also left, after a spirited scene with Miss Fowler, and took the housemaid with her. Miss Fowler gazetted Nellie, Cheape's seventeen-year-old daughter, to the vacant post; Mrs. Cheape to the rank of cook, with occasional cleaning bouts; and the reduced establishment moved forward smoothly.

Wynn demanded an increase in his allowance. Miss Fowler, who always looked facts in the face, said, "He must have it. The chances are he won't live long to draw it, and if three hundred makes him happy—"

Wynn was grateful, and came over, in his tight-buttoned uniform, to say so. His training centre was not thirty miles away, and his talk was so technical that it had to be explained by charts of the various types of machines. He gave Mary such a chart.

"And you'd better study it, Postey," he said. "You'll be seeing a lot of 'em soon." So Mary studied the chart, but when Wynn next arrived to swell and exalt himself before his womenfolk, she failed badly in cross-examination, and he rated her as in the old days.

"You *look* more or less like a human being," he said in his new Service voice. "You *must* have had a brain at some time in your past. What have you done with it? Where d'you keep it? A sheep would know more than you do, Postey. You're lamentable. You are less use than an empty tin can, you dowey old cassowary."

"I suppose that's how your superior officer talks to *you?*" said Miss Fowler from her chair.

"But Postey doesn't mind," Wynn replied. "Do you, Packthread?"

"Why? Was Wynn saying anything? I shall get this right next time you come," she muttered, and knitted her pale brows again over the diagrams of Taubes, Farmans, and Zeppelins.

In a few weeks the mere land and sea battles which she read to Miss Fowler after breakfast passed her like idle breath. Her heart and her interest were high in the air with Wynn, who had finished "rolling" (whatever that might be) and had gone on from a "taxi" to a machine more or less his own. One morning it circled over their very chimneys, alighted on Vegg's Heath, almost outside the garden gate, and Wynn came in, blue with cold, shouting for food. He and she drew Miss Fowler's bath-chair, as they had often done, along the Heath footpath to look at the biplane. Mary observed that "it smelt very badly."

"Postey, I believe you think with your nose," said Wynn. "I know you don't with your mind. Now, what type's that?"

"I'll go and get the chart," said Mary.

"You're hopeless! You haven't the mental capacity of a white mouse," he cried, and explained the dials and the sockets for bomb-dropping till it was time to mount and ride the wet clouds once more.

"Ah!" said Mary, as the stinking thing flared upward. "Wait till our Flying Corps gets to work! Wynn says it's much safer than in the trenches."

"I wonder," said Miss Fowler. "Tell Cheape to come and tow me home again."

"It's all downhill. I can do it," said Mary, "if you put the brake on." She laid her lean self against the pushing-bar and home they trundled.

"Now, be careful you aren't heated and catch a chill," said over-dressed Miss Fowler.

"Nothing makes me perspire," said Mary. As she bumped the chair under the porch she straightened her long back. The exertion had given her a colour, and the wind had loosened a wisp of hair across her forehead. Miss Fowler glanced at her.

"What do you ever think of, Mary?" she demanded suddenly.

"Oh, Wynn says he wants another three pairs of stockings—as thick as we can make them."

"Yes. But I mean the things that women think about. Here you are, more than forty—"

"Forty-four," said truthful Mary.

"Well?"

"Well?" Mary offered Miss Fowler her shoulder as usual.

"And you've been with me ten years now."

"Let's see," said Mary. "Wynn was eleven when he came. He's twenty now, and I came two years before that. It must be eleven."

"Eleven! And you've never told me anything that matters in all that while. Looking back, it seems to me that *I've* done all the talking."

"I'm afraid I'm not much of a conversationalist. As Wynn says, I haven't the mind. Let me take your hat."

Miss Fowler, moving stiffly from the hip, stamped her rubber-tipped stick on the tiled hall floor. "Mary, aren't you *anything* except a companion? Would you *ever* have been anything except a companion?"

Mary hung up the garden hat on its proper peg. "No," she said after consideration. "I don't imagine I ever should. But I've no imagination, I'm afraid."

She fetched Miss Fowler her eleven-o'clock glass of Contrexeville.

That was the wet December when it rained six inches to the month, and the women went abroad as little as might be. Wynn's flying chariot visited them several times, and for two mornings (he had warned her by postcard) Mary heard the thresh of his propellers at dawn. The second time she ran to the window, and stared at the whitening sky. A little blur passed overhead. She lifted her lean arms towards it.

That evening at six o'clock there came an announcement in an official envelope that Second Lieutenant W. Fowler had been killed during a trial flight. Death was instantaneous. She read it and carried it to Miss Fowler.

"I never expected anything else," said Miss Fowler; "but I'm sorry it happened before he had done anything."

The room was whirling round Mary Postgate, but she found herself quite steady in the midst of it.

"Yes," she said. "It's a great pity he didn't die in action after he had killed somebody."

"He was killed instantly. That's one comfort," Miss Fowler went on.

"But Wynn says the shock of a fall kills a man at once—whatever happens to the tanks," quoted Mary.

The room was coming to rest now. She heard Miss Fowler say impatiently, "But why can't we cry, Mary?" and herself replying, "There's nothing to cry for. He has done his duty as much as Mrs. Grant's son did."

"And when he died, *she* came and cried all the morning," said Miss Fowler. "This only makes me feel tired—terribly tired. Will you help me to bed, please, Mary?—And I think I'd like the hot-water bottle."

So Mary helped her and sat beside her, talking of Wynn in his riotous youth.

"I believe," said Miss Fowler suddenly, "that old people and young people slip from under a stroke like this. The middle-aged feel it most."

"I expect that's true," said Mary, rising. "I'm going to put away the things in his room now. Shall we wear mourning?"

"Certainly not," said Miss Fowler. "Except, of course, at the funeral. I can't go. You will. I want you to arrange about his being buried here. What a blessing it didn't happen at Salisbury!"

Everyone, from the Authorities of the Flying Corps to the Rector, was most kind and sympathetic. Mary found herself for the moment in a world where bodies were in the habit of being despatched by all sorts of conveyances to all sorts of places. And at the funeral two young men in buttoned-up uniforms stood beside the grave and spoke to her afterwards.

"You're Miss Postgate, aren't you?" said one. "Fowler told me about you. He was a good chap—a first-class fellow—a great loss."

"How high did he fall from?" Mary whispered.

"Pretty nearly four thousand feet, I should think, didn't he? You were up that day, Monkey?"

"All of that," the other child replied. "My bar made three thousand, and I wasn't as high as him by a lot."

"Then *that's* all right," said Mary. "Thank you very much."

They moved away as Mrs. Grant flung herself weeping on Mary's flat chest, under the lych-gate, and cried, "*I* know how it feels! *I* know how it feels!"

"But both his parents are dead," Mary returned, as she fended her off. "Perhaps they've all met by now," she added vaguely as she escaped towards the coach.

"I've thought of that too," wailed Mrs. Grant; "but then he'll be practically a stranger to them. Quite embarrassing!"

Mary faithfully reported every detail of the ceremony to Miss Fowler, who, when she described Mrs. Grant's outburst, laughed aloud.

"Oh, how Wynn would have enjoyed it! He was always utterly unreliable at funerals. D'you remember——" And they talked of him again, each piecing out the other's gaps. "And now," said Miss Fowler, "we'll pull up the blinds and we'll have a general tidy. That always does us good. Have you seen to Wynn's things?"

"Everything—since he first came," said Mary. "He was never destructive—even with his toys."

They faced that neat room.

"It can't be natural not to cry," Mary said at last. "I'm *so* afraid you'll have a reaction."

"As I told you, we old people slip from under the stroke. It's you I'm afraid for. Have you cried yet?"

"I can't. It only makes me angry with the Germans."

"That's sheer waste of vitality," said Miss Fowler. "We must live till the war's finished." She opened a full wardrobe. "Now, I've been thinking things over. This is my plan. All his civilian clothes can be given away—Belgian refugees, and so on."

Mary nodded. "Boots, collars, and gloves?"

"Yes. We don't need to keep anything except his cap and belt."

"They came back yesterday with his Flying Corps clothes"—Mary pointed to a roll on the little iron bed.

"Ah, but keep his Service things. Someone may be glad of them later. Do you remember his sizes?"

"Five feet eight and a half; thirty-six inches round the chest. But he told me he's just put on an inch and a half. I'll mark it on a label and tie it on his sleeping-bag."

"So that disposes of *that*," said Miss Fowler, tapping the palm of one hand with the ringed third finger of the other. "What waste it all is! We'll get his old school trunk tomorrow and pack his civilian clothes."

"And the rest?" said Mary. "His books and pictures and the games and the toys—and—and the rest?"

"My plan is to burn every single thing," said Miss Fowler. "Then we shall know where they are and no one can handle them afterwards. What do you think?"

"I think that would be much the best," said Mary. "But there's such a lot of them."

"We'll burn them in the destructor," said Miss Fowler.

This was an open-air furnace for the consumption of refuse; a little circular four-foot tower of pierced brick over an iron grating. Miss Fowler had noticed the design in a gardening journal years ago, and had had it built at the bottom of the garden. It suited her tidy soul, for it saved unsightly rubbish heaps, and the ashes lightened the stiff clay soil.

Mary considered for a moment, saw her way clear, and nodded again. They spent the evening putting away well-remembered civilian suits, underclothes that Mary had marked, and the regiments of very gaudy socks and ties. A second trunk was needed, and, after that, a little packing-case, and it was late next day when Cheape and the local carrier lifted them to the cart. The Rector luckily knew of a friend's son, about five feet eight and a half inches high, to whom a complete Flying Corps outfit would be most acceptable, and sent his gardener's son down with a barrow to take delivery of it. The cap was hung up in Miss Fowler's bedroom, the belt in Miss Postgate's; for, as Miss Fowler said, they had no desire to make tea-party talk of them.

"That disposes of *that*," said Miss Fowler. "I'll leave the rest to you, Mary. I can't run up and down the garden. You'd better take the big clothes-basket and get Nellie to help you."

"I shall take the wheelbarrow and do it myself," said Mary, and for once in her life closed her mouth.

Miss Fowler, in moments of irritation, had called Mary deadly methodical. She put on her oldest waterproof and gardening-hat and her ever-slipping goloshes, for the weather was on the edge of more rain.

She gathered fire-lighters from the kitchen, a half-scuttle of coals, and a faggot of brushwood. These she wheeled in the barrow down the mossed paths to the dank little laurel shrubbery where the destructor stood under the drip of three oaks. She climbed the wire fence into the Rector's glebe just behind, and from his tenant's rick pulled two large armfuls of good hay, which she spread neatly on the fire-bars. Next, journey by journey, passing Miss Fowler's white face at the morning-room window each time, she brought down in the towel-covered clothes-basket on the wheelbarrow, thumbed and used Hentys, Marryats, Levers, Stevensons, Baroness Orczys, Garvices, schoolbooks, and atlases, unrelated piles of the *Motor Cyclist*, the *Light Car*, and catalogues of Olympia Exhibitions; the remnants of a fleet of sailing-ships from ninepenny cutters to a three-guinea yacht; a prep-school dressing-gown; bats from three-and-sixpence to twenty-four shillings; cricket and tennis balls; disintegrated steam and clockwork locomotives with their twisted rails; a grey and red tin model of a submarine; a dumb gramophone and cracked records; gold-clubs that had to be broken across the knee, like his walking-sticks, and an assegai; photographs of private and public school cricket and football elevens, and his O.T.C. on the line of march; Kodaks and film-rolls; some pewters, and one real silver cup, for boxing competitions and Junior Hurdles; sheaves of school photographs; Miss Fowler's photograph; her own which he had borne off in fun and (good care she took not to ask!) had never returned; a playbox with a secret drawer; a load of flannels, belts, and jerseys, and a pair of spiked shoes, unearthed in the attic; a packet of all the letters that Miss Fowler and she had ever written to him, kept for some absurd reason through all these years; a five-day attempt at a diary; framed pictures of racing motors in full Brooklands career, and load upon load of undistinguishable wreckage of tool-boxes, rabbit-hutches, electric batteries, tin soldiers, fret-saw outfits, and jig-saw puzzles.

Miss Fowler at the window watched her come and go, and said to herself, "Mary's an old woman. I never realized it before."

After lunch she recommended her to rest.

"I'm not in the least tired," said Mary. "I've got it all arranged. I'm going to the village at two o'clock for some paraffin. Nellie hasn't enough, and the walk will do me good."

She made one last quest round the house before she started, and found that she had overlooked nothing. It began to mist as soon as she had skirted Vegg's Heath, where Wynn used to descend—it seemed to her that she could almost hear the beat of his propellers overhead, but there was nothing to see. She hoisted her umbrella and lunged into the blind wet till she had reached the shelter of the empty village. As she came out of Mr. Kidd's shop with a bottle full of paraffin in her string shopping-bag, she met Nurse Eden, the village nurse, and fell into talk with her, as usual, about the village children. They were just parting opposite the "Royal Oak," when a gun, they fancied, was fired immediately behind the house. It was followed by a child's shriek dying into a wail.

"Accident!" said Nurse Eden promptly, and dashed through the empty bar, followed by Mary. They found Mrs. Gerritt, the publican's wife, who could only gasp and point to the yard, where a little cart-lodge was sliding sideways amid a clatter of tiles. Nurse Eden snatched up a sheet drying before the fire, ran out, lifted something from the ground, and flung the sheet round it. The sheet turned scarlet and half her uniform too, as she bore the load into the kitchen. It was little Edna Gerritt, aged nine, whom Mary had known since her perambulator days.

"Am I hurted bad?" Edna asked, and died between Nurse Eden's dripping hands. The sheet fell aside and for an instant, before she could shut her eyes, Mary saw the ripped and shredded body.

"It's a wonder she spoke at all," said Nurse Eden. "What in God's name was it?"

"A bomb," said Mary.

"One o' the Zeppelins?"

"No. An aeroplane. I thought I heard it on the Heath, but I fancied it was one of ours. It must have shut off its engines as it came down. That's why we didn't notice it."

"The filthy pigs!" said Nurse Eden, all white and shaken. "See the pickle I'm in! Go and tell Dr. Hennis, Miss Postgate." Nurse looked at the mother, who had dropped face down on the floor. "She's only in a fit. Turn her over."

Mary heaved Mrs. Gerritt right side up, and hurried off for the doctor. When she told her tale, he asked her to sit down in the surgery till he got her something.

"But I don't need it, I assure you," said she. "I don't think it would be wise to tell Miss Fowler about it, do you? Her heart is so irritable in this weather."

Dr. Hennis looked at her admiringly as he packed up his bag.

"No. Don't tell anybody till we're sure," he said, and hastened to the "Royal Oak," while Mary went on with the paraffin. The village behind her was as quiet as usual, for the news had not yet spread. She frowned a little to herself, her large nostrils expanding uglily, and from time to time she muttered a phrase which Wynn, who never restrained himself before his womenfolk, had applied to the enemy. "Bloody pagans! They *are* bloody pagans. But," she continued, falling back on the teaching that had made her what she was, "one mustn't let one's mind dwell on these things."

Before she reached the house Dr. Hennis, who was also a special constable, overtook her in his car.

"Oh, Miss Postgate," he said, "I wanted to tell you that that accident at the 'Royal Oak' was due to Gerritt's stable tumbling down. It's been dangerous for a long time. It ought to have been condemned."

"I thought I heard an explosion too," said Mary.

"You might have been misled by the beams snapping. I've been looking at 'em. They were dry-rotted through and through. Of course, as they broke, they would make a noise just like a gun."

"Yes?" said Mary politely.

"Poor little Edna was playing underneath it," he went on, still holding her with his eyes, "and that and the tiles cut her to pieces, you see?"

"I saw it," said Mary, shaking her head. "I heard it too."

"Well, we cannot be sure." Dr. Hennis changed his tone completely. "I know both you and Nurse Eden (I've been speaking to her) are perfectly trustworthy, and I can rely on you not to say anything—yet at least. It is no good to stir up people unless—"

"Oh, I never do—anyhow," said Mary, and Dr. Hennis went on to the country town.

After all, she told herself, it might, just possibly, have been the collapse of the old stable that had done all those things to poor little Edna. She was sorry she had even hinted at other things, but Nurse Eden was discretion itself. By the time she reached home the affair seemed increasingly remote by its very monstrosity. As she came in, Miss Fowler told her that a couple of aeroplanes had passed half an hour ago.

"I thought I heard them," she replied. "I'm going down the garden now. I've got the paraffin."

"Yes, but—what *have* you got on your boots? They're soaking wet. Change them at once."

Not only did Mary obey but she wrapped the boots in a newspaper, and put them into the string bag with the bottle. So, armed with the longest kitchen poker, she left.

"It's raining again," was Miss Fowler's last word, "but—I know you won't be happy till that's disposed of."

"It won't take long. I've got everything down there, and I've put the lid on the destructor to keep the wet out."

The shrubbery was filling with twilight by the time she had completed her arrangements and sprinkled the sacrificial oil. As she lit the match that would burn her heart to ashes, she heard a groan or a grunt behind the dense Portugal laurels.

"Cheape?" she called impatiently, but Cheape, with his ancient lumbago, in his comfortable cottage would be the last man to profane the sanctuary. "Sheep," she concluded, and threw in the fusee. The pyre went up in a roar, and the immediate flame hastened night around her.

"How Wynn would have loved this!" she thought, stepping back from the blaze.

By its light she saw, half hidden behind a laurel not five paces away, a bare-headed man sitting very stiffly at the foot of one of the oaks. A broken branch lay across his lap—one booted leg protruding from beneath it. His head moved ceaselessly from side to side, but his body was as still as the tree's trunk. He was dressed—she moved sideways to look more closely—in a uniform something like Wynn's, with a flap buttoned across the chest. For an instant, she had some idea that it might be one of the young flying men she had met at the funeral. But their heads were dark and glossy. This man's was as pale as a baby's, and so closely cropped that she could see the disgusting pinky skin beneath. His lips moved.

"What do you say?" Mary moved towards him and stooped.

"Laty! Laty! Laty!" he muttered, while his hands picked at the dead wet leaves. There was no doubt as to his nationality. It made her so angry that she strode back to the destructor, though it was still too hot to use the poker there. Wynn's books seemed to be catching well. She looked up at the oak behind the man; several of the light upper and two or three rotten lower branches had broken and scattered their rubbish on the shrubbery path. On the lowest fork a helmet with dependent strings, showed like a bird's-nest in the light of a long-tongued flame. Evidently this person had fallen through the tree.

Wynn had told her that it was quite possible for people to fall out of aeroplanes. Wynn told her too, that trees were useful things to break an aviator's fall, but in this case the aviator must have been broken or he would have moved from his queer position. He seemed helpless except for his horrible rolling head. On the other hand, she could see a pistol case at his belt—and Mary loathed pistols. Months ago, after reading certain Belgian reports together, she and Miss Fowler had had dealings with one—a huge revolver with flat-nosed bullets, which latter, Wynn said, were forbidden by the rules of war to be used against civilized enemies. "They're good enough for us," Miss Fowler had replied. "Show Mary how it works." And Wynn, laughing at the mere possibility of any such need, had led the craven winking Mary into the Rector's disused quarry, and had shown her how to fire the terrible machine. It lay now in the top left-hand drawer of her toilet-table—a memento not included in the burning. Wynn would be pleased to see how she was not afraid.

She slipped up to the house to get it. When she came through the rain, the eyes in the head were alive with expectation. The mouth even tried to smile. But at sight of the revolver its corners went down just like Edna Gerritt's. A tear trickled from one eye, and the head rolled from shoulder to shoulder as though trying to point out something.

"Cassée. Tout cassée," it whimpered.

"What do you say?" said Mary disgustedly, keeping well to one side, though only the head moved.

"Cassée," it repeated. "Che me rends. Le médicin! Toctor!"

"Nein!" said she, bringing all her small German to bear with the big pistol. "Ich haben der todt Kinder gesehn."

The head was still. Mary's hand dropped. She had been careful to keep her finger off the trigger for fear of accidents. After a few moments' waiting, she returned to the destructor, where the flames were falling, and churned up Wynn's charring books with the poker.

Again the head groaned for the doctor.

"Stop that!" said Mary, and stamped her foot. "Stop that, you bloody pagan!"

The words came quite smoothly and naturally. They were Wynn's own words, and Wynn was a gentleman who for no consideration on earth would have torn little Edna into those vividly coloured strips and strings. But this thing hunched under the oak-tree had done that thing. It was no question of reading horrors out of newspapers to Miss Fowler. Mary had seen it with her own eyes on the "Royal Oak" kitchen table. She must not allow her mind to dwell upon it. Now Wynn was dead, and everything connected with him was lumping and rustling and tinkling under her busy poker into red black dust and grey leaves of ash. The thing beneath the oak would die too. Mary had seen death more than once. She came of a family that had a knack of dying under, as she told Miss Fowler, "most distressing circumstances." She would stay where she was till she was entirely satisfied that It was dead—dead as dear papa in the late eighties; Aunt Mary in 'eighty-nine; mamma in 'ninety-one; and Cousin Dick in 'ninety-five; Lady McCausland's housemaid in 'ninety-nine; Lady McCausland's sister in nineteen hundred and one; Wynn buried five days ago; and Edna Gerritt still waiting for decent earth to hide her. As she thought—her underlip caught up by one faded canine, brows knit and nostrils wide—she wielded the poker with lunges that jarred the grating at the bottom, and careful scrapes round the brickwork above. She looked at her wrist-watch. It was getting on to half-past four, and the rain was coming down in earnest. Tea would be at five. If It did not die before that time, she would be soaked and would have to change. Meantime, and this occupied her, Wynn's things were burning well in spite of the hissing wet, though now and again a book-back with a quite distinguishable title would be heaved up out of the mass. The exercise of stoking had given her a glow which seemed to reach to the marrow of her bones. She hummed—Mary never had a voice—to herself. She had never believed in all those advanced views—though Miss Fowler herself leaned a little that way—of woman's work in the world; but now she saw there was much to be said for them. This, for instance, was *her* work—work which no man, least of all Dr. Hennis, would ever have done. A man, at such a crisis, would be what Wynn called a "sportsman"; would leave everything to fetch help, and would certainly bring It into the house. Now a woman's business was to make a happy home for—for a husband and children. Failing these—it was not a thing one should allow one's mind to dwell upon—but——

"Stop it!" Mary cried once more across the shadows. "Nein, I tell you! Ich haben der todt Kinder gesehn."

But it was a fact. A woman who had missed these things could still be useful—more useful than a man in certain respects. She thumped like a pavior through the settling ashes at the secret thrill of it. The rain was damping the fire, but she could feel—it was too dark to see—that her work was done. There was a dull red glow at the bottom of the destructor, not enough to char the wooden lid if she slipped it half over against the driving wet. This arranged, she leaned on the poker and waited, while an increasing rapture laid hold on her. She ceased to think. She gave herself up to feel. Her long pleasure was broken by a sound that she had waited for in agony several times in her life. She leaned forward and listened, smiling. There could be no mistake. She closed her eyes and drank it in. Once it ceased abruptly.

"Go on," she murmured, half aloud. "That isn't the end."

Then the end came very distinctly in a lull between two rain-gusts. Mary Postgate drew her breath short between her teeth and shivered from head to foot. "*That's* all right," said she contentedly, and went up to the house, where she scandalized the whole routine by taking a luxurious hot bath before tea, and came down looking, as Miss Fowler said when she saw her lying all relaxed on the other sofa, "quite handsome!"

PATRICK O'BRIAN

THE WALKER

*I*N THE COUNTRY around this village it is not as simple as one could wish to find a pleasant, easy path for walking. The roads inland are all uphill, and although it is true that they lead through magnificent, dramatic country—bold, falling rock with terraces of vines and olive trees standing among the dried-up, barren mountains—they are roads that have to be climbed with attention: the landscape makes continual demands upon one; the winding, rock-strewn paths need perpetual care, and both these things interfere with the real aim of a walk, which for me is a half-conscious gentle physical exercise, the perfect accompaniment to reflection. I do not say that the countryside is anything but superb, and for one who walks to see magnificence these paths are ideal: but that is not my aim, and sometimes I long for an ordinary sober country lane, a way through the level cornfields or a towpath along a quiet river or a sea wall between salt flats and a marsh. Then there is the heat: for a big, heavy man that is important, and in the summer (it lasts from April to November here) all these roads are tilted to the blazing sun throughout the day.

The alternative is to walk along the sea. It is fresher in the summer, but there again it is not the kind of walking that I like best, for the sea is bordered by high cliffs: the sea comes right to their feet, and there is no way along the shore; one must be climbing or descending all the time.

When I was a little boy I lived for a time in a place where there was an immense stretch of sand, hard, pounded sand upon which you could walk for miles and miles. You never had to watch your feet on the level sand: walking was effortless, and the rhythm of your steps and the half-heard incessant thunder of the sea induced that trance in which one can go on and on for ever, singing perhaps, or taking to the air. There were shells, too, far better than the shells are here, delicately stranded at the watermark, and all kinds of sea-wrecked things, trawlers' floats, kelp, sea purses, spindrift, tarred or whitened planks of wood.

That is the sort of beach or strand that is lacking here; for here, as I say, there is no way along the sea except by the cliffs, and although they do sometimes go down to a little bay of shingle, it is only to rise again abruptly within a hundred yards. It is not a coast for general wander-ing: it is not a shore where one can stroll at all, and that is my only complaint against this place. I have no others. My lodgings are clean and orderly, the people are used to me, they are quiet and civil, and nobody interferes with my work or my set habits.

However, there is one walk that is neither violent nor exhausting. It is not a very good walk: it is an illogical, synthetic walk, but it is the best that I have been able to find and I have gone over the paths of it so often now that my feet find their way by themselves, leaving my mind free, to meditate or drift in vacancy, just as it pleases; and that is all that one can ask.

I go out of the back of the village, past the fort: for this is a bad part, for the quarter's rubbish dump is by the fort, and there is always a car-rion smell and the thin dogs hunt about in shameful, mean-looking bands. The rubbish is supposed to be burned in that square concrete box, but although a cloud of stinking smoke drifts over it, the amount is never the less. I pass it and hurry over the bare drying-ground: the wind is almost always in the right direction, and as soon as I am on the level field the reek is blown away, so by the time I am halfway over it the unpleasant feeling has quite gone. This is the place where the women spread their washing out to dry, and in certain months of the year the men bring their nets to lie in the sun.

Beyond the drying field one must branch off to the left, to the main road, and follow it to the entrance of a broad cart track: this is where the walk begins. The track dips down between high banks, and very soon there are hedges on either side. These are the only hedges for miles around, and if it were not for the prickly pears that show here and there and the pomegranates that form part of the hedge itself, one might suppose the track an English lane. On the far side there are orange trees and vines, which destroy the effect, but all around the farmhouse that stands on the downward slope an ordinary market garden gives the green in ordered rows again—broad beans, cauliflowers and cabbages, lettuce, carrots, familiar plants. Farther down, the bushes close overhead and the lane becomes a tunnel through the green; then at the bottom there is the river. For nearly all the year the bed is dry, and even when there is some water flowing it is always possible to cross dry-shod. Now I turn to the right and follow the path downstream. Here there are laurels, a few willows, tamarisks and those tall, thin bushes that have purple sprays of flowers—the kind that bloom in the late summer and draw flights of peacock butterflies.

Among the bushes there are dragonflies, for the river, flowing underground, leaves stagnant pools in the hollows: and up and down the river bed, low under the trees, innumerable swallows dash through the light; there are martins, too, and in the evening, when the bats are out and the swallows are no more than dark blurs, more sensed than seen, the white bottoms of the martins show, disembodied, weaving up and down.

I follow the river then, and come to its mouth. This is in one of the little bays that I have mentioned: it stands between the cliffs on either hand, a half-moon of shingle, with tall reeds at the back of it and behind them an orchard of fig and orange trees. The river, when it is flowing, hugs the right-hand side, cutting along at the foot of the cliff itself, and the beach shows no sign of having a river in it at all.

It is a shingle beach, with large pebbles at the back and small ones by the sea. Nearly always there is a high-water mark of broken reeds, bushes, driftwood and grass-like seaweed: this line of vegetable rubbish (it is as much as two feet high sometimes) stays unmoved from one big storm to another. Only at the equinox, when the wind comes straight in from the sea, do the waves beat in so far, and then there is nearly always rain inland, so that the river brings down more dead reeds and bushes, and these, being unable to drive out to sea, drift in the little bay and are thrown in to the same high-water mark.

It is only at these times, too, that the one boat that lives on that beach is hauled up far from the sea. It is a blue boat, shaped like those one made from paper as a child; the old man of the orchard uses it to fish for congers. He spends more time in his boat than working on his land, and it is said that he knows the rocks at the bottom of that bay better than most men know the rooms of the house they live in. But he is a savage old man, a solitary, and I do not speak to him nor he to me.

When I am on the beach I usually walk up and down it. It is not that it is agreeable to walk upon—the shingle is so loose and shifting that one's feet plunge deep and walking is painful—but it is the end of my walk. One must either go back the way one came (an unsatisfactory retreat) or else climb up the cliff, which is not walking any more. It is the cliff path that I nearly always take, up past the destroyed German searchlight and to the huge domed gun-emplacements home; but I walk up and down first to consider it.

I walk, naturally, by whatever water mark there may be. Not the high ridge-like mark of the great storms, for that so rarely changes, but by the sea itself; and sometimes, when there has been a swell, or a storm in Africa, there are shells or wreckage on the beach.

Once I found a wet brass ring. It had just arrived from who knows what rolling in the sea. It was a cheap ring, the kind that is sold in fairs: the sea had pitted it with eatings-out and dents, which gave it the look of vast antiquity. But in low relief on the flat part of it there was a swastika, and no doubt it had belonged to one of the Germans drowned here in the war. The ring filled me with repulsion, like a thing unclean: the round was so much the answering shape to the finger that had fitted it that I shuddered and threw it far into the sea, wiping my hands on the pebbles afterward. A human finger, by itself without a hand, is a disgusting thing. A human finger in the sea.

The pelvis that I found did not have the same effect. It was not long after the ring, and it lay within a yard or two of the place where I had picked it up: but I did not connect it with the Germans drowned— nor, indeed, with mankind at all.

It was by itself, white, dry and smooth, symmetrical and polished to inhumanity by the sea. It was only by a conscious effort that I could feel that this had been a piece of a man—only by running my hand round my own hip to my spine and tracing the same rise and curve that I saw on the bleached and diagrammatic bone in front of me. It had been in some way human, that was true; but is a shell the shellfish? This pelvis was very like a shell. Ordinarily, I suppose, a human bone would raise some emotion, some emotion resembling piety; it would be a distur- bance of decency, a kind of profanation on the shore. But I felt no such emotion as I sat looking at this bone: I connected it with death, but with no particular death. A specimen in an anatomical museum could more easily have been clothed with living flesh than this white basin in the sun.

One's mental processes, and especially the wandering fantasies that pass through one's mind as one walks, are linked by a chain of association so slight that it usually cannot be traced. A bramble will claw out from a thicket: one pushes on automatically, and then in half an hour one will find that one has been dwelling on the Passion for the last mile of the road. That is why I speak of this bone: it provides the obvious and unfortuitous start for the recollections that unfolded in my head as I walked up the cliff path and high along the edge of the sea to the ruined batteries, where the camouflaged concrete still lies among the thistles and the asphodel, with its reinforcing steel rods all standing like the prickles of some prodigious monster of the earth.

When first I came to this village I lodged in a house belonging to an elderly couple named Joseph and Martine Albère. It was a large house, but I was the only lodger: it was a tall, gaunt place, always cold and damp, even in the height of the summer, and from the outside you would have said that it was uninhabited. But it was in good repair, a solid, middle-class house, much richer than the terrace-cottages in which most of the villagers lived: only the presbytery and the doctor's house were better; and from this I judged that the owner would be a man of some standing in the village. I learned, too, that my landlord was the owner and the equipper, the *armateur*, as they say, of three fishing boats: his boats, then, were the direct means of livelihood for nearly forty of the men of the place—a considerable proportion of the working inhabitants.

However, I soon gathered the impression that Albère was not a man of high standing. It is difficult to say how one forms an impression of this nature: it is built up of so many little things—gestures, tones of voice, a look cast backward, and avoiding eye—but in the end it grows into certainty. On the concrete, demonstrable side there was the fact that he never ran for municipal office, that he was president of none of the many co-operative or political associations and that he never appeared at any of the funerals or public feasts.

He seemed to be rich but unconsidered: a contradiction of common experience. At one time I asked myself whether in fact he was rich. Would a rich man take in a lodger? He did not seem to like letting the room I had; but when upon some trifling disagreement (he did not allow his lodgers the front-door key) I suggested that I should find a room elsewhere, he showed so much concern that I could not but suppose he was in earnest. He at once proposed a much lower rent if I would give up my point, and after a little more discussion I agreed to stay. This caused him a disproportionate satisfaction.

Then I learned that he had a fourth boat building on the stocks, which disposed of my idea that he was poor, for at that time a new boat was a very costly undertaking. As for the letting of rooms, that might indicate much or little: after all, in a big house one might let rooms to keep the house lived in, simply to prevent that decay that always comes in an empty place.

But still he remained a curious man to me. He did not like me, and he did not like having me in the house: yet he did not want me to leave it. The rent that I paid was a trifle to him even before he reduced it, yet he forced himself to be amiable to me, provided my room with the meagre best of the furniture in the house, and waited up every night to let me in after my evening walk.

He was a small, dark man, about sixty-five years of age: he was always carelessly dressed, dirty and unshaved, and his air of brutality contrasted strangely with the house he lived in. How did this brutal air appear? He was not obviously vicious: he spoke politely enough to me (though it was patently constrained) and I can only say that it must have been his lurching walk, the set expression on his face and the way he terrorized his wife that made me think, "Albère? A brutish man." His wife I hardly saw: she was utterly effaced, and she moved about the darkened house furtively, with the sound of a person who is trying to make no noise—this was when she was going about her obvious, everyday duties. She was much more like an imprisoned servant than the mistress of the house. Whenever she spoke to me he would appear and, whatever she was saying, she would stop and hurry downstairs. Yet I had the impression, that in spite of this domination they were allies. Sometimes, in the dead quiet of night, I would hear them talking, two whispers, urgent and hurrying, that would answer one to the other in the basement of the house. They slept in the kitchen, and I do not think they ever used any other room.

When I had been there some time I learnt something of their habits. They did not sleep very much, and every few hours one or another of them (or sometimes both) would creep up to the top of the house, along the passage that traversed its length, opening every door softly and softly closing it again, then down the stairs to the middle landing, very silently past my door to the room beyond, and there they would pause, perhaps for as long as half an hour, before coming out, crossing quietly to the other side of the house, back to the stairs, and so down again to the hall and their kitchen.

But I have my nocturnal habits, too: and more than once I have been there before them, fixed silent in a corner just off their trodden beat (for their patrol was so settled by long routine that their feet stepped in exactly the same places night after night), silent and unbreathing, watching their shadows.

However, this was much later: at first I merely noted that they never left the house together, and that when one was gone the other always waited in the hall or near it to open the door.

They appeared to have no relations. At least nobody ever came to visit them; and as far as I could see they were always in the house except when Albère was on the beach, conducting his business with the crews of his boats or when the woman was out for shopping. She never went to church: nor, of course, did he.

I had been there a long time before I found out what was the matter with them. It was a long time, for there were two difficulties in my way: the one was that the people of the village were not unduly open—they may know for generations, but they will not go out of their way to tell strangers—and the other, that I do not talk readily either. I do not go to cafés nor make acquaintance with the loungers on the quay. My form of recreation after my work is to walk. I like to go for long, uninterrupted walks.

Eventually it was a Dutch painter who told me what I had to know. He was a fat, exuberant man—spoke the language perfectly, having been brought up in Rheims—and he almost forced himself upon me. All he wanted was an audience: he loved to talk, and the smallest word of attention would keep him talking on the quay for hours. He was not my idea of a Dutchman. He knew all the fishermen and all the shop-keepers: he was hail-fellow-well-met with all of them before he had been here a month, and he stayed for a long time. It was a local man who told him about Albère: or perhaps "local man" is inexact, for he was a waiter who had married a local girl and settled down here: he did not have the same sense of a closed community. The facts were common knowledge, and I often came across references to them afterwards. Albère was originally a sailor, a seaman employed on the packet boats that run between France and North Africa. On his ship, the *Jules-Bastide*, there were two other men from this village.

One night, about thirty years ago, the *Jules-Bastide* put out from Marseilles in a black gale of wind: there were very few passengers, for it was mid-winter, and most of those few went straight to their cabins. Only a few Algerian deck passengers huddled on the fo'c'sle, and one solitary priest, indifferent to the weather, stayed on the afterdeck. He carried a black valise wherever he went. When he went below for dinner he kept it with him, and afterwards, when he returned to the deck, in spite of the wild seas, he carried it still. He paced up and down in the gale, always carrying this valise. There were three men on duty on this part of the ship at this particular time, Albère and his two fellow-villagers.

In the morning the priest was missing. Nobody knew anything about it: the official inquiry revealed nothing whatever. There was even some mystery about the identity of the priest, as there had been a mistake in the list of passengers, and the person who had arranged for the priest's ticket could not be traced.

Shortly afterwards the three men left the sea. One bought a café in the town ten miles up the coast; the second took an important farm some way inland; and Albère bought the house where I was staying and the three fishing boats.

Within a year the first man and his wife were burned alive in a fire that destroyed their house and café. Two years later the second man, already overcome by misfortune in all his enterprises, lost his only son: the boy was killed riding a motor bicycle that his father had bought him. The man returned to this village by foot, walked to the graveyard, and hanged himself in the daylight.

Ever since, the Albères had been waiting for their turn. They had taken me in as some kind of protection (the lightning, they thought, would not strike a house where a just man lived) but still they did not think that my presence was enough: they were still in dread, and I remembered how one night, early in my stay, I had gone out about three in the morning (I had thought that it might be the beginning of the day of wrath, but when I looked at the stars I found that I was wrong: I had been unable to move Aldebaran) and I had unbolted the door without a sound. When I came back and closed it after me, I heard the stifled gasp that Albère made as he stood silently behind the door, and in the moonlight from the landing window I saw that he had a gun. He muttered something about thieves, but, as I thought at the time, you shoot thieves down. Thieves had their hands cut off in former days; they were also stoned to death. Some thieves were nailed and hung up alive.

Nothing has ever given me a livelier pleasure than my realization that they had taken me in as a protection. And it came to me quite slowly, as I was walking by the river, that once again I had been chosen as the hand of God. After such a long time it had come again: all my anxious waiting was rewarded. The wickedness of my doubt was overlooked— for at times I had wavered—and now once again I was the elected vessel. I had hoped for so long: and to hope for such an election twice in one lifetime seemed presumptuous indeed. But now I was the hand of God again; the wrath of a jealous God Who spoke through the prophet and ploughed the Amalekites into the ground. And without any knowledge I had been set there in my place for a long year past: oh, it was the sweetest realization in the world, this kindness done to me.

Clearly I knew that it was not for the murder I had been sent: no, no; it was for accidie. These wicked people had despaired of all forgiveness: they had hardened their hearts, and for that last wickedness they were to be destroyed in this world as they were already damned in the next.

I waited for the dream that would direct my hand: it had been so clear before. It had been so clear and explicit, and twice repeated, on the last occasion, the sawing of the blasphemer in Newtownards. But it did not come at once this time, and in my lightness of spirits I could not sleep. Between half-past three and four o'clock they were on the upper corridor, together; and the spirit of delight was so strong in me that I could not resist the pleasure of running out with my black coat over my nakedness, barefoot up behind them. They were in the far room, listening; I was fast in the black shadow of the corner, and as they crept by I sprang on them shrieking, "The priest, the valise, the priest, ha ha ha ha ha." I leaped and sprang, but with the shrieking and the laughter I could hardly run as fast as they did. They were some way ahead, the man before the woman, and I am a very big, heavy man; but I cut them off at the head of the stairs and hunted them into the farthest room: I howled and howled in the room. And I let them escape me there while I ran to leap and shriek all through the house. Then I had them on the stairs half down, the man dragging the woman by the arm. They were trying to reach the door, and the laughing nearly choked my breath. From up there I flew, I say I *flew*, and smashed them down on to the far stone floor.

But it was finished then. It was finished almost before it had begun. I had meant a full night's inspired, enormous ecstasy, and I had wasted it in half an hour. Before it had started it was done: they had died without a mark; and I had not set the sign.

NADINE GORDIMER

COUNTRY LOVERS

*T*HE FARM CHILDREN play together when they are small; but once the white children go away to school they soon don't play together any more, even in the holidays. Although most of the black children get some sort of schooling, they drop every year further behind the grades passed by the white children; the childish vocabulary, the child's exploration of the adventurous possibilities of dam, koppies, mealie lands and veld—there comes a time when the white children have surpassed these with the vocabulary of boarding-schools and the possibilities of inter-school sports matches and the kind of adventures seen at the cinema. This usefully coincides with the age of twelve or thirteen; so that by the time early adolescence is reached, the black children are making, along with the bodily changes common to all, an easy transition to adult forms of address, beginning to call their old playmates *missus* and *baasie*—little master.

The trouble was Paulus Eysendyck did not seem to realise that Thebedi was now simply one of the crowd of farm children down at the kraal, recognisable in his sisters' old clothes. The first Christmas holidays after he had gone to boarding-school he brought home for Thebedi a painted box he had made in his woodwork class. He had to give it to her secretly because he had nothing for the other children at the kraal. And she gave him, before he went back to school, a bracelet she had made of thin brass wire and the grey-and-white beans of the castor-oil crop his father cultivated. (When they used to play together, she was the one who had taught Paulus how to make clay oxen for their toy spans.) There was a craze, even in the *platteland* towns like the one where he was at school, for boys to wear elephant-hair and other bracelets beside their watch-straps; his was admired, friends asked him to get similar ones for them. He said the natives made them on his father's farm and he would try.

When he was fifteen, six feet tall, and tramping round at school dances with the girls from the "sister" school in the same town; when he had learnt how to tease and flirt and fondle quite intimately these girls who were the daughters of prosperous farmers like his father; when he had even met one who, at a wedding he had attended with his parents on a nearby farm, had let him do with her in a locked storeroom what people did when they made love—when he was as far from his childhood as all this, he still brought home from a shop in town a red plastic belt and gilt hoop ear-rings for the black girl, Thebedi. She told her father the missus had given these to her as a reward for some work she had done—it was true she sometimes was called to help out in the farmhouse. She told the girls in the kraal that she had a sweetheart nobody knew about, far away, away on another farm, and they giggled, and teased, and admired her. There was a boy in the kraal called Njabulo who said he wished he could have bought her a belt and ear-rings.

When the farmer's son was home for the holidays she wandered far from the kraal and her companions. He went for walks alone. They had not arranged this; it was an urge each followed independently. He knew it was she, from a long way off. She knew that his dog would not bark at her. Down at the dried-up river-bed where five or six years ago the children had caught a leguaan one great day—a creature that combined ideally the size and ferocious aspect of the crocodile with the harmlessness of the lizard—they squatted side by side on the earth bank. He told her traveller's tales: about school, about the punishments at school, particularly, exaggerating both their nature and his indifference to them. He told her about the town of Middleburg, which she had never seen. She had nothing to tell but she prompted with many questions, like any good listener. While he talked he twisted and tugged at the roots of white stinkwood and Cape willow trees that looped out of the eroded earth around them. It had always been a good spot for children's games, down there hidden by the mesh of old, ant-eaten trees held in place by vigorous ones, wild asparagus bushing up between the trunks, and here and there prickly-pear cactus sunken-skinned and bristly, like an old man's face, keeping alive sapless until the next rainy season. She punctured the dry hide of a prickly-pear again and again with a sharp stick while she listened. She laughed a lot at what he told her, sometimes dropping her face on her knees, sharing amusement with the cool shady earth beneath her bare feet. She put on her pair of shoes—white sandals, thickly Blanco-ed against the farm dust—when he was on the farm, but these were taken off and laid aside, at the river-bed.

One summer afternoon when there was water flowing there and it was very hot she waded in as they used to do when they were children, her dress bunched modestly and tucked into the legs of her pants. The schoolgirls he went swimming with at dams or pools on neighbouring farms wore bikinis but the sight of their dazzling bellies and thighs in the sunlight had never made him feel what he felt now, when the girl came up the bank and sat beside him, the drops of water beading off her dark legs the only points of light in the earth-smelling, deep shade.

They were not afraid of one another, they had known one another always; he did with her what he had done that time in the storeroom at the wedding, and this time it was so lovely, so lovely, he was surprised . . . and she was surprised by it, too—he could see in her dark face that was part of the shade, with her big dark eyes, shiny as soft water, watching him attentively: as she had when they used to huddle over their teams of mud oxen, as she had when he told her about detention weekends at school.

They went to the river-bed often through those summer holidays. They met just before the light went, as it does quite quickly, and each returned home with the dark—she to her mother's hut, he to the farmhouse—in time for the evening meal. He did not tell her about school or town any more. She did not ask questions any longer. He told her, each time, when they would meet again. Once or twice it was very early in the morning; the lowing of the cows being driven to graze came to them where they lay, dividing them with unspoken recognition of the sound read in their two pairs of eyes, opening so close to each other.

He was a popular boy at school. He was in the second, then the first soccer team. The head girl of the "sister" school was said to have a crush on him; he didn't particularly like her, but there was a pretty blonde who put up her long hair into a kind of doughnut with a black ribbon round it, whom he took to see films when the schoolboys and girls had a free Saturday afternoon. He had been driving tractors and other farm vehicles since he was ten years old, and as soon as he was eighteen he got a driver's licence and in the holidays, this last year of his school life, he took neighbours' daughters to dances and to the drive-in cinema that had just opened twenty kilometres from the farm. His sisters were married, by then; his parents often left him in charge of the farm over the weekend while they visited the young wives and grandchildren.

When Thebedi saw the farmer and his wife drive away on a Saturday afternoon, the boot of their Mercedes filled with fresh-killed poultry and vegetables from the garden that it was part of her father's work to tend, she knew that she must come not to the river-bed but up to the house. The house was an old one, thick-walled, dark against the heat. The kitchen was its lively thoroughfare, with servants, food supplies, begging cats and dogs, pots boiling over, washing being damped for ironing, and the big deep-freeze the missus had ordered from town, bearing a crocheted mat and a vase of plastic irises. But the dining-room with the bulging-legged heavy table was shut up in its rich, old smell of soup and tomato sauce. The sitting-room curtains were drawn and the T.V. set silent. The door of the parents' bedroom was locked and the empty rooms where the girls had slept had sheets of plastic spread over the beds. It was in one of these that she and the farmer's son stayed together whole nights—almost: she had to get away before the house servants, who knew her, came in at dawn. There was a risk someone would discover her or traces of her presence if he took her to his own bedroom, although she had looked into it many times when she was helping out in the house and knew well, there, the row of silver cups he had won at school.

When she was eighteen and the farmer's son nineteen and working with his father on the farm before entering a veterinary college, the young man Njabulo asked her father for her. Njabulo's parents met with hers and the money he was to pay in place of the cows it is customary to give a prospective bride's parents was settled upon. He had no cows to offer; he was a labourer on the Eysendyck farm, like her father. A bright youngster; old Eysendyck had taught him brick-laying and was using him for odd jobs in construction, around the place. She did not tell the farmer's son that her parents had arranged for her to marry. She did not tell him, either, before he left for his first term at the veterinary college, that she thought she was going to have a baby. Two months after her marriage to Njabulo, she gave birth to a daughter. There was no disgrace in that; among her people it is customary for a young man to make sure, before marriage, that the chosen girl is not barren, and Njabulo had made love to her then. But the infant was very light and did not quickly grow darker as most African babies do. Already at birth there was on its head a quantity of straight, fine floss, like that which carries the seeds of certain weeds in the veld. The unfocused eyes it opened were grey flecked with yellow. Njabulo was the matt, opaque coffee-grounds colour that had always been called black; the colour of Thebedi's legs on which beaded water looked oyster-shell blue, the same colour as Thebedi's face, where the black eyes, with their interested gaze and clear whites, were so dominant.

Njabulo made no complaint. Out of his farm labourer's earnings he bought from the Indian store a cellophane-windowed pack containing a pink plastic bath, six napkins, a card of safety pins, a knitted jacket, cap and bootees, a dress, and a tin of Johnson's Baby Powder, for Thebedi's baby.

When it was two weeks old Paulus Eysendyck arrived home from the veterinary college for the holidays. He drank a glass of fresh, still-warm milk in the childhood familiarity of his mother's kitchen and heard her discussing with the old house-servant where they could get a reliable substitute to help out now that the girl Thebedi had had a baby. For the first time since he was a small boy he came right into the kraal. It was eleven o'clock in the morning. The men were at work in the lands. He looked about him, urgently; the women turned away, each not wanting to be the one approached to point out where Thebedi lived. Thebedi appeared, coming slowly from the hut Njabulo had built in white man's style, with a tin chimney, and a proper window with glass panes set in straight as walls made of unfired bricks would allow. She greeted him with hands brought together and a token movement representing the respectful bob with which she was accustomed to acknowledge she was in the presence of his father or mother. He lowered his head under the doorway of her home and went in. He said, "I want to see. Show me."

She had taken the bundle off her back before she came out into the light to face him. She moved between the iron bedstead made up with Njabulo's checked blankets and the small wooden table where the pink plastic bath stood among food and kitchen pots, and picked up the bundle from the snugly-blanketed grocer's box where it lay. The infant was asleep; she revealed the closed, pale, plump tiny face, with a bubble of spit at the corner of the mouth, the spidery pink hands stirring. She took off the woollen cap and the straight fine hair flew up after it in static electricity, showing gilded strands here and there. He said nothing. She was watching him as she had done when they were little, and the gang of children had trodden down a crop in their games or transgressed in some other way for which he, as the farmer's son, the white one among them, must intercede with the farmer. She disturbed the sleeping face by scratching or tickling gently at a cheek with one finger, and slowly the eyes opened, saw nothing, were still asleep, and then, awake, no longer narrowed, looked out at them, grey with yellowish flecks, his own hazel eyes.

He struggled for a moment with a grimace of tears, anger and self-pity. She could not put out her hand to him. He said, "You haven't been near the house with it?"

She shook her head.

"Never?"

Again she shook her head.

"Don't take it out. Stay inside. Can't you take it away somewhere? You must give it to someone—"

She moved to the door with him.

He said, "I'll see what I will do. I don't know." And then he said: "I feel like killing myself."

Her eyes began to glow, to thicken with tears. For a moment there was the feeling between them that used to come when they were alone down at the river-bed.

He walked out.

Two days later, when his mother and father had left the farm for the day, he appeared again. The women were away on the lands, weeding, as they were employed to do as casual labour in summer; only the very old remained, propped up on the ground outside the huts in the flies and the sun. Thebedi did not ask him in. The child had not been well; it had diarrhoea. He asked where its food was. She said, "The milk comes from me." He went into Njabulo's house, where the child lay; she did not follow but stayed outside the door and watched without seeing an old crone who had lost her mind, talking to herself, talking to the fowls who ignored her.

She thought she heard small grunts from the hut, the kind of infant grunt that indicates a full stomach, a deep sleep. After a time, long or short she did not know, he came out and walked away with plodding stride (his father's gait) out of sight, towards his father's house.

The baby was not fed during the night and although she kept telling Njabulo it was sleeping, he saw for himself in the morning that it was dead. He comforted her with words and caresses. She did not cry but simply sat, staring at the door. Her hands were cold as dead chickens' feet to his touch.

Njabulo buried the little baby where farm workers were buried, in the place in the veld the farmer had given them. Some of the mounds had been left to weather away unmarked, others were covered with stones and a few had fallen wooden crosses. He was going to make a cross but before it was finished the police came and dug up the grave and took away the dead baby: someone—one of the other labourers? their women?—had reported that the baby was almost white, that, strong and healthy, it had died suddenly after a visit by the farmer's son. Pathological tests on the infant corpse showed intestinal damage not always consistent with death by natural causes.

Thebadi went for the first time to the country town where Paulus had been to school, to give evidence at the preparatory examination into the charge of murder brought against him. She cried hysterically in the witness box, saying yes, yes (the gilt hoop ear-rings swung in her ears), she saw the accused pouring liquid into the baby's mouth. She said he had threatened to shoot her if she told anyone.

More than a year went by before, in that same town, the case was brought to trial. She came to court with a new-born baby on her back. She wore gilt hoop ear-rings; she was calm, she said she had not seen what the white man did in the house.

Paulus Eysendyck said he had visited the hut but had not poisoned the child.

The defence did not contest that there had been a love relationship between the accused and the girl, or that intercourse had taken place, but submitted there was no proof that the child was the accused's.

The judge told the accused there was strong suspicion against him but not enough proof that he had committed the crime. The court could not accept the girl's evidence because it was clear she had committed perjury either at this trial or at the preparatory examination. There was the suggestion in the mind of the court that she might be an accomplice in the crime; but, again, insufficient proof.

The judge commended the honourable behavior of the husband (sitting in court in a brown-and-yellow-quartered golf cap bought for Sundays) who had not rejected his wife and had "even provided clothes for the unfortunate infant out of his slender means."

The verdict on the accused was "not guilty."

The young white man refused to accept the con1gratulations of press and public and left the court with his mother's raincoat shielding his face from photographers. His father said to the press, "I will try and carry on as best I can to hold up my head in the district."

Interviewed by the Sunday papers, who spelled her name in a variety of ways, the black girl, speaking in her own language, was quoted beneath her photograph: "It was a thing of our childhood, we don't see each other any more."

WILLIAM FAULKNER

MONK

I WILL HAVE to try to tell about Monk. I mean, actually try—a deliberate attempt to bridge the inconsistencies in his brief and sordid and unoriginal history, to make something out of it, not only with the nebulous tools of supposition and inference and invention, but to employ these nebulous tools upon the nebulous and inexplicable material which he left behind him. Because it is only in literature that the paradoxical and even mutually negativing anecdotes in the history of a human heart can be juxtaposed and annealed by art into verisimilitude and credibility.

He was a moron, perhaps even a cretin; he should never have gone to the penitentiary at all. But at the time of his trial we had a young District Attorney who had his eye on Congress, and Monk had no people and no money and not even a lawyer, because I don't believe he ever understood why he should need a lawyer or even what a lawyer was, and so the Court appointed a lawyer for him, a young man just admitted to the bar, who probably knew but little more about the practical functioning of criminal law than Monk did, who

perhaps pleaded Monk guilty at the direction of the Court or maybe
forgot that he could have entered a plea of mental incompetence,
since Monk did not for one moment deny that he had killed the
deceased. They could not keep him from affirming or even reiterat-
ing it, in fact. He was neither confessing nor boasting. It was almost
as though he were trying to make a speech, to the people who held
him beside the body until the deputy got there, to the deputy and to
the jailor and to the other prisoners—the casual niggers picked up
for gambling or vagrancy or for selling whiskey in alleys—and to the
J.P. who arraigned him and the lawyer appointed by the Court, and
to the Court and the jury. Even an hour after the killing he could not
seem to remember where it had happened; he could not even
remember the man whom he affirmed that he had killed; he named
as his victim (this on suggestion, prompting) several men who were
alive, and even one who was present in the J.P.'s office at the time.
But he never denied that he had killed somebody. It was not insis-
tence; it was just a serene reiteration of the fact in that voice bright,
eager, and sympathetic while he tried to make his speech, trying to
tell them something of which they could make neither head nor tail
and to which they refused to listen. He was not confessing, not trying to establish grounds for lenience in order to escape what he had
done. It was as though he were trying to postulate something, using
this opportunity to bridge the hitherto abyss between himself and
the living world, the world of living men, the ponderable and travailing earth—as witness the curious speech which he made on the
gallows five years later.

But then, he never should have lived, either. He came—emerged:
whether he was born there or not, no one knew—from the pine hill
country in the eastern part of our county: a country which twenty-
five years ago (Monk was about twenty-five) was without roads
almost and where even the sheriff of the county did not go—a coun-

try impenetrable and almost uncultivated and populated by a clan-
nish people who owned allegiance to no one and no thing and whom
outsiders never saw until a few years back when good roads and
automobiles penetrated the green fastnesses where the denizens with
their corrupt Scotch-Irish names intermarried and made whiskey
and shot at all strangers from behind log barns and snake fences. It
was the good roads and the fords which not only brought Monk to
Jefferson but brought the half-rumored information about his origin.
Because the very people among whom he had grown up seemed to
know almost as little about him as we did—a tale of an old woman
who lived like a hermit, even among those fiercely solitary people, in
a log house with a loaded shotgun standing just inside the front door,
and a son who had been too much even for that country and people,
who had murdered and fled, possibly driven out, where gone none
knew for ten years, when one day he returned, with a woman—a
woman with hard, bright, metallic, city hair and a hard, blonde, city
face seen about the place from a distance, crossing the yard or just
standing in the door and looking out upon the green solitude with
an expression of cold and sullen and unseeing inscrutability: and
deadly, too, but as a snake is deadly, in a different way from their
almost conventional ritual of warning and then powder. Then they
were gone. The others did not know when they departed nor why,
any more than they knew when they had arrived nor why. Some said
that one night the old lady, Mrs. Odlethrop, had got the drop on
both of them with the shotgun and drove them out of the house and
out of the country.

But they were gone; and it was months later before the neighbors
discovered that there was a child, an infant, in the house; whether
brought there or born there—again they did not know. This was
Monk; and the further tale how six or seven years later they began to
smell the body and some of them went into the house where old

Mrs. Odlethrop had been dead for a week and found a small creature in a single shift made from bedticking trying to raise the shotgun from its corner beside the door. They could not catch Monk at all. That is, they failed to hold him that first time, and they never had another chance. But he did not go away. They knew that he was somewhere watching them while they prepared the body for burial, and that he was watching from the undergrowth while they buried it. They never saw him again for some time, though they knew that he was about the place, and on the following Sunday they found where he had been digging into the grave, with sticks and with his bare hands. He had a pretty big hole by then, and they filled it up and that night some of them lay in ambush for him, to catch him and give him food. But again they could not hold him, the small furious body (it was naked now) which writhed out of their hands as if it had been greased, and fled with no human sound. After that, certain of the neighbors would carry food to the deserted house and leave it for him. But they never saw him. They just heard, a few months later, that he was living with a childless widower, an old man named Fraser who was a whiskey maker of wide repute. He seems to have lived there for the next ten years, until Fraser himself died. It was probably Fraser who gave him the name which he brought to town with him, since nobody ever knew what old Mrs. Odlethrop had called him, and now the country got to know him or become familiar with him, at least—a youth not tall and already a little pudgy, as though he were thirty-eight instead of eighteen, with the ugly, shrewdly foolish, innocent face whose features rather than expression must have gained him his nickname, who gave to the man who had taken him up and fed him the absolute and unquestioning devotion of a dog and who at eighteen was said to be able to make Fraser's whiskey as well as Fraser could.

That was all that he had ever learned to do—to make and sell whiskey where it was against the law and so had to be done in secret, which further increases the paradox of his public statement when they drew the black cap over his head for killing the warden of the penitentiary five years later. That was all he knew: that, and fidelity to the man who fed him and taught him what to do and how and when; so that after Fraser died and the man, whoever it was, came along in the truck or the car and said, "All right, Monk. Jump in," he got into it exactly as the homeless dog would have, and came to Jefferson. This time it was a filling station two or three miles from town, where he slept on a pallet in the back room, what time the pallet was not already occupied by a customer who had got too drunk to drive his car or walk away, where he even learned to work the gasoline pump and to make correct change, though his job was mainly that of remembering just where the half-pint bottles were buried in the sand ditch five hundred yards away. He was known about town now, in the cheap, bright town clothes for which he had discarded his overalls—the colored shirts which faded with the first washing, the banded straw hats which dissolved at the first shower, the striped shoes which came to pieces on his very feet—pleasant, impervious to affront, talkative when anyone would listen, with that shrewd, foolish face, that face at once cunning and dreamy, pasty even beneath the sunburn, with that curious quality of imperfect connection between sense and ratiocination. The town knew him for seven years until that Saturday midnight and the dead man (he was no loss to anyone, but then as I said, Monk had neither friends, money, nor lawyer) lying on the ground behind the filling station and Monk standing there with the pistol in his hand—there were two others present, who had been with the dead man all evening—trying to tell the ones who held him and then the deputy himself whatever it was that he was trying to say in his eager, sympathetic voice, as though the sound of the shot had broken the barrier behind which he had lived for twenty-five years and that he had now crossed the chasm into the world of living men by means of the dead body at his feet.

Because he had no more conception of death than an animal has—of that of the man at his feet nor of the warden's later nor of his own. The thing at his feet was just something that would never walk or talk or eat again and so was a source neither of good nor harm to anyone; certainly not of good nor use. He had no comprehension of bereavement, irreparable finality. He was sorry for it, but that was all. I don't think he realized that in lying there it had started a train, a current of retribution that someone would have to pay. Because he never denied that he had done it, though denial would have done him no good, since the two companions of the dead man were there to testify against him. But he did not deny it, even though he was never able to tell what happened, what the quarrel was about, nor (as I said), later, even where it had occurred and who it was that he had killed, stating once (as I also said) that his victim was a man standing at the moment in the crowd which had followed him into the J.P.'s office. He just kept on trying to say whatever it was that had been inside him for twenty-five years and that he had only now found the chance (or perhaps the words) to free himself of, just as five years later on the scaffold he was to get it (or something else) said at last, establishing at last that contact with the old, fecund, ponderable, travailing earth which he wanted but had not been able to tell about because only then had they told him how to say what it was that he desired. He tried to tell it to the deputy who arrested him and to the J.P. who arraigned him; he stood in the courtroom with that expression on his face which people have when they are waiting for a chance to speak, and heard the indictment read: . . . *against the peace and dignity of the Sovereign State of Mississippi, that the aforesaid Monk Odlethrop did willfully and maliciously and with premeditated—* and interrupted, in a voice reedy and high, the sound of which in dying away left upon his face the same expression of amazement and surprise which all our faces wore:

"My name ain't Monk; it's Stonewall Jackson Odlethrop."

You see? If it were true, he could not have heard it in almost twenty years since his grandmother (if grandmother she was) had died: and yet he could not even recall the circumstances of one month ago when he had committed a murder. And he could not have invented it. He could not have known who Stonewall Jackson was, to have named himself. He had been to school in the country, for one year. Doubtless old Fraser sent him, but he did not stay. Perhaps even the first-grade work in a country school was too much for him. He told my uncle about it when the matter of his pardon came up. He did not remember just when, nor where the school was, nor why he had quit. But he did remember being there, because he had liked it. All he could remember was how they would all read together out of the books. He did not know what they were reading, because he did not know what the book said; he could not even write his name now. But he said it was fine to hold the book and hear all the voices together and then to feel (he said he could not hear his own voice) his voice too, along with the others, by the way his throat would buzz, he called it. So he could never have heard of Stonewall Jackson. Yet there it was, inherited from the earth, the soil, transmitted to him through a self-pariahed people—something of bitter pride and indomitable undefeat of a soil and the men and women who trod upon it and slept within it.

They gave him life. It was one of the shortest trials ever held in our county, because, as I said, nobody regretted the deceased and nobody except my Uncle Gavin seemed to be concerned about Monk. He had never been on a train before. He got on, handcuffed to the deputy, in a pair of new overalls which someone, perhaps the sovereign state whose peace and dignity he had outraged, had given him, and the still new, still pristine, gaudy-banded, imitation Panama hat (it was still only the first of June, and he had been in jail six weeks) which he had just bought during the week of the fatal Saturday night. He had the window side in the car and he sat there looking at us with his warped, pudgy, foolish face, waving the fingers of the hand, the free arm propped in the window until the train began to move, accelerating slowly, huge and dingy as the metal gangways clashed, drawing him from our sight hermetically sealed and leaving upon us a sense of finality more irrevocable than if we had watched the penitentiary gates themselves close behind him, never to open again in his life, the face looking back at us, craning to see us, wan and small behind the dingy glass, yet wearing that expression questioning yet unalarmed, eager, serene, and grave. Five years later one of the dead man's two companions on that Saturday night, dying of pneumonia and whiskey, confessed that he had fired the shot and thrust the pistol into Monk's hand, telling Monk to look at what he had done.

My Uncle Gavin got the pardon, wrote the petition, got the signatures, went to the capitol and got it signed and executed by the Governor, and took it himself to the penitentiary and told Monk that he was free. And Monk looked at him for a minute until he understood, and cried. He did not want to leave. He was a trusty now; he had transferred to the warden the same doglike devotion which he had given to old Fraser. He had learned to do nothing well, save manufacture and sell whiskey, though after he came to town he had learned to sweep out the filling station. So that's what he did here; his life now must have been something like that time when he had gone to school. He swept and kept the warden's house as a woman would have, and the warden's wife had taught him to knit; crying, he showed my uncle the sweater which he was knitting for the warden's birthday and which would not be finished for weeks yet.

So Uncle Gavin came home. He brought the pardon with him,

though he did not destroy it, because he said it had been recorded and that the main thing now was to look up the law and see if a man could be expelled from the penitentiary as he could from a college. But I think he still hoped that maybe some day Monk would change his mind; I think that's why he kept it. Then Monk did set himself free, without any help. It was not a week after Uncle Gavin had talked to him; I don't think Uncle Gavin had even decided where to put the pardon for safekeeping, when the news came. It was a headline in the Memphis papers next day, but we got the news that night over the telephone: how Monk Oglethrop, apparently leading an abortive jailbreak, had killed the warden with the warden's own pistol, in cold blood. There was no doubt this time; fifty men had seen him do it, and some of the other convicts overpowered him and took the pistol away from him. Yes. Monk, the man who a week ago cried when Uncle Gavin told him that he was free, leading a jailbreak and committing a murder (on the body of the man for whom he was knitting the sweater which he cried for permission to finish) so cold-blooded that his own confederates had turned upon him.

Uncle Gavin went to see him again. He was in solitary confinement now, in the death house. He was still knitting on the sweater. He knitted well, Uncle Gavin said, and the sweater was almost finished. "I ain't got but three days more," Monk said. "So I ain't got no time to waste."

"But why, Monk?" Uncle Gavin said. "Why? Why did you do it?" He said that the needles would not cease nor falter, even while Monk would look at him with that expression serene, sympathetic, and almost exalted. Because he had no conception of death. I don't believe he had ever connected the carrion at his feet behind the filling station that night with the man who had just been walking and talking, or that on the ground in the compound with the man for whom he was knitting the sweater.

"I knowed that making and selling that whiskey wasn't right," he said. "I knowed that wasn't it. Only I . . . " He looked at Uncle Gavin. The serenity was still there, but for the moment something groped behind it: not bafflement nor indecision, just seeking, groping.

"Only what?" Uncle Gavin said. "The whiskey wasn't it? Wasn't what? It what?"

"No. Not it." Monk looked at Uncle Gavin. "I mind that day on the train, and that fellow in the cap would put his head in the door and holler, and I would say 'Is this it? Is this where we get off?' and the deppity would say No. Only if I had been there without that deppity to tell me, and that fellow had come in and hollered, I would have . . ."

"Got off wrong? Is that it? And now you know what is right, where to get off right? Is that it?"

"Yes," Monk said. "Yes. I know right, now."

"What? What is right? What do you know now that they never told you before?"

He told them. He walked up onto the scaffold three days later and stood where they told him to stand and held his head docilely (and without being asked) to one side so they could knot the rope comfortably, his face still serene, still exalted, and wearing that expression of someone waiting his chance to speak, until they stood back. He evidently took that to be his signal, because he said, "I have sinned against God and man and now I have done paid it out with my suffering. And now—" they say he said this part loud, his voice clear and serene. The words must have sounded quite loud to him and irrefutable, and his heart uplifted, because he was talking inside the black cap now: "And now I am going out into the free world, and farm."

You see? It just does not add up. Granted that he did not know that he was about to die, his words still do not make sense. He could have known but little more about farming than about Stonewall Jackson; certainly he had never done any of it. He had seen it, of course, the cotton and the corn in the fields, and men working it.

But he could not have wanted to do it himself before, or he would have, since he could have found chances enough. Yet he turns and murders the man who befriended him and, whether he realized it or not, saved him from comparative hell and upon whom he had transferred his capacity for doglike fidelity and devotion and on whose account a week ago he had refused a pardon: his reason being that he wanted to return into the world and farm land—this, the change, to occur in one week's time and after he had been for five years more completely removed and insulated from the world than any nun. Yes, granted that this could be the logical sequence in that mind which he hardly possessed and granted that it could have been powerful enough to cause him to murder his one friend (Yes, it was the warden's pistol; we heard about that: how the warden kept it in the house and one day it disappeared and to keep word of it getting out the warden had his Negro cook, another trusty and who would have been the logical one to have taken it, severely beaten to force the truth from him. Then Monk himself found the pistol, where the warden now recalled having hidden it himself, and returned it.)—granted all this, how in the world could the impulse have reached him, the desire to farm land have got into him where he now was? That's what I told Uncle Gavin.

"It adds up, all right," Uncle Gavin said. "We just haven't got the right ciphers yet. Neither did they."

"They?"

"Yes. They didn't hang the man who murdered Gambrell. They just crucified the pistol."

"What do you mean?" I said.

"I don't know. Maybe I never shall. Probably never shall. But it adds up, as you put it, somewhere, somehow. It has to. After all, that's too much buffooning even for circumstances, let alone a mere flesh-and-blood imbecile. But probably the ultimate clowning of circumstances will be that we won't know it."

But we did know. Uncle Gavin discovered it by accident, and he never told anyone but me, and I will tell you why.

At that time we had for Governor a man without ancestry and with but little more divulged background than Monk had; a politician, a shrewd man who (some of us feared, Uncle Gavin and others about the state) would go far if he lived. About three years after Monk died he declared, without warning, a kind of jubilee. He set a date for the convening of the Pardon Board at the penitentiary, where he inferred that he would hand out pardons to various convicts in the same way that the English king gives out knighthoods and garters on his birthday. Of course, all the Opposition said that he was frankly auctioning off the pardons, but Uncle Gavin didn't think so. He said that the Governor was shrewder than that, that next year was election year, and that the Governor was not only gaining votes from the kin of the men he would pardon but was laying a trap for the purists and moralists to try to impeach him for corruption and then fail for lack of evidence. But it was known that he had the Pardon Board completely under his thumb, so the only protest the Opposition could make was to form committees to be present at the time, which step the Governor—oh, he was shrewd—courteously applauded, even to the extent of furnishing transportation for them. Uncle Gavin was one of the delegates from our county.

He said that all these unofficial delegates were given copies of the list of those slated for pardon (the ones with enough voting kin to warrant it, I suppose)—the crime, the sentence, the time already served, prison record, etc. It was in the mess hall; he said he and the other delegates were seated on the hard, backless benches against one wall, while the Governor and his Board sat about the table on the raised platform where the guards would sit while the men ate, when the convicts were marched in and halted. Then the Governor called the first name on the list and told the man to come forward to the table. But nobody moved. They just huddled there in their striped overalls, murmuring to one another while the guards began to holler at the man to come out and the Governor looked up from the paper and looked at them with his eyebrows raised. Then somebody said from back in the crowd: "Let Terrel speak for us, Governor. We done 'lected him to do our talking."

Uncle Gavin didn't look up at once. He looked at his list until he found the name: *Terrel, Bill. Manslaughter. Twenty years. Served since May 9, 19—. Applied for pardon January, 19—. Vetoed by Warden C. L. Gambrell. Applied for pardon September, 19—. Vetoed by Warden C. L. Gambrell. Record, Troublemaker.* Then he looked up and watched Terrel walk out of the crowd and approach the table—a tall man, a huge man, with a dark aquiline face like an Indian's, except for the pale yellow eyes and a shock of wild, black hair—who strode up to the table with a curious blend of arrogance and servility and stopped and, without waiting to be told to speak, said in a queer, high singsong filled with that same abject arrogance: "Your Honor, and honorable gentlemen, we have done sinned against God and man but now we have done paid it out with our suffering. And now we want to go out into the free world, and farm."

Uncle Gavin was on the platform almost before Terrel quit speaking, leaning over the Governor's chair, and the Governor turned with his little, shrewd, plump face and his inscrutable, speculative eyes toward Uncle Gavin's urgency and excitement. "Send that man back for a minute," Uncle Gavin said. "I must speak to you in private." For a moment longer the Governor looked at Uncle Gavin, the puppet Board looking at him too, with nothing in their faces at all, Uncle Gavin said.

"Why, certainly, Mr. Stevens," the Governor said. He rose and followed Uncle Gavin back to the wall, beneath the barred window, and the man Terrel still standing before the table with his head jerked suddenly up and utterly motionless and the light from the window in his yellow eyes like two match flames as he stared at Uncle Gavin.

"Governor, that man's a murderer," Uncle Gavin said. The Governor's face did not change at all.

"Manslaughter, Mr. Stevens," he said. "Manslaughter. As private and honorable citizens of the state, and as humble servants of it, surely you and I can accept the word of a Mississippi jury."

"I'm not talking about that," Uncle Gavin said. He said he said it like that, out of his haste, as if Terrel would vanish if he did not hurry; he said that he had a terrible feeling that in a second the little inscrutable, courteous man before him would magic Terrel out of reach of all retribution by means of his cold will and his ambition and his amoral ruthlessness. "I'm talking about Gambrell and that half-wit they hanged. That man there killed them both as surely as if he had fired the pistol and sprung that trap."

Still the Governor's face did not change at all. "That's a curious charge, not to say serious," he said. "Of course you have proof of it."

"No. But I will get it. Let me have ten minutes with him, alone. I will get proof from him. I will make him give it to me."

"Ah," the Governor said. Now he did not look at Uncle Gavin for a whole minute. When he did look up again, his face still had not altered as to expression, yet he had wiped something from it as he might have done physically, with a handkerchief. ("You see, he was paying me a compliment," Uncle Gavin told me. "A compliment to my intelligence. He was telling the absolute truth now. He was paying me the highest compliment in his power.") "What good do you think that would do?" he said.

"You mean . . . " Uncle Gavin said. They looked at one another. "So you would still turn him loose on the citizens of this state, this country, just for a few votes?"

"Why not? If he murders again, there is always this place for him to come back to." Now it was Uncle Gavin who thought for a minute, though he did not look down.

"Suppose I should repeat what you have just said. I have no proof of that, either, but I would be believed. And that would——"

"Lose me votes? Yes. But you see, I have already lost those votes because I have never had them. You see? You force me to do what, for all you know, may be against my own principles too—or do you grant me principles?" Now Uncle Gavin said the Governor looked at him with an expression almost warm, almost pitying—and quite curious. "Mr. Stevens, you are what my grandpap would have called a gentleman. He would have snarled it at you, hating you and your kind; he might very probably have shot your horse from under you someday from behind a fence—for a principle. And you are trying to bring the notions of 1860 into the politics of the nineteen hundreds. And politics in the twentieth century is a sorry thing. In fact, I sometimes think that the whole twentieth century is a sorry thing, smelling to high heaven in somebody's nose. But, no matter." He turned now, back toward the table and the room full of faces watching them. "Take the advice of a well-wisher even if he cannot call you friend, and let this business alone. As I said before, if we let him out and he murders again, as he probably will, he can always come back here."

"And be pardoned again," Uncle Gavin said.

"Probably. Customs do not change that fast, remember."

"But you will let me talk to him in private, won't you?" The Governor paused, looking back, courteous and pleasant.

"Why certainly, Mr. Stevens. It will be a pleasure to oblige you."

They took them to a cell, so that a guard could stand opposite the barred door with a rifle. "Watch yourself," the guard told Uncle Gavin. "He's a bad egg. Don't fool with him."

"I'm not afraid," Uncle Gavin said; he said he wasn't even careful now, though the guard didn't know what he meant. "I have less reason to fear him than Mr. Gambrell even, because Monk Odlethrop is dead now." So they stood looking at one another in the bare cell—Uncle Gavin and the Indian-looking giant with the fierce, yellow eyes.

"So you're the one that crossed me up this time," Terrel said, in that queer, almost whining singsong. We knew about that case, too; it was in the Mississippi reports, besides it had not happened very far away, and Terrel not a farmer, either. Uncle Gavin said that that was it, even before he realized that Terrel had spoken the exact words which Monk had spoken on the gallows and which Terrel could not have heard or even known that Monk had spoken; not the similarity of the words, but the fact that neither Terrel nor Monk had ever farmed anything, anywhere. It was another filling station, near a railroad this time, and a brakeman on a night freight testified to seeing two men rush out of the bushes as the train passed, carrying something which proved later to be a man, and whether dead or alive at the time the brakeman could not tell, and fling it under the train. The filling station belonged to Terrel, and the fight was proved, and Terrel was arrested. He denied the fight at first, then he denied that the deceased had been present, then he said that the deceased had seduced his (Terrel's) daughter and that his (Terrel's) son had killed the man, and he was merely trying to avert suspicion from his son. The daughter and the son both denied this, and the son proved an alibi, and they dragged Terrel, cursing both his children, from the courtroom.

"Wait," Uncle Gavin said. "I'm going to ask you a question first. What did you tell Monk Odlethrop?"

"Nothing!" Terrel said. "I told him nothing!"

"All right," Uncle Gavin said. "That's all I wanted to know." He turned and spoke to the guard beyond the door. "We're through. You can let us out."

"Wait," Terrel said. Uncle Gavin turned. Terrel stood as before, tall and hard and lean in his striped overalls, with his fierce, depthless, yellow eyes, speaking in that half-whining singsong. "What do you want to keep me locked up in here for? What have I ever done to you? You, rich and free, that can go wherever you want, while I have to—" Then he shouted. Uncle Gavin said he shouted without raising his voice at all, that the guard in the corridor could not have heard him: "Nothing, I tell you! I told him nothing!" But this time Uncle Gavin didn't even have time to begin to turn away. He said that Terrel passed him in two steps that made absolutely no sound at all, and looked out into the corridor. Then he turned and looked at Uncle Gavin. "Listen," he said. "If I tell you, will you give me your word not to vote agin me?"

"Yes," Uncle Gavin said. "I won't vote agin you, as you say."

"But how will I know you ain't lying?"

"Ah," Uncle Gavin said. "How will you know, except by trying it?" They looked at one another. Now Terrel looked down; Uncle Gavin said Terrel held one hand in front of him and that he (Uncle Gavin) watched the knuckles whiten slowly as Terrel closed it.

"It looks like I got to," he said. "It just looks like I got to." Then he looked up; he cried now, with no louder sound than when he had shouted before: "But if you do, and if I ever get out of here, then look out! See? Look out."

"Are you threatening me?" Uncle Gavin said. "You, standing there, in those striped overalls, with that wall behind you and this locked door and a man with a rifle in front of you? Do you want me to laugh?"

"I don't want nothing," Terrel said. He whimpered almost now. "I just want justice. That's all." Now he began to shout again, in that repressed voice, watching his clenched, white knuckles too apparently. "I tried twice for it; I tried for justice and freedom twice. But it was him. He was the one; he knowed I knowed it too. I told him I was going to—" He stopped, as sudden as he began; Uncle Gavin said he could hear him breathing, panting.

"That was Gambrell," Uncle Gavin said. "Go on."

"Yes. I told him I was. I told him. Because he laughed at me. He didn't have to do that. He could have voted agin me and let it go at that. He never had to laugh. He said I would stay here as long as he did or could keep me, and that he was here for life. And he was. He stayed here all his life. That's just exactly how long he stayed." But he wasn't laughing, Uncle Gavin said. It wasn't laughing.

"Yes. And so you told Monk——"

"Yes. I told him. I said here we all were, pore ignorant country folks that hadn't had no chance. That God had made to live outdoors in the free world and farm His land for Him; only we were pore and ignorant and didn't know it, and the rich folks wouldn't tell us until it was too late. That we were pore ignorant country folks that never saw a train before, getting on the train and nobody caring to tell us where to get off and farm in the free world like God wanted us to do, and that he was the one that held us back, kept us locked up outen the free world to laugh at us agin the wishes of God. But I never told him to do it. I just said 'And now we can't never get out because we ain't got no pistol. But if somebody had a pistol we would walk out into the free world and farm it, because that's what God aimed for us to do and that's what we want to do. Ain't that what we want to do?' and he said, 'Yes. That's it. That's what it is.' And I said, 'Only we ain't got nara pistol.' And he said, 'I can get a pistol.' And I said, 'Then we will walk in the free world because we have sinned against God but it wasn't our fault because they hadn't told us what it was He aimed for us to do. But now we know what it is because we want to walk in the free world and farm for God!' That's all I told him. I never told him to do nothing. And now go tell them. Let them hang me too. Gambrell is rotted, and that batbrain is rotted, and I just as soon rot under ground as to

WILLIAM FAULKNER

rot in here. Go on and tell them."

"Yes," Uncle Gavin said. "All right. You will go free."

For a minute he said Terrel did not move at all. Then he said, "Free?"

"Yes," Uncle Gavin said. "Free. But remember this. A while ago you threatened me. Now I am going to threaten you. And the curious thing is, I can back mine up. I am going to keep track of you. And the next time anything happens, the next time anybody tries to frame you with a killing and you can't get anybody to say you were not there nor any of your kinsfolks to take the blame for it— You understand?" Terrel had looked up at him when he said Free, but now he looked down again. "Do you?" Uncle Gavin said.

"Yes," Terrel said. "I understand."

"All right," Uncle Gavin said. He turned; he called to the guard. "You can let us out this time," he said. He returned to the mess hall, where the Governor was calling the men up one by one and giving them their papers and where again the Governor paused, the smooth, inscrutable face looking up at Uncle Gavin. He did not wait for Uncle Gavin to speak.

"You were successful, I see," he said.

"Yes. Do you want to hear——"

"My dear sir, no. I must decline. I will put it stronger than that: I must refuse." Again Uncle Gavin said he looked at him with that expression warm, quizzical, almost pitying, yet profoundly watchful and curious. "I really believe that you never have quite given up hope that you can change this business. Have you?"

Now Uncle Gavin said he did not answer for a moment. Then he said, "No. I haven't. So you are going to turn him loose? You really are?" Now he said that the pity, the warmth vanished, that now the face was as he first saw it: smooth, completely inscrutable, completely false.

"My dear Mr. Stevens," the Governor said. "You have already convinced me. But I am merely the moderator of this meeting; here are the votes. But do you think that you can convince these gentlemen?" And Uncle Gavin said he looked around at them, the identical puppet faces of the seven or eight of the Governor's battalions and battalions of factory-made colonels.

"No," Uncle Gavin said. "I can't." So he left then. It was in the middle of the morning, and hot, but he started back to Jefferson at once, riding across the broad, heat-miraged land, between the cotton and the corn of God's long-fecund, remorseless acres, which would outlast any corruption and injustice. He was glad of the heat, he said; glad to be sweating, sweating out of himself the smell and the taste of where he had been.

VIRGINIA WOOLF

THE WIDOW
AND THE PARROT:
A TRUE STORY

SOME FIFTY YEARS AGO Mrs. Gage, an elderly widow, was sitting in her cottage in a village called Spilsby in Yorkshire. Although lame, and rather short sighted she was doing her best to mend a pair of clogs, for she had only a few shillings a week to live on. As she hammered at the clog, the postman opened the door and threw a letter into her lap.

It bore the address "Messrs. Stagg and Beetle, 67 High Street, Lewes, Sussex."

Mrs. Gage opened it and read:

"Dear Madam; We have the honour to inform you of the death of your brother Mr. Joseph Brand."

"Lawk a mussy," said Mrs. Gage. "Old brother Joseph gone at last!"

"He has left you his entire property," the letter went on, "which consists of a dwelling house, stable, cucumber frames, mangles, wheelbarrows &c &c in the village of Rodmell, near Lewes. He also bequeaths to you his entire fortune; Viz: £3,000. (three thousand pounds) sterling."

Mrs. Gage almost fell into the fire with joy. She had not seen her brother for many years, and, as he did not even acknowledge the Christmas card which she sent him every year, she thought that his miserly habits, well known to her from childhood, made him grudge even a penny stamp for a reply. But now it had all turned out to her advantage. With three thousand pounds, to say nothing of house &c &c, she and her family could live in great luxury for ever.

She determined that she must visit Rodmell at once. The village clergyman, the Rev. Samuel Tallboys, lent her two pound ten, to pay her fare, and by next day all preparations for her journey were complete. The most important of these was the care of her dog Shag during her absence, for in spite of her poverty she was devoted to animals, and often went short herself rather than stint her dog of his bone.

She reached Lewes late on Tuesday night. In those days, I must tell you, there was no bridge over the river at Southease, nor had the road to Newhaven yet been made. To reach Rodmell it was necessary to cross the river Ouse by a ford, traces of which still exist, but this could only be attempted at low tide, when the stones on the river bed appeared above the water. Mr. Stacey, the farmer, was going to Rodmell in his cart, and he kindly offered to take Mrs. Gage with him. They reached Rodmell about nine o'clock on a November night and Mr. Stacey obligingly pointed out to Mrs. Gage the house at the end of the village which had been left her by her brother. Mrs. Gage knocked at the door. There was no answer. She knocked again. A very strange high voice shrieked out "Not at home." She was so much taken aback that if she had not heard footsteps coming she would have run away. However the door was opened by an old village woman, by name Mrs. Ford.

"Who was that shrieking out 'Not at home'?" said Mrs. Gage.

"Drat the bird!" said Mrs. Ford very peevishly, pointing to a large grey parrot. "He almost screams my head off. There he sits all day humped up on his perch like a monument screeching 'Not at home' if ever you go near his perch." He was a very handsome bird, as Mrs. Gage could see; but his feathers were sadly neglected. "Perhaps he is unhappy, or he may be hungry," she said. But Mrs. Ford said it was temper merely; he was a seaman's parrot and had learnt his language in the east. However, she added, Mr. Joseph was very fond of him, and called him James; and, it was said, talked to him as if he were a rational being. Mrs. Ford soon left. Mrs. Gage at once went to her box and fetched some sugar which she had with her and offered it to the parrot, saying in a very kind tone that she meant him no harm, but was his old master's sister, come to take possession of the house, and she would see to it that he was as happy as a bird could be. Taking a lantern she next went round the house to see what sort of property her brother had left her. It was a bitter disappointment. There were holes in all the carpets. The bottoms of the chairs had fallen out. Rats ran along the mantelpiece. There were large toadstools growing through the kitchen floor. There was not a stick of furniture worth seven pence halfpenny; and Mrs. Gage only cheered herself by thinking of the three thousand pounds that lay safe and snug in Lewes Bank.

She determined to set off to Lewes next day in order to claim her money from Messrs. Stagg and Beetle the solicitors, and then to return home as quick as she could. Mr. Stacey, who was going to market with some fine Berkshire pigs, again offered to take her with him, and told her some terrible stories of young people who had been drowned through trying to cross the river at high tide, as they drove. A great disappointment was in store for the poor old woman directly she got in to Mr. Stagg's office.

"Pray take a seat, Madam," he said, looking very solemn and grunting slightly. "The fact is," he went on, "that you must prepare to face some very disagreeable news. Since I wrote to you I have gone carefully through Mr. Brand's papers. I regret to say that I can find no trace whatever of the three thousand pounds. Mr. Beetle, my partner, went himself to Rodmell and searched the premises with the utmost care. He found absolutely nothing—no gold, silver, or valuables of any kind—except a fine grey parrot which I advise you to sell for whatever he will fetch. His language, Benjamin Beetle said, is very extreme. But that is neither here nor there. I much fear you have had your journey for nothing. The premises are dilapidated; and of course our expenses are considerable." Here he stopped, and Mrs. Gage well knew that he wished her to go. She was almost crazy with disappointment. Not only had she borrowed two pound ten from the Rev. Samuel Tallboys, but she would return home absolutely empty handed, for the parrot James would have to be sold to pay her fare. It was raining hard, but Mr. Stagg did not press her to stay, and she was too beside herself with sorrow to care what she did. In spite of the rain she started to walk back to Rodmell across the meadows.

Mrs. Gage, as I have already said, was lame in her right leg. At the best of times she walked slowly, and now, what with her disappointment and the mud on the bank her progress was very slow indeed. As she plodded along, the day grew darker and darker, until it was as much as she could do to keep on the raised path by the river side. You might have heard her grumbling as she walked, and complaining of her crafty brother Joseph, who had put her to all this trouble "Express," she said, "to plague me. He was always a cruel little boy when we were children," she went on. "He liked worrying the poor insects, and I've known him trim a hairy caterpillar with a pair of scissors before my very eyes. He was such a miserly varmint too. He used to hide his pocket money in a tree, and if anyone gave him a piece of iced cake for tea, he cut the sugar off and kept it for his supper. I make no doubt he's all aflame at this very moment in Hell fire, but what's the comfort of that to me?" she asked, and indeed it was very little comfort, for she ran slap into a great cow which was coming along the bank, and rolled over and over in the mud.

She picked herself up as best she could and trudged on again. It seemed to her that she had been walking for hours. It was now pitch dark and she could scarcely see her own hand before her nose. Suddenly she bethought her of Farmer Stacey's words about the ford. "Lawk a mussy," she said, "however shall I find my way across? If the tide's in, I shall step into deep water and be swept out to sea in a jiffy! Many's the couple that been drowned here; to say nothing of horses, carts, herds of cattle, and stacks of hay."

Indeed what with the dark and the mud she had got herself into a pretty pickle. She could hardly see the river itself, let alone tell whether she had reached the ford or not. No lights were visible anywhere, for, as you may be aware, there is no cottage or house on that side of the river nearer than Asheham House, lately the seat of Mr. Leonard Woolf. It seemed that there was nothing for it but to sit down and wait for the morning. But at her age, with the rheumatics in her system, she might well die of cold. On the other hand, if she tried to cross the river it was almost certain that she would be drowned. So miserable was her state that she would gladly have changed places with one of the cows in the field. No more wretched old woman could have been found in the whole county of Sussex; standing on the river bank, not knowing whether to sit or to swim, or merely to roll over in the grass, wet though it was, and sleep or freeze to death, as her fate decided.

At that moment a wonderful thing happened. An enormous light shot up into the sky, like a gigantic torch, lighting up every blade of grass, and showing her the ford not twenty yards away. It was low tide, and the crossing would be an easy matter if only the light did not go out before she had got over.

"It must be a Comet or some such wonderful monstrosity," she said as she hobbled across. She could see the village of Rodmell brilliantly up in front of her.

"Bless us and save us!" she cried out. "There's a house on fire— thanks be to the Lord"—for she reckoned that it would take some minutes at least to burn a house down, and in that time she would be well on her way to the village.

"It's an ill wind that blows nobody any good," she said as she hobbled along the Roman road. Sure enough, she could see every inch of the way, and was almost in the village street when for the first time it struck her, "Perhaps it's my own house that's blazing to cinders before my eyes!"

She was perfectly right.

A small boy in his nightgown came capering up to her and cried out, "Come and see old Joseph Brand's house ablaze!"

All the villagers were standing in a ring round the house handing buckets of water which were filled from the well in Monks House kitchen, and throwing them on the flames. But the fire had got a strong hold, and just as Mrs. Gage arrived, the roof fell in.

"Has anybody saved the parrot?" she cried.

"Be thankful you're not inside yourself, Madam," said the Rev. James Hawkesford, the clergyman. "Do not worry for the dumb creatures. I make no doubt the parrot was mercifully suffocated on his perch."

But Mrs. Gage was determined to see for herself. She had to be held back by the village people, who remarked that she must be crazy to hazard her life for a bird.

"Poor old woman," said Mrs. Ford, "she has lost all her property, save one old wooden box, with her night things in it. No doubt we should be crazed in her place too."

So saying, Mrs. Ford took Mrs. Gage by the hand and led her off to her own cottage, where she was to sleep the night. The fire was now extinguished, and everybody went home to bed.

But poor Mrs. Gage could not sleep. She tossed and tumbled thinking of her miserable state, and wondering how she could get back to Yorkshire and pay the Rev. Samuel Tallboys the money she owed him.

At the same time she was even more grieved to think of the fate of the poor parrot James. She had taken a liking to the bird, and thought that he must have an affectionate heart to mourn so deeply for the death of old Joseph Brand, who had never done a kindness to any human creature. It was a terrible death for an innocent bird, she thought; and if only she had been in time, she would have risked her own life to save his.

She was lying in bed thinking these thoughts when a slight tap at the window made her start. The tap was repeated three times over. Mrs. Gage got out of bed as quickly as she could and went to the window. There, to her utmost surprise, sitting on the window ledge was an enormous parrot. The rain had stopped and it was a fine moonlight night. She was greatly alarmed at first, but soon recognised the grey parrot, James, and was overcome with joy at his escape. She opened the window, stroked his head several times, and told him to come in. The parrot replied by gently shaking his head from side to side, then flew to the ground, walked away a few steps, looked back as if to see whether Mrs. Gage were coming, and then returned to the window sill, where she stood in amazement.

"The creature has more meaning in its acts than we humans know," she said to herself. "Very well, James," she said aloud, talking to him as though he were a human being, "I'll take your word for it. Only wait a moment while I make myself decent."

So saying she pinned on a large apron, crept as lightly as possible downstairs, and let herself out without rousing Mrs. Ford.

The parrot James was evidently satisfied. He now hopped briskly a few yards ahead of her in the direction of the burnt house. Mrs. Gage followed as fast as she could. The parrot hopped, as if he knew his way perfectly, round to the back of the house, where the kitchen had originally been. Nothing now remained of it except the brick floor, which was still dripping with the water which had been thrown to put out the fire. Mrs. Gage stood still in amazement while James hopped about, pecking here and there, as if he were testing the bricks with his beak. It was a very uncanny sight, and had not Mrs. Gage been in the habit of living with animals, she would have lost her head, very likely, and hobbled back home. But stranger things yet were to happen. All this time the parrot had not said a word. He suddenly got into a state of the greatest excitement, fluttering his wings, tapping the floor repeatedly with his beak, and crying so shrilly, "Not at home! Not at home!" that Mrs. Gage feared that the whole village would be roused.

"Don't take on so James; you'll hurt yourself," she said soothingly. But he repeated his attack on the bricks more violently than ever.

"Whatever can be the meaning of it?" said Mrs. Gage, looking carefully at the kitchen floor. The moonlight was bright enough to show her a slight unevenness in the laying of the bricks, as if they had been taken up and then relaid not quite flat with the others. She had fastened her apron with a large safety pin, and she now prised this pin between the bricks and found that they were only loosely laid together. Very soon she had taken one up in her hands. No sooner had she done this than the parrot hopped onto the brick next to it, and, tapping it smartly with his beak, cried, "Not at home!" which Mrs. Gage understood to mean that she was to move it. So they went on taking up the bricks in the moonlight until they had laid bare a space some six feet by four and a half. This the parrot seemed to think was enough. But what was to be done next?

Mrs. Gage now rested, and determined to be guided entirely by the behaviour of the parrot James. She was not allowed to rest for long. After scratching about in the sandy foundations for a few minutes, as you may have seen a hen scratch in the sand with her claws, he unearthed what at first looked like a round lump of yellowish stone. His excitement became so intense, that Mrs. Gage now went to his help. To her amazement she found that the whole space which they had uncovered was packed with long rolls of these round yellow stones, so neatly laid together that it was quite a job to move them. But what could they be? And for what purpose had they been hidden here? It was not until they had removed the entire layer on the top, and next a piece of oil cloth which lay beneath them, that a most miraculous sight was displayed before their eyes—there, in row after row, beautifully polished, and shining brightly in the moonlight, were thousands of brand new sovereigns!!!!

This, then, was the miser's hiding place; and he had made sure that no one would detect it by taking two extraordinary precautions. In the first place, as was proved later, he had built a kitchen range over the spot where his treasure lay hid, so that unless the fire had destroyed it, no one could have guessed its existence; and secondly he had coated the top layer of sovereigns with some sticky substance, then rolled them in the earth, so that if by chance one had been laid bare no one would have suspected that it was anything but a pebble such as you may see for yourself any day in the garden. Thus, it was only by the extraordinary coincidence of the fire and the parrot's sagacity that old Joseph's craft was defeated.

Mrs. Gage and the parrot now worked hard and removed the whole hoard—which numbered three thousand pieces, neither more nor less—placing them in her apron which was spread upon the ground. As the three thousandth coin was placed on the top of the pile, the parrot flew up into the air in triumph and alighted very gently on the top of Mrs. Gage's head. It was in this fashion that they returned to Mrs. Ford's cottage, at a very slow pace, for Mrs. Gage was lame, as I have said, and now she was almost weighted to the ground by the contents of her apron. But she reached her room without any one knowing of her visit to the ruined house.

Next day she returned to Yorkshire. Mr. Stacey once more drove her into Lewes and was rather surprised to find how heavy Mrs. Gage's wooden box had become. But he was a quiet sort of man, and merely concluded that the kind people at Rodmell had given her a few odds and ends to console her for the dreadful loss of all her property in the fire. Out of sheer goodness of heart Mr. Stacey offered to buy the parrot off her for half a crown; but Mrs. Gage refused his offer with such indignation, saying that she would not sell the bird for all the wealth of the Indies, that he concluded that the old woman had been crazed by her troubles.

It now only remains to be said that Mrs. Gage got back to Spilsby in safety; took her black box to the Bank; and lived with James the parrot and her dog Shag in great comfort and happiness to a very great age.

It was not till she lay on her death bed that she told the clergyman (the son of the Rev. Samuel Tallboys) the whole story, adding that she was quite sure that the house had been burnt on purpose by the parrot James, who, being aware of her danger on the river bank, flew into the scullery, and upset the oil stove which was keeping some scraps warm for her dinner. By this act, he not only saved her from drowning, but brought to light the three thousand pounds, which could have been found in no other manner. Such, she said, is the reward of kindness to animals.

The clergyman thought that she was wandering in her mind. But it is certain that the very moment the breath was out of her body, James the parrot shrieked out, "Not at home! Not at home!" and fell off his perch stone dead. The dog Shag had died some years previously.

Visitors to Rodmell may still see the ruins of the house, which was burnt down fifty years ago, and it is commonly said that if you visit it in the moonlight you may hear a parrot tapping with his beak upon the brick floor, while others have seen an old woman sitting there in a white apron.

W. S. GILBERT

MY MAIDEN BRIEF

Late on a certain May morning, as I was sitting at a modest breakfast in my "residence chambers," Pump Court, Temple, my attention was claimed by a single knock at an outer door, common to the chambers of Felix Polter and of myself, Horace Penditton, both barristers-at-law of the Inner Temple.

The outer door was not the only article common to Polter and myself. We also shared what Polter (who wrote farces) was pleased to term a "property" clerk, who did nothing at all, and a "practicable" laundress, who did everything. There existed also a communion of interest in tea cups, razors, gridirons, candlesticks, et cetera; for although neither of us was particularly well supplied with the necessaries of domestic life, each happened to possess the very articles in which the other was deficient. So we got on uncommonly well together, each regarding his friend in the light of an indispensable other self. We had both embraced the "higher walk" of the legal profession, and were patiently waiting for the legal profession to return the compliment.

The single knock raised some well-founded fears in both our minds.

"Walker," said I to the property clerk.

"Sir?"

"If that knock is for me, I'm out, you know."

"Of course, sir."

"And Walker," cried Polter.

"Sir?"

"If it's for me, I'm not at home."

Walker opened the door. "Mr. Penditton's a-breakfasting with the Master of the Rolls, if it's him you want; and if it isn't, Mr. Polter's with the Attorney-General."

"You don't say so!" remarked the visitor; "then you'll give this to Mr. Penditton, as soon as the Master can make up his mind to part with him."

And so saying, the visitor handed Walker a lovely parcel of brief paper, tied up neatly with a piece of red tape, and minuted—

Central Criminal Court, May Sessions, 187-. —The Queen on the prosecution of Ann Black v. Elizabeth Briggs. Brief for the prisoner. Mr. Penditton, one guinea. —Poddle and Shaddery, Brompton Square.

So it had come at last! Only an Old Bailey brief, it is true—but still a brief. We scarcely knew what to make of it. Polter looked at me, and I looked at Polter, and then we both looked at the brief.

It turned out to be a charge against Elizabeth Briggs, widow, of picking pockets in an omnibus. It appeared from my "instructions," that my client was an elderly lady, and religious. On the 2nd of April last, she entered an Islington omnibus, with the view of attending a tea and prayer meeting in Bell Court, Islington. A woman in the omnibus missed her purse, and accused Mrs. Briggs, who sat on her right, of having stolen it. The poor soul, speechless with horror at the charge, was dragged out of the omnibus, and as the purse was found in a pocket in the left-hand side of her dress, she was given into custody. As it was stated by the police that she had been "in trouble" before, the magistrate committed her for trial.

"There, my boy, your fortune's made," said Polter.

"But I don't see the use of my taking it," said I. "There's nothing to be said for her."

"Not take it? Won't you though? I'll see about that. You shall take it, and you shall get her off, too! Highly respectable old lady—attentive member of well-known congregation—parson to speak for her character, no doubt. As honest as you are!"

"But the purse was found on her!"

"Well, sir, and what of that? Poor woman left-handed, and pocket in left side of her dress. Robbed woman right-handed, and pocket in right side of her dress. Poor woman sat on right of robbed woman. Robbed woman, replacing her purse, slipped it accidentally into poor woman's pocket. Ample folds of dress, you know—crinolines overlapping, and all that. Splendid defence for you!"

"Well, but she's an old hand, it seems. The police know her."

"Police always do. 'Always know everybody'—police maxim. Swear anything, they will."

Polter really seemed so sanguine about it that I began to look at the case hopefully, and to think that something *might* be done with it. He talked to me with such effect that he not only convinced me that there was a good deal to be said in Mrs. Briggs's favour, but I actually began to look upon her as an innocent victim of circumstantial evidence, and determined that no effort should be wanting on my part to procure her release from a degrading but unmerited confinement.

Of the firm of Poddle and Shaddery I knew nothing whatever, and how they came to entrust Mrs. Briggs's case to me I could form no conception. As we (for Polter took so deep a personal interest in the success of Mrs. Briggs's case that he completely identified himself, in my mind, with her fallen fortunes) resolved to go to work in a thoroughly businesslike manner, we determined to commence operations by searching for the firm of Poddle and Shaddery in the *Law List*.

To our dismay the *Law List* of that year had no record of Poddle, neither did Shaddery find a place in its pages. This was serious, and Polter did not improve matters by suddenly recollecting that he once heard an old Q.C. say that, as a rule, the further west of Temple Bar, the shadier the attorney; so that assuming Polter's friend to have been correct on this point, a firm from Brompton Square whose name did not appear in Mr. Dalbiac's *Law List* was a legitimate object of suspicion.

But Polter, who took a hopeful view of anything which he thought might lead to good farce "situations," and who probably imagined that my first appearance on any stage as counsel for the defence was likely to be rich in suggestions, remarked that they might possibly have been certificated since the publishing of the last *Law List;* and as for the *dictum* about Temple Bar, why, the case of Poddle and Shaddery might be one of those very exceptions whose existence is necessary to the proof of every general rule. So Polter and I determined to treat the firm in a spirit of charity, and accept their brief.

As the May sessions did not commence until the 8th, I had four clear days in which to study my brief and prepare my defence. Besides, there was a murder case, and a desperate burglary or two, which would probably be taken first, so that it was unlikely that the case of the poor soul whose cause I had espoused would be tried before the 12th. So I had plenty of time to master what Polter and I agreed was one of the most painful cases of circumstantial evidence ever submitted to a British jury; and I really believe that by the first day of the May sessions I was intimately acquainted with the details of every case of pocket-picking reported in *Cox's Criminal Cases* and *Buckler's Shorthand Reports*.

On the night of the 11th I asked Bodger of Brasenose, Norton of Gray's Inn, Cadbury of the Lancers, and three or four other men, college chums principally, to drop in at Pump Court and hear a rehearsal of my speech for the defence, in the forthcoming *cause célèbre* of the Queen on the prosecution of Ann Black v. Elizabeth Briggs.

At nine o'clock they began to appear, and by ten all were assembled. Pipes and strong waters were produced, and Norton of Gray's was forthwith raised to the Bench by the style and dignity of Sir Joseph Norton, one of the Barons of Her Majesty's Court of Exchequer; Cadbury, Bodger, and another represented the jury; Wilkinson of Lincoln's Inn was counsel for the prosecution, Polter was clerk of arraigns, and Walker, my clerk, was the prosecutrix.

Everything went satisfactorily; Wilkinson broke down in his speech for the prosecution; his witness prevaricated and contradicted himself in a preposterous manner; and my speech for the defence was voted to be one of the most masterly specimens of forensic ingenuity that had ever come before the notice of the Court; and the consequence was that the prisoner (inadequately represented by a statuette of the Greek slave) was discharged, and Norton, who would have looked more like a Baron of the Exchequer if he had looked less like a tipsy churchwarden, remarked that she left the Court without a stain on her character.

The Court then adjourned for refreshment, and the conversation took a general turn, after canvassing the respective merits of "May it please your ludship," and "May it please you, my lud," as an introduction to a counsel's speech—a discussion which ended in favour of the latter form, as being a trifle more independent in its character. I remember proposing that the health of Elizabeth Briggs should be drunk in a solemn and respectful bumper; and as the evening wore on, I am afraid I became exceedingly indignant with Cadbury, because he had taken the liberty of holding up to public ridicule an imaginary (and highly undignified) *carte de visite* of my unfortunate client.

The 12th of May, big with the fate of Penditton and of Briggs, dawned in the usual manner. At ten o'clock Polter and I drove up in wigs and gowns to the Old Bailey. Impressed with a sense of the propriety of the occasion, I had taken remarkable pains with my toilet. I had the previous morning shaved off a flourishing moustache, and sent Walker out for half a dozen serious collars, as substitutes for the unprofessional "lay-downs" I usually wore. I was dressed in a correct evening suit and wore a pair of thin gold spectacles; and Polter remarked that I looked "the sucking Bencher to the life." Polter, whose interest in the accuracy of my "get-up" was almost fatherly, had totally neglected his own: he made his appearance in the raggedest of beards and moustaches under his wig, and the sloppiest of cheap drab lounging-coats under his gown.

I modestly took my place in the back row of the seats allotted to the Bar; Polter took his in the very front in order to have an opportunity, at the close of the case, of telling the leading counsel, in the hearing of the attorneys, the name and address of the young and rising barrister who had just electrified the Court. In various parts of the building I detected Cadbury, Wilkinson, and others, who had represented judge, jury, and counsel on the previous evening. They had been instructed by Polter (who had had some experience in "packing" a house) to distribute themselves about the Court and at the termination of the speech for the defence, to give vent to their feelings in that applause which is always so quickly suppressed by the officers of a court of justice.

I was rather annoyed at this, as I did not consider it altogether legitimate; and my annoyance was immensely increased when I found that my three elderly maiden aunts, to whom I had been foolish enough to confide, were seated in state in that portion of the room allotted to friends of the Bench and Bar, and busied themselves by informing everybody within whisper-shot that I was to defend Elizabeth Briggs, and that this was my first brief.

At length the clerk called the case of Briggs, and with my heart in my mouth I began to try to recollect the opening words of my speech for the defence; but I was interrupted in that hopeless task by the appearance of Elizabeth in the dock.

She was a pale, elderly widow, rather buxom, and neatly dressed in slightly rusty mourning. Her hair was arranged in two sausage curls, one on each side of her head, and looped in two festoons over the forehead. She appeared to feel her position acutely, and although she did not weep, her red eyes showed evident traces of recent tears. She grasped the edge of the dock, and rocked backwards and forwards, accompanying the motion with a low moaning sound that was extremely touching. Polter looked back at me with an expression which plainly said, "If ever an innocent woman appeared in that dock, that woman is Elizabeth Briggs!"

The clerk now proceeded to charge the jury. "Gentlemen of the jury, the prisoner at the bar, Elizabeth Briggs, is indicted for that she did, on the second of April last, steal from the person of Ann Black a purse containing ten shillings and fourpence, the money of the said Ann Black. There is another count to the indictment, charging her with having received the same, knowing it to have been stolen. To both of these counts the prisoner has pleaded 'Not Guilty,' and it is your charge to try whether she is guilty or not guilty." Then to the Bar, "Who appears in this case?"

Nobody replying on behalf of the Crown, I rose and remarked that I appeared for the defence.

A counsel here said that he believed that the brief for the prosecution was entrusted to Mr. Porter, but that that gentleman was engaged at the Middlesex Sessions in a case which was likely to occupy several hours, and that he (Mr. Porter) did not expect that Briggs's case would come on that day.

A consultation then took place between the judge and the clerk. At its termination, the latter functionary said, "Who is the junior counsel present?"

To my horror, up jumped Polter, and said, "I think it's very likely that I am the junior counsel in court. My name is Polter, and I was only called last term!"

A titter ran through the crowd, but Polter, whose least fault was bashfulness, only smiled benignly at those around him.

Another whispering between judge and clerk. At its conclusion the clerk handed a bundle of papers to Polter, saying, at the same time:

"Mr. Polter, his lordship wishes you to conduct the prosecution."

"Certainly," said Polter; and he opened the papers, glanced at them, and rose to address the court.

He began by requesting that the jury would take into consideration the fact that he had only that moment been placed in possession of the brief for the prosecution of the prisoner, who appeared from what he had gathered from a glance at his instructions to have been guilty of as heartless a robbery as ever disgraced humanity. He would endeavour to do his duty, but he feared that, at so short a notice, he should scarcely be able to do justice to the brief with which he had been most unexpectedly entrusted.

He then went on to state the case in a masterly manner, appearing to gather the facts (with which, of course, he was perfectly intimate) from the papers in his hand. He commented on the growing frequency of omnibus robberies, and then went on to say:

"Gentlemen, I am at no loss to anticipate the defence on which my learned friend will base his hope of inducing you to acquit that wretched woman. I don't know whether it has ever been your misfortune to try criminal cases before, but if it has, you will be able to anticipate his defence as certainly as I can. He will probably tell you, because the purse was found in the left-hand pocket of that miserable woman's dress, that she is left-handed, and on that account wears her pocket on the left side; and he will then, if I am not very much mistaken, ask the prosecutrix if she is not right-handed; and lastly, he will ask you to believe that the prosecutrix, sitting on the prisoner's left, slipped the purse accidentally into the prisoner's pocket.

"But gentlemen, I need not remind you that the facts of these omnibus robberies are always identical. The prisoner always *is* left-handed, the prosecutrix always *is* right-handed, and the prosecutrix always *does* slip the purse accidentally into the prisoner's pocket instead of her own. My lord will tell you that this is so, and you will know how much faith to place upon such a defence, should my friend think proper to set it up."

He ended by entreating the jury to give the case their attentive consideration, and stated that he relied confidently on an immediate verdict of "Guilty." He then sat down, saying to the usher, "Call Ann Black."

Ann Black, who was in court, shuffled up into the witness box, and was duly sworn. Polter then drew out her evidence, bit by bit, helping her with leading questions of the most flagrant description. I knew that I ought not to allow this, but I was too horrified at the turn matters had taken to interfere. At the conclusion of the examination Polter sat down triumphantly, and I rose to cross-examine.

"You are right-handed, Mrs. Black?" *(Laughter.)*

"Oh, yes, sir!"

"Very good. I've nothing else to ask you."

So Mrs. Black stood down, and the omnibus conductor took her place. His evidence was not material, and I declined to cross-examine. The policeman who had charge of the case followed the conductor, and his evidence was to the effect that the purse was found in Elizabeth Briggs's pocket.

I felt that this witness ought to be cross-examined, but not having anything ready, I allowed him to stand down. A question, I am sorry to say, then occurred to me, and I requested his lordship to allow the witness to be recalled.

"You say you found the purse in her pocket, my man?"

"Yes, sir."

"Did you find anything else?"

"Yes, sir."

"What?"

"Two other purses, a watch, three handkerchiefs, two silver pencil cases, and a hymn book." *(Roars of laughter.)*

"You may stand down."

"This is the case, my lord," said Polter.

It was now my turn to address the court. What could I say? I believe I observed that, undeterred by my learned friend's opening speech, I did intend to set up the defence he had anticipated. I set it up, but I don't think it did much good. The jury, who were perfectly well aware that this was Polter's first case, had no idea but that I was an old hand at it; and no doubt thought me an uncommonly clumsy one. They had made every allowance for Polter, who needed nothing of the kind, and they made none at all for me, who needed all they had at their disposal.

I soon relinquished my original line of defence, and endeavoured to influence the jury by vehement assertions of my personal conviction of the prisoner's innocence. I warmed with my subject (for Polter had not anticipated me here), and I believe I grew really eloquent. I think I staked my professional reputation on her innocence, and I sat down expressing my confidence in a verdict that would restore the unfortunate lady to a circle of private friends, several of whom were waiting in the court to testify to her excellent character.

"Call witnesses to Mrs. Briggs's character," said I.

"Witnesses to the character of Briggs!" shouted the crier.

The cry was repeated three or four times outside the court; but there was no response.

"No witnesses to Briggs's character here, my lord!" said the crier.

Of course I knew this very well; but it sounded respectable to expect them.

"Dear, dear," said I, "this is really most unfortunate. They must have mistaken the day."

"Shouldn't wonder," observed Polter, rather drily.

I was not altogether sorry that I had no character witnesses, as I am afraid that they would scarcely have borne the test of Polter's cross-examination.

Mr. Baron Bounderby then proceeded to sum up, grossly against the prisoner, as I thought at the time, but, as I have since had reason to believe, most impartially. He went carefully over the evidence and told the jury that if they believed the witnesses for the prosecution, they should find the prisoner guilty, and if they did not—why, they should acquit her.

The jury were then directed by the crier to "consider their verdict," which they couldn't possibly have done, for they immediately returned the verdict of "Guilty." The prisoner not having anything to say in arrest of judgement, the learned judge proceeded to pronounce sentence—inquiring, first of all, whether anything was known about her?

A policeman stepped forward and stated that she had twice been convicted of felony in this court, and once at the Middlesex Sessions.

Mr. Baron Bounderby, addressing the prisoner, told her that she had been most properly convicted, on the clearest possible evidence; that she was an accomplished and dangerous thief; and that the sentence of the court was that she be imprisoned and kept at hard labour for the space of eighteen calendar months.

No sooner had the learned judge pronounced this sentence than the poor soul stooped down and, taking off a heavy boot, flung it at my head, as a reward for my eloquence on her behalf; accompanying the assault with a torrent of invective against my abilities as a counsel, and my line of defence. The language in which her oration was couched was perfectly shocking. The boot missed me, but hit a reporter on the head, and to this fact I am disposed to attribute the unfavourable light in which my speech for the defence was placed in a leading daily paper next morning.

I hurried out of court as quickly as I could and, hailing a hansom, I dashed back to chambers, pitched my wig at a bust of Lord Brougham, bowled over Mrs. Briggs's prototype with my gown, packed up, and started that evening for the west coast of Cornwall. Polter, on the other hand, remained in town, and got plenty of business in that and the ensuing session, and afterwards on circuit. He is now a flourishing Old Bailey counsel, doing very well, while I am as briefless as ever.

AN ACT OF
VENGEANCE

O N THAT GLORIOUS noonday when Dulce Rosa Orellano was crowned with the jasmines of Carnival Queen, the mothers of the other candidates murmured that it was unfair for her to win just because she was the only daughter of the most powerful man in the entire province, Senator Anselmo Orellano. They admitted that the girl was charming and that she played the piano and danced like no other, but there were other competitors for the prize who were far more beautiful. They saw her standing on the platform in her organdy dress and with her crown of flowers, and as she waved at the crowd they cursed her through their clenched teeth. For that reason, some of them were overjoyed some months later when misfortune entered the Orellanos' house sowing such a crop of death that thirty years were required to reap it.

On the night of the queen's election, a dance was held in the Santa Teresa Town Hall, and young men from the remotest villages came to meet Dulce Rosa. She was so happy and danced with such grace that many failed to perceive that she was not the most beautiful, and when they returned to where they had come from they all declared that they had never before seen a face like hers. Thus she acquired an unmerited reputation for beauty and later testimony was never able to prove to the contrary. The exaggerated descriptions of her translucent skin and her diaphanous eyes were passed from mouth to mouth, and each individual added something to them from his own imagination. Poets from distant cities composed sonnets to a hypothetical maiden whose name was Dulce Rosa.

Rumors of the beauty who was flourishing in Senator Orellanos' house also reached the ears of Tadeo Céspedes, who never dreamed he would be able to meet her, since during all his twenty-five years he had neither had time to learn poetry nor to look at women. He was concerned only with the Civil War. Ever since he had begun to shave he had had a weapon in his hands, and he had lived for a long time amidst the sound of exploding gunpowder. He had forgotten his mother's kisses and even the songs of mass. He did not always have reason to go into battle, because during several periods of truce there were no adversaries within reach of his guerrilla band. But even in times of forced peace he lived like a corsair. He was a man habituated to violence. He crossed the country in every direction, fighting visible enemies when he found them, and battling shadows when he was forced to invent them. He would have continued in the same way if his party had not won the presidential election. Overnight he went from a clandestine existence to wielding power, and all pretext for continuing the rebellion had ended for him.

Tadeo Céspedes's final mission was the punitive expedition against Santa Teresa. With a hundred and twenty men he entered the town under cover of darkness to teach everyone a lesson and eliminate the leaders of the opposition. They shot out the windows in the public buildings, destroyed the church door, and rode their horses right up to the main altar, crushing Father Clemente when he tried to block their way. They burned the trees that the Ladies' Club had planted in the square; amidst all the clamor of battle, they continued at a gallop toward Senator Orellano's house which rose up proudly on top of the hill.

After having locked his daughter in the room at the farthest corner of the patio and turned the dogs loose, the Senator waited for Tadeo Céspedes at the head of a dozen loyal servants. At that moment he had regretted, as he had so many other times in his life, not having had male descendants who could help him to take up arms and defend the honor of his house. He felt very old, but he did not have time to think about it, because he had spied on the hillside the terrible flash of a hundred and twenty torches that terrorized the night as they advanced. He distributed the last of the ammunition in silence. Everything had been said, and each of them knew that before morning he would be required to die like a man at his battle station.

"The last man alive will take the key to the room where my daughter is hidden and carry out his duty," said the Senator as he heard the first shots.

All the men had been present when Dulce Rosa was born and had held her on their knees when she was barely able to walk; they had told her ghost stories on winter afternoons; they had listened to her play the piano and they had applauded in tears on the day of her coronation as Carnival Queen. Her father could die in peace, because the girl would never fall alive into the hands of Tadeo Céspedes. The one thing that never crossed Senator Orellano's mind was that, in spite of his recklessness in battle, he would be the last to die. He saw his friends fall one by one and finally realized that it was useless to continue resisting. He had a bullet in his stomach and his vision was blurred. He was barely able to distinguish the shadows that were climbing the high walls surrounding his property, but he still had the presence of mind to drag himself to the third patio. The dogs recognized his scent despite the sweat, blood, and sadness that covered him and moved aside to let him pass. He inserted the key in the lock and through the mist that covered his eyes saw Dulce Rosa waiting for him. The girl was wearing the same organdy dress that she had worn for the Carnival and had adorned her hair with the flowers from the crown.

"It's time, my child," he said, cocking his revolver as a puddle of blood spread about his feet.

"Don't kill me, father," she replied in a firm voice. "Let me live so that I can avenge us both."

Senator Anselmo Orellano looked into his daughter's fifteen-year-old face and imagined what Tadeo Céspedes would do to her, but he saw great strength in Dulce Rosa's transparent eyes, and he knew that she would survive to punish his executioner. The girl sat down on the bed and he took his place at her side, pointing his revolver at the door.

When the uproar from the dying dogs had faded, the bar across the door was shattered, the bolt flew off, and the first group of men burst into the room. The Senator managed to fire six shots before losing consciousness. Tadeo Céspedes thought he was dreaming when he saw an angel crowned in jasmines holding a dying old man in her arms. But he did not possess sufficient pity to look for a second time, since he was drunk with violence and enervated by hours of combat.

"The woman is mine," he said, before any of his men could put his hands on her.

A leaden Friday dawned, tinged with the glare from the fire. The silence was thick upon the hill. The final moans had faded when Dulce Rosa was able to stand and walk to the fountain in the garden. The previous day it had been surrounded by magnolias, and now it was nothing but a tumultuous pool amidst the debris. After having removed the few strips of organdy that were all that remained of her dress, she stood nude before what had been the fountain. She submerged herself in the cold water. The sun rose behind the birches, and the girl watched the water turn red as she washed away the blood that flowed from between her legs along with that of her father which had dried in her hair. Once she was clean, calm, and without tears, she returned to the ruined house to look for something to cover herself. Picking up a linen sheet, she went outside to bring back the Senator's remains. They had tied him behind a horse and dragged him up and down the hillside until little remained but a pitiable mound of rags. But guided by love, the daughter was able to recognize him without hesitation. She wrapped him in the sheet and sat down by his side to watch the dawn grow into day. That is how her neighbors from Santa Teresa found her when they finally dared to climb up to the Orellano villa. They helped Dulce Rosa to bury her dead and to extinguish the vestiges of the fire. They begged her to go and live with her godmother in another town where no one knew her story, but she refused. Then they formed crews to rebuild the house and gave her six ferocious dogs to protect her.

From the moment they had carried her father away, still alive, and Tadeo Céspedes had closed the door behind them and unbuckled his leather belt, Dulce Rosa lived for revenge. In the thirty years that followed, that thought kept her awake at night and filled her days, but it did not completely obliterate her laughter nor dry up her good disposition. Her reputation for beauty increased as troubadors went everywhere proclaiming her imaginary enchantments until she became a living legend. She arose every morning at four o'clock to oversee the farm and household chores, roam her property on horseback, buy and sell, haggling like a Syrian, breed livestock, and cultivate the magnolias and jasmines in her garden. In the afternoon she would remove her trousers, her boots, and her weapons, and put on the lovely dresses which had come from the capital in aromatic trunks. At nightfall visitors would begin to arrive and would find her playing the piano while the servants prepared trays of sweets and glasses of orgeat. Many people asked themselves how it was possible that the girl had not ended up in a straitjacket in a sanitarium or as a novitiate with the Carmelite nuns. Nevertheless, since there were frequent parties at the Orellano villa, with the passage of time people stopped talking about the tragedy and erased the murdered Senator from their memories. Some gentlemen who possessed both fame and fortune managed to overcome the repugnance they felt because of the rape and, attracted by Dulce Rosa's beauty and sensitivity, proposed marriage. She rejected them all, for her only mission on Earth was vengeance.

Tadeo Céspedes was also unable to get that night out of his mind. The hangover from all the killing and the euphoria from the rape left him as he was on his way to the capital a few hours later to report the results of his punitive expedition. It was then that he remembered the child in a party dress and crowned with jasmines, who endured him in silence in that dark room where the air was impregnated with the odor of gunpowder. He saw her once again in the final scene, lying on the floor, barely covered by her reddened rags, sunk in the compassionate embrace of unconsciousness, and he continued to see her that way every night of his life just as he fell asleep. Peace, the exercise of government, and the use of power turned him into a settled, hard-working man. With the passage of time, memories of the Civil War faded away and the people began to call him Don Tadeo. He bought a ranch on the other side of the mountains, devoted himself to administering justice, and ended up as mayor. If it had not been for Dulce Rosa Orellano's tireless phantom, perhaps he might have attained a certain degree of happiness. But in all the women who crossed his path, he saw the face of the Carnival Queen. And even worse, the songs by popular poets, often containing verses that mentioned her name, would not permit him to expel her from his heart. The young woman's image grew within him, occupying him completely, until one day he could stand it no longer. He was at the head of a long banquet table celebrating his fifty-fifth birthday, surrounded by friends and colleagues, when he thought he saw in the tablecloth a child lying naked among jasmine blossoms, and understood that the nightmare would not leave him in peace even after his death. He struck the table with his fist, causing the dishes to shake, and asked for his hat and cane.

"Where are you going, Don Tadeo?" asked the Prefect.

"To repair some ancient damage," he said as he left without taking leave of anyone.

It was not necessary for him to search for her, because he always knew that she would be found in the same house where her misfortune had occurred, and it was in that direction that he pointed his car. By then good highways had been built and distances seemed shorter. The scenery had changed during the decades that had passed, but as he rounded the last curve by the hill, the villa appeared just as he remembered it before his troops had taken it in the attack. There were the solid walls made of river rock that he had destroyed with dynamite charges, there the ancient wooden coffers he had set afire, there the trees where he had hung the bodies of the Senator's men, there the patio where he had slaughtered the dogs. He stopped his vehicle a hundred meters from the door and dared not continue because he felt his heart exploding inside his chest. He was going to turn around and go back to where he came from, when a figure surrounded by the halo of her skirt appeared in the yard. He closed his eyes, hoping with all his might that she would not recognize him. In the soft twilight, he perceived that Dulce Rosa Orellano was advancing toward him, floating along the garden paths. He noted her hair, her candid face, the harmony of her gestures, the swirl of her dress, and he thought he was suspended in a dream that had lasted for thirty years.

"You've finally come, Tadeo Céspedes," she said as she looked at him, not allowing herself to be deceived by his mayor's suit or his gentlemanly gray hair, because he still had the same pirate's hands.

"You've pursued me endlessly. In my whole life I've never been able to love anyone but you," he murmured, his voice choked with shame.

Dulce Rosa gave a satisfied sigh. At last her time had come. But she looked into his eyes and failed to discover a single trace of the executioner, only fresh tears. She searched her heart for the hatred she had cultivated throughout those thirty years, but she was incapable of finding it. She evoked the instant that she had asked her father to make his sacrifice and let her live so that she could carry out her duty; she relived the embrace of the man whom she had cursed so many times, and remembered the early morning when she had wrapped some tragic remains in a linen sheet. She went over her perfect plan of vengeance, but did not feel the expected happiness; instead she felt its opposite, a profound melancholy. Tadeo Céspedes delicately took her hand and kissed the palm, wetting it with his tears. Then she understood with horror that by thinking about him every moment, and savoring his punishment in advance, her feelings had become reversed and she had fallen in love with him.

During the following days both of them opened the floodgates of repressed love and, for the first time since their cruel fate was decided, opened themselves to receive the other's proximity. They strolled through the gardens talking about themselves and omitting nothing, even that fatal night which had twisted the direction of their lives. As evening fell, she played the piano and he smoked, listening to her until he felt his bones go soft and the happiness envelop him like a blanket and obliterate the nightmares of the past. After dinner he went to Santa Teresa where no one still remembered the ancient tale of horror. He took a room in the best hotel and from there organized his wedding. He wanted a party with fanfare, extravagance, and noise, one in which the entire town would participate. He discovered love at an age when other men have already lost their illusions, and that returned to him his youthful vigor. He wanted to surround Dulce Rosa with affection and beauty, to give her everything that money could buy, to see if he could compensate in his later years for the evil he had done as a young man. At times panic possessed him. He searched her face for the smallest sign of rancor, but he saw only the light of shared love and that gave him back his confidence. Thus a month of happiness passed.

Two days before their wedding, when they were already setting up the tables for the party in the garden, slaughtering the birds and pigs for the feast, and cutting the flowers to decorate the house, Dulce Rosa Orellano tried on her wedding dress. She saw herself reflected in the mirror, just as she had on the day of her coronation as Carnival Queen, and realized that she could no longer continue to deceive her own heart. She knew that she could not carry out the vengeance she had planned because she loved the killer, but she was also unable to quiet the Senator's ghost. She dismissed the seamstress, took the scissors, and went to the room on the third patio which had remained unoccupied during all that time.

Tadeo Céspedes searched for her everywhere, calling out to her desperately. The barking of the dogs led him to the other side of the house. With the help of the gardeners he broke down the barred door and entered the room where thirty years before he had seen an angel crowned with jasmines. He found Dulce Rosa Orellano just as he had seen her in his dreams every night of his existence, lying motionless in the same bloody organdy dress. He realized that in order to pay for his guilt he would have to live until he was ninety with the memory of the only woman his soul could ever love

—Translated by E. D. Carter, Jr.

A. A. MILNE

IN VINO VERITAS

I am in a terrible predicament, as you will see directly. I don't know what to do. . . .

"One of the maxims which I have found most helpful in my career," the Superintendent was saying, "apart, of course, from employing a good press agent, has been the simple one that appearances are not always deceptive. A crime may be committed exactly as it seems to have been committed, and exactly as it was intended to be committed." He helped himself and passed the bottle.

"I don't think I follow you," I said, hoping thus to lead him on.

I am a writer of detective stories. If you have never heard of me, it can only be because you don't read detective stories. I wrote *Murder on the Back Stairs* and *The Mystery of the Twisted Eglantine*, to mention only two of my successes. It was this fact, I think, which first interested Superintendent Frederick Mortimer in me, and, of course, me in him. He is a big fellow with the face of a Roman Emperor; I am rather the small neat type. We gradually became friends, and so got into the habit of dining together once a month, each in turn being host in his own flat. He liked talking about his cases and naturally I liked listening. I may say now that *Blood on the Eiderdown* was suggested to me by an experience of his at Crouch End. He also liked putting me right when I made mistakes, as so many of us do, over such technical matters as finger-prints and Scotland Yard procedure. I had always supposed, for instance, that you could get good finger-prints from butter. This, apparently, is not the case. From buttery fingers on other objects, yes, but not from the pat of butter itself, or, anyhow, not in hot weather. This, of course, was a foolish mistake of mine, as in any case Lady Sybil would not have handled the butter directly in this way, as my detective should have seen. My detective, by the way, is called Sherman Flagg, and is pretty well known by now. Not that this is germane to my present story.

"I don't think I follow you," I said.

"I mean that the simple way of committing a murder is often the best way. This doesn't mean that the murderer is a man of simple mind. On the contrary. He is subtle enough to know that the simple solution is too simple to be credible."

This sounded anything but simple, so I said, "Give me an example."

"Well, take the case of the magnum of Tokay which was sent to the Marquis of Hedingham on his lordship's birthday. Have I never told you about it?"

"Never," I said, and I too helped myself and passed the bottle.

He filled his glass and considered. "Give me a moment to get it clear," he said. "It was a long time ago." While he closed his eyes, and let the past drift before him, I fetched another bottle of the same; a Château Latour '78, of which I understand there is very little left in the country.

"Yes," said Mortimer, opening his eyes, "I've got it now."

I leant forward, listening eagerly. This is the story he told me.

The first we heard of it at the Yard (said Mortimer) was a brief announcement over the telephone that the Marquis of Hedingham's butler had died suddenly at his lordship's town house in Brook Street, and that poison was suspected. This was at seven o'clock. We went round at once. Inspector Totman had been put in charge of the case; I was a young Detective Sergeant at the time, and I generally worked under Totman. He was a brisk, military sort of fellow, with a little prickly ginger moustache, good at his job in a showy, orthodox way, but he had no imagination, and he was thinking all the time of what Inspector Totman would get out of it. Quite frankly I didn't like him. Outwardly we kept friendly, for it doesn't do to quarrel with one's superiors; indeed, he was vain enough to think that I had a great admiration for him; but I knew that he was just using me for his own advantage, and I had a shrewd suspicion that I should have been promoted before this, if he hadn't wanted to keep me under him so that he could profit by my brains.

We found the butler in his pantry, stretched out on the floor. An open bottle of Tokay, a broken wine-glass with the dregs of the liquid still in it, the medical evidence of poisoning, all helped to build the story for us. The wine had arrived about an hour before, with the card of Sir William Kelso attached to it. On the card was a typewritten message, saying, "Bless you, Tommy, and here's something to celebrate it with." Apparently it was his lordship's birthday, and he was having a small family party for the occasion, of about six people. Sir William Kelso, I should explain, was his oldest friend and a relation by marriage, Lord Hedingham having married his sister; in fact, he was to have been one of the party present that evening. He was a bachelor about fifty, and a devoted uncle to his nephew and nieces.

Well, the butler had brought up the bottle and the card to his lordship—this was about six o'clock; and Lord Hedingham, as he told us, had taken the card, said something like "Good old Bill, we'll have that tonight, Perkins," and Perkins had said, "Very good, my lord," and gone out again with the bottle, and the card had been left lying on the table. Afterwards, there could be little doubt what had happened. Perkins had opened the bottle with the intention of decanting it, but had been unable to resist the temptation to sample it first. I suspect that in his time he had sampled most of his lordship's wine, but had never before come across a Tokay of such richness. So he had poured himself out a full glass, drunk it, and died almost immediately.

"Good Heavens!" I interrupted. "But how extremely providential— I mean, of course, for Lord Hedingham and the others."

"Exactly," said the Superintendent.

The contents of the bottle were analyzed (he went on) and found to contain a more than fatal dose of prussic acid. Prussic acid isn't a diffi- cult thing to get hold of, so that didn't help much. Of course we did all the routine things, and I and young Roberts, a nice young fellow who often worked with us, went round all the chemists' shops in the neighbourhood, and Totman examined everybody from Sir William and Lord Hedingham downwards, and Roberts and I took the bottle round to all the well-known wine-merchants, and at the end of a week all we could say was this:

1. The murderer had a motive for murdering Lord Hedingham; or, possibly, somebody at his party; or, possibly the whole party. In accor- dance, we learnt, with the usual custom, his lordship would be the first to taste the wine. A sip would not be fatal, and in a wine of such richness the taste might not be noticeable; so that the whole party would then presumably drink his lordship's health. He would raise his glass to them, and in this way they would all take the poison, and be affected according to how deeply they drank. On the other hand, his lordship might take a good deal more than a sip in the first place, and so be the only one to suffer. My deduction from this was that the motive was revenge rather than gain. The criminal would revenge

himself on Lord Hedingham, if his lordship or *any* of his family were seriously poisoned; he could only profit if *definite* people were definitely *killed.* It took a little time to get Totman to see this, but he did eventually agree.

2. The murderer had been able to obtain one of Sir William Kelso's cards, and knew that John Richard Mervyn Plantaganet Carlow, 10th Marquis of Hedingham, was called "Tommy" by his intimates. Totman deduced from this that he was therefore one of the Hedingham-Kelso circle of relations and friends. I disputed this. I pointed out: (a) that it was rather to strangers than to intimate friends that cards were presented; except in the case of formal calls, when they were left in a bowl or tray in the hall, and anybody could steal one; (b) that the fact that Lord Hedingham was called Tommy must have appeared in Society papers and be known to many people; and, most convincing of all, (c) that the murderer did *not* know that Sir William Kelso was to be in the party that night. For obviously some reference would have been made to the gift, either on his arrival or when the wine was served; whereupon he would have disclaimed any knowledge of it, and the bottle would immediately have been suspected. As it was, of course, Perkins had drunk from it before Sir William's arrival. Now both Sir William and Lord Hedingham assured us that they *always* dined together on each other's birthday, and they were convinced that any personal friend of theirs would have been aware of the fact. I made Totman question them about this, and he then came round to my opinion.

3. There was nothing to prove that the wine in the bottle corresponded to the label; and wine-experts were naturally reluctant to taste it for us. All they could say from the smell was that it was a Tokay of sorts. This, of course, made it more difficult for us. In fact I may say that neither from the purchase of the wine nor the nature of the poison did we get any clue.

We had, then, the following picture of the murderer. He had a cause of grievance, legitimate or fancied, against Lord Hedingham, and did not scruple to take the most terrible revenge. He knew that Sir William Kelso was a friend of his lordship's and called him Tommy, and that he might reasonably give him a bottle of wine on his birthday. He did *not* know that Sir William would be dining there that night; that is to say, *even as late as six o'clock that evening, he did not know.* He was not likely, therefore, to be anyone at present employed or living in Lord Hedingham's house. Finally, he had had an opportunity, for what this was worth, to get hold of a card of Sir William's.

As it happened, there was somebody who fitted completely into this picture. It was a fellow called—wait a bit, Merrivale, Medley—oh well, it doesn't matter. Merton, that was it. Merton. He had been his lordship's valet for six months, had been suspected of stealing, and dismissed without a character. Just the man we wanted. So for a fortnight we searched for Merton. And then, when at last we got on to him, we discovered that he had the most complete *alibi* imaginable. *(The Superintendent held up his hand, and it came into my mind that he must have stopped the traffic as a young man with just that gesture.)* Yes, I know what you're going to say, what you detective-story writers always say— the better an *alibi*, the worse it is. Well, sometimes, I admit; but not in this case. For Merton was in gaol, under another name, and he had been inside for the last two months. And what do you think he was suspected of, and now waiting trial for? Oh well, of course you guess, I've as good as told you. He was on a charge of murder—and murder, mark you, by poison.

"Good Heavens," I interjected. I seized the opportunity to refill my friend's glass. He said, "Exactly," and took a long drink. I thought fancifully that he was drinking to drown that terrible disappointment of so many years ago.

You can imagine (he went on) what a shock this was to us. You see, a certain sort of murder had been committed; we had deduced that it was done by a certain man without knowing whether he was in the least capable of such a crime; and now, having proved to the hilt that he was capable of it, we had simultaneously proved that he didn't do it. We had proved ourselves right—and our case mud.

I said to Totman, "Let's take a couple of days off, and each of us think it out, and then pool our ideas and start afresh."

Totman frisked up his little moustache, and laughed in his conceited way.

"You don't think I'm going to admit myself wrong, do you, when I've just proved I'm right?" Totman saying "I," when he had got everything from me! "Merton's my man. He'd got the bottle ready, and somebody else delivered it for him. That's all. He had to wait for the birthday, you see, and when he found himself in prison, his wife or somebody—"

"—took round the bottle, all nicely marked 'Poison; not to be delivered till Christmas Day.'" I had to say it, I was so annoyed with him.

"Don't be more of a damned fool than you can help," he shouted, "and don't be insolent, or you'll get into trouble."

I apologised humbly, and told him how much I liked working with him. He forgave me—and we were friends again. He patted me on the shoulder.

"You take a day off," he said kindly, "you've been working too hard. Take a 'bus into the country and make up a good story for me; the story of that bottle, and how it came from Merton's lodging to Brook Street, and who took it and why. I admit I don't see it at present, but that's the bottle, you can bet your life. I'm going down to Leatherhead. Report here on Friday morning, and we'll see what we've got. My birthday as it happens, and I feel I'm going to be lucky." Leatherhead was where this old woman had been poisoned. That was the third time in a week he'd told me when his entirely misconceived birthday was. He was like that.

I took a 'bus to Hampstead Heath. I walked round the Leg of Mutton Pond twenty times. And each time that I went round, Totman's theory seemed sillier than the last time. And each time I felt more and more strongly that we were being *forced* into an entirely artificial interpretation of things. It sounds fantastic, I know, but I could almost feel the murderer behind us, pushing us along the way he wanted us to go.

I sat down on a seat, and I filled a pipe and I said, "Right! The murderer's a man who wanted me to believe all that I have believed. When I've told myself that the murderer intended to do so-and-so, he intended me to believe that, and therefore he didn't do so-and-so. When I've told myself that the murderer wanted to mislead me, he wanted me to think he wanted to mislead me, which meant that the truth was exactly as it seemed to be. Now then, Fred, you'll begin all over again, and you'll take things as they are, and won't be too clever about them. Because the murderer expects you to be clever, and wants you to be clever, and from now on you aren't going to take your orders from *him*."

And of course, the first thing which leaped to my mind was that the murderer *meant* to murder the butler!

It seemed incredible now that we could ever have missed it. Didn't every butler sample his master's wines? Why, it was an absolute certainty that Perkins would be the first victim of a poisoned bottle of a very special vintage. What butler could resist pouring himself out a glass as he decanted it?

Wait, though. Mustn't be in a hurry. Two objections, One: Perkins might be the one butler in a thousand who wasn't a wine-sampler. Two: Even if he were like any other butler, he might be out of sorts on that particular evening, and have put by a glass to drink later. Wouldn't it be much too risky for a murderer who only wanted to destroy Perkins, and had no grudge against Lord Hedingham's family, to depend so absolutely on the butler drinking first?

For a little while this held me up, but not for long. Suddenly I saw the complete solution.

It would *not* be risky if (a) the murderer had certain knowledge of the butler's habits; and (b) could, if necessary, at the last moment, prevent the family from drinking. In other words, if he were an intimate of the family, were himself present at the party, and without bringing suspicion on himself, could bring the wine under suspicion.

In other words, and only, and finally, and definitely—if he were Sir William Kelso. For Sir William was the only man in the world who could say, "Don't drink this wine. I'm supposed to have sent it to you, and I didn't, so that proves it's a fake." The *only* man.

Why hadn't we suspected him from the beginning? One reason, of course, was that we had supposed the intended victim to be one of the Hedingham family, and of Sir William's devotion to his sister, brother-in-law, nephew and nieces, there was never any doubt. But the chief reason was our assumption that the last thing a murderer would do would be to give himself away by sending his own card round with the poisoned bottle. "The *last* thing a murderer would do"—and therefore the *first* thing a really clever murderer would do. For it couldn't be explained as "the one mistake which every murderer makes"; he couldn't send his own card accidentally. "Impossible," we said, that a murderer should do it deliberately! But the correct answer was, Impossible that we should not be deceived if it were done deliberately—and therefore brilliantly clever.

To make my case complete to myself, for I had little hope as yet of converting Totman, I had to establish motive. Why should Sir William want to murder Perkins? I gave myself the pleasure of having tea that afternoon with Lord Hedingham's cook-housekeeper. We had caught each other's eye on other occasions when I had been at the house, and—well, I suppose I can say it now—I had a way with the women in those days. When I left, I knew two things. Perkins had been generally unpopular, not only downstairs, but upstairs; "it was a wonder how they put up with him." And her ladyship "had been a different woman lately."

"How different?" I asked.

"So much younger, if you know what I mean, Sergeant Mortimer. Almost like a girl again, bless her heart."

I did know. And that was that. Blackmail.

What was I to do? What did my evidence amount to? Nothing. It was all corroborative evidence. If Kelso had done one suspicious thing, or left one real clue, then the story I had made up would have convinced any jury. As it was, in the eyes of a jury he had done one completely unsuspicious thing, and left one real clue to his innocence—his visiting-card. Totman would just laugh at me.

I disliked the thought of being laughed at by Totman. I wondered how I could get the laugh of him. I took a 'bus to Baker Street, and walked into Regent's Park, not minding where I was going, but just thinking. And then, as I got opposite Hanover Terrace, who should I see but young Roberts.

"Hallo, young fellow, what have *you* been up to?"

"Hallo, Sarge," he grinned. "Been calling on my old school-chum, Sir Woppity Wotsit—or rather, his valet. Tottie thought he might have known Merton. Speaking as one valet to another, so to speak."

"Is Inspector Totman back?" I asked.

Roberts stood to attention, and said, "No, Sergeant Mortimer, Inspector Totman is not expected to return from Leatherhead, Surrey, until a late hour to-night."

You couldn't be angry with the boy. At least I couldn't. He had no respect for anybody, but he was a good lad. And he had an eye like a hawk. Saw everything and forgot none of it.

"I suppose by Sir Woppity Wotsit you mean Sir William Kelso," I said. "I didn't know he lived up this way."

Roberts pointed across the road. "Observe the august mansion. Five minutes ago you'd have found me in the basement, talking to a cock-eyed churchwarden who thought Merton was in Surrey. As it is, of course."

I had a sudden crazy idea.

"Well, now you're going back there," I said. "I'm going to call on Sir William, and I want you handy. Would they let you in at the basement again, or are they sick of you?"

"Sarge, they just love me. When I went, they said, 'Must you go?'"

We say at the Yard, "Once a murderer, always a murderer." Perhaps that was why I had an absurd feeling that I should like young Roberts within call. Because I was going to tell Sir William Kelso what I'd been thinking about by the Leg of Mutton Pond. I'd only seen him once, but he gave me the idea of being the sort of man who wouldn't mind killing, but didn't like lying. I thought he would give himself away . . . and then—well, there might be a rough house, and young Roberts would be useful.

As we walked in at the gate together, I looked in my pocket-book for a card. Luckily I had one left, though it wasn't very clean. Roberts, who never missed anything, said, "Personally I always use blotting-paper," and went on whistling. If I hadn't known him, I shouldn't have known what he was talking about. I said, "Oh, do you?" and rang the bell. I gave the maid my card, and asked if Sir William could see me, and at the same time Roberts gave her a wink, and indicated the back door. She nodded to him, and asked me to come in. Roberts went down and waited for her at the basement. I felt safer.

Sir William was a big man, as big as I was. But of course a lot older.

He said, "Well, Sergeant, what can I do for you?" twiddling my card in his fingers. He seemed quite friendly about it. "Sit down, won't you?"

I said, "I think I'll stand, Sir William. I wanted just to ask you one question if I might." Yes, I know I was crazy, but somehow I felt kind of inspired.

"By all means," he said, obviously not much interested.

"When did you first discover that Perkins was blackmailing Lady Hedingham?"

He was standing in front of his big desk, and I was opposite to him. He stopped fiddling with my card, and became absolutely still; and there was a silence so complete that I could feel it in every nerve of my body. I kept my eyes on his, you may be sure. We stood there, I don't know how long.

"Is that the only question?" he asked. The thing that frightened me was that his voice was just the same as before. Ordinary.

"Well, just one more. Have you a Corona typewriter in your house?" You see, we knew that a Corona had been used, but there was nothing distinctive about it, and it might have been any one in a thousand. Just corroborative evidence again, that's all. But it told him that I knew.

He gave a long sigh, tossed the card into the waste-paper basket, and walked to the window. He stood there with his back to me, looking out but seeing nothing. Thinking. He must have stood there for a couple of minutes. Then he turned round, and to my amazement he had a friendly smile on his face. "I think we'd both better sit down," he said. We did.

"There is a Corona in the house which I sometimes use," he began. "I daresay you use one too."

"I do."

"And so do thousands of other people—including, it may be, the murderer you are looking for."

"Thousands of people including the murderer," I agreed.

He noticed the difference, and smiled. "People" I had said, not "other people." And I didn't say I was looking for him. Because I had found him.

"So much for that. There is nothing in the actual wording of the typed message to which you would call my attention?"

"No. Except that it was exactly right."

"Oh, my dear fellow, anyone could have got it right. A simple birthday greeting."

"Anyone in your own class, Sir William, who knew you both. But that's all. It's Inspector Totman's birthday tomorrow—" (as he keeps telling us, damn him, I added to myself). "If I sent him a bottle of whisky, young Roberts—that's the constable who's in on this case, you may have seen him about, he's waiting for me now down below"—I thought this was rather a neat way of getting that in—"Roberts could make a guess at what I'd say, and so could anybody at the Yard who knows us both, and they wouldn't be far wrong. But *you* couldn't, Sir William."

He looked at me. He couldn't take his eyes off me. I wondered what he was thinking. At last he said:

"A long life and all the best, with the admiring good wishes of — — how's that?"

It was devilish. First that he had really been thinking it out, when he had so much else to think about, and then that he'd got it so right. That "admiring"; which meant that he'd studied Totman just as he was studying me, and knew how I'd play up to him.

"You see," he smiled, "it isn't really difficult. And the fact that my card was used is in itself convincing evidence of my innocence, don't you think?"

"To a jury perhaps," I said, "but not to me."

"I wish I could convince *you,*" he murmured to himself. "Well, what are you doing about it?"

"I shall, of course, put my re-construction of the case in front of Inspector Totman to-morrow."

"Ah! A nice birthday surprise for him. And, knowing your Totman, what do you think he will do?"

He had me there, and he knew it.

"I think *you* know him too, Sir," I said.

"I do," he smiled.

"And me, I daresay, and anybody else you meet. Quick as lightning. But even ordinary men like me have a sort of sudden understanding of people sometimes. As I've got of you, Sir. And I've a sort of feeling that, if ever we get you into a witness-box, and you've taken the oath, you won't find perjury so much to your liking as murder. Or what the Law calls murder."

"But *you* don't?" he said quickly.

"I think," I said, "that there are a lot of people who ought to be killed. But I'm a policeman, and what I think isn't evidence. You killed Perkins, didn't you?"

He nodded; and said, almost with a grin at me, "A nervous affection of the head, if you put it in evidence. I could get a specialist to swear to it." My God, he was a good sort of man. I was really sorry when they found him next day on the Underground. Or what was left of him. And yet what else could he do?

I was furious with Fred Mortimer. That was no way to end a story. Suddenly, like that, as if he were tired of it. I told him so.

"My dear little Cyril," he said, "it isn't the end. We're just coming to the exciting part. This will make your hair curl."

"Oh!" I said sarcastically. "Then I suppose all that you've told me so far is just introduction?"

"That's right. Now listen. On the Friday morning, before we heard of Sir William's death, I went in to report to Inspector Totman. He wasn't there. Nobody knew where he was. They rang up his block of flats. Now hold tight to the leg of the table or something. When the porter got into his flat, he found Totman's body. Poisoned."

"Good Heavens!" I ejaculated.

"You may say so. There he was, and on the table was a newly opened bottle of whisky, and by the side of it was a visiting-card. And whose card do you think it was? *Mine!* And what do you think it said? A long life and all the best with the admiring good wishes of— *me!* Lucky for me I had had young Roberts with me. Lucky for me he had this genius for noticing and remembering. Lucky for me he could swear to the exact shape of the smudge of ink on that card. And I might add, lucky for me that they believed me when I told them word for word what had been said at my interview with Sir William, as I have just told you. I was reprimanded, of course, for exceeding my duty, as I most certainly had, but that was only official. Unofficially they were very pleased with me. We couldn't prove anything, naturally, and Sir William's death had looked as accidental as anything could, so we just had to leave it. But a month later I was promoted to Inspector."

He filled his glass and drank, while I revolved his extraordinary story in my mind.

"The theory," I said, polishing my *pince-nez* thoughtfully, "was, I suppose, this. Sir William sent the poisoned whisky, not so much to get rid of Totman, from whom he had little to fear, as to discredit you by bringing you under suspicion, and entirely to discredit your own theory of the other murder."

"Exactly."

"And then, at the last moment he realised that he couldn't go on with it, or the weight of his crimes became suddenly too much for him, or—"

"Something of the sort. Nobody ever knew, of course."

I looked across the table with sudden excitement; almost with awe.

"Do you remember what he said to you?" I asked, giving the words their full meaning as I slowly quoted them. "'The fact that my card was used is convincing evidence of my innocence.' And you said, 'Not to me.' And he said, 'I wish I could convince you.' *And that was how he did it!* The fact that your card was used *was* convincing evidence of your innocence!"

"With the other things. The proof that he was in possession of the particular card of mine which was used, and the certainty that he had committed the other murder. Once a poisoner, always a poisoner."

"True . . . yes. . . . Well, thanks very much for the story, Fred. All the same, you know," I said, shaking my head at him, "it doesn't altogether prove what you set out to prove."

"What was that?"

"That the simple explanation is generally the true one. In the case of Perkins, yes. But not in the case of Totman."

"Sorry, I don't follow."

"My dear fellow," I said, putting up a finger to emphasise my point, for he seemed a little hazy with the wine suddenly; "the *simple* explanation of Totman's death—surely?—would have been that *you* had sent him the poisoned whisky."

Superintendent Mortimer looked a little surprised.

"But I did," he said.

So now you see my terrible predicament. I could hardly listen as he went on dreamily: "I never liked Totman, and he stood in my way; but I hadn't seriously thought of getting rid of him, until I got that card into my hands again. As I told you, he dropped it into the basket, and turned to the window, and I thought, Damn it, *you* can afford to chuck about visiting-cards, but I can't, and it's the only one I've got left, and if you don't want it, I do. So I bent down very naturally to do up my boot-lace, and felt in the basket behind me, because of course it was rather an undignified thing to do, and I didn't want to be seen; and it was just as I was putting it into my pocket that I saw that ink-smudge again, and I remembered Roberts had seen it. And in a flash the whole plan came to me; simple; fool-proof. And from that moment everything I said to him was in preparation of it. Course we were quite alone, but you never know who might be listening, and besides"—he twiddled the stem of his empty wine-glass—"p'raps I'm like Sir William, rather tell the truth than not, and it *was* true, all of it as I told the Super, how Sir William came to know about Totman's birthday, and knew that those were the very words I should have used. Made it very convincing, me just repeating to the Super what had really been said. Don't think I wanted to put anything on to Sir William that wasn't his. I liked him. But he as good as told me he wasn't going to wait for what was coming to him and he'd done one murder anyway. That was why I slipped down with the bottle that evening, and left it outside Totman's flat. Didn't dare wait till the morning, in case Sir William closed his account that night." He stood up and stretched himself. "Ah, well, it was a long time ago. Good-bye, old man, I must be off. Thanks for a grand dinner. Don't forget, you're dining with *me* next month. I've got a new cocktail for you. You'll like it."— He swaggered out, leaving me to my thoughts.

"Once a murderer, always a murderer. . . . " And to-morrow he will wake up and remember what he has told me! And I shall be the only person in the world who knows his secret! . . .

Perhaps he won't remember. Perhaps he was drunk. . . .

In vino veritas. Wasn't it the younger Pliny who said that? A profound observation. Truth in the bottle. . . .

"Once a poisoner, always a poisoner. . . . "

"I've got a new cocktail for you. You'll like it."

Yes, but—shall I?

MURIEL SPARK

THE PORTOBELLO ROAD

O NE DAY in my young youth at high summer, lolling with my lovely companions upon a haystack, I found a needle. Already and privately for some years I had been guessing that I was set apart from the common run, but this of the needle attested the fact to my whole public: George, Kathleen and Skinny. I sucked my thumb, for when I had thrust my idle hand deep into the hay, the thumb was where the needle had stuck.

When everyone had recovered George said, "She put in her thumb and pulled out a plum." Then away we were into our merciless hacking-hecking laughter again.

The needle had gone fairly deep into the thumby cushion and a small red river flowed and spread from this tiny puncture. So that nothing of our joy should lag, George put in quickly,

"Mind your bloody thumb on my shirt."

Then hac-hec-hoo, we shrieked into the hot Borderland afternoon. Really I should not care to be so young of heart again. That is my thought every time I turn over my old papers and come across the photograph. Skinny, Kathleen and myself are in the photo atop the haystack. Skinny had just finished analysing the inwards of my find.

"It couldn't have been done by brains. You haven't much brains but you're a lucky wee thing."

Everyone agreed that the needle betokened extraordinary luck. As it was becoming a serious conversation, George said,

"I'll take a photo."

I wrapped my hanky round my thumb and got myself organised. George pointed up from his camera and shouted,

"Look, there's a mouse!"

Kathleen screamed and I screamed although I think we knew there was no mouse. But this gave us an extra session of squalling hee-hoo's. Finally we three composed ourselves for George's picture. We look lovely and it was a great day at the time, but I would not care for it all over again. From that day I was known as Needle.

One Saturday in recent years I was mooching down the Portobello Road, threading among the crowds of marketers on the narrow pavement when I saw a woman. She had a haggard, careworn, wealthy look, thin but for the breasts forced-up high like a pigeon's. I had not seen her for nearly five years. How changed she was! But I recognised Kathleen, my friend; her features had already begun to sink and protrude in the way that mouths and noses do in people destined always to be old for their years. When I had last seen her, nearly five years ago, Kathleen, barely thirty, had said,

"I've lost all my looks, it's in the family. All the women are handsome as girls, but we go off early, we go brown and nosey."

I stood silently among the people, watching. As you will see, I wasn't in a position to speak to Kathleen. I saw her shoving in her avid manner from stall to stall. She was always fond of antique jewellery and of bargains. I wondered that I had not seen her before in the Portobello

Road on my Saturday morning ambles. Her long stiff-crooked fingers pounced to select a jade ring from amongst the jumble of brooches and pendants, onyx, moonstone and gold, set out on the stall.

"What do you think of this?" she said.

I saw then who was with her. I had been half-conscious of the huge man following several paces behind her, and now I noticed him.

"It looks all right," he said. "How much is it?"

"How much is it?" Kathleen asked the vendor.

I took a good look at this man accompanying Kathleen. It was her husband. The beard was unfamiliar, but I recognised beneath it his enormous mouth, the bright sensuous lips, the large brown eyes forever brimming with pathos.

It was not for me to speak to Kathleen, but I had a sudden inspiration which caused me to say quietly,

"Hallo, George."

The giant of a man turned round to face the direction of my face. There were so many people—but at length he saw me.

"Hallo, George," I said again.

Kathleen had started to haggle with the stall-owner, in her old way, over the price of the jade ring. George continued to stare at me, his big mouth slightly parted so that I could see a wide slit of red lips and white teeth between the fair grassy growths of beard and moustache.

"My God!" he said.

"What's the matter?" said Kathleen.

"Hallo, George!" I said again, quite loud this time, and cheerfully.

"Look!" said George. "Look who's there, over beside the fruit stall."

Kathleen looked but didn't see.

"Who is it?" she said impatiently.

"It's Needle," he said. "She said 'Hallo, George'."

"*Needle*," said Kathleen. "Who do you mean? You don't mean our old friend *Needle* who—"

"Yes. There she is. My God!"

He looked very ill, although when I had said "Hallo, George" I had spoken friendly enough.

"I don't see anyone faintly resembling poor Needle," said Kathleen looking at him. She was worried.

George pointed straight at me. "Look *there*. I tell you that is Needle."

"You're ill, George. Heavens, you must be seeing things. Come on home. Needle isn't there. You know as well as I do, Needle is dead."

I must explain that I departed this life nearly five years ago. But I did not altogether depart this world. There were those odd things still to be done which one's executors can never do properly. Papers to be looked over, even after the executors have torn them up. Lots of business except, of course, on Sundays and Holidays of Obligation, plenty to take an interest in for the time being. I take my recreation on Saturday mornings. If it is a wet Saturday I wander up and down the substantial lanes of Woolworth's as I did when I was young and visible. There is a pleasurable spread of objects on the counters which I now perceive and exploit with a certain detachment, since it suits with my condition of life. Creams, toothpastes, combs and hankies, cotton gloves, flimsy flowering scarves, writing-paper and crayons, ice-cream cones and orangeade, screwdrivers, boxes of tacks, tins of paint, of glue, of marmalade; I always liked them but far more now that I have no need of any. When Saturdays are fine I go instead to the Portobello Road where formerly I would jaunt with Kathleen in our grown-up days. The barrow-loads do not change much, of apples and rayon vests in common blues and low-taste mauve, of silver plate, trays and teapots long since changed hands from the bygone citizens to dealers, from shops to the new flats and breakable homes, and then over to the barrow-stalls and the dealers again: Georgian spoons, rings, ear-rings of turquoise and opal set in the butterfly pattern of true-lovers' knot, patch-boxes with miniature paintings of ladies on ivory, snuff-boxes of silver with Scotch pebbles inset.

Sometimes as occasion arises on a Saturday morning, my friend Kathleen, who is a Catholic, has a Mass said for my soul, and then I am in attendance, as it were, at the church. But most Saturdays I take my delight among the solemn crowds with their aimless purposes, their eternal life not far away, who push past the counters and stalls, who handle, buy, steal, touch, desire and ogle the merchandise. I hear the tinkling tills, I hear the jangle of loose change and tongues and children wanting to hold and have.

That is how I came to be in the Portobello Road that Saturday morning when I saw George and Kathleen. I would not have spoken had I not been inspired to it. Indeed it's one of the things I can't do now—to speak out, unless inspired. And most extraordinary, on that morning as I spoke, a degree of visibility set in. I suppose from poor George's point of view it was like seeing a ghost when he saw me standing by the fruit barrow repeating in so friendly a manner, "Hallo, George!"

We were bound for the south. When our education, what we could get of it from the north, was thought to be finished, one by one we were sent or sent for to London. John Skinner, whom we called Skinny, went to study more archaeology, George to join his uncle's tobacco farm, Kathleen to stay with her rich connections and to potter intermittently in the Mayfair hat shop which one of them owned. A little later I also went to London to see life, for it was my ambition to write about life, which first I had to see.

"We four must stick together," George said very often in that yearning way of his. He was always desperately afraid of neglect. We four looked likely to shift off in different directions and George did not trust the other three of us not to forget all about him. More and more as the time came for him to depart for his uncle's tobacco farm in Africa he said,

"We four must keep in touch."

And before he left he told each of us anxiously,

"I'll write regularly, once a month. We must keep together for the sake of the old times." He had three prints taken from the negative of that photo on the haystack, wrote on the back of them "George took this the day that Needle found the needle" and gave us a copy each. I think we all wished he could become a bit more callous.

During my lifetime I was a drifter, nothing organised. It was difficult for my friends to follow the logic of my life. By the normal reckonings I should have come to starvation and ruin, which I never did. Of course, I did not live to write about life as I wanted to do. Possibly that is why I am inspired to do so now in these peculiar circumstances.

I taught in a private school in Kensington for almost three months, very small children. I didn't know what to do with them but I was kept fairly busy escorting incontinent little boys to the lavatory and telling the little girls to use their handkerchiefs. After that I lived a winter holiday in London on my small capital, and when that had run out I found a diamond bracelet in the cinema for which I received a reward of fifty pounds. When it was used up I got a job with a publicity man, writing speeches for absorbed industrialists, in which the dictionary of quotations came in very useful. So it went on. I got engaged to Skinny, but shortly after that I was left a small legacy, enough to keep me for six months. This somehow decided me that I didn't love Skinny so I gave him back the ring.

But it was through Skinny that I went to Africa. He was engaged with a party of researchers to investigate King Solomon's mines, that series of ancient workings ranging from the ancient port of Ophir, now called Beira, across Portuguese East Africa and Southern Rhodesia to the mighty jungle-city of Zimbabwe whose temple walls still stand by the approach to an ancient and sacred mountain, where the rubble of that civilisation scatters itself over the surrounding Rhodesian waste. I accompanied the party as a sort of secretary. Skinny vouched for me, he paid my fare, he sympathised by his action with my inconsequential life although when he spoke of it he disapproved. A life like mine annoys most people; they go to their jobs every day, attend to things, give orders, pummel typewriters, and get two or three weeks off every year, and it vexes them to see someone else not bothering to do these things and yet getting away with it, not starving, being lucky as they call it. Skinny, when I had broken off our engagement, lectured me about this, but still he took me to Africa knowing I should probably leave his unit within a few months.

We were there a few weeks before we began enquiring for George, who was farming about four hundred miles away to the north. We had not told him of our plans.

"If we tell George to expect us in his part of the world he'll come rushing to pester us the first week. After all, we're going on business," Skinny had said.

Before we left Kathleen told us, "Give George my love and tell him not to send frantic cables every time I don't answer his letters right away. Tell him I'm busy in the hat shop and being presented. You would think he hadn't another friend in the world the way he carries on."

We had settled first at Fort Victoria, our nearest place of access to the Zimbabwe ruins. There we made enquiries about George. It was clear he hadn't many friends. The older settlers were the most tolerant about the half-caste woman he was living with, as we found, but they were furious about his methods of raising tobacco which we learned were most unprofessional and in some mysterious way disloyal to the whites. We could never discover how it was that George's style of tobacco farming gave the blacks opinions about themselves, but that's what the older settlers claimed. The newer immigrants thought he was unsociable and, of course, his living with that nig made visiting impossible.

I must say I was myself a bit off-put by this news about the brown woman. I was brought up in a university town to which came Indian, African and Asiatic students in a variety of tints and hues. I was brought up to avoid them for reasons connected with local reputation and God's ordinances. You cannot easily go against what you were brought up to do unless you are a rebel by nature.

Anyhow, we visited George eventually, taking advantage of the offer of transport from some people bound north in search of game. He had heard of our arrival in Rhodesia and though he was glad, almost relieved, to see us he pursued a policy of sullenness for the first hour.

"We wanted to give you a surprise, George."

"How were we to know that you'd get to hear of our arrival, George? News here must travel faster than light, George."

"We did hope to give you a surprise, George."

At last he said, "Well, I must say it's good to see you. All we need now is Kathleen. We four simply must stick together. You find when you're in a place like this, there's nothing like old friends."

He showed us his drying sheds. He showed us a paddock where he was experimenting with a horse and a zebra mare, attempting to mate them. They were frolicking happily, but not together. They passed each other in their private play time and again, but without acknowledgment and without resentment.

"It's been done before," George said. "It makes a fine strong beast, more intelligent than a mule and sturdier than a horse. But I'm not having any success with this pair, they won't look at each other."

After a while, he said, "Come in for a drink and meet Matilda."

She was dark brown, with a subservient hollow chest and round shoulders, a gawky woman, very snappy with the house-boys. We said pleasant things as we drank on the stoep before dinner, but we found George difficult. For some reason he began to rail at me for breaking off my engagement to Skinny, saying what a dirty trick it was after all those good times in the old days. I diverted attention to Matilda. I supposed, I said, she knew this part of the country well?

"No," said she, "I been a-shellitered my life. I not put out to working. Me nothing to go from place to place is allowed like dirty girls does." In her speech she gave every syllable equal stress.

George explained, "Her father was a white magistrate in Natal. She had a sheltered upbringing, different from the other coloureds, you realise."

"Man, me no black-eyed Susan," said Matilda, "no, no."

On the whole, George treated her as a servant. She was about four months advanced in pregnancy, but he made her get up and fetch for him, many times. Soap: that was one of the things Matilda had to fetch. George made his own bath soap, showed it proudly, gave us the recipe which I did not trouble to remember; I was fond of nice soaps during my lifetime and George's smelt of brillantine and looked likely to soil one's skin.

"D'yo brahn?" Matilda asked me.

George said, "She is asking if you go brown in the sun."

"No, I go freckled."

"I got sister-in-law go freckles."

She never spoke another word to Skinny nor to me, and we never saw her again.

Some months later I said to Skinny,

"I'm fed up with being a camp-follower."

He was not surprised that I was leaving his unit, but he hated my way of expressing it. He gave me a Presbyterian look.

"Don't talk like that. Are you going back to England or staying?"

"Staying, for a while."

"Well, don't wander too far off."

I was able to live on the fee I got for writing a gossip column in a local weekly, which wasn't my idea of writing about life, of course. I made friends, more than I could cope with, after I left Skinny's exclusive little band of archaeologists. I had the attractions of being newly out from England and of wanting to see life. Of the countless young men and go-ahead families who purred me along the Rhodesian roads, hundred after hundred miles, I only kept up with one family when I returned to my native land. I think that was because they were the most representative, they stood for all the rest: people in those parts are very typical of each other, as one group of standing stones in that wilderness is like the next.

I met George once more in a hotel in Bulawayo. We drank highballs and spoke of war. Skinny's party were just then deciding whether to remain in the country or return home. They had reached an exciting part of their research, and whenever I got a chance to visit Zimbabwe he would take me for a moonlight walk in the ruined temple and try to make me see phantom Phoenicians flitting ahead of us, or along the walls. I had half a mind to marry Skinny; perhaps, I thought, when his studies were finished. The impending war was in our bones: so I remarked to George as we sat drinking highballs on the hotel stoep in the hard bright sunny July winter of that year.

George was inquisitive about my relations with Skinny. He tried to pump me for about half an hour and when at last I said, "You are becoming aggressive, George," he stopped. He became quite pathetic. He said, "War or no war I'm clearing out of this."

"It's the heat does it," I said.

"I'm clearing out in any case. I've lost a fortune in tobacco. My uncle is making a fuss. It's the other bloody planters; once you get the wrong side of them you're finished in this wide land."

"What about Matilda?" I asked.

He said, "She'll be all right. She's got hundreds of relatives."

I had already heard about the baby girl. Coal black, by repute, with George's features. And another on the way, they said.

"What about the child?"

He didn't say anything to that. He ordered more highballs and when they arrived he swizzled his for a long time with a stick. "Why didn't you ask me to your twenty-first?" he said then.

"I didn't have anything special, no party, George. We had a quiet drink among ourselves, George, just Skinny and the old professors and two of the wives and me, George."

"You didn't ask me to your twenty-first," he said. "Kathleen writes to me regularly."

This wasn't true. Kathleen sent me letters fairly often in which she said, "Don't tell George I wrote to you as he will be expecting word from me and I can't be bothered actually."

"But you," said George, "don't seem to have any sense of old friend-ships, you and Skinny."

"Oh, George!" I said.

"Remember the times we had," George said. "We used to have times." His large brown eyes began to water.

"I'll have to be getting along," I said.

"Please don't go. Don't leave me just yet. I've something to tell you."

"Something nice?" I laid on an eager smile. All responses to George had to be overdone.

"You don't know how lucky you are," George said.

"How?" I said. Sometimes I got tired of being called lucky by every-body. There were times when, privately practising my writings about life, I knew the bitter side of my fortune. When I failed again and again to reproduce life in some satisfactory and perfect form, I was the more imprisoned, for all my carefree living, within my craving for this satisfaction. Sometimes, in my impotence and need I secreted a venom which infected all my life for days on end and which spurted out indiscriminately on Skinny or on anyone who crossed my path.

"You aren't bound by anyone," George said. "You come and go as you please. Something always turns up for you. You're free, and you don't know your luck."

"You're a damn sight more free than I am," I said sharply. "You've got your rich uncle."

"He's losing interest in me," George said. "He's had enough."

"Oh well, you're young yet. What was it you wanted to tell me?"

"A secret," George said. "Remember we used to have those secrets."

"Oh, yes we did."

"Did you ever tell any of mine?"

"Oh no, George." In reality, I couldn't remember any particular secret out of the dozens we must have exchanged from our schooldays onwards.

"Well, this is a secret, mind. Promise not to tell."

"Promise."

"I'm married."

"Married, George! Oh, who to?"

"Matilda."

"How dreadful!" I spoke before I could think, but he agreed with me.

"Yes, it's awful, but what could I do?"

"You might have asked my advice," I said pompously.

"I'm two years older than you are. I don't ask advice from you, Needle, little beast."

"Don't ask for sympathy then."

"A nice friend you are," he said, "I must say after all these years."

"Poor George!" I said.

"There are three white men to one white woman in this country," said George. "An isolated planter doesn't see a white woman and if he sees one she doesn't see him. What could I do? I needed the woman."

I was nearly sick. One, because of my Scottish upbringing. Two, because of my horror of corny phrases like "I needed the woman," which George repeated twice again.

"And Matilda got tough," said George, "after you and Skinny came to visit us. She had some friends at the Mission, and she packed up and went to them."

"You should have let her go," I said.

"I went after her," George said. "She insisted on being married, so I married her."

"That's not a proper secret, then," I said. "The news of a mixed marriage soon gets about."

"I took care of that," George said. "Crazy as I was, I took her to the Congo and married her there. She promised to keep quiet about it."

"Well, you can't clear off and leave her now, surely," I said.

"I'm going to get out of this place. I can't stand the woman and I can't stand the country. I didn't realise what it would be like. Two years of the country and three months of my wife has been enough."

"Will you get a divorce?"

"No, Matilda's Catholic. She won't divorce."

George was fairly getting through the highballs, and I wasn't far behind him. His brown eyes floated shiny and liquid as he told me how he had written to tell his uncle of his plight, "Except, of course, I didn't say we were married, that would have been too much for him. He's a prejudiced hardened old colonial. I only said I'd had a child by a coloured woman and was expecting another, and he perfectly understood. He came at once by plane a few weeks ago. He's made a settlement on her, providing she keeps her mouth shut about her association with me."

"Will she do that?"

"Oh, yes, or she won't get the money."

"But as your wife she has a claim on you, in any case."

"If she claimed as my wife she'd get far less. Matilda knows what she's doing, greedy bitch she is. She'll keep her mouth shut."

"Only, you won't be able to marry again, will you, George?"

"Not unless she dies," he said. "And she's as strong as a trek ox."

"Well, I'm sorry, George," I said.

"Good of you to say so," he said. "But I can see by your chin that you disapprove of me. Even my old uncle understood."

"Oh, George, I quite understand. You were lonely, I suppose."

"You didn't even ask me to your twenty-first. If you and Skinny had been nicer to me, I would never have lost my head and married the woman, never."

"You didn't ask me to your wedding," I said.

"You're a catty bissom, Needle, not like what you were in the old times when you used to tell us your wee stories."

"I'll have to be getting along," I said.

"Mind you keep the secret," George said.

"Can't I tell Skinny? He would be very sorry for you, George."

"You mustn't tell anyone. Keep it a secret. Promise."

"Promise," I said. I understood that he wished to enforce some sort of bond between us with this secret, and I thought, "Oh well, I suppose he's lonely. Keeping his secret won't do any harm."

I returned to England with Skinny's party just before the war.

I did not see George again till just before my death, five years ago.

After the war Skinny returned to his studies. He had two more exams, over a period of eighteen months, and I thought I might marry him when the exams were over.

"You might do worse than Skinny," Kathleen used to say to me on our Saturday morning excursions to the antique shops and the junk stalls.

She too was getting on in years. The remainder of our families in

Scotland were hinting that it was time we settled down with husbands. Kathleen was a little younger than me, but looked much older. She knew her chances were diminishing but at that time I did not think she cared very much. As for myself, the main attraction of marrying Skinny was his prospective expeditions to Mesopotamia. My desire to marry him had to be stimulated by the continual reading of books about Babylon and Assyria; perhaps Skinny felt this, because he supplied the books and even started instructing me in the art of deciphering cuneiform tablets.

Kathleen was more interested in marriage than I thought. Like me, she had racketed around a good deal during the war; she had actually been engaged to an officer in the U.S. navy, who was killed. Now she kept an antique shop near Lambeth, was doing very nicely, lived in a Chelsea square, but for all that she must have wanted to be married and have children. She would stop and look into all the prams which the mothers had left outside shops or area gates.

"The poet Swinburne used to do that," I told her once.

"Really? Did he want children of his own?"

"I shouldn't think so. He simply liked babies."

Before Skinny's final exam he fell ill and was sent to a sanatorium in Switzerland.

"You're fortunate after all not to be married to him," Kathleen said. "You might have caught T.B."

I was fortunate, I was lucky . . . so everyone kept telling me on different occasions. Although it annoyed me to hear, I knew they were right, but in a way that was different from what they meant. It took me very small effort to make a living; book reviews, odd jobs for Kathleen, a few months with the publicity man again, still getting up speeches about literature, art and life for industrial tycoons. I was waiting to write about life and it seemed to me that the good fortune lay in this, whenever it should be. And until then I was assured of my charmed life, the necessities of existence always coming my way and I with far more leisure than anyone else. I thought of my type of luck after I became a Catholic and was being confirmed. The Bishop touches the candidate on the cheek, a symbolic reminder of the sufferings a Christian is supposed to undertake. I thought, how lucky, what a feathery symbol to stand for the hellish violence of its true meaning.

I visited Skinny twice in the two years that he was in the sanatorium. He was almost cured, and expected to be home within a few months. I told Kathleen after my last visit.

"Maybe I'll marry Skinny when he's well again."

"Make it definite, Needle, and not so much of the maybe. You don't know when you're well off," she said.

This was five years ago, in the last year of my life. Kathleen and I had become very close friends. We met several times each week, and after our Saturday morning excursions in the Portobello Road very often I would accompany Kathleen to her aunt's house in Kent for a long week-end.

One day in the June of that year I met Kathleen specially for lunch because she had phoned me to say she had news.

"Guess who came into the shop this afternoon," she said.

"Who?"

"George."

We had half imagined George was dead. We had received no letters in the past ten years. Early in the war we had heard rumours of his keeping a night club in Durban, but nothing after that. We could have made enquiries if we had felt moved to do so.

At one time, when we discussed him, Kathleen had said,

"I ought to get in touch with poor George. But then I think he would write back. He would demand a regular correspondence again."

"We four must stick together," I mimicked.

"I can visualise his reproachful limpid orbs," Kathleen said.

Skinny said, "He's probably gone native. With his coffee concubine and a dozen mahogany kids."

"Perhaps he's dead," Kathleen said.

I did not speak of George's marriage, nor of any of his confidences in the hotel at Bulawayo. As the years passed we ceased to mention him except in passing, as someone more or less dead so far as we were concerned.

Kathleen was excited about George's turning up. She had forgotten her impatience with him in former days; she said,

"It was so wonderful to see old George. He seems to need a friend, feels neglected, out of touch with things."

"He needs mothering, I suppose."

Kathleen didn't notice the malice. She declared, "That's exactly the case with George. It always has been, I can see it now."

She seemed ready to come to any rapid new and happy conclusion about George. In the course of the morning he had told her of his wartime night club in Durban, his game-shooting expeditions since. It was clear he had not mentioned Matilda. He had put on weight, Kathleen told me, but he could carry it.

I was curious to see this version of George, but I was leaving for Scotland next day and did not see him till September of that year, just before my death.

While I was in Scotland I gathered from Kathleen's letters that she was seeing George very frequently, finding enjoyable company in him, looking after him. "You'll be surprised to see how he has developed." Apparently he would hang round Kathleen in her shop most days, "it makes him feel useful" as she maternally expressed it. He had an old relative in Kent whom he visited at week-ends; this old lady lived a few miles from Kathleen's aunt, which made it easy for them to travel down together on Saturdays, and go for long country walks.

"You'll see such a difference in George," Kathleen said on my return to London in September. I was to meet him that night, a Saturday. Kathleen's aunt was abroad, the maid on holiday, and I was to keep Kathleen company in the empty house.

George had left London for Kent a few days earlier. "He's actually helping with the harvest down there!" Kathleen told me lovingly.

Kathleen and I planned to travel down together, but on that Saturday she was unexpectedly delayed in London on some business. It was arranged that I should go ahead of her in the early afternoon to see to the provisions for our party; Kathleen had invited George to dinner at her aunt's house that night.

"I should be with you by seven," she said. "Sure you won't mind the empty house? I hate arriving at empty houses, myself."

I said no, I liked an empty house.

So I did, when I got there. I had never found the house more likeable. A large Georgian vicarage in about eight acres, most of the rooms shut and sheeted, there being only one servant. I discovered that I wouldn't need to go shopping, Kathleen's aunt had left many and delicate supplies with notes attached to them: "Eat this up please do, see also fridge" and "A treat for three hungry people see also 2 bttles beaune for yr party on back kn table." It was like a treasure hunt as I followed clue after clue through the cool silent domestic quarters. A house in which there are no people—but with all the signs of tenancy—can be a most tranquil good place. People take up space in a house out of proportion to their size. On my previous visits I had seen the rooms overflowing as it seemed, with Kathleen, her aunt, and the little fat maidservant; they were always on the move. As I wandered through that part of the house which was in use, opening windows to let in the pale yellow air of September, I was not conscious that I, Needle, was taking up any space at all, I might have been a ghost.

The only thing to be fetched was the milk. I waited till after four when the milking should be done, then set off for the farm which lay across two fields at the back of the orchard. There, when the byreman was handing me the bottle, I saw George.

"Hallo, George," I said.

"Needle! What are you doing here?" he said.

"Fetching milk," I said.

"So am I. Well, it's good to see you, I must say."

As we paid the farm-hand, George said, "I'll walk back with you part of the way. But I mustn't stop, my old cousin's without any milk for her tea. How's Kathleen?"

"She was kept in London. She's coming on later, about seven, she expects."

We had reached the end of the first field. George's way led to the left and on to the main road.

"We'll see you tonight, then?" I said.

"Yes, and talk about old times."

"Grand," I said.

But George got over the stile with me.

"Look here," he said. "I'd like to talk to you, Needle."

"We'll talk tonight, George. Better not keep your cousin waiting for the milk." I found myself speaking to him almost as if he were a child.

"No, I want to talk to you alone. This is a good opportunity."

We began to cross the second field. I had been hoping to have the house to myself for a couple more hours and I was rather petulant.

"See," he said suddenly, "that haystack."

"Yes," I said absently.

"Let's sit there and talk. I'd like to see you up on a haystack again. I still keep that photo. Remember that time when—"

"I found the needle," I said very quickly, to get it over.

But I was glad to rest. The stack had been broken up, but we managed to find a nest in it. I buried my bottle of milk in the hay for coolness. George placed his carefully at the foot of the stack.

"My old cousin is terribly vague, poor soul. A bit hazy in her head. She hasn't the least sense of time. If I tell her I've only been gone ten minutes she'll believe it."

I giggled, and looked at him. His face had grown much larger, his lips full, wide and with a ripe colour that is strange in a man. His brown eyes were abounding as before with some inarticulate plea.

"So you're going to marry Skinny after all these years?"

"I really don't know, George."

"You played him up properly."

"It isn't for you to judge. I have my own reasons for what I do."

"Don't get sharp," he said, "I was only funning." To prove it, he lifted a tuft of hay and brushed my face with it.

"D'you know," he said next, "I didn't think you and Skinny treated me very decently in Rhodesia."

"Well, we were busy, George. And we were younger then, we had a lot to do and see. After all, we could see you any other time, George."

"A touch of selfishness," he said.

"I'll have to be getting along, George." I made to get down from the stack.

He pulled me back. "Wait, I've got something to tell you."

"O.K., George, tell me."

"First promise not to tell Kathleen. She wants it kept a secret so that she can tell you herself."

"All right. Promise."

"I'm going to marry Kathleen."

"But you're already married."

Sometimes I heard news of Matilda from the one Rhodesian family with whom I still kept up. They referred to her as "George's Dark Lady" and of course they did not know he was married to her. She had apparently made a good thing out of George, they said, for she minced around all tarted up, never did a stroke of work and was always unsettling the respectable coloured girls in their neighbourhood. According to accounts, she was a living example of the folly of behaving as George did.

"I married Matilda in the Congo," George was saying.

"It would still be bigamy," I said.

He was furious when I used that word bigamy. He lifted a handful of hay as if he would throw it in my face, but controlling himself meanwhile he fanned it at me playfully.

"I'm not sure that the Congo marriage was valid," he continued. "Anyway, as far as I'm concerned, it isn't."

"You can't do a thing like that," I said.

"I need Kathleen. She's been decent to me. I think we were always meant for each other, me and Kathleen."

"I'll have to be going," I said.

But he put his knee over my ankles, so that I couldn't move. I sat still and gazed into space.

He tickled my face with a wisp of hay.

"Smile up, Needle," he said; "let's talk like old times."

"Well?"

"No one knows about my marriage to Matilda except you and me."

"And Matilda," I said.

"She'll hold her tongue so long as she gets her payments. My uncle left an annuity for the purpose, his lawyers see to it."

"Let me go, George."

"You promised to keep it a secret," he said, "you promised."

"Yes, I promised."

"And now that you're going to marry Skinny, we'll be properly coupled off as we should have been years ago. We should have been—but youth!—our youth got in the way, didn't it?"

"Life got in the way," I said.

"But everything's going to be all right now. You'll keep my secret, won't you? You promised." He had released my feet. I edged a little further from him.

I said, "If Kathleen intends to marry you, I shall tell her that you're already married."

"You wouldn't do a dirty trick like that, Needle? You're going to be happy with Skinny, you wouldn't stand in the way of my—"

"I must, Kathleen's my best friend," I said swiftly.

He looked as if he would murder me and he did. He stuffed hay into my mouth until it could hold no more, kneeling on my body to keep it still, holding both my wrists tight in his huge left hand. I saw the red full lines of his mouth and the white slit of his teeth last thing on earth. Not another soul passed by as he pressed my body into the stack, as he made a deep nest for me, tearing up the hay to make a groove the length of my corpse, and finally pulling the warm dry stuff in a mound over this concealment, so natural-looking in a broken haystack. Then George climbed down, took up his bottle of milk and went his way. I suppose that was why he looked so unwell when I stood, nearly five years later, by the barrow in the Portobello Road and said in easy tones, "Hallo, George!"

The Haystack Murder was one of the notorious crimes of that year.

My friends said, "A girl who had everything to live for."

After a search that lasted twenty hours, when my body was found, the evening papers said, "'Needle' is found: in haystack!"

Kathleen, speaking from that Catholic point of view which takes some getting used to, said, "She was at Confession only the day before she died—wasn't she lucky?"

The poor byre-hand who sold us the milk was grilled for hour after hour by the local police, and later by Scotland Yard. So was George. He admitted walking as far as the haystack with me, but he denied lingering there.

"You hadn't seen your friend for ten years?" the Inspector asked him.

"That's right," said George.

"And you didn't stop to have a chat?"

"No. We'd arranged to meet later at dinner. My cousin was waiting for the milk, I couldn't stop."

The old soul, his cousin, swore that he hadn't been gone more than ten minutes in all, and she believed it to the day of her death a few months later. There was the microscopic evidence of hay on George's jacket, of course, but the same evidence was on every man's jacket in the district that fine harvest year. Unfortunately, the byreman's hands were even brawnier and mightier than George's. The marks on my wrists had been done by such hands, so the laboratory charts indicated when my post-mortem was all completed. But the wrist-marks weren't enough to pin down the crime to either man. If I hadn't been wearing my long-sleeved cardigan, it was said, the bruises might have matched up properly with someone's fingers.

Kathleen, to prove that George had absolutely no motive, told the police that she was engaged to him. George thought this a little foolish. They checked up on his life in Africa, right back to his living with Matilda. But the marriage didn't come out—who would think of looking up registers in the Congo? Not that this would have proved any motive for murder. All the same, George was relieved when the enquiries were over without the marriage to Matilda being disclosed. He was able to have his nervous breakdown at the same time as Kathleen had hers, and they recovered together and got married, long after the police had shifted their enquiries to an Air Force camp five miles from Kathleen's aunt's home. Only a lot of excitement and drinks came of those investigations. The Haystack Murder was one of the unsolved crimes that year.

Shortly afterwards the byre-hand emigrated to Canada to start afresh, with the help of Skinny who felt sorry for him.

After seeing George taken away home by Kathleen that Saturday in the Portobello Road, I thought that perhaps I might be seeing more of him in similar circumstances. The next Saturday I looked out for him, and at last there he was, without Kathleen, half-worried, half-hopeful.

I dashed his hopes. I said, "Hallo, George!"

He looked in my direction, rooted in the midst of the flowing mar-ket-mongers in that convivial street. I thought to myself, "He looks as if he had a mouthful of hay." It was the new bristly maize-coloured beard and moustache surrounding his great mouth which suggested the thought, gay and lyrical as life.

"Hallo, George!" I said again.

I might have been inspired to say more on that agreeable morning, but he didn't wait. He was away down a side street and along another street and down one more, zig-zag, as far and as devious as he could take himself from the Portobello Road.

Nevertheless he was back again next week. Poor Kathleen had brought him in her car. She left it at the top of the street, and got out with him, holding him tight by the arm. It grieved me to see Kathleen ignoring the spread of scintillations on the stalls. I had myself seen a charming Battersea box quite to her taste, also a pair of enamelled sil-ver earrings. But she took no notice of these wares, clinging close to George, and, poor Kathleen—I hate to say how she looked.

And George was haggard. His eyes seemed to have got smaller as if he had been recently in pain. He advanced up the road with Kathleen on his arm, letting himself lurch from side to side with his wife bob-bing beside him, as the crowds asserted their rights of way.

"Oh, George!" I said. "You don't look at all well, George."

"Look!" said George. "Over there by the hardware barrow. That's Needle."

Kathleen was crying. "Come back home, dear," she said.

"Oh, you don't look well, George!" I said.

They took him to a nursing home. He was fairly quiet, except on Saturday mornings when they had a hard time of it to keep him indoors and away from the Portobello Road.

But a couple of months later he did escape. It was a Monday.

They searched for him in the Portobello Road, but actually he had gone off to Kent to the village near the scene of the Haystack Murder. There he went to the police and gave himself up, but they could tell from the way he was talking that there was something wrong with the man.

"I saw Needle in the Portobello Road three Saturdays running," he explained, "and they put me in a private ward but I got away while the nurses were seeing to the new patient. You remember the murder of Needle—well, I did it. Now you know the truth, and that will keep bloody Needle's mouth shut."

Dozens of poor mad fellows confess to every murder. The police obtained an ambulance to take him back to the nursing home. He wasn't there long. Kathleen gave up her shop and devoted herself to looking after him at home. But she found that the Saturday mornings were a strain. He insisted on going to see me in the Portobello Road and would come back to insist that he'd murdered Needle. Once he tried to tell her something about Matilda, but Kathleen was so kind and solicitous, I don't think he had the courage to remember what he had to say.

Skinny had always been rather reserved with George since the murder. But he was kind to Kathleen. It was he who persuaded them to emigrate to Canada so that George should be well out of reach of the Portobello Road.

George has recovered somewhat in Canada but of course he will never be the old George again, as Kathleen writes to Skinny. "That Haystack tragedy did for George," she writes, "I feel sorrier for George sometimes than I am for poor Needle. But I do often have Masses said for Needle's soul."

I doubt if George will ever see me again in the Portobello Road. He broods much over the crumpled snapshot he took of us on the haystack. Kathleen does not like the photograph, I don't wonder. For my part, I consider it quite a jolly snap, but I don't think we were any of us so lovely as we look in it, gazing blatantly over the ripe cornfields, Skinny with his humorous expression, I secure in my difference from the rest, Kathleen with her head prettily perched on her hand, each reflecting fearlessly in the face of George's camera the glory of the world, as if it would never pass.

ACKNOWLEDGMENTS

Every effort has been made to contact the appropriate copyright holders. In the event of an inadvertent omission or error, the editor should be notified c/o St. Martin's Press. No portion of this book may be reprinted without permission of the copyright holders listed below.

"Montraldo" by John Cheever. Copyright © 1978 by John Cheever. Reprinted by permission of The Wylie Agency, Inc.

"The Hitch-Hikers" by Eudora Welty. From *A Curtain of Green and Other Stories*. Copyright © 1939 and renewed 1967 by Eudora Welty. Reprinted by permission of Harcourt Brace & Company.

"Success or Failure" by T. H. White. Copyright © 1937 by the Trustees of the Estate of T. H. White. Reprinted by permission of David Higham Associates, London.

"By a Person Unknown" by Naguib Mahfouz. From *The Time and the Place and Other Stories*. Copyright © 1991 by the American University in Cairo Press. Reprinted by permission of Doubleday, a division of Bantam Doubleday Dell Publishing Group, Inc.

"How Did I Get Away with Killing One of the Biggest Lawyers in the State? It Was Easy." by Alice Walker. From *You Can't Keep a Good Woman Down*. Copyright © 1980 by Alice Walker. Reprinted by permission of Harcourt Brace & Company.

"The Hotel of the Idle Moon" by William Trevor. Copyright © 1967, 1983, 1992. Published by permission of the author and the author's agent.

"The Fat Man" by Isak Dinesen. From *Carnival: Entertainments and Posthumous Tales*. Copyright © 1975 by Rungstedlundfonden. Copyright © 1977 by the University of Chicago. Reprinted by permission of The University of Chicago Press.

"An Act of Vengeance" by Isabel Allende. Reprinted by permission of the publisher of *Short Stories by Latin American Women: The Magic and the Real* (Houston: Arte Público Press—University of Houston, 1990).

"In Vino Veritas" by A. A. Milne. Copyright © 1949 by A. A. Milne. Reprinted by permission of Curtis Brown, London.

"The Portobello Road" by Muriel Spark. Copyright © 1985 by Copyright Administration Limited. From *The Stories of Muriel Spark* (E.P. Dutton). Reprinted by permission of the author and the author's agents.

MICHELE SLUNG edited the anthologies *Crime on Her Mind* (1975); *Women's Wiles* (1979); *I Shudder at Your Touch: Tales of Sex and Horror* (1991) and its sequel, *Shudder Again* (1993); and *Murder for Halloween* (1994, in collaboration with Roland Hartman).

Her critical writing on crime and mystery has appeared in *The New York Times Book Review*, *The Washington Post Book World*, *USA Today*, *Newsday*, *Ms.* magazine, *The New Republic*, and *The Armchair Detective*, as well as in such volumes as *Twentieth-Century Crime and Mystery Writers*, *Murder Ink*, *Whodunit?*, *The Sleuth and the Scholar*, and *The Penguin Encyclopedia of Horror and the Supernatural.*

Her other works include *The Absent-Minded Professor's Memory Book* (1985); *The Only Child Book* (1989); *Hear! Here* (1994); and the best-selling *Momilies®: As My Mother Used to Say* (1985) and *More Momilies* (1986). She is also the editor of two collections of original erotic writing by women, *Slow Hand* (1992) and *Fever* (1994).